KUAN'S WONDERLAND

HENRY TAM

Dedicated to:

All who with noble defiance
Challenge dubious internment
To secure the innocent's return

Contents

Chapter 1

Not Home

The past was a sanctuary to which no return was possible.

A child in his own home. Everything conceivably bad shut out. Cocooned in safety, laughter without fear. He had all that not so long ago. But one moment changed his life. Was it his fault he allowed it to happen? What could he do? It all happened so quickly before he had a chance to turn back.

It was too late now. Shivering and wet, he was desperate to know where he was.

He must have passed out. The featureless darkness made him rigid with fear. Not that he could move if he wanted to. There were straps tying his arms and legs to a cold floor. He could taste the saline cocktail of regurgitated seawater and panic tears trickling down him.

Ten-year old boys don't cry, father had told him. So many things he shouldn't do. Like climbing out of his bedroom window at night to check out a noise on the beach behind their home.

For as long as he could remember, he had lived in his tiny room, tucked away in a corner of that drab building by the sea. He was newly born when father left China with him to start a new life. They settled at a remote spot that was deserted except for their single storey dwelling. A slab of grey in the middle of nowhere, it relied on a decrepit generator for electricity. Freezing cold in the winter, boiling hot in the summer. It was a forgotten nook of the twenty-first century.

The boy never complained. He had his own space. A tatty poster of a Shaolin warrior was stuck on the door of his plastic wardrobe. There was a dusty paper lantern hanging at the foot of the top bunk in which he slept. No one had ever occupied the bed below, simply an old football and his favourite comic book, *The Monkey King*.

Father wished frivolities would not so easily distract the child. He home-schooled him to cultivate his potential for more important things. Books on history, science, Chinese literature, and politics would pile up along the narrow corridor, loaned out from his study for the boy's absorption.

Occasional flashes of understanding and insightful comments would suggest his son did have something special in him. He would offer an idea for a clever experiment with electricity or point to a flaw in the practices of ancient Athenians that even his father had not thought about. Often it would happen when they were having their meals together, plain rice and a dish of stir-fried vegetables.

But once their chopsticks were down, the boy would take up his position by the kitchen sink and all remnants left on their plates, along with any deeper knowledge he might have momentarily possessed, would be swiftly washed away.

His father could never fathom why his mind would soar so briefly to surprising heights and fall back completely to infantile vacuity. Ineffectually wiping his thin gold-rimmed glasses and replacing them on his weathered face, he looked in vain for a change for the better. For his son, it was a constant strain to avert father's gaze of disappointment. He could not help being ten years old. If not for the curse of having random surges of intelligence, he would not be so burdened with expectations.

Of course it was not all pressure. Their rambles through the nearby woods were mostly carefree moments. Father would talk about the wildlife, distant galaxies, or the fossils underfoot, and he would occasionally tune in. All the while he was free to search for amphibians, follow the flight of butterflies, and make up games, in which once in a while father would take part.

Excursions over, father would retreat to his study. So long as he had finished his assigned homework for the day, the boy could resume his imaginative play. He probably did not get enough credit for conjuring up games and adventures with a stick, a football, and an ever-expanding cast of invisible foes and allies. There was no television or computer in the house. Modernity's reach stopped at the nearest town about two hours' walk away. Given their isolation, there was hardly ever any visitor either.

Having exhausted himself with countless battles, he would reread the latest clashes between the monkey king and assorted demons before getting himself ready for bed. He liked his sleep. The only trouble was that often he would be kept awake at night by the tapping noise made by his father on one of those old-fashioned typewriters. He would not trust any electronic device that could be hacked into from a distance. No one else was allowed into his study, not even his son. Rapid bursts of key bashing would be followed by long stretches of silence. Then, just as the boy thought father had at last retired to bed, the typing would resume, hesitantly at first, and then ferociously, until another long pause set in.

Then came that evening when, unable to sleep, the boy sat up to stare out of the opened window. It was uncomfortably warm, and the thought that he should have done more to prepare for the test scheduled by father for the next day was weighing on his mind when he noticed an odd sound amidst the routine flow of the waves.

3

It was a peculiar splash – like nothing he had ever come across before. It was too dark for him to make out from a distance what might be causing it, but all the more reason for him to sneak out to take a closer look. Wearing his tangerine T-shirt and baggy pajama bottoms, he went out through his bedroom window.

Armed with a torch and a whistle, he walked through the pebbles and rocks to get as near as he could to the sea. Not detecting anything out of the ordinary, he took one step, then another, nearer the water. He pointed his searchlight randomly across the undulating greyness. Less in fear than in hope that he could be making a dramatic discovery, he put the whistle to his mouth. If he could have something extraordinary to talk about in the morning, father might just postpone the test to another day.

He had to find out what caused that strange noise.

Imperceptibly he was edging into the murky water. After a few minutes, detecting nothing unusual, he was about to turn back to the shore when, quite distinctly, he heard that splash again. He swung to his left and then his right, sweeping his torch in all directions. But he could not see anything. Then suddenly a howling wave hit him full on and dragged him into the sea. The whistle fell out of his mouth.

He was a poor swimmer. His legs kicked frantically in search of firm ground below. The current was pulling him out further. The more he tried to stay afloat, the heavier he felt. Spitting out the water he had gulped, he desperately moved his arms to no effect.

There was something moving towards him from underneath. He looked down. A bright light was circulating below him. Gripped with fright, he was unable to move. He wanted to scream for help but his voice deserted him. A powerful stream of freezing cold water surged past his rigid body. A dark shape was approaching from the depths. He was convinced something had got hold of him by his waist. It was dragging him under the sea. Water gushed into his lungs, and everything faded from his mind.

Was there any chance he would open his eyes and find himself back in his room? The trick with nightmares was to know how to wake up from them. If he absolutely refused to believe that anything distressing had happened to him, he might recover the tranquillity of his earlier life. Ultimately it was down to him.

He was trembling, but he told himself he could stop it if he was determined enough. It was a ploy of the mind. All he had to do was to slowly open his eyes. Finding himself lying on the top bunk, he would reach over to the side to flick the light switch on, and discover his room exactly as it ever was. Reality could be a stubborn obstacle though. His arms could not be lifted, however much he tried to break free.

Who had done this to him? Father was always worried about people spying on him, plotting against him. This could be the work of his enemies. Not to exact a ransom, for they were poor. The only thing father had plenty of were books and manuscripts. It might be to give him a warning. They would cut off one of his son's fingers and post it to him. The boy visualised his blood-soaked severed finger dropping into an envelope. He clenched his fists to give his little digits token shelter.

Suddenly, he felt the floor moving. It tilted forward and lurched to the right. Then after a few seconds it steadied itself. Not a sound could be heard. Nothing to be seen in the blackness of his confinement.

Father could be on his way already, he thought. Peering at the sea through his heavily smudged glasses, he would have worked out what had happened. It was only a matter of time before the boy was rescued. But he didn't hear any typing that night. Father had been frequently away that summer. What if he were still out, and he hadn't even realised his son had disappeared?

Faint voices could be heard approaching. A very bright light came on, forcing the boy to squint. The mechanical sound of a door smoothly sliding open was heard. He strained to raise his head but could not see anyone. The narrow ceiling and the walls were all metallic, enclosing him in a small cell.

The door was now closed. Three cats came up to him. The one in front, a tailless Manx with a serious tabby face, covered in a thick grey and white coat, tilted its head to one side and stared at the boy. The other two cats circled him and returned to the side of the Manx. The one on its right was a large, dark blue, virtually black, Chartreux. To the left was a lithe Abyssinian with bright red hair.

To the boy's astonishment, the Manx moved closer to him and at the same time grew ever taller with skin and cloth displacing its fur until it had transformed into a middle-aged man wearing a sombre naval uniform. His long silvery hair was swept back, revealing a pale, stern face. Bending down over the boy, he kept his gaze fixed on the young captive.

"You made it after all", said the naval man in a slow drawl.

The boy tried to pull himself free but the straps tied him firmly to the floor.

"An interesting specimen," he remarked to his feline companions.

He took half a step back, straightened his back and put his hand inside his jacket. Watched intently by the boy, he slowly pulled out a pipe.

"What's your name?"

"Kuan."

6

The questioner arched one of his greying eyebrows.

"Kuan, what were you doing in our territorial waters?"

What could he mean by *their* waters?

"I heard this odd sound near the beach and suddenly I was swept out to sea."

His whole body was shaking beyond his control. The naval man took no notice of it, and casually put the pipe in his mouth.

"What kind of sound?"

"Like a splash, but different. I can't describe it."

It had to be a dream. Cats did not turn into naval officers. But he could not ignore what was standing in front of him. His mind raced through countless possibilities of what might be done to him, and his fear cut ever deeper into his chest.

"And because of this sound, you went near the water just when our submarine was sailing by? Quite a coincidence, wouldn't you say?"

Kuan swallowed hard. He could not make sense of any of the information swelling up painfully inside his head. How could a submarine snatch him off the beach? Had he drifted far out into the sea? And why was he being interrogated?

"You should tell us everything. We always find out in the end, and we invariably execute those who lie to us."

Kuan pictured a heavy sword crashing down on the back of his neck. His body wanted to curl up but the restraints held firm.

"Who are you working for?"

The boy looked blank and terrified.

"You want us to believe that you're doing this alone? That no one's going to come after you?"

"I hope father's coming."

7

No sooner had he said it, Kuan was anxious that he should perhaps have said nothing about him. What if the naval man and the cats were the secret enemies father had dreaded all these years?

"Your father?"

He pushed a loose strand of his silvery hair to the back of his head and moved the pipe out of his mouth so he could point the mouthpiece at Kuan.

"When did you last see your father alive?"

Kuan was at a loss. It could have been earlier that day. Or was it the day before? He could not actually remember. But the way the question was asked, was there a suggestion that something had happened to father? Fluids intruded once more into the boy's eyes.

The man was about to resume his questioning when the red Abyssinian cat began to morph. Waves of human features and woven textile flowed over the rising feline form and a tall woman came into view. She wore a light blue blouse underneath an immaculate white coat, which accentuated her thick flowing scarlet hair. There was a subtle fragrant scent about her. She whispered in the ear of the interrogator and he acceded to her intervention.

She crouched down by the boy, smoothed the tears on his face, and gently ran her fingers through those damp and tangled locks. For his part, he could not stop staring back at her mesmerising green eyes.

"Kuan, I'm Dr. Erica Lee. I'm here to make sure you're given proper medical treatment. As Captain Ma indicated, there are security issues we have to deal with. You went somewhere you shouldn't have, and I think you know that, so now you have to help us with a few questions. Once those questions are satisfactorily answered, you'll be free to go."

"You won't let them hurt me?"

"Everything will be alright."

Kuan deeply wanted to believe the doctor without any reservation.

"I'm not too far from home, am I?" he asked, yearning for reassurance.

"Depends where home is. It's difficult to say when you're from outside Shiyan. But there's nothing we can't work out. For now, you should try to get some rest. I'm sorry about the restraints, but it's standard procedure. Tomorrow things will be different. If you need medical attention ask for me, Dr. Erica Lee."

She stood up to leave. The captain stepped back to let her go first. Before following Captain Ma out of the cell, the black Chartreux cat took a sideway glance at Kuan. There might have been a hint of pity in there, or it could just be disdain.

The cell was plunged back into darkness.

In his own room back home, a faint glow from the moon would be enough to enable him to make out the outlines of what were around him. The silhouette of the paper lantern was always reassuring for him. In his mind, he had on more than one occasion drawn power from it to fight off evil spirits trying to sneak into the human world. But now, he was shrouded in black, and held captive in a world controlled by shape-changing cats.

Did father know about this Shiyan world when he set up their home at a location so close to what was allegedly *their* territorial waters? He could have deliberately moved there to keep an eye on what they were up to. It was not surprising that they would cause father such anxiety, and make him behave so furtively whenever he left the house.

At least they appeared to have left him alone for the time being. Danger might no longer be imminent. From the kindness of her eyes, the boy had no doubt that the doctor just wanted to look after him. Erica would untie the straps for him the next day, and help him get in touch with father who would swiftly come to take him back. The captain was only interested in frightening him. All that execution talk was probably his way of scaring answers out of his captives. Same reason why he was messing with his head about seeing father alive.

As for the muscular black cat, Kuan didn't like the meanness he glimpsed in those narrow copper brown eyes of the creature. It would harm him given half a chance. If the other two were not around, it might come back and claw out his throat, just for the fun of it. But Dr. Erica Lee would not allow that to happen.

He wondered if father might already have a plan to deal with these creatures of Shiyan. This could even be a trap to lure them into a false sense of security. Yet what could father possibly do on his own?

He would have to put aside his suspicions and go into the town to get help. There was just one snag. They might jump to the conclusion that he had something to do with the boy's disappearance? How could he explain what had really happened? Who would believe him? He wished father had not so persistently kept away from others.

There was a noise coming from the door. It was actually from the wall to his left. A scratching or crackling kind of sound. One thing was certain, something was trying to creep into the cell. He pumped all the energy he had into his arms to break out of the straps. They would not budge. Tied firmly to the ground, he felt his heart punching against his chest. A presence was heading towards him.

"Help! Erica!" he screamed.

"Be quiet", a voice instructed him.

The boy froze. It was the voice of a young girl, or so he would normally assume.

"Not another word, or we'd both be dead."

Kuan turned his head to where the voice was coming from. It must be very close to his face. Suddenly there was a tiny combustion in the air as though a match had been struck. And there, he could see, right in front of him, was a flame the size of his thumb. It gently flickered before him.

"You're not one of them", the voice assured herself.

"Who are you?" the boy whispered. By squeezing his eyelids as close together as possible, he thought he might at least make out the shape of the person speaking to him.

"Like you, I'm what they would classify as an outsider. We do not belong here."

"Are we really held in a submarine?"

"This is the *FSS Castle*, one of their Class A submarines. You're not the only one they've captured. To my knowledge, they have never let any of their prisoners go free."

The boy could not imagine why he would be held captive in a submarine commanded by shape-shifting creatures. But who was the stranger talking to him at that moment?

"Could you show yourself a little, so I could see who you are?"

"That's what I'm doing."

Kuan's frown ran deep.

"If you could move just slightly to the side of the flame."

"I am the flame."

"You're a flame?"

"No. I can express myself as a flame, but that's not what I am."

"How did they capture you then?"

"They didn't. I was stranded here. I must get back to my own world."

"Do you know how to do that?"

"That's what I am trying to work out."

"They have no idea you're on board their submarine."

"No, and you must not tell anyone about me."

"I won't tell anyone. Would you hurt them if they found out?"

"It is not my intention to hurt anyone."

"But you can burn them if they try to capture you?"

"I don't have time to talk with you any further. I only came in here to see if there was any escape route I could use."

Kuan watched incredulously as the flame floated around the cell.

"It's another dead end."

"Can't you just go through the submarine and make your way to the surface?"

"I cannot survive in water. I'll have to go and look elsewhere."

The flame was retreating.

"Wait. Could you help me remove these straps? I want to go with you."

"Until I have an escape plan worked out, you coming with me won't help either of us. You have to stay here. And those straps will have to be left as they are, or else they'd suspect you're getting help."

"But once you have found a way to get away from this submarine, you won't leave me behind, will you?"

The flame's pause seemed endless. Kuan was desperate to secure her help. Father was not likely to navigate the ocean and retrieve his son from an impregnable submarine. This amorphous being flickering before him was his only realistic hope. At last she gave him her response.

"I'll come back for you when the time's right."

"You won't leave without me."

"You have my word."

The flame blew itself out and there was no trace of anything left. Kuan sensed that the voice he heard would ordinarily belong to a girl about his age, but the tone suggested she was much older. And beneath that matter-of-fact persona, there was a tense yearning to be back where she belonged, in another world. It was a yearning with which the boy deeply empathised.

Chapter 2

<u>Nausea</u>

At some point in the night sheer exhaustion sent Kuan to sleep. Phantoms of dread shocked him into spasmodic awakening. In the end he was so drained of energy that not even fear could rouse him anymore. He had no idea how much time had elapsed when a cold voice summoned him to get up.

The black Chartreux cat brusquely introduced himself as Agent Tan before removing the straps deftly with his mouth, and instructing the boy to change into a black jumpsuit. Kuan followed the cat into a small cubicle next door where a large meal was displayed before him: noodles, dumplings, vegetable buns, and spring rolls.

Kuan was already famished, and the aroma of the delicious dishes made his stomach ache. He half expected to be clawed at as soon as he approached the food, but he took one mouthful, and then another. There was no catch. The boy decided to gorge himself without worrying about Tan, who sat motionless like an ice sculpture with his eyes half closed, his feelings concealed.

Once Kuan had finished, he was told it was time to head for the assessment centre. They stepped outside to a long, narrow passageway that went on for some distance before it ended with a steep staircase, which wound downward into an empty hall. With its spacious interiors, the submarine must overall be extraordinarily large. Kuan wanted to ask Tan what the assessment centre was about, but he could sense not much of an answer would be forthcoming.

As they were halfway through the hall, the boy thought he saw Dr. Erica Lee standing in the far corner, with her red hair tied back on this occasion, but he was immediately told by Tan to keep up with him. He had hoped to catch her comforting eyes. If she saw him being led away by the black Chartreux, she would make sure nothing untoward would happen to him.

The doctor did not notice him going by.

Tan and the boy entered a dark room with screens showing blips in different directions. The cat stopped to listen to some amplified sonar signals. Without a word, he continued through a wide corridor that bent gradually to the top of another staircase. All the while, Kuan was trying to memorise every feature, every turn, so that he could map out in his head where to go when the moment of escape came.

Down they went to the lowest level, where Kuan was shown into a padded cell with a single stainless steel chair by the wall. Up until that point he had been confident that he could handle any question they might have in store for him at his assessment. But the sight of the solitary chair filled his ribcage with a bitter cold draught.

Agent Tan told him to sit down. Kuan knew he had no choice and complied. Instantly metallic bands clasped around his waist and wrists. Was that meant to be his last meal? He racked his brain for some line to plead with Tan, but the cat struck him as devoid of sympathy.

A screen emerged from the floor in front of Kuan. The black Chartreux spoke impassively.

"You will be asked a number of questions. You must answer them truthfully, or else, as Captain Ma made clear, you will be killed. Before we commence the process, there is a recording for you to watch so you can see how it should or shouldn't be done. Remember it's not an actor you're about to see. This is the footage from an actual assessment – with an outsider intercepted a year ago, if I'm not mistaken. But that's of no consequence."

Kuan's eyes were fixed on the screen. What looked like a chimpanzee in a black jumpsuit was sitting in exactly the same chair he was in. An unseen questioner was asking him questions in a monotonous voice: what was his name, where was he from, how he got lost, what was on his mind when he wandered into Shiyan territories, and he earnestly answered each one. Then came the question: "Are you working with the Potokans?"

Tan looked up at Kuan's face.

On screen, the chimpanzee was silent.

"Tell us, the name of the Potokan you're working with."

Terror slowly filled his face.

"Answer me", commanded the interrogator.

"I don't know any Potokan. I don't even know what a Potokan is."

Around the chimp's wrists and waist, sparks flew. From underneath the metallic band, smoke began to spread. He was in unspeakable agony. In seconds his jumpsuit was on fire and his arms and belly were intensely grilled. He was shaking uncontrollably. Against the back of the chair he kept banging his head. His whole body was by then engulfed in flame. Layers of burnt flesh peeled off him, he was dead.

Kuan convulsed forward and vomited up what he had just eaten. His stomach felt as though it had been washed in acid and wrung dry by a pair of rusty clamps. He gasped for air. Tan remained motionless as the screen retreated into the floor.

"Now answer the questions I have for you", said the black cat coldly.

Kuan could barely pull himself to sit upright. He was going to die. It would have been so much better to have drowned in the sea.

"Who did you live with, apart from your father?"

"No one, it was just the two of us." Kuan could not help trembling.

"And your mother?"

"She left us soon after I was born."

"What do you mean she left? She died? She walked away from your father? They divorced?"

"She disappeared. Father never talked about it." Kuan was getting very nervous for fear of giving the wrong answer though it was the truth.

"You've not seen her since."

The boy shook his head.

"Disappeared? First his wife disappeared, now his son has disappeared. Why do you think he's so prone to losing those close to him? Is he a particularly careless man?"

Kuan looked up at the cat's expressionless face. There was nothing he could do but reply as honestly as he could.

"No, father is a very careful man. He's always thinking ahead about what might be dangerous."

"In my experience, only those with something to hide obsess about the dangers that might be lying in wait. Your father, Kuan, what's his secret?"

"I don't know what you mean?"

"A secret he has tried to hide, most possibly with your help."

"I have no idea what secret you could be talking about."

"I think you do."

"I really don't know."

"Do you want to end up like the other outsider?"

Kuan rapidly shook his head.

"Did your father tell you about our submarine patrolling off the coastline?"

"No."

"So who told you about us?" Tan jumped up onto Kuan's left shoulder and peered down into his eyes. His claws protruding through the fabric of the boy's jumpsuit, threatening without words to tear into the tender skin.

"No one. I heard a strange sound, and I went out to find out what it was. Next thing I knew I was being dragged into what turned out to be your ship."

"We rescued you by bringing you onto our boat. You would have drowned out there. The key is that sound. Someone engineered it. Someone wanted to get you into the water when we were sailing by."

The black cat leapt down to the floor, and slowly glanced back at Kuan.

"It must have been a Potokan."

The very mention of 'Potokan' filled Kuan with fear.

"What's the name of this Potokan who led you to us?"

Images of the chimp burning in his head, Kuan sat mouth-opened, unable to utter a word.

"Time's running out."

"I don't know any Potokan!"

Kuan looked down at his wrists and his waist. They felt hot. He put all his energy into pushing forward, but it made no difference. Within seconds, he would smell his own flesh being fried. What could he possibly say to bargain his way out of an excruciating death? Tingling sensations crawled all over his body. He stared wretchedly at Tan, who slowly looked away from him – the metallic bands retracted. Nothing was burning. Kuan ran out of the chair to the opposite side of the room where he collapsed on the floor.

The Chartreux cat walked up to the door and told Kuan to follow him. Kuan's assessment was, he maintained, inconclusive. If the boy had lied about his knowledge of Potokans he would have been executed like the chimp. But his ignorance seemed genuine enough. However, Agent Tan still suspected him of holding something back, and he was to remain under custodial supervision.

Kuan assumed that he would be allowed to live for now. But nothing else made much sense. His head was filled with questions. He had no answers. Dread pervaded each breath he drew. If for some arbitrary reason he should arouse their suspicion, he could be instantly executed. He could not remain there. Yet there was still no sign of father. For all he knew the submarine was taking him ever further away from home.

It was only when Kuan found himself back in his bare metallic cell that he realised he had completely failed to map out the layout of the submarine. He couldn't see any hope of ever working out an escape route by himself. He needed that flame he encountered last night to show him a way out. Somehow he found her small yet serious voice reassuring. Whatever obstacles there were, she would come up with a plan.

He was accustomed to leaving difficult matters to father. He never had to worry about anything other than getting his homework done and passing the tests set him. Father would take care of any problem that might come their way. There was never even the suggestion that he might have to cope with any tricky situation on his own. It was the one thing he felt he could take for granted, until he was snatched from his own home and thrown into an incomprehensible world.

Surveying every surface in his cell, which he could now at least do without being strapped down to the floor, he tried to look for even the faintest burn mark on the floor or the walls. There was no sign whatsoever. Could he have dreamt the fire up? His memory of her presence was so vivid he could not doubt she was real.

Kuan was still looking around when Agent Tan ordered him to take up his new duty with the Elephantium Team. Life on board *FSS Castle* was full of the most unpleasant surprises.

From then on, the only time the boy had outside his cell was to be spent with the Team: a group of detained outsiders. Despite their superficial resemblance to chimpanzees and gorillas, and one had the appearance of an orangutan, they were from another world the Shiyanese called the Simian Galaxy. They were all clothed in ill-fitting black jumpsuits and tasked with collecting elephantium wherever it was found on the submarine and transporting it as quickly as possible before its potency declined to the fuel converter in the engine room.

It transpired that elephantium was a highly valued fuel generated by the privileged class of Shiyanese known as the Mauveans, who had managed to acquire the precious ability of transforming from their cat form into mauve-coloured elephant-shaped beings. As they alone could provide through their excremental deposit an endless supply of elephantium, which was an essential source of power to sustain Shiyan's numerous mechanised activities, they were treated with the utmost deference.

On board a Class A submarine such as *FSS Castle*, Mauveans were permitted, indeed encouraged, to defecate at will, so that their waste product could be frequently gathered to keep the boat running. Unfortunately, the material's unrivalled economic value was matched by its odorous repugnance, and Kuan soon found out there was no easy way to endure the experience. Day in, day out, alongside the others, he would have to shovel up elephantium and bring it to the engine room. Apart from the brief respite of being locked back in his cell, he would be running after the lumbering elephants to clean up the repulsive mess they casually left behind on all decks.

Days, then weeks, went by. He was caught in the disgusting routine with no sign that he might escape from it any time soon. Agent Tan seemed to have lost interest in the secret he was previously adamant that Kuan was harbouring. Something else preoccupied the mind of the black cat, who would often be seen sitting on his hind legs staring into the distance, and not even acknowledging other Shiyanese when they, in whatever form, walked by.

Once when Kuan tried to raise the subject of his release, Tan just reminded him of the importance of focusing on doing his duty. Asking for Dr. Erica Lee was equally futile as his request was dismissed as non-medical. The boy began to look at other members of the Elephantium Team to see how they coped.

Most of the gorillas appeared to have adapted to their situation by losing their sense of smell. It could be just mud they were scooping up for all they cared. He wished he had the genetic capability to copy their mutation. The orangutan always stood apart and kept a vow of silence. He went through the motion of what had to be done, but cut out all interactions with other living creatures. His small eyes would sometimes betray a glint of sadness, but not one word would be shared with the world outside his mind.

By contrast, the gregarious chimpanzees preferred to distract themselves with incessant chat. Accurately or not, they had gathered a considerable amount of information about the Federation of Shiyan that they were more than happy to pass on to Kuan. According to them, a minute portal in Shiyan had always provided a link to both the human universe and the Simian Galaxy.

For thousands of years, however, the Shiyanese showed no interest in their neighbouring worlds because in their view Shiyan was far superior to them in every way. Then gradually Shiyan sank into a state of crippling decline. It could not even defend itself anymore. Some talked of Shiyan being repeatedly invaded by outsiders and suffering great humiliation in those dark times. Recently the Federation's fortune appeared to be in the ascendant again. Growing ever more powerful, its formidable submarine fleet was increasingly sailing near the adjoining worlds, rounding up any outsiders who had strayed into Shiyan.

One of the chimpanzees known as Max had a habit of winking and curling up his lips whenever they were talking about such matters, leaving Kuan not sure if he should believe any of it. It was Max who told him about zamenhof particles, a substance abundant in the atmosphere of Shiyan, which filtered the thought patterns of all those passing through them so they could communicate in a mutually understandable manner. Thus the outsiders could speak with each other as well as with the Shiyanese.

What Max was most animated in pontificating about was Shiyan's Circles of Challenge. Apparently, the basic Shiyanese form was that of the small cat. But if certain challenges were met, one could rise to a higher Circle and be granted the privilege to morph into other forms of being. These might be that of a wolf dog, a human, a tiger or the most enviable of all, a mauve elephant.

Max claimed that anyone, including outsiders, could take up the challenges and through them rise through successive Circles. The challenges had to be approved by the Council of Mauveans. They ultimately controlled the route to acquire the precious ability to change oneself into the most revered form in the whole of Shiyan. Mauveans could do as they pleased, and everyone else had to defer to them.

At first the prospect of entering the Circles of Challenge appealed to Kuan. It would give him a chance to rise above his pathetic position. As a mauve elephant he could demand to be returned home, where he could then morph back to his human form. On a good day he could outwit anyone in a challenge, he was convinced, though he had no idea what it might involve. But when he asked Max how they could actually get into the Circles of Challenge, the chimp confessed he had not got a clue. At that point Max burst into a laughing fit and skipped back to clearing up elephantium.

Fed up with listening to the chimp's endless drivel of false hope, Kuan began to get more and more resigned to being held indefinitely on board *FSS Castle*. Far from there being any prospect of becoming one of the mauve elephants, he was condemned to getting rid of their nauseating waste for the rest of his life.

In time, he would have to become like that solitary orangutan, fulfilling his assigned function with deadened feelings, displacing his longing for home with a numb quietude. There was no help coming. Father must have kept walking alone along the rocky beach, not knowing what he could do. He had probably given up hope of ever finding his son again. Removing his glasses, he would stare out towards the sea's empty blurriness.

Kuan wished he had not wandered off onto the beach. He wanted to load himself with so much recrimination that no one would have the heart to attach any more blame to him. But who else apart from father would remotely care about what he did? Father would be disappointed that the boy left the house alone in the middle of the night. He would not be angry with him though, not for long anyway.

What he would give to be surrounded by the grown-up books he found so tedious to have to plough through. He did understand some of what he read occasionally - more than understood in fact. He could dismantle arguments and put forward more cogent interpretations. But ever so fleetingly. If he had worked as hard as father wanted, perhaps he could now analyse the submarine holding him captive and deduce how he could escape from it.

He was quietly rebuking himself as usual when he turned into one of the labyrinthine corridors. Begrudgingly, he shoveled up the elephantium in front of him. Agent Tan came up from around the corner. The burly black cat addressed the boy as he checked the sharpness of his own claws.

"Until you've done your quota, you won't be allowed to rest."

Kuan did not respond.

"And you won't be allowed to eat either."

"Please don't talk about food."

The cat took a few steps closer.

"Kuan, I have a question for you."

"I have no secrets to tell you, Agent Tan."

Tan was about to explain when a scarlet streak shot past them. It was the sleek Abyssinian, tail lowered, galloping to some emergency.

Kuan's eyes widened, looking in the direction the red cat had gone.

The Chartreux briefly turned his head.

"There goes Lee again. It's probably one of the outsiders trapped in a decompression tank trying to escape. She gets so concerned about it. You'd have thought that having been in her job all this time, she wouldn't get so wound up anymore. And yet she does, without fail."

Kuan picked up his shovel and container to head for the engine room, but Tan padded in front of him.

"You may think we've been through this already. But search your mind, do you really not know who sent you to us? Or more importantly, why you were sent to us?"

"If I knew, why wouldn't I tell you? I was promised that if I answered your questions, you would let me go. But I've told you everything I know, and I'm still here."

"It's possible you've forgotten why you're here."

"It was an accident, my own bad luck, that I should end up here."

"But beneath all this, you know there's something more. When you remember it, things could change, quite radically."

"The only change I care about is being able to return home. Could you arrange that?"

Tan frowned. With his intense eyes, it was difficult to tell if it was a look of disapproval or an inner frustration tethered by something he could not reveal. He made another attempt to press Kuan.

"You said you heard the sound. You had no doubt about that?"

"Yes, it was like a splash."

"That was meant to be the trigger, the signal. Do you really have no recollection what you're supposed to do here?"

The boy thought if he looked closely at the cat, he might detect some sense of what he was getting at. But those copper brown eyes set in the bluish black head reflected back every inspection. Was he trying to trick him? Get him to say something he could use against him? Have him executed?

"No one sent me. There is no reason why I've ended up here. It's just my own bad luck. It's that simple. Of all the people in the world, I have to be the one. I've done nothing to deserve this. But I'm sure you still don't believe me."

Tan was about to respond but paused when footsteps pulled his attention to an approaching figure. It was Erica Lee, now in human form wearing her long white coat, carrying some small creature in her cupped hands. Utterly despondent, water dripping down through her fingers, she admonished herself, "yet another one I've failed to save."

"Why do you get so upset?" Tan spoke with some emotion, but it wasn't sympathy. "They try to escape, and they drown. It's the same story every time. Why let it get to you?"

"Because it matters. You'll never understand, Tan." She walked away.

Kuan tried to construct a sentence to engage the red-haired doctor, but he was too slow. He was counting on eye contact being established to pave the way for some simple line of reconnection. Yet she did not look in his direction.

Tan waited for Dr. Lee to be out of earshot before telling Kuan that he must think harder and they would need to talk again about the true reason he was brought to Shiyan.

Kuan left Tan and continued with his unpleasant duty. The last thing he wanted was to answer any more of Tan's questions. It then struck him that the flame, whose return he had been awaiting for weeks, could have been killed in one of her attempts to find a way out. She said she could not survive in water so she must have drowned in one of those decompression tanks, which were routinely flooded for some reason. That was probably her, or some tiny physical remains, dead in Erica's hands. A few wet ashes.

But why didn't the doctor even notice Kuan? Not even a fleeting glance. He told himself that she was so dejected with another loss of life that she was momentarily unaware of his presence. Yet a subtle pang betrayed his lack of conviction in his own explanation. He was after all just an outsider.

Chapter 3

A Plan

Another month or more had gone by. The summer sun continued to direct the flow of the season. But its warm rays could not penetrate the depth of the sea. Far beneath the surface, time drifted strangely in an enclosed space cut off from the rest of the world, disorientating its inhabitants, leaving them uncertain about their memories. Was it really a strange noise that attracted him towards the sea that night? Or did he notice a shadowy figure standing in the dark on the edge of the beach? No, he was alone.

Kuan was standing in one of the narrow passageways on board *FSS Castle*, going yet again over the moments that led to his captivity when the black cat strolled by without stopping. Agent Tan no longer kept a close eye on the outsiders in the Elephantium Team. As far as he was concerned, so long as they got the substance off the boat's deck into the energy converter, they could get their ration of food and be sent back to their cell for the night. He had even given up asking Kuan questions which the boy had long deemed unanswerable. What was preoccupying him much more of late was a growing suspicion that he would not be able to fulfill his real mission. He licked his thick fur in a half-hearted attempt to forget about the dire consequences that could follow his failure.

With Tan's attention drifting elsewhere Max, the talkative chimpanzee, started to boast openly about his plan to enter one of the Circles of Challenge. He seemed to think the young human would still be interested.

"Kuan, don't you want to know how we can get out of here?"

The boy was tired of Max's fanciful ideas.

"Max, what is it this time?"

"I can get them to let me take on a challenge. All I have to do is to utter one simple word."

Kuan looked wearily at the grinning chimp in his crumpled jumpsuit.

"You know what that word is? Go on, guess."

The boy would not be drawn.

"Just one word, and they would be listening to me. That word is 'Potokan'."

"You want to get yourself killed? They killed an outsider from your world just because they suspected he knew something about the Potokans. They showed me a recording of his execution. It was horrible. You talk about Potokans and what do you think they'll do to you?"

"Relax, Kuan, I know what I'm doing. I've heard about these executions. Lots of outsiders get electrocuted. But that's the point. The Shiyanese are paranoid about the Potokans. They're convinced they could be under attack from them at any time. When I tell them I've got some useful information for them, they wouldn't think twice about agreeing to my demand, which is no less than being entered into one of the Circles of Challenge."

"Max, they wouldn't think twice about torturing you before killing you."

"They would do nothing of the kind if they want the information from me."

"But what information have you got? What do you know about the Potokans?"

"I haven't made it up yet."

"You're going to make it up?"

"Apart from them being the mortal enemy of Shiyan, I know nothing about Potokans, so I have to make something up. But I'm good at that."

"Max, you haven't thought this through, have you?"

"Of course I have. I'll give them some convoluted intelligence I have supposedly picked up from one of my outsider contacts who's visited Potoka. By the time they realise that it's all bogus, I will have made my way to the top of the Circles of Challenge and become one of the privileged Mauveans. They won't be able to touch me then."

Dragging his knuckles beside him as he strutted forward, Max could not be prouder of his plan.

"Max, whatever you're going to make up, talk it through with me first. You may need to refine it."

"Kuan, don't worry, I'll share my idea with you so you can use it too. One day soon we'll both be mauve elephants in Shiyan, and we'll look back at this moment as the beautiful turning point."

The chimp peeled back his lips and chuckled as though his salvation was already secured. It would take him just a couple of days to come up with some concocted story about a Potokan plot he could help to foil.

On the morning Kuan was meant to hear from Max about what he had come up with, the team was called to an emergency assignment. Half a dozen mauve elephants had decided to have a drunken celebration through the night. Their precious deposit was left all over the hall built for their exclusive recreation. As Kuan did his best to suppress his retching instinct, he noticed that Max was nowhere to be seen. He was not to be seen again the following week, or the week after that.

Was Max so foolish that he went to Agent Tan with some Potokan story he made up and got himself executed? Or did he, like so many others, end up drowning in a decompression tank in a futile attempt to get away from *FSS Castle*?

Night after night, Kuan sat by a wall and stared into the unremitting darkness of his cell. There could be no escape. The truth was like a rusty nail slowly screwed into his wrist. He did not want it, but he could not repel it. There was no conceivable way to regain his freedom.

The only route out of the hermetically-sealed submarine seemed to lead invariably to those randomly flooded chambers. And since none of father's books was about how to carry out an underwater rescue, he would know nothing about tracking his son's whereabouts, let alone saving him. As for Dr. Erica Lee, she was no different from any of the other Shiyanese. She assured him he would be free to go once he had answered the questions put to him. Yet all this time had elapsed and he was still held captive. No wonder she was always avoiding his gaze.

As he contemplated his bleak future, he heard a faint noise approaching him. Kuan tensed and looked down. A fire lit up by itself.

"You're alive!"

"Keep your voice down."

"I thought you were dead, but you're alive!" Kuan exclaimed but as quietly as he could.

"It's taken me longer than I had hoped. I'm here to tell you I've found a way out."

"Not the decompression tank?"

"No. This would safely get us off the submarine."

She commanded Kuan's total attention.

"You know storage bay J on deck 4? Tomorrow night, 22:00 hour, meet me there."

"But 22:00", said Kuan in a confused tone, "I'll be locked up in here."

"You have to come up with an excuse. Tell them you've got some elephantium to clear up. That won't be hard for them to believe. You will have to focus, because this is your one chance."

"So what's in storage bay K? I mean J."

"It's 'J'. Storage bay J, deck 4, 22:00 hours. You must remember that. Your life depends on it."

"Tell me more. How are we going to make our escape?"

"There's no time for that now. Just meet me there tomorrow night."

Her voice was calm, but not without a hint of fear.

"I'll be there."

"If you're late, I can't wait for you." The flame lowered itself as it was about to go out.

"Wait, wait, what's your name?"

"You can call me *Amo*."

"Amo, thank you for coming back for me."

"A promise is a promise."

"And my name is Kuan."

"I know."

The boy wanted to ask Amo how she knew his name, but the flame went out and vanished. He repeated it in his head: Storage bay J, Deck 4, 22:00 hours; storage bay J, Deck 4, 22:00 hours, and so on until he dozed off on the floor.

The Elephantium Team was summoned the next morning to a meeting with Captain Ma who was in his human form. Once they had gathered before him, he stepped forward, tugging the front of his much decorated tunic to make sure it was suitably resplendent.

"Team, in a few days' time, and it could be sooner than that as the schedules for these things are kept under wraps, Governor Pui, special envoy to the Vice President, will be coming on board *FSS Castle* to carry out a mission that could affect the lives of millions of inhabitants in our world. Tensions have continued to rise between us and our Potokan enemies. The governor will conduct a series of meetings here and report back to the Vice-President about what actions Shiyan should take to protect our safety. I cannot overstate the critical significance this visit has for us. Agent Tan, over to you."

The black cat walked in front of his commander, then turned slowly towards the assembled crew as a mixture of tedium and bewilderment draped across his face.

"Thank you, Captain Ma. It is up to us to make sure the governor's stay on *FSS Castle* meets the highest standards. Therefore, members of the Elephantium Team, in addition to your usual duty, you will over the next two days be required to clean every surface on this submarine. It is essential for Governor Pui to find our boat in pristine condition. Any questions?"

He did not wait.

"None. Good. Detailed instructions will be passed to you from 08:00. Dismissed!"

For the rest of the day, Kuan worked doubly hard so as not to arouse any suspicion about him, although if Tan had been watching carefully, that sort of unusual behaviour was precisely what would have struck him as odd. But the Chartreux's mind was weighed down by other concerns.

Kuan got rid of the usual elephantium deposited all over the submarine, brought it to the engine room and then scrubbed as best he could any spot showing the least bit of dirt or stain. Any other day he would be thinking what was the point when the most extensive cleaning would soon be ruined by the thoughtless bowels of the wandering Mauveans. But today he had a plan. It was Amo's plan, but if fortune would just for once side with him, he would be part of it too.

The timer on the wall was ticking ever closer to 22:00. To Kuan's immense relief, the black cat was nowhere to be seen. He started to head down to Deck 4. When he reached Deck 2, he was sure he took a wrong turn. Scratching his head, he attempted to retrace his steps. Not too good with his sense of direction, he anxiously paced up and down in the hope that the correct way would dawn on him.

Without looking up, he backed into a lion. Kuan jumped and became even more nervous when he realised it was Len-Wu, the Head of Security who, with his huge frame and golden mane, had the most intimidating presence. The one saving grace for the boy was that Len-Wu, for reasons he never shared with anyone, detested the Mauveans, and had always felt sorry for those having to shovel up elephantium all day long. Kuan raced through in his mind the various questions Len-Wu could be firing at him any second now. As for the possible answers he could bounce back, he was drawing a blank.

"You look lost", said Len-Wu in his characteristically matter of fact way.

"Lost, yes, trying to find the stairs to get down to the next level." He held up his shovel in one hand and his elephantium container in the other.

"Thought I had finished for the day, but then some of our Mauvean guests felt like relieving themselves, again, apparently because they could, whenever they wanted to."

Len-Wu shook his head in dismay.

"Now which way is it to get down to Deck 3? I forget every time."

The lion went round Kuan and with his nose pointed to an exit on the left. "Through there and you'll see the stairs down."

With a gentle sigh, Len-Wu padded away.

Kuan rushed down to Deck 3, remembering that a similar route must take him to the stairs for Deck 4. The timer read 21:56. He was right about the stairs, but as he was going down, up came in the opposite direction Xian, the chief engineer, a work-obsessed leopard who often, as at that moment, took on the semi-morphed form of a human body in a tight blue naval overalls while retaining her fierce leopard head.

With her searching red eyes, Xian stared at the juvenile human. There were rumours that she once cracked the skull of one of the cat engineers working for her because he made a foolish mistake. Kuan took a deep breath as he squeezed himself tightly to one side of the stairs. The chief engineer moved past Kuan, who was transfixed by the sight of her protruding fangs, and disappeared up the stairs.

21:58. Kuan reached Deck 4. Where was storage bay J? It had to be at the end of that corridor, and from there, a right turn. A minute left. He ran and ran. It was the shortest and yet the longest minute of his life. There it was. Storage bay J. 22:00. He made it. But where was Amo? A side door was left open. In he walked. Still no sign of her. There were hundreds of boxes in the bay. Smoke was coming out of the top of one of those nearest to Kuan. Kuan lifted it and there was Amo burning gently without scorching anything around her. She told Kuan to hide his shovel and container in one of the other boxes, then get himself into the box with her and a collection of food pellets, and finally bring the lid of the box back down over both of them.

They were now all set, ensconced inside a large box that, Amo explained, would soon be delivered along with the others to Potoka. The shipment would be sent in a waterproof transporter to ensure an unspoilt delivery of the pellets, which had been developed to appeal to gluttonous Potokans. When they reach their destination, they would be left out in the open, the Potokans would gorge themselves on them and never have any offspring after that. It was something the Shiyanese had recently started to do as part of their strategy to deal with the Potokan threat.

"Kuan, I'm not sure what effect they might have on non-Potokans, so best for you to leave them alone."

"What about you?"

"I don't eat, not food as such."

Amo had extinguished her flame form but Kuan could still hear her.

"You must need something for energy?"

"There's no need to worry about me."

"If I can help, just let me know."

"We can talk more when we get to Potoka."

"Amo, do you know what Potokans are like?"

"I've never come across one up to now."

They heard the mechanised packing system kicking in. They were being placed in a transport tube with all the coordinates programmed in. Very soon, they would be on the move. He was so excited. There was now a real of prospect of being back with father again. For the first time in a long while, Kuan smiled.

Chapter 4

<u>Blessed</u>

A dark cavern. Large boxes were left lying around. Some were on their side with their cargo spilled in all directions. Shadows moved around in fits and starts. Barely audible voices mixed up in faint echoes. Suddenly, the lid of one of the boxes flew open and landed on the ground. The noise it made reverberated. All motion halted.

Eyes dotting the blackness blinked in guarded silence. Transient seconds passed to give way once more to random movements of unseen creatures. Kuan had a cautious look as he stood up, before he climbed down from the crammed container in which he had been travelling. His vision was finding it hard to pick out anything. Amo manifested her fiery self as best she could beside him, but it barely showed up what was a step or two from them. She was weak and tired.

Out of nowhere a large cluster of what appeared to be fireflies floated into the cavern like a mobile searchlight. The swaying brightness drifted right and left. With his hand shielding his unbelieving eyes, the boy took stock of the creatures crawling around the cool, rocky surface. They were small and grey, like cats that had been shrunken to the size of a squirrel. But their eyes were white with no discernible iris, and each creature had an extra pair of legs protruding from its abdomen. Disturbed by the intrusion of unwelcome light, they scurried towards shaded crevices. They did not stay out of sight for long. Something was drawing them back out of their hiding places.

Sensing that the biped standing in front of them posed little threat, they sniffed their way back towards the scattered food pellets. Kuan tried to warn them about the side effects, but they just carried on regardless. Supported by their four hind legs, they picked up the pellets with their front paws to devour them.

Amo dimmed to a flicker and then faded into invisibility.

"Amo, where are you?"

He was afraid of losing her.

"Kuan, I must find a means to revive me."

"Let me help."

"You stay safe here for the time being. I can move about without being seen, but we can't risk you being captured again."

"I don't think we need to worry about that. These Potokans look more scared than scary."

"Appearances can deceive. We know nothing about them."

"Shouldn't you rest first?"

"If I rest now, this could be my last conscious moment. I must go."

She left.

Kuan crouched down to take a closer look at the diminutive Potokans. One moment they would barely move as though they were weighed down with foreboding. Then they scampered spasmodically, chasing their own shadows. Why would the Shiyanese be so fearful of such beings?

They were beginning to congregate around a pile of food pellets. He leaned forward to watch them but lost his footing and toppled over onto his knees. The sudden movement startled the six-legged creatures. The one closest to the boy bared its sharp fangs and hissed at him. Then it slowly backed away.

Were they more dangerous than he suspected? Appearances could deceive. Once he was with father on one of their rare journeys into town. It was early summer before it got unpleasantly warm even at night.

Approaching the checkpoint at the outskirt of the town, father started to pat his pockets nervously to assure himself he had the right documentation with him. There would usually be two sour-faced guards making demands in a monotonous tone.

But on that day, there was a different one wearing a thin moustache and a broad smile as father and son walked up to him. He observed that it was going to be a long hot summer with little rain. Kuan looked up at father nodding, knowing how he cringed at small talk about the weather, or anything else for that matter.

The smiley guard noticed the briefcase father was tightly holding and asked if he could take a look. Reluctantly, for it contained a typescript he wanted to show someone in town whose name he never mentioned to Kuan, he passed the briefcase to the guard. The smile vanished. The guard opened the briefcase and tipped it upside down with all the papers falling onto the ground. Father went down on all fours to gather his writings, and the guard kicked him in the stomach. He strolled away laughing. Before turning back to help father up, Kuan fetched the few sheets attempting to get away on the wind.

Back home that night father talked as usual to Kuan about his latest reading over supper, and said nothing about the incident earlier in the day. The boy wanted to know how he felt, but father just wanted to press him on what he thought could have prevented the rise of the ancient Qin Empire in China. He vaguely recollected he came up with a couple of ideas which seemed quite original, but he then lost track of what the conflict was about. By the time he finished doing the washing up, father had disappeared back into his study. He was left on his own, as he was now in the unstably lit cavern.

A grey mass was sweeping away from him, heading deeper into the cavern. Something was attractive enough to pull the Potokans away from their new-found food. Kuan followed them and at a distance saw an almost human figure glowing in blue, waving his arms at those who had gathered before him. He threw out small blue objects at a selected few. These seized their prize with their front paws and ran off in different directions.

One of them stopped by a rock near Kuan and squeezed itself into what it must have thought a safe enough space. It was holding a tiny crystalline globe glowing a cold shade of blue. It rolled onto its back, its white eyes half closed, and fell into a trance.

Those disappointed by not getting a blue globe were growling around the lone figure, who stood his ground while gesticulating wildly. In the end that was sufficient to disperse them. Kuan walked closer and discovered that there in front of him, with that trademark grin, was the missing, presumed dead, chimpanzee.

"Max, is that really you?"

"Who's that?" The chimp snapped his fingers and a platoon of fireflies assembled above him. On closer inspection, they appeared very much like tiny electrical bulbs with fiberglass legs and wings.

"Kuan, it's you! How did you manage to find your way here? I always thought there was more to you than meets the eye. Hidden potential, that's what you've got, and I could use someone like you."

"I thought you had got yourself killed."

"Is that what they told you?"

"No. After you disappeared, nobody said a word. Agent Tan acted as if nothing had happened."

"He would. He had no idea how I escaped."

"How did you escape?"

"It's all about who you know, Kuan. I asked a friend of a friend about what I could convincingly say about Potokans. Suddenly I had all this information about Potoka and how I could make my way here without anyone noticing."

Kuan's eyes were drawn to a small round object still glowing out of Max's long blue coat, which was worn over his garishly pink shirt and trousers. The chimp casually fetched it out from an inside pocket and twirled it around in his hand.

"Max, will that help you complete the rest of your journey?"

"What journey?"

"Back to your home world, the Simian Galaxy you told me about?"

"Why would I want to go back? The life I had was worse than being in the Elephantium Team. I was treated like dirt round the clock. I was everywhere an utter nobody. It's the last place in the universe I'd want to be."

"What about your family?"

Max covered his face with his large hand in mock distress.

"They're all dead. That's one lucky break I've had in my whole life, not to be tied to that sorry bunch of no-hopers."

"You don't mean that, Max."

"You haven't met them. Don't tell me you like your family."

"It's just my father, and I do wish I could be with him again."

A rare look of seriousness clouded the chimp's face.

"You don't approve?" asked Kuan.

"How you feel about your father is your business. But getting back to your own world from here would be a little difficult unless you can bypass the laws of nature."

"If I could get here, surely I can go back."

"You wouldn't say that about time, would you, young Kuan? And the inter-dimensional traffic from your world to this is a lot like time. You can arrive here, but you can't get back."

"Why?"

"Do I look like a scientist to you?"

"There must be a way."

Max scratched his head as though he was trying to think of a way, though of course he wasn't.

"If I can't go back, it's still possible for father to come here. He could have got a boat and started rowing out to sea. Without knowing it he would have entered this world and it's only a matter of time before we find each other."

"That's possible. But it's more likely your father would have been captured by one of the subs patrolling the borders. And we know what they're like with outsiders, don't we? The whole assessment centre routine is just an excuse for them to show us they can do what they want. You may not believe this, but there was an outsider who was asked if he liked the colour red, and he said yes because that was the truth, and they fried him alive in the interrogation chair. Just like that."

"Who told you that?"

"I hear things. If I were you, I would not pin too much hope on your family reunion. That might sound cruel, but you need to be realistic."

Echoes of a rainstorm filled Kuan's head. On that day, father was saying something important to him, but he could not hear the words. The rain pinned him to the spot. Father disappeared into the gushing water. Why didn't he run after him? What happened that day?

The unrelenting downpour slowly drowned out his hope for their reunion.

Max put his long arm around his shoulder and tossed the glowing blue globe up in the air a few times before Kuan's unblinking eyes.

"Do you know what this is?"

The boy shook his head.

"This is Blessing, only to be given to those who are truly worthy."

The chimp threw the tiny globe at Kuan who caught it in his hand. It was a little bigger than the marbles he played with when he was younger. It continued to glow brightly blue by itself and felt cold in his palm.

"What do I do with this, Max?"

"I believe you're worthy, Kuan, so consider yourself Blessed. Keep hold of it in your hand, and you will find inner peace."

"Will it help me find father?"

"Sit yourself down, Kuan, now hold it tightly. Close your eyes, and relax."

The boy did as he was told. A cold, but not unpleasant, sensation floated up to his head and transported him to a theatre hidden deep in his mind. On the giant screen he saw a young boy with gold-rimmed glasses walk into a mansion with marble floor and golden columns. He climbed up a long spiral staircase. Out of breath, he entered a study shielded by rows of tall bookcases filled with dusty volumes. In the middle was a small wooden table with a typewriter on it. The boy sat down, pushed his glasses up, inserted a piece of paper, and started typing. Like a concert pianist he pressed on the keys with rhythmic precision, transmuting the blankness before him into a vessel for his innermost feelings. One after another he pulled out the sheets of freshly cast text. When he had come to the end he gathered up his typescript and put them in a briefcase.

A scream was heard. He clasped the briefcase close to his chest and ran down the corridor into a steam-filled room. He peered hopelessly over his glasses. The steam drifted out through the open door, and eventually the blurred image came into focus.

The boy recognised the man ahead of him, the long white hair and beard, submerged in a large bath, his head half severed from his body. Behind the dead man stood a masked woman with heavily mascaraed eyes, wearing an over-large tunic suit, and holding an enormous carving knife with blood and water dripping down it.

"You finished what he asked you to write?" she asked without emotion.

The boy started to back out of the room.

"Give it to me, and I will spare you."

He turned and ran. Going down the stairs, he tripped and fell. He could barely pull himself up. His broken glasses were hanging pathetically off him. The masked woman, her grey suit stained red, descended the stairs. She kicked the boy before picking up the briefcase he had dropped. She then pressed her knife against his thigh and asked where the rest of the papers were. He just shook his head, and she pushed the tip of the knife into his flesh.

Kuan cried out in pain. A Potokan had sunk its cat fangs into his thigh. It was small enough for him to swat away. But a dozen or so others had come up, drawn by the smell of blood. Their white eyes were gleaming with irrepressible hunger. He was still too much in a dazed state to pick himself up and run. The six-legged creatures moved closer to him. He wanted to shout out for help but his lungs were too enfeebled to pump out a sound.

A flame erupted from the ground, flexing its raw brightness. The Potokans stared incredulously at the intense blaze, quivered and scuttled away. The fire contracted to a tiny flicker. Amo had returned in time. Kuan wanted to tell her that after receiving Blessing from Max, he discovered something about his father, a family secret which had been kept hidden from him. In a sympathetic but firm voice she told him they must leave the cavern for a safer place. He looked in his hand when he was standing up, and found the blue globe had melted away completely.

Through a narrow opening of the cavern, they made their way out into a vast cave, shaped like the interiors of a succession of monumental cathedrals joined together with no partitions. High above, a dense cloud of fireflies shone like an infant sun on the multitude below. The creatures outside were not dissimilar in appearance to the Potokans he had earlier encountered, but they showed no interest in Kuan. It could be that in striding forward, even with a slight limp, he was no longer a ready-meal lying down flat for dinner guests to arrive. There must be thousands of them, white eyes scanning, legs sprawling. Eager scavengers carried away boxes of the surreptitiously delivered food pellets.

It was not a long walk to where Amo suggested, but he found it most tiring. It might have been partly the effect of the Blessing. It did not stop him recounting to her what had happened after she left. Quietly, invisibly, she listened as she floated alongside him.

She guided him to a short, twisted tree where he was finally able to rest. The leaves had the shapes and colourful patterns of butterfly wings. According to Amo, the Potokans believed that was a sign of it being haunted and were unlikely to go near them when they stayed by it. For Kuan, that information was more unnerving than reassuring.

"In what way is it haunted?" he asked.

"It isn't. It can't be, since haunting requires an after-death presence."

"But the Potokans think ghosts come here?"

"They are obviously superstitious."

"You don't believe in ghosts?"

"I can't believe in what does not exist."

"I've just seen a ghost. She killed my father's dad. She then tried to kill father too, when he was just a boy."

"That was in the dream you had after you took the Blessing."

A gust of air flew by, causing the oddly shaped leaves of the tree to flutter like real butterfly wings. Father told him that some people in ancient China actually believed that the souls of the dead would rest in a chrysalis before they were transformed into butterflies so they could visit the loved ones they had left behind. He recounted it to the boy not to soften his concerns about death, but to illustrate how people could believe just about anything. Ever since, Kuan felt an ineffable sadness at the sight of butterflies.

"It wasn't a dream. I saw what must have been troubling father for years. His father taught him to write down something which was obviously important, but the woman wanted to stop it. She would kill anyone who got in her way. That's why father wanted so much for me to learn from him so I could carry on his work. But this woman, or her ghost, is out to get us."

"Did you see what was actually written?"

"No, it was all gathered up and put in his briefcase."

"And your grandfather was killed because of it."

"It sounds crazy, to kill someone just because he or his son wrote something. It's horrible."

"Kuan, did you know your grandfather?"

"No."

"Has your father ever said anything about him or how he died?"

"He doesn't like talking about family matters."

"So they were just random hallucinations induced by the Blessing."

"I didn't dream those things up. They happened, and the Blessing helped me find the truth. Father was frightened that I would be hurt so he sent me away. That's what Agent Tan was getting at. He knew someone deliberately sent me here. Father knew that I would be safe in this world, and he could join me later."

"Kuan, you now want to wait for your father to come here rather than find your way home?"

"Amo, maybe you didn't know this, but none of us can return to our own world. It's like a one-way street. We can arrive here but we cannot go back."

"What evidence have you got for this?"

"I was told on good authority."

"You mean Max, who told you he would one day become a mauve elephant, but having escaped from the Shiyanese, he's dispensing hallucinatory Blessing to the gullible."

"I think Max just wants to make things better for himself and his friends. We don't want to chase after the impossible, do we? If you believe we can get back to our own worlds, have you figured out how to get back to yours?"

The tone of Amo's reply, when it came after a long pause, made Kuan feel uncomfortable.

"I have not. I fear I won't be able to."

He should be more sensitive about her feelings. But what could he say?

"Your parents might come looking for you here."

"We don't have parents. We come into being if our life force attains self-consciousness. Once we do, we continue to exist so long as we have enough positive energy to sustain us."

"If you haven't got parents, you can't miss them."

It didn't sound right to him as soon as he said it.

"We miss each other, everyone of us who is a part of the totality of our world. It's not divided into individuals or family units. We constitute one integrated sentient nebula. I don't know how I came to be separated off and drifted into this world. I cannot survive for long on my own. I have to get back or I perish."

"Max does get things wrong. One-way streets can become two-ways, can't they?"

"He must be wrong. I would have known if I had come through a uni-directional portal. I would have sensed it."

"Maybe it stops us going back but not you, because you're different from us."

"I don't accept that anyone of us has to be confined here forever. Nor should you, Kuan. Don't accept the false serenity of surrendering hope. We will find a way back to where we belong."

Her words lifted the boy's spirits, and symbiotically, a surge of energy infused Amo.

Chapter 5

<u>A Second Chance</u>

Kuan had spent almost a week in the Potokan cave. While Amo continued to search for a way out to the open space beyond, the boy was learning to gather tiny berries and nuts for his sustenance. These were so unfailingly bitter that he was on more than one occasion tempted to try some of the modified food pellets still left lying around. So far he had resisted, but his patience was running out.

The bleak dullness of life there was wearing him down. At night everything was shrouded by a chilling blackness, and when daytime arrived with the bulb-like fireflies, a pandemonium of screeching and scampering would once again break out.

The Potokans did not seem to have anything in particular to occupy their time, except for this morning when Kuan was woken up by an unprecedented display of carpentry. Surprisingly dexterous with their front paws, the cat-like creatures were using wooden hammers and splints to forge together a large frame on the ground. It could be an attempt to mark out an area to grow vegetables. They could do with a little more variety, or even just something more palatable.

He was stabbed with hunger pangs. He gave his own cheeks a squeeze the way father used to when he was worried the boy was not eating enough. His face had never felt so bony. Meals were never luxurious at home, but they were dependable and comforting. Food on the table, deep if fleeting discussions with father, happy eating, and then everything washed up and tidied away ready for the next meal.

The notion drifted into his head that another Blessing would help him. It had opened his mind to buried memories, so he assumed. Whether or not he could go back to his home, he was more convinced than ever that father would look for him. But there were too many anxieties clouding his mind. Only the clarity afforded by another one of those glowing blue globes could help to reveal how he and father were to find each other again.

While father encouraged him to read so many books, he never showed him what he had written himself. The masked woman could be a Shiyanese in human form. Having known the threat she posed to them, father was careful to protect him, making sure he knew nothing of what he was working on. Why then did he send the boy to Shiyan? Or did the plan he had in mind go wrong? Perhaps the intended sanctuary was Potoka, in which case that would be where father would be heading, if he had not arrived already. But how would he find his way to this particular cave?

A Potokan crawled towards the twisted tree under which Kuan was lost in a haze of speculation. It made a guttural sound too quiet for the boy to notice. Another came up and when both of them were making a similar noise, he looked up in alarm. Was he being seen as their next meal? It was difficult to read their intention behind the solid whiteness of their eyes. He clung to the tree trunk like a talisman to protect him. The two growled more urgently.

"They mean you no harm."

Amo had returned.

"Light yourself up. They're getting closer."

"Kuan, I need to conserve my energy. There's no need to worry."

"It's alright for you, they can't bite you."

"They're just asking for your advice."

Kuan stared disbelievingly at the two creatures with their heads bowed low.

"You know what they're saying?"

"I'm sure you would too if they speak up. For some reason they're not projecting their voices beyond a whisper."

Holding themselves up with their four hindlegs, they held their front paws together in a gesture of supplication.

"Amo, what do they want?"

"They're imploring you to tell them why you're chosen for the Blessing. They have been begging for it for a long time and were always ignored. And yet you showed up from nowhere and straightaway you were given the Blessing."

Kuan turned to the pair of cat creatures desperate for guidance.

"To receive the Blessing, you need to be worthy."

They glanced at each other in mutual puzzlement and fixed their gaze back at Kuan, white eyes blinking.

"You need to have something inside you. Something that shouldn't be left there. I have these memories of father I didn't know I had. Without them, I'd be completely lost. I can't see a way of getting back to him, and I don't know how he can make it alive coming to look for me. But with the Blessing, I'm finding what father wanted me to know so I can be waiting for him."

Both Potokans were firmly unenlightened. A third one scurried up to them and they exchanged views in a highly agitated tone. The first two nodded, then shook their heads despairingly. And in glum silence all three departed.

"What were they saying?"

"They have other things to worry about besides Blessing. The Potokan who just came up had heard about an imminent Shiyanese attack. If it's true, this cave could soon be demolished."

"A Shiyanese attack? What are we going to do? We can't stay here."

Amo was well aware that they could not stay around with an invasion looming. Of course it could be an unfounded rumour. She had noticed Potokans dreading pernicious Shiyanese plots wherever they went. Ironically that had not prevented them from eating the food pellets engineered to stop them reproducing. Being paranoid but not smart, these creatures might not be able to put up much of a fight when the enemy actually launched their offensive.

Unfortunately, Amo had not found a way out. She had explored one side of the cave extensively, but it left her wondering if it backed onto the sea or an underground lake. Every time she found a tunnel that did not eventually double back on itself, it led to a dead-end behind which she unmistakably sensed the presence of water. She could not go through it without a protective vehicle. Her only hope was that despite the area's general backwardness, more advanced transport machinery might have been left there by previous visitors. In the meantime, there was the other side of the cave which might hold the secret of an escape from Potoka.

In her invisible form Amo set off on her journey. She had tried to assure Kuan that she would soon track down a viable route out of the cave, but he was palpably not convinced. It was impossible to tell how much time she had. Whether the Shiyanese attacked in the next few days or weeks, she could not remain intact if she was kept too long from rejoining her home nebula. Pushing ahead over the dry, craggy surface, she had to focus on the prospect, however remote, of achieving her goal. Anxiety weighed heavily on her.

The numbing stillness of the air had left Kuan with the impression that they had been dropped into an abandoned well. The cave walls enclosed all who dwelt within them. Did the Potokans think it would afford them the greatest security, or had they trapped themselves in the worst possible hole? Some of them must know of a secret passageway out even if they were not inclined to share that knowledge with others.

The grey creatures were now crowding around the frame they had noisily constructed. Over it they pulled a large sheet of material, made of very rough cloth or what could have been dead leaves and other vegetation unevenly knitted together. They nailed it tightly to the frame. Each in turn sniffed and checked if the work done by its immediate neighbour was up to scratch. The contraption looked like a giant piece of carpet, neither suited for sitting on nor for mounting onto the cave wall as a drab piece of decoration. But they all seemed very satisfied with it. Perhaps it was their way of diverting themselves from the thought that they would not be able to move anywhere else.

Father had talked about setting up another new home for a number of years. He did not like being near the sea. He feared that the water was getting ever closer. Kuan didn't know how true that was, but father was genuinely uncomfortable about it. And since nobody else had ever chosen to live there, it suggested that there might be good reasons to settle elsewhere. But they never did anything.

Father might have belatedly concluded that it was better to leave their world behind altogether. Did he have somewhere in mind already? What would make him opt for this barely habitable cave? What was his plan? Father never did anything without working out every step in his head first.

With another Blessing, he told himself, he could probably delve deeper and uncover what father would want him to do in circumstances the old man would have lamented as most unpropitious. Planted in his subconscious would be where they should meet, or at least how he and father could find their way to each other again in this alien world. But what would they do with Amo? If she had no idea how to get back to some distant nebula, they were unlikely to be of much assistance to her either. Yet it would be out of the question to abandon her.

As Kuan's mind raced ahead to wrestle with one intractable problem after another, a vast shadow crawled across the cave. The whispered mutterings between the Potokans came to an abrupt end as they gazed up at the changes fermenting above. The multi-coloured leaves of his twisted tree all at once turned the darkest shade of grey. The fireflies which had every morning arrived to greet the ground dwellers began to dim their light. Their replacements were approaching in a dense cloud, linked together by the chain of saturated sponges they held aloft.

Potokans with thick branches pushed them under the large frame and in unison raised the edifice off the ground. It was a shelter and as some of the creatures crawled underneath it, a few water droplets began to trickle down here and there. Then in one single coordinated move, the sponges were squeezed and the rain poured. In no time he was wet through. He hated the clammy sensation of soaked cloth clinging onto his skin. But that was nothing compared with what would happen to his friend.

"Amo!"

She had long disappeared into the distant wilderness.

Such a sustained downpour could well be fatal for her. He ran in random directions, half realising he would not be able to see her. It did not stop him though. Watery arrows shot down at him relentlessly. He screamed out her name over and over again.

Although quite a few Potokans were now hiding under the makeshift tarpaulin, many of them did not seem to mind. Sprawled on all sixes, they appeared to enjoy the rain. At the sight of Kuan, they casually turned their heads, bemused by his erratic behaviour. Others started to run alongside him assuming he might know something they did not. But when it became clear even to them that his darting about conformed to no coherent pattern, they trailed off. He was wandering by himself again, his feet dragging through the thickening mud. Squinting as much as he could to look through the curtain of rain across his eyelids, the boy's desperation grew. There was no sign of her.

Minute after minute of captivity under the omnipresent waterfall, the drenching was starting to dissolve his concentration, filling his mind instead with suffocating memories of being dragged under the sea. It paralysed him. If the water softened the ground any more, he would sink right through. A small band of Potokans were hopping about in a haphazard line, attempting to stand on their two hind legs and wave the other four with little rhythmic regularity, giving a poor impression of some Hindu deity dancing for the rebirth of the universe. Just beyond the clumsy troupe, Kuan saw a tiny flicker of flame. He wiped his eyes and caught a momentary flare again. He fixed the point and sprinted towards it.

By the time he reached where he was sure the briefly visible fire had been, there was no sign of Amo. He turned frantically in a circle calling out to her, until he became so dizzy that he fell on his knees. That serious young girl's voice of hers was not to be heard. He thumped the ground in anger. He had been so preoccupied with finding father that he had allowed Amo to go out without any protection against what was lethal to her. She had helped him escape, first from the Shiyanese and then the hungry Potokans. And that was how he repaid her. With the rain masking his tears, he sobbed.

A Potokan came up to him and nudged his thigh with its head. Its cat face looked up for his attention. A second one joined in and rubbed its cheek on the boy's mud-caked knee. Together they called to him with that strangled sound in their throat. Their tense expression was filled with meaning. He bent down closer to them. They croaked some word. The same word. At last he knew what they were saying.

"Blessing."

With grief-dampened gentleness, he stroked them and followed their lead. He was back in the cavern where he and Amo first reached Potoka. Outside the downpour was getting even heavier. The repetitive drumming on the ground echoed through the hollow chamber. Watery keys were typing out the epitaph of his friend. His companions did not want him to linger and urged him to move further in.

Blue light and mingling shadows marked their destination. Preachers and clowns, the thought came to him. For some reason, from the earliest age Kuan had allergically disliked preachers and clowns. Father was not a churchgoer, but occasionally when he had brought the boy with him when he visited the town, he would leave him at the back of the church while he attended to whatever business he had elsewhere. At other times, when the circus came, he would buy a ticket for his son to sit through the show so he could go unencumbered to one of his many meetings.

The visits to the town were rare. But when they happened he would too often end up sitting in front of preachers and clowns. Instead of expecting to be filled with awe or laughter, the only feeling he had was a suspicion of abandonment. Their eyes staring, demanding an exclamation of joy; their arms waving, commanding the heart to overlook its inner melancholy; their mouths smiling, but their faces betraying indifference.

There was Max, the chimpanzee glowing in his blue and pink outfit, speaking with an air of solemnity, but grinning with irreverence. Preacher and clown. He told those gathered around him that the days of hatred were numbered. He clapped his hands and flipped a back somersault on the spot. It was time for the chosen ones to be Blessed, and for the Blessed to prepare to embrace the second chance coming their way. There was much entanglement of legs as many tried to push their way to the front.

Max told them all to accept their fate, for it was fixed. A residual of jostling rumbled on. He raised his thick brows to signal disapproval until there was quiet compliance throughout. There was a message which they must reflect on day and night. Never lament one's destiny. Suffering was inseparable from finding the right path. Those already chosen would soon find themselves with the once-in-all-eternity chance to be truly fulfilled. They must cast all doubt aside and give every fibre of their being when the moment came. Not one of them had even the slightest inkling of what he was hinting at, but fervently they nodded.

Like a magician juggler, Max swirled his arms around and out came dozens of the glowing blue globes flying towards the selected few to receive the Blessing. They clutched their prizes and scampered away to where they could devote themselves to their quiet meditation.

To those left disappointed, he reminded them he would return next week, and the week after. They should never give up hope that they might yet be chosen. It was hard to believe for those who had turned up each time only to come away again with nothing. Yet they kept on believing, or blindly yearning, that they would be in line for the Blessing the next time. For now, drawn and despondent, they reluctantly dispersed.

Max leapt up to an overhang in the cavern ceiling and swung to land by the side of Kuan.

"Back for more Blessing, young Kuan?"

"I was just following the others. But I have been thinking that another Blessing might help me."

"Help? Blessing would transform your life!"

"There's not much left to transform. Everyone I care about is taken away from me."

"But not everyone who cares about you has given up on you."

"Who do you mean?"

Max wrapped his long arm around the boy and led him into a narrow tunnel off the side of the cavern. Their path was lit by a couple of fireflies the chimpanzee had summoned. A few minutes on, just before the path was to slope sharply downwards, there was a cleft in the sandstone passage, where Max gestured to Kuan to rest himself. He put in the boy's palm a glowing blue globe and folded his fingers back to close the little hand.

"Sit back and receive your Blessing. You will see that you're not alone. Sometimes you have to lose many things before you realise you may yet attain everything. When you are ready, come and join us in the valley tonight. Just follow the tunnel down and keep going until you come out to an opening. All those who have had the privilege of being Blessed will be gathering together to embrace their second chance. The Curator will be there himself."

"Who's the Curator?"

Kuan stared up at Max's murky, yellowish eyes.

"The Curator is responsible for the collection."

A cold sensation was streaming into his head. His eyes were tiring. Max's face was blurring, and it was as though another voice was speaking through the chimp.

"Whatever you have lost, forget about it. Whatever you have been seeking, let it go. You are at the threshold of a new life. Surrender the pain, and you will attain victory over despair. Accept your future."

He was in his old home. Unusually, the door to the study was left ajar. Through the gap he could see father's back as he bashed away at the typewriter. He stopped, took off his glasses, wiped them on his shirt, swiped at the carriage return lever, and resumed typing. Kuan noticed an unfamiliar staircase and walked up it until he could see the steam drifting out of the bathroom at the end of the corridor. Against his own judgement, he entered. The man with the half severed head rolled his eyes towards Kuan.

"Where's my boy?"

"He's typing downstairs."

"Has he nearly finished it?"

"I don't know. What is he supposed to be writing?"

"It's better you don't know."

"Shall I call a doctor?"

"It's too late for that. Just make sure he gets it done."

"Is someone going to hurt him?"

"They'll hurt him, then they'll hurt you."

"What should we do?"

His eyes had given up his spirit. Slowly he slid into the water until he was completely submerged. The bath started to overflow. Blood and water poured onto the floor. Kuan ran back outside. Startled by his own reflection in the mirror at the top of the staircase, he froze, only to see that behind his image was the blood-stained figure of the masked woman.

"Is your father still trying to hide from me?"

Kuan could barely lift his legs.

"Like father, like son." She coldly remarked.

The red water was spreading into the corridor. He finally managed to run down the stairs. The study's door was locked. He banged on it, screaming out to father as footsteps trailed him down the stairs. The front door was open. He must have left the house. Kuan sprinted outside.

An insipid grey was painted across the cloud-ridden sky and the rocky beach. No sign of father. The waves crashed boldly, encroaching on the shrinking land barrier. The boy could see the water was swelling towards him. He started retreating towards the house, calling out for father all the while. He backed into the hallway and shut the door as the sea was arriving on the threshold. Watery blood was dripping from the ceiling. A hand grabbed him by the neck and forced him to sit in a chair. His arms were tied behind his back. A steady stream was pouring down onto his face. He tried in vain to push himself away. The ceiling gave way.

He was tucked away in the cleft in the passageway behind the cavern. It was subtly harder to breathe. He wanted to cough up imagined fluids in his lungs, but his mouth was dry. The blue globe was gone. He gazed up. There was just one firefly left hovering above him, and it was tapping its bulb head with one of its fiberglass limbs to see if its filament brain was still fired up. It flew erratically. Not much energy left. Its flying partner had already collapsed. It landed delicately next to it, bent its weakened joints, lay down and expired.

Kuan was left in darkness. He pulled himself up. Which way should he turn? Was the Blessing helping him? It brought him nightmares, but knowing them to be nightmares gave him a strange sense of reassurance. He should not wonder what would happen to him or father, because everything would turn out right for those who were Blessed.

A loud squeal shot through the dark space. Hair sprung up across his tightly stretched skin. To be Blessed was to know there was nothing to fear. He listened intently. There was a hammering sound, followed by a harrowing cry of pain. Was someone being tortured? He must at least find out if there was anything he could do. Leaning against the side of the tunnel, Kuan gingerly moved forward. With his hopeless night vision, he was afraid of stumbling over. But then came another hammering sound, and another heart-crunching cry. He crept forward more quickly and slipped down the sharply downward path.

Pulling himself up, he could see a faint light glowing round the corner. He moved closer to it. A solitary Potokan came into view. The creature was standing upright with his back flat against the tunnel wall. One of his front paws, held above his head, was nailed to the stone. A shrunken but still glowing blue globe lay on the ground, casting an eerie upward shadow on an emaciated face. With one of the limbs hanging out of his midriff, he was grasping a hammer. His white eyes reached out to Kuan with a plea. The boy bent down to pick up the globe.

"No!"

He was straining his throat to its limit to project his voice.

"No more Blessing."

His eyes were directed just beyond the small globe. Kuan patted the ground and felt a tiny object. It was a hard, rusty nail.

"Must stop myself."

"Why?" asked Kuan, still holding on to the nail.

"Stay away from the valley."

"Let me help you. I can try to pull the nail out."

"No. It stops here."

He held out his middle paw requesting the nail Kuan had picked up.

"Please."

The boy was not sure what he should do.

"Resist Blessing." The Potokan whimpered.

"Why?"

"Keep away from it."

His paw demanded the nail.

"You're bleeding badly," said Kuan at the distressing sight.

"I've had enough of the curse."

"There has to be another way."

"The nail, pass me the nail."

As soon as it was reluctantly passed to him, it was elevated into position in line with his other front paw, and without hesitation he hammered it through his flesh into the stony wall. He screeched out in agony but barely paused before he struck another blow on the nail.

Kuan could not bear to look. Could Blessing drive you insane? Or did it depend on how well you managed to cope with its revelations? Not everyone could have their minds open to hidden knowledge and act calmly. That must be what being worthy was about. Though the Blessing might have been too much for that Potokan, he must go on until he was ready to step beyond his present state and begin a new life. Father could be waiting for him already, at some location his

Blessed experiences were pointing to. He must not be distracted by doubt.

A thud on the ground turned his head. The hammer was dropped. The Potokan's two forelimbs were fixed above his drooping head – a pose of victorious defiance, or abject surrender. Kuan crouched down by the motionless creature. Life had deserted him. He had turned his back on Blessing and for him, things could not get any worse. The boy did not want to throw away his second chance. He carried on down the path. Not far ahead now was a dim light. Deep within him he would seize the courage to discover how he and his father would find each other again.

Chapter 6

<u>The Unexpected</u>

At last Kuan made it out of the tunnel. He found himself in an underground oasis, with a steep rocky slope rising on either side. There had been no rain in here. The ground was dry, but the air was fragrant. Enough fireflies were overhead to keep darkness at bay. Discarded boxes which had earlier carried dubious food pellets from Shiyan had made their way down here with their contents long gone.

There was an incongruous breeze sweeping his hair back. Glancing in the direction it was coming from, he detected a patch of blue shimmering in the distance. In his mind there was an image of father leaving the house, walking away without once turning back until he came to a deserted shoreline. His silhouette was superimposed on the blue sea behind. That would be the rendezvous point. Overwhelmed by a sense of certainty, he started to run towards what must be the sea. Close to the edge of the blue were geometrical shapes. They had to be parts of the boat father had sailed in.

It must have been the proximity of the sea that put Amo off from exploring this part of the cave, which opened up to the ocean where different worlds connected. If only she had not been caught in that furious downpour. She would be safe in father's boat as they travelled together to another land. It might still be far from her home, but it would have offered Amo a chance to edge closer to the desired destination. But none of that mattered now.

Father would probably prefer to stay somewhere like Potoka precisely because it was a backwater. He would be safe from tracking and hacking. But what about that ghostly vision of the murderous masked

woman he saw in his Blessed state? Father would know
if they should fear her. She might be no more than a
dreaded memory. A phantom that could be transported
back to her own time and laid to rest.

Kuan wanted to go faster but his jogging slowed.
He never had the stamina to run for long. What if father
were still angry that he sneaked out of the house that
night? What if he opened his arms and father just yelled
at him for his stupidity? Too much time had gone by. It
must be two or nearly three months. Father would just
be so glad to see him, to find him alive.

The verdant ground was beginning to give way
to desiccated soil. The valley was much less welcoming
beyond its grassy centre. The cloud of fireflies grew
brighter, polishing the surface of the not so far off blue
patch into a blinding glare. Kuan virtually closed his
eyes as his legs went into automatic mode. He was
getting closer with every step, to the reunion he had
achingly yearned for. It was going to be the happiest
moment of his life. He wanted to savour it in slow
motion. But should he allow himself to be so
optimistic?

Far above, the fireflies dimmed their light, and
the gloss was stripped away from his sight. Clumps of
moss and dwarf cacti paved the way leading up to the
edge. It was not the edge of a sea, but a basin of blue
sand. There was no boat, just old boxes left in a
mangled heap.

Might father still appear? Seconds took minutes
to tick by. The raw cut of disappointment scratched ever
so slowly down the chalkboard. Blessing was all a lie.
It played with his head, confusing him with shocking
imagery and deceptive notions. It had nothing to do
with father. Just a trick he fell for.

No wonder that Potokan nailed himself to his
death rather than have anything more to do with it. Why

did he allow himself to be taken in? He visualised a blue globe resting in his hand. The enchanted purity of hope, sullied by false promises. It was all to keep him in the Potokan cave. He would not accept it. He stepped over the edge and dived into the blue sand. With whatever strength he had left, he would swim away through sand if that's what it would take.

But the little strength he had was not enough to keep him afloat on the quicksand he had plunged into. The more he splashed his arms and legs, the more he sank. He kept his mouth tightly shut, but the sandy mush was streaming into his ears and nostrils. The solidity of granite weighed down his exhausted limbs. He twisted his neck as much as he could to catch some air. One act of rash folly to leave his home. Another to exit life altogether.

A plank of wood thrashed down by his face. Instinctively he grabbed on to it and felt it pulled in fits and jerks towards the dry bank. He could feel the arid soil and his fingers scrambled to find a suitable grip. But before he detected anything to hold on to, a concerted force yanked him out of the blue quicksand.

Clearing his nose and throat, he blinked his eyes to identify his saviour. Or saviours. Seven or eight pairs of white eyes were fixed on him. A wave of relief swept across their small cat faces. He thanked them for saving him, and they meekly nodded back.

He rolled over onto his back and surveyed the smooth cave ceiling towering above him. Each time in church when asked to pray he would look up at the ceiling, wondering if an angel, or even God Himself, would make a quick appearance. Just long enough to assure him that even though father had wandered off again, he would never be really alone. But the ceiling refused to offer any revelation.

"You must not give up."

One of the Potokans spoke in a parched, feminine voice.

Kuan wearily sat himself up.

"What's the point? I'm stuck here on my own."

"You're not alone."

Father's gone. Amo's gone. Of course he was alone.

"Come with us."

Behind her, the other six-legged Potokans scratched around in the soil, unearthing a few seeds, catching the odd worm, feeding off what they could find.

"I'm not hungry."

"Come with us to the Final Blessing."

He showed no interest while his fingers combed out the wet sand in his hair.

"Your second chance with a new life."

"What new life? Blessing leads nowhere. It drags you around in a circle, and you end up where you started. I'm grateful you saved my life, but could you leave me alone now?"

"You shan't be alone. Soon you can join the others."

"What others?"

"We'll all join for a new life."

Kuan stood up and brushed himself down.

"Tell that to your friend who nailed himself to the wall in the tunnel rather than get mixed up any more with the Blessing."

She bowed her head momentarily.

"It's sad that some lose their way."

The others had finished their snack and now stood behind her.

"If you want to help me, tell me how I can leave this place. I don't care what anyone says, I'm going to make my way home. It's ridiculous to suggest father would even try to get into this world. I know him. He'd do nothing of the kind. He's staying at home, waiting for me."

She made a sound resembling a sigh.

"There is no way out of here. You must understand. In this life, this is where we're all confined. To be free, embrace your second chance and find a new life beyond."

"I'm not having any more of this."

Kuan turned away from the Potokans, but facing the blue sand there was no obvious path he could take. A small cluster of fireflies broke away from the main cloud and hurtled towards Kuan and his rescue party. The radiant ball suspended itself in midair and flashed out signals.

"You must come with us", insisted the Potokan who had been speaking to him.

"Why?" asked Kuan.

"The Final Blessing is about to commence. We must go together."

"I'm not interested. Who are they to tell me what to do anyway?"

"Together or nothing. If you don't come, we won't get our Final Blessing."

"That might not be a bad thing."

"Without it, we'd be stuck here forever. No hope, no escape."

"But I don't want any more Blessing."

"Please come with us. Decline your Blessing if you will. But at least come with us."

"Why should I?"

"Please, for our sake."

"If I come, you can take your Final Blessing, but I can walk away if I want to?"

"Of course."

"Why don't you just go ahead yourselves?"

The fireflies flashed brightly.

"The Curator wishes to see you there."

"Who's the Curator?"

"He's responsible for the collection."

"What collection?"

"We will soon find out."

"Why does he want to see me?"

"You have to ask him yourself."

"I'll go, but I'm only doing this for you. We'll go there together. You get your Final Blessing. Then I'm off."

The ball of fireflies flew off ahead, like a shooting star heralding a momentous change. Kuan and the band of Potokans followed in tow. Thinking back to his life on board *FSS Castle*, Kuan could see that he was at a total loss when it came to trying to escape from the submarine. The prospect of finding a way out only ever surfaced when he spoke with Amo and Max. Amo did help him reach Potoka, but she was gone. Max, on the other hand, seemed to be all talk at one stage, yet he did actually get away without Agent Tan even noticing. He had no idea what was behind Max's involvement with giving out Blessing, but the chimp knew how to get round obstacles. Even if he really thought the boy could not get back to his own world, he might be open to helping him get off Potoka at least, so long as Kuan was prepared to do him some favour in return. There could be no harm in asking. He would make sure he had nothing to do with any more Blessing, and just press Max until he was ready to help him out.

The fireflies rejoined their brethren in the vast cloud hovering above. They exchanged charges and sparked off shots of light which fanned out like fireworks. Below, standing near the front of a semi-circular stone platform, right at the heart of the valley, was Max dressed in a red tuxedo and an open-necked frilly green shirt. The chimp clapped his hands and slapped his thighs, laughing like a warm-up act who was not the least worried if he was funny or not. Converging on the platform were hundreds of Potokans who had been Blessed and given a special invitation to attend this gathering. They were all visibly consumed with excitement.

Kuan waved at the chimp. He just wanted to find out how he could leave Potoka and get away from the valley before more Blessing was dispensed. Max leapt off his stage and put his big hands on the boy's face. Kuan recoiled from their sweaty odour.

"I heard you took a plunge in the wrong pool. You must be more careful."

Kuan wanted to tell him how ridiculous he looked in his outfit.

"It's nothing. Max, I need your help. I want to get away from this place."

"Very soon, my friend. You and your Blessed companions here will all get your second chance and leave this place behind."

"I don't want to get Blessed. I want to really get away from here. I know what you said about going back to my world is impossible, but let me worry about that. Just tell me how I can get out of this cave. I'll do you a favour in return."

"I'm not looking for any favours from you. Kuan, what do you take me for? I want to help you because it's the right thing to do. And I *am* going to help you."

"So how do I get out? Is there a secret passageway like the tunnel you showed me to get down to this valley?"

"You don't get it, do you? The only way out is to take your second chance."

"But I don't want to take my second chance, whatever that's supposed to be."

"Listen to yourself. You don't know what you're talking about. Stick around, see for yourself, and I bet you'll want to take your second chance. Otherwise, you'll be stuck here till the end of time."

Max broke out a huge grin.

"Can you imagine that?"

"Max, are you going to help me or not?"

"Kuan, trust me, and in the end you'll thank me."

The chimp put his hands on his chest and lowered his head.

"But there won't be any need for you to thank me, because helping others is what I do."

With a flourish of his arm, Max acrobatically jumped back onto the bare stage. Tugging the lapels of his jacket, he called the congregation to order. Noisy chatters simmered down to a few odd whispers. His searching eyes seemed to be looking into each one of them individually.

"This is what you have all been waiting for. Each Blessing has brought you closer to this moment. You have proven your worthiness and shall be given a second chance to live a life beyond Potoka, a life that will be richer, greater than any you can imagine. Forget the talk of impending attacks from the Shiyanese, the threat of inescapable suffering. A different path is to open up for you, and you alone. Raise your eyes to our harbingers of the New Beginning, reach out for your Final Blessing."

Max shot his arms upward, while quietly lowering his own head. A swarm of fireflies descended into the valley clutching the glowing blue globes. As these were dropped and caught by those below, a euphoric cry erupted. Instinctively Kuan had put his hand out and plucked one of the falling globes. His face, like those of the gathered Potokans, was wrapped in a blue glow, which rapidly intensified while every Blessing held shot out a beam of light towards the centre of the stone platform. The hundreds of beams dived into a common point and appeared to pull a column of pure radiance out of the ground. The column rose and blossomed into a tulip-shaped luminosity.

"Behold, the Curator!" announced the chimp.

The brightness lit up the valley. Max pirouetted twice and somersaulted off the stage.

"Hold on tight to your Final Blessing, and step forward to meet the Curator who will grant you your second chance."

Kuan began to wonder if he had been too hasty in what he said to Max. Why shouldn't he try to take the second chance?

The Potokans were flocking onto the platform. The beams of light originating from their blue globes were reeling them towards the unseen Curator, ensconced in brilliance. One after another the six-legged creatures were pulled into the giant flower of light and disappeared. That only encouraged others to rush forward faster still. One Potokan dropped his blue globe as he ran onto the stage. He looked dazed, indeed shocked when his hind legs were dragged by an invisible force towards the light. Just before he was fully absorbed into it, he cried inaudibly. Kuan saw the look on his face. A chill crept into the boy.

More of the Blessed were clamouring to reach the Curator. The light was like a porous membrane sucking the furry supplicants into its inner mystery.

A pair of Potokans tried to push each other out of the way to get just a few steps ahead but ended up knocking their blue globes out of their grasp. The glowing spheres bounced once and rolled away. Their Blessing was gone. Their white eyes flashed a dawning of realisation. It was not actually their wish to give themselves up to the light. Kuan caught their despairing faces calling out for help. But it was too late. They were already too close and in but a split second, they were blended into the intense whiteness.

The boy's grip loosened, and the blue globe fell out of his hand.

"Aren't you going up?"

It was the Potokan who earlier on had helped to save him from the blue quicksand.

"No. Neither should you."

"The second chance is the only chance left for us", she said while moving up onto the platform.

"It's not what you think it is."

"Nobody knows. You have to have faith."

She glanced back at him, her white eyes half closed in sadness. For him? Or for herself? She carried on towards the light.

Kuan called to her to stop. He was darting forward to pull her back but a long arm blocked his way.

"What do you think you're doing?" asked Max, his face screwed up in consternation.

"I want to stop her. She's going to be melted into nothing. There's no second chance."

"You're a clueless little boy."

Kuan watched her approach the point of no return. He tried to push forward but Max was too strong for him.

"You must let me stop her."

Max wouldn't budge. She looked back one last time as she was swallowed into the voracious light.

"Kuan, we are your friends. Don't make us your enemies."

The chimp lowered his arm and swung behind the boy to grab hold of his shoulders. Ever so gently but resolutely he pushed him forward towards the centre of the platform.

"Let go of me, Max. I don't want this."

"Too late. You've been chosen. You're Blessed. There's no turning back."

Kuan dug his feet into the ground as much as he could, but he was skidding forward just the same.

"Max, don't do this."

"It is the Curator's wish."

The chimpanzee was poised to give the boy one final push when a stentorian command thundered out of the darkness: "Let the boy go!"

The remaining Potokans parted to reveal a massive black rhinoceros setting its sight on Max. It commenced its charge. With a living locomotive bearing down on him, the panic-stricken simian threw Kuan in the direction of the oncoming rhino. But it simply dropped its shoulder, avoided the boy without even breaking stride. With gathered momentum it rammed its horn into the chimp's chest and in the same move tossed the limp and blood-drenched body onto the platform where it was absorbed into the bulbous brightness.

The black rhino saw some of the blue globes that had been dropped on the ground and crushed them with its feet. Those who had stayed out of the light threw theirs away. Almost immediately the brightness in the centre dimmed. Layers of radiance peeled away in quick succession until the light was gone. The survivors dispersed, leaving Kuan lying on his back looking at the approaching rhino. His consciousness was fading. Darkness was closing in, and he was not sure how he had escaped Max's treachery.

"Where am I?" he asked in a very low voice.

"Kuan, don't worry," said the rhino as it morphed into the black Chartreux cat known to the boy as Agent Tan, "you're on board *FSS Castle*."

74

Chapter 7

<u>The Accused</u>

Within the darkening chrysalis, the body decomposed into momentarily freed cells, swimming frantically for an independent life. Against the pre-ordained tide, sloshing back and forth in a thick organic soup, they struggled in vain. Slowly they were drawn together by the intimate bonds of blood. To their collective metamorphosis, they succumbed in silence. The crystalline shell cracked, secreting a new creature. Its legs sniffed the air. A spectrum of colours inflated its wings, bedecked with two pairs of unblinking eyes, one set gleaming in scarlet and yellow, the other staring out in blue and lilac, all framed by a symmetry of red, white and black. The Peacock butterfly took off.

He wanted to chase after it. Father firmly said no. Seek the simple beauty of the Orange Tip, the ragged shape of the Comma, or the playful Small Tortoiseshell with its black and white keyboard across its forewings, but do not follow the Peacock. They were on a field trip dedicated to Lepidoptera. He had very strong views about what his son should pursue. But on this occasion there was no need to chase after any of them. A sea of butterflies swept towards father and son. The rainbow cut to a thousand papery pieces flapping above his head.

His eyes slowly opened, looking up at the butterfly-wing shaped leaves of the twisted tree which had given him some semblance of shelter. Why was he lying here? The residual effect of the Blessing was still stirring up memories of father, true or false he knew not. Back in the valley he dropped the blue globe and escaped with his life, though he did not manage that alone. A shadow approached. He pinched himself painfully to rule out more delusional dreaming. It was the doctor.

"Erica?"

"Kuan, how are you feeling?"

"What are you doing here in Potoka? This is Potoka, isn't it?"

"Of course it is. I heard you might need medical help, getting mixed up with Blessing."

"How did you know? I had no idea what it was. But I feel fine now."

"I wouldn't be so sure. It can really affect you over time. Let me check you over."

Dr. Lee, her long red hair tied back, knelt down by Kuan. Her face came right up close to him. A sweet smell like serene ocean air wafting ashore. She pointed a light into one of his eyes, and then the other. Her green stare rendered him immaculately still. Pensively he studied her steel-smooth cheeks and calmingly thin, flat eyebrows. She felt his neck and behind his head. Comfort flowed from her fingers into his delicate frame. Taking the stethoscope from her coat pocket she asked him to sit up and listened to his breathing. At last she smiled and pushed his hair back.

"It doesn't seem to have done any permanent damage. But you should be careful."

"I'm not going to have anything to do with Blessing again."

She reached out to feel the butterfly-wing leaves of the tree.

"This is the home you've made for yourself here."

"It's hardly a home."

"Everyone was quite insistent this is where you should be left to rest."

"It's supposed to be haunted."

"By what?" asked Erica.

He wished Amo's ghost would come back.

"Erica, who brought me back up here?"

"Try to remember."

"I was in the valley. I refused to go to the Curator."

"Who's the Curator?"

"The curator of the collection. I saw him. Not directly. There was just this intense light. And there would be nothing of me left had I gone to him. Max was forcing me to."

The confrontation with the chimp was dripping back into his mind. He was about to be pushed into the ravenous brightness when he was rescued.

"I think I can remember it now. Except for when I was saved from the light by ..."

The pause made her quizzical.

"... Agent Tan. That must be a dream. He told me I was on board *FSS Castle*."

The doctor's expression was unsettling.

"Kuan, you did see Tan. He was the one who brought you back up here from the valley."

She hesitated. He did not want her to go on.

"And, I'm afraid, you are on board *FSS Castle*."

He did not believe those words came out of her lips. An unstoppable fear was swallowing him whole from within his soul.

"Erica, I asked you, and you said this is Potoka!"

"This is Potoka, in a sense. I suppose it could be confusing if you're from elsewhere. Potoka, how can I put it, is not a place on its own. It is a collection of enclaves spread across Shiyan, some on land, and some on vessels, like here for example. This is Castle de Potoka, meaning it's where Potokans are gathered on the submarine, *FSS Castle*."

The boy's shield of incredulity was splintering under the force of the doctor's explanation. Shards of pain were breaking through with the bleak realisation that he had not left the submarine at all.

"This place is in what's called the subterranean deck of our submarine. Most Class A subs have it so the Potokans can be more easily confined to one large sealed off area, and there is no travelling allowed between the subterranean deck and the rest of the boat, unless it's been authorised by the captain."

"But I thought I had managed to escape."

"No life form can leave the submarine without being detected."

"I hid in one of those boxes, sent faraway to Potoka, to give them poisoned food so they can't reproduce. I tried to stop them, but they wouldn't listen. But I was convinced I had got away from the submarine."

His eyes were drifting out of focus.

"Tell me I'm not on the submarine anymore."

She knew the symptom. It's the lingering effect of the Blessing. His brain was shutting itself down.

"Kuan, stay with me!"

"I'm safe. I got away."

The traumatic shock was about to throw his mind into a prolonged state of hibernation. He did not want to know that even his one faint hope of having fled *FSS Castle* was but an illusion. After all he had endured, he was no closer to father.

"Can you hear me, Kuan?"

She fumbled in her pocket, drew out a black tube and sprayed a fine mist over the boy's face. He convulsed and keeled over. The sourest sensation gnawed at his throat. Diving into the light would have been a better choice. Even if the Curator only wanted to add his corpse to whatever collection he was amassing, Kuan would have been liberated from this interminable confinement. He wanted to curl up and end it, but something had reached into his lungs, giving them a new vitality. From the deep chasm greeting him, he was yanked back up by his arms. Standing on his own two feet, he wiped his eyes.

"Kuan, you mustn't allow yourself to be cut off like that. You've got to accept it. I don't know how you found out about this place. You must have somehow got into the transportation chute which led you here, but Castle de Potoka is still a part of our submarine."

She held out her hand so he could steady himself.

"Want to know a secret?" she asked in the hope of distracting him.

He gave no reply.

"The boxes of food sent down here are not actually harmful to the Potokans in any way. In fact, they're made with added vitamins to help them fight off nutritional deficiency."

Vaguely he blinked in her direction.

"You mustn't tell anyone though. There are those high up the command chain who wanted to test out ways to make Potokans sterile. They asked me to lead the project and I took the chance to alter the formula for the food pellets being made. None of them has a clue about what I've done. If they did, I'd probably be executed."

That grabbed his attention. He held her hand tightly. His predicament was atrocious, but her death would be unpardonable. However much he detested his ill fortune, he instinctively wanted her to be out of harm's way.

"But they're not going to find out, are they?" she softly checked with him.

"Why do you risk your life to help the Potokans?"

"Just look at them, Kuan."

And he did. Small cats with an unsightly extra pair of legs. White eyes searching without hope. Indecipherable whines mingled with sharp screeches. They crawled around sniffing for food, scratching the ground on mostly futile missions for something worth eating.

"Do they know they're stuck here, in the bottom of a submarine?"

"In the beginning maybe. But over time, they seem to forget. It could be part of their natural adaptation. Potokans are moved around a lot, depending on what space is available at any time."

"Why do Shiyanese hate them so much?"

"Not all Shiyanese."

"All I ever hear is that Shiyanese want to attack them, get rid of them."

"It doesn't have to be like that. Some of us would …"

Erica stopped as soon as she saw the black Chartreux cat approaching. Kuan dreaded his presence but at the same time he could not eradicate all trace of gratitude to someone who had saved his life.

Agent Tan scrutinised the boy with his reddish brown eyes and announced it was time to return to the main part of the submarine. She tried to make the case to let him rest a little longer, but Tan was adamant they must leave straightaway. There was something on the agent's mind he would not share with anyone. When previously Tan asked Dr. Lee to join him in tracking down two escaped outsiders in the subterranean deck, all he would reveal was that they were probably involved in the unauthorised giving of Blessing, which could have very damaging side-effects that only the doctor knew how to treat.

Through his network of spies, Tan had known that Max had sneaked down to Castle de Potoka where he had attracted a following amongst the natives. He was already under close surveillance when he appeared to have recruited Kuan into his activities.

On the grounds of preventing any unsavory alliance built up between Potokans and outsiders, Tan obtained the captain's clearance to break up whatever racket Max had put together. He was particularly concerned about the role Kuan might have taken on, and he was immensely relieved, perhaps even encouraged, when he found the boy wilfully obstructing Max's plan in the valley even when it was at great risk to himself. That could suggest that he was beginning to realise why he was sent to Shiyan. The moment of revelation might be drawing near. Until then, Tan must continue to conceal his own intentions.

The black cat led the way with relentless strides. He did not look back once, knowing Kuan would follow with the doctor. The fireflies high above in the cave's arch ceiling shone brightly. Tan followed a narrow path up onto a steep slope lined with Potokan skeletons. Some of the six-legged creatures tailing them up to that point growled at each other before finally turning back. The three of them were now on their own. At the top of the slope still some distance away was a large crimson stone.

Kuan glanced back at the cave with dimmed hope of catching a small flame flickering. He was not surprised at not picking up any sign of her. The rain had extinguished her, washing away a bond that had only begun to be forged. She would never return to her world, just as he was doomed to be stranded in Shiyan without ever seeing father again.

The doctor held out her hand to the boy.

"Kuan, we must keep up."

He took her hand and reluctantly continued the journey back to the wretched life on board *FSS Castle*.

"I'll have to go back to clearing up elephantium, won't I?"

"That would be up to Captain Ma."

"That's a 'yes'."

"You can't tell. From what I've heard from Tan, what you did down in the valley was extremely brave, and it helped to stop the illegal Blessing. The captain might look favourably on that."

"I'm sure he won't."

"I'll put in a good word for you."

And not the slightest difference that would make, he told himself. Nothing good was going to come out of this life.

"Erica, do you think we have some kind of life after we die?"

"I doubt it. Why do you ask?"

"Why do you doubt it?"

"Once we lose our physical form, there wouldn't be anything left for a life."

"But you lose your form every time you change. You're not just a cat, or just a human, there's something else. Why can't that part of you live on when you're no longer a cat, or a human, or anything else?"

"Because when I die, that part will disintegrate too. There'll be nothing left of me. You shouldn't be thinking about death anyway. You have a long life ahead of you."

"What a life, scooping up mauve elephants' mess by day, locked up in a cell by night."

It pained her that she could offer him no solace.

"Don't worry, Erica, I believe it won't be the end when I die in this life. I can never get back to my world, and father will never find his way here. But when we're both dead, we'll be together again."

She looked deep into the big black eyes staring back at her, and forbade herself from contradicting him.

"I wish you could meet father. He's full of ideas, always setting them down on his typewriter. You'd like him. He doesn't believe there's life after death either. But once in a while he gets things wrong too. And he's wrong on this one. How else can those who have been wrenched apart ever be together again?"

She squeezed his hand and raised a smile full of unspoken sadness.

In front of them, Tan leapt onto the crimson stone and with a claw delicately tapped in a code on a well concealed metal pad to its side. The stone moved forward just enough for the three of them to go through, and quickly closed behind them. A light came on instantly to reveal they were standing on a circular disc that steadily rose upward until it reached the subterranean portal, through which they stepped onto the familiar deck 4 of the submarine. Len-Wu, the Head of Security, was waiting for them, flanked by a pair of sleek cheetahs. The lion greeted them with a stern announcement.

"You're under arrest."

"Len-Wu, I'll deal with the boy. He left his duty without proper authorisation, but I'll speak to Captain Ma about that."

Tan moved protectively in front of Kuan as he spoke, but they were both dwarfed by the hulking presence of the lion.

"Agent Tan, *you* are under arrest."

The Chartreux cat could not believe what he just heard.

"For what? Let me speak to the captain at once."

"For the murder of the eleven Mauveans on board *FSS Castle*. It was Captain Ma who ordered your arrest. Guards, take him away."

Tan's eyes flared with suspicion but he went silently with the two cheetahs.

"Dr. Lee, could you take the human child back to his cell? We then need you to carry out the autopsy of the victims. Captain Ma insisted we wait until you were back. He wouldn't trust anyone else with it."

"When did all this happen?" asked the doctor.

"In the last 24 hours, we believe. Governor Pui was to have a final meeting at 09:00 with the Mauveans after concluding his visit to *FSS Castle*. When none of them showed, we went to check and found each and every one of them dead in their own room. The governor had delayed going back to the capital because he said he might have to amend his report to the Vice-President. It's most unfortunate, and all happening on my watch."

"But Tan couldn't have done it. He's been with either me or Kuan all that time down in Castle de Potoka. Who could even think of accusing him of doing such a thing?"

"It'll all come out in the trial when it begins tomorrow. You have until 16:00 to submit your autopsy report."

The hall reserved for the exclusive use by mauve elephants, where their meeting with Governor Pui would have taken place, had been converted into a sombre courtroom. Causing serious injury to Mauveans, fatal or otherwise, was punishable by death. The governor, perched on a golden lectern placed next to the judge's bench, fanned out his commanding feathers to start the proceedings. His rich plumage, adorned by a purple crown, was second to none by virtue of the fact that he was granted special presidential privilege to be the only Shiyanese permitted to assume the form of a peacock. Apart from his subservience to the Mauveans, who included the President and Vice-President in their ranks, he had supreme power over all others. In the last three days he had met with Captain Ma; Chief Engineer Xian, the one with the leopard head atop her human body; Head of Security, Len-Wu; and the President's military adviser, General Chi-Ling, to discuss whether *FSS Castle* should spearhead the launch of a preemptive strike against the Potokans. But with all the mauve elephants dead, and the supply of elephantium depleted, the submarine was in every sense powerless to do anything. Indeed if Potokans from other enclaves managed to launch an attack now, the sub would not be able to defend itself.

"I cannot overstate the gravity of our current situation." The governor began.

"Taking the life of any of our most venerated Shiyanese is a heinous crime, but to murder a group of them so as to sabotage a Class A submarine is treason of the highest order. Not only must we find out who is responsible, it is imperative we establish what conspiracy lies behind this so that we can extinguish it with alacrity."

He pecked out each point like a surgical incision, focused on drawing blood, so as to remove a malignant threat.

"I have to leave now to prepare for my meeting with Vice-President Dao tomorrow evening. He will be expecting a full report from me, which will in turn inform his discussion with the President herself about the Potokan Question. The findings of this court will provide critical evidence. I have therefore asked Captain Ma to preside over this trial, ensuring it is open and fair, and to deliver its conclusions to me by 14:00 tomorrow."

The peacock drew his glistening cape together and beckoned Captain Ma to join him on the dais. As the silver-haired officer took his seat behind the judge's bench, the governor whispered to him, "Ma, I'm counting on you."

Then with a cold stare at the assembled personnel, he solemnly nodded to signify the court was now in session. With a flourish of his translucent feathers, he exited.

Captain Ma, his pale face drawn down by heavy expectations, put the pipe in his mouth and wondered how he could reconcile his conflicting loyalties. Directly in front of him stood the accused, Agent Tan, who had been told he would be entitled to claim a less painful form of execution if he agreed to save the court's time by confessing to his crime. The black cat, tail relaxed, stared defiantly ahead.

Kuan sat waiting nervously in the gallery. He had been designated the key witness and he would be questioned last. First up was Dr. Lee who padded up to the witness box in her red Abyssinian cat form, but morphed into the human doctor before she presented her autopsy report. The eleven mauve elephants on board *FSS Castle* had all died from asphyxiation. It had happened sometime after midnight but no later than 02.00. There was no sign of any physical assault. She wanted to add that Agent Tan was with her on an authorised mission during that time to deal with illegal Blessing taking place in Castle de Potoka. Captain Ma ruled that it was a separate issue they would return to later and asked her to step down after thanking her for the speed and thoroughness with which she had conducted the autopsy.

Next came Xian, the chief engineer who was as usual in her close-fitting blue naval overalls. The leopard with the human body took the witness stand. Her fiery red eyes turned on Tan. Gnashing her teeth, she reported that the airflow system had been tampered with. It was no thoughtless act of vandalism, because the individual responsible cut off the oxygen supply to the eleven rooms in question precisely between 01:00 and 02:00. He wanted to kill all the Mauveans on board, risking the general oxygen balance of the boat, and depleting the level of elephantium available to fuel the submarine. She accused him of betraying Shiyan in carrying out the most deplorable acts. She would not be surprised if he turned out to be a double-agent for the Potokans. Any form of execution would be too lenient for him, he should instead be sent to Hades for an eternity of suffering.

Captain Ma had heard enough and told Xian to stand down. It was not for her to talk about sentencing options, least of all the Hades punishment.

Xian stepped down from the witness box and exchanged a gentle nod with Len-Wu who was next up to give his testimony. Her account of the deliberate tampering of the oxygen supply was corroborated by the Head of Security, whose investigation confirmed there was a re-programming of the airflow system carried out at 00:46. There was no reported sighting of any unauthorised personnel in the restricted engineering area where any re-programming had to be carried out. That suggested someone with security clearance had managed to get into the area unseen to make the lethal adjustment.

Captain Ma then called General Chi-Ling to give what turned out to be the most damning evidence against Agent Tan. Chi-Ling was a fearsome tiger, as big as the lion Len-Wu. As he took the witness stand he adopted the semi-morphed form with a human body in camouflage combat uniform, while his head remained that of a tiger. He could crush the black cat with his bare hand, but when he spoke, it was in a calm and considered tone. He regretted having to break the confidence of a fellow officer, but the integrity of the trial required no less than putting all pertinent information in plain view.

It was the day after the general arrived on *FSS Castle* to take part in Governor Pui's top level discussions that he had a chance to speak with Agent Tan in private. He sought his views on the Potokan situation and was struck by Tan's claim that the problem was not so much with the Potokans as with the Mauveans. When pressed to elaborate what he meant, Tan allegedly responded by saying that the mauve elephants had to be "taken out of the equation". The whole courtroom gasped.

"What I actually said was …" Tan tried to explain himself but Captain Ma silenced him by banging his pipe like a gavel on the bench.

"Agent Tan, your turn will come. In the meantime, refrain from interrupting proceedings."

Chi-Ling folded his arms across his broad chest and continued.

"At the time I thought it was just a throwaway remark and didn't consider it necessary to mention it to anyone else. In the light of what has happened, I regret not alerting the Head of Security."

The face of the tiger glanced briefly at Tan. Two inscrutable stares clashed in silence. The general marched back to the gallery.

Ma wiped the sweat from his forehead and called Kuan to the witness box. The boy made his way forward. He stood there holding on to the edge of the box. There was no chair. He looked over at Tan whose eyes tracked every move made by the increasingly uncomfortable captain.

"Kuan, we have reached the point where your testimony can settle this trial conclusively. It is noted by our security guards that the defendant left deck 4 with Dr. Lee through the subterranean portal just after midnight two nights ago. After they reached the main cave of Castle de Potoka, he claimed he had to separate from Dr. Lee to go down to the valley to look for you. He further claimed that he was with you in the valley when an unauthorised Blessing event was successfully disrupted, which local sources put at around 00:35 to 00:50. If that were true, there would be insufficient time for him to get back up to deck 4 to re-programme the oxygen supply before or after the incident in the valley. However, if there were any doubt in your mind, then his alibi would collapse. Remember, you have already given a statement to the Head of Security indicating that someone with a rhinoceros form was responsible for your rescue in the valley. It is a matter of military record that Tan has not reached a high enough level in the Circles of Challenge to be able to morph into a rhino. So could you tell the court to the best of your recollection if it was Tan you saw, without any reasonable doubt, or having been Blessed that night, you hallucinated and merely thought you saw the agent."

The boy searched his memory hard. He had momentarily disbelieved that it could be Tan standing in front of him when he was lying there in the valley. But that was because he did not want to believe it. It only shook him up so much since deep down, he knew it was true.

"Captain Ma, I was not hallucinating, it was Agent Tan that I …"

"This court is adjourned until 09:00 tomorrow!"

Agitated outbursts shattered the silence of the courtroom. Ma transformed into his grey Manx cat form and disappeared out of a side door.

Chapter 8

Quid Pro Quo

Kuan had not been back in his cell long before someone called on him. He could sense it was Erica Lee before she even stepped through the door. His heart raced ahead the moment that scent of hope swept towards him. It was an association that planted itself in him though he was convinced no good news would ever be forthcoming.

The doctor asked him to come urgently with her. She took him down the corridor to another cell similar to his. Inside, lying weakly on the floor was the golden brown orangutan he used to work with in the Elephantium Team, the one who never spoke with anyone. Kuan knelt down beside him. The orangutan blinked his small weary eyes and spoke softly.

"I heard you were back."

The boy clasped the emaciated arm of his fellow outsider.

"We never got to know each other. My fault. Not good with words." The orangutan continued.

Kuan had never heard that mellow, thoughtful voice before. If only they had got to know each other. But the time had passed.

"I asked the good doctor if she could bring you here so I could ask you a favour."

He took out something from his black jumpsuit and gently placed it in Kuan's opening palm. It was a small emerald green pebble.

"My son gave me this when we were on a family outing once by the sea. I don't know how long ago it was now. Less painful if you don't count the days. I was showing off, diving into the water to catch a fish. The only thing caught that day was me."

The boy looked down at the gleaming stone in his hand.

"One day, if it so pleases heaven, you will meet my son. It would mean so much to me if you wouldn't mind returning this token to him. Tell him Batya loves him."

Kuan nodded with hollow affirmation, watched through the stoic eyes of the doctor standing behind him.

Batya drew a long, deep breath.

"Thank you."

And those were his last words.

The boy held the pebble tightly as he bore witness to a life passing.

The orangutan had acquired the notion that with all the mauve elephants on board dead, the Elephantium Team would be disbanded and the outsiders who had been pressganged into its service would be released. The thought of returning to his family ignited a yearning which had lain dormant for years. When told that more Mauveans would soon be arriving, and he was not going anywhere, his spirit came crashing down from the boundless heights to which it had soared. There was nothing to keep him alive anymore.

Kuan slowly stood up. Dr. Lee held him close to her. He put his arms around her waist and wished she would never let go of him. Father was not coming for him. He had no memory of a mother. Stranded alone in the desert of his mind, he had to cling on even to a mirage if he was not to be buried by a random sandstorm, erasing his existence from the face of a dubious world.

The doctor stepped aside from Kuan to stare at the corpse before her.

"We used to be a beacon of hope to the world. Now we rip it out of every poor soul who looks to us for mercy."

She took the boy back to his cell, and having pushed his hair behind his ears, kissed his forehead and walked away.

The future was condensed into one bleak moment. There would be no escape. Even though Erica Lee wanted to help him, she could do nothing to alter the fate to which he had been arbitrarily condemned. If she had stayed with him a little longer, he could perhaps fix his eyes on her and momentarily ignore the chains of futility that bound him. But ultimately he could see no way out of his predicament. Whatever attempt he made, some fateful force would drag him back to this solitary confinement. He took another look at the pebble and put it in the trouser pocket of his dirt-encrusted jumpsuit.

The cell door slid open. The Manx cat entered cautiously and walked along each wall of the cell, carrying out his silent inspection with meticulous care. In one corner, he sniffed for a moment only to conclude there was nothing to be concerned with. Satisfied with the condition, he morphed into the captain's human form. He flicked some dust off his sleeve and gave the boy an anxious look.

"Kuan, I know you haven't been exactly happy since coming on board *FSS Castle*. In spite of that, you've maintained a positive attitude. I have heard about the role you played in challenging that rogue simian and bringing his Blessing racket to an end. That was very brave of you. You can't always count on outsiders to do the right thing. But you're an impressive exception. Therefore, I'm prepared to make you a proposition. I will guarantee your immediate release from custody on this boat, and return you to where we first found you, provided you tell the court tomorrow that you never saw Agent Tan in the valley down in Castel de Potoka two nights ago."

If his first thought was whether he could seriously trust Captain Ma to stand by such an offer, his second rapidly caught up to remind him that he did indeed see Tan in the valley that night. If he chose to lie, he would be responsible for getting an innocent individual executed. How could he live with himself if he did that?

"It doesn't matter if you claim the Blessing affected you, or fatigue after battling the chimp caused you to imagine you saw someone resembling Tan. What you must categorically maintain when you're in the witness box is that having reflected at length, you did not see Agent Tan in the valley that night."

The boy's face was riven with doubt.

"You don't understand the complications we've got here. But we must secure a guilty verdict as quickly as possible. And all the evidence points to Tan. No one else had the ability *and* the motive to tamper with the oxygen supply. He told General Chi-Ling that Mauveans were the problem. You don't know Agent Tan as well as I do, but once he's set his mind on something, he'll find a way to do it."

Kuan was not convinced. Captain Ma tracked down his pipe in one of his uniform's many pockets and put it in his mouth for barely a second before taking it out again.

"You have no idea how devious he can be. There's probably a multitude of ways he could make you think you saw him when he was actually in the engineering room cutting off the oxygen supply to his victims. Subterfuge, that's what he's good at. Don't be fooled by him. You need to help us convict the true culprit of this terrible crime."

"But what if he had nothing to do with it? And he ends up being executed because I give testimony that isn't true."

"Kuan, who says your testimony won't be true? You don't know that. How can you be absolutely sure about what you did or didn't see? And how could you, a ten-year old human outsider, understand better than those of us in charge of the investigation and trial of this critical case for Shiyan, what really happened?"

The captain put his hands on the boy's shoulders. Kuan could feel them shaking.

"He must have done it. It could not be any other way."

Kuan looked down at the floor. What would father want him to do? Father who was despairing at home over the disappearance of his son, pining for his return.

"Think about it, Kuan. On the one hand you can cling to what you think you might have seen, and the trial is prolonged, the uncertainties drive Shiyan into declaring war against the Potokans, and Tan will still most likely be executed – because someone has to be when such an atrocious crime against a group of Mauveans has been committed. On the other hand, you can help us wrap this up, I get my report off to Governor Pui, Tan is spared the dreadful wait before his unavoidable execution, and you get to go home. You do want to go home, don't you?"

Put like that, Kuan could not see how he could choose differently.

"Captain Ma, if I said in court I didn't see Agent Tan in the valley, would you have me taken back to my home immediately?"

"Absolutely."

"But I've heard it's not possible for outsiders to return to our own world once we've come into Shiyan."

"Who told you that? Just because no outsider has returned to their own world, it doesn't mean it can't be done. One can leave Shiyan as easily as coming into it."

"You're sure?"

"Without a doubt. With my many years as a sub-mariner, I have come to know all there is to know about traversing between different worlds. You give me the testimony we need, I will personally take you back to where you're from at once."

Arms folded, Captain Ma stared at Kuan so intensely that one would think his naval career, even his life, depended on the boy agreeing to his deal.

"Captain, I'll go along with what you've suggested, but I've got to see Agent Tan one last time to thank him for saving my life. I couldn't go through with it otherwise."

"But in the witness box, you wouldn't say anything about him saving your life in the valley."

Kuan shook his head.

It was a measure of Ma's desperation that he eventually consented to the boy seeing Tan. With his authorisation, Kuan was allowed to go over to Tan's cell. He was able to speak with him alone, though the cheetahs standing guard outside would leap in if the boy were threatened in any way. Tan's temperament was deemed unpredictable.

Alone with Tan, Kuan told him about the captain's offer. The black cat was not at all surprised, and he calmly thanked Kuan for informing him. He insisted that an ordinary outsider would have just taken the deal, but something was now directing the boy to the true path.

Kuan could not believe that Tan would at this point still bring up his mystifying obsession with some secret reason for which he was brought to Shiyan.

"You have to look within yourself, Kuan. You were sent here for a purpose, and this is the beginning of your realisation."

"What purpose? The only thing I know is that nothing makes sense. You saved my life in the valley. But not long ago you threatened to kill me in that interrogation chair."

"That had to be done. I needed to know if you were the one sent to us."

"Who's supposed to have sent me to this place? Who would be so cruel?"

The black cat momentarily lowered his eyes.

"And if I weren't the one, you would have killed me like you did that other outsider in the chair?"

"No, I had nothing to do with what happened to him. What you saw was a recording of some other agent's work. But that is how things are done around here, whatever I may think about it."

"And that's how they will continue to be?"

"They can change. They ought to change. No doubt it will become clearer to you soon."

"This much is clear. I go along with the captain, and I'm putting you to death. I say no, and I lose my one real chance of getting home."

"Or you could find the real killer."

"How could I possibly do that? I'm a prisoner on this ship. Besides, Captain Ma is set on finding you guilty. His mind is made up."

"Ma is a master of naval manoeuvres, but he hasn't got a clue how to deal with politicians like Governor Pui. He's under pressure to deliver a verdict, and he's got no other suspect. That's why he's going for me. It's nothing personal."

"But you didn't do it. Did you?"

"I was there in the valley when the reprogramming of the oxygen supply was done. You saw me."

"I saw the black rhino which changed into you. But they said you couldn't become a rhino."

"There's a lot they don't know about me."

"Why don't you tell them? Or better still, show them you can do it."

"Nothing will change their mind unless they have a suspect who will as good as own up to the crime."

Kuan sat down furtively close to the Chartreux cat who whispered to him what he should do.

Back in his cell, Kuan found the hatch to a secret passageway Tan told him about. Through it he crawled into an air vent, and after a couple of false turns he arrived at the engineering room. The panel controlling the airflow system was very close by, and whoever tampered with the oxygen supply would have had to key in a personalised security code to alter the standard programme. Although it was reported that the panel recorded no such code, that could only happen if someone was able to enter a secondary code to wipe out the initial entry.

While the secondary code was not detectable by a routine inspection, one could retrieve it with the right password and use it to identify the perpetrator. Agent Tan did not have the authorization for such a password, but nonetheless possessed one. Kuan quietly opened the panel and was about to use the password Tan gave him to discover whose secondary code was deployed to wipe the information when he heard footsteps approaching. He quickly closed the panel and hid behind the large energy converter next to it. The female voice he heard was distinctly that of Xian, the leopard-faced Chief Engineer.

"General Chi-Ling, our elephantium level is critically low. Even with more Mauveans arriving in the next few days, and of course we can't hurry them, it would take us at least a week to get back up to optimum operational capacity. To flood the subterranean deck as soon as the death sentence is passed on Tan tomorrow would provoke a Potokan attack on *FSS Castle* that we're in no position to defend against."

"Wait. An outsider." Chi-Ling interrupted.

Kuan held his breath.

The tiger-head general glared at the room, his fingers morphing into extended claws. But Xian, wiping her hands in a cloth she pulled out from the pocket of her overalls, was not the least perturbed.

"We use outsiders to bring elephantium to the energy converter here. Their smell tends to linger."

"My guards are outside. No one's come past them apart from us." The lion-shaped Len-Wu was there too.

Chi-Ling returned his hand to fully human form. His eyes, which Kuan could spy from his hiding place, still glowed with suspicion.

"Xian, Len-Wu, you don't seem to understand how this works. Governor Pui will get his report from Captain Ma saying Tan has committed an act of treason. He will tell Vice-President Dao, who will then have no choice but to press the President to declare war on the Potokans at once. I have to prepare the army for this, and you in the navy have to be able to look after your own fleet."

"No, I don't understand', protested Len-Wu, the vast shadow of his lion form sweeping towards Kuan. "Nobody knows why Tan has done this, and it may have nothing to do with the Potokans."

"Len-Wu, isn't it obvious that Tan's in league with the Potokans? Why else would he do such a thing? I've never trusted him."

The lion shook his mane at Xian's riposte. General Chi-Ling resumed his explanation of what would happen at the conclusion of the trial.

"It doesn't matter what we think. War is going to be declared, and Potokans everywhere will attack us. And if you're not ready to flood your subterranean deck and drown all the Potokans on your boat with one strike, you will have to face their deranged onslaught. I have fought against them in the past. They don't abide by our rules of engagement. Once they launch an attack, they will destroy everything in their way. Len-Wu, even if you were able to increase your security force tenfold, you would not be able to protect this submarine from them."

"General, with due respect, isn't that a factor Governor Pui must take into account when he speaks to the Vice-President? Strike against the Potokans by all means if that's the final consensus, but surely the timing has to be right." Len-Wu spoke with restrained agitation.

"Governor Pui will take into account what he decides to take into account. My job is to carry out orders when they're given." Chi-Ling replied.

"But General, you're the military adviser to the President. You have a direct line of communication to her. Can't you persuade her to delay any declaration of war?"

"If I give any advice contrary to what Vice-President Dao would give, I might as well hand in my resignation now."

"So we have to approach this differently." Xian interjected.

Kuan peeped from the side of the energy converter. The lion paced up and down, growling in deep frustration. General Chi-Ling, arms behind his mountainous back, tried to be patient. For some reason, Xian was uncharacteristically enthusiastic.

"The time has come to broach the subject of an alternative to elephantium. There's a prototype for solar conversion. I can have it set up to use the sun's energy to power everything, and we would be ready to fight any war without the delay with elephantium. Shouldn't the President seriously consider that?"

"Are you trying to downgrade the status of the Mauveans? The President would never permit such heresy. And if Vice-President Dao hears about this, you could be demoted, or even court-martialed. You cannot suggest anything which implies that we can do without the most revered Shiyanese."

"Xian, your alternative technology is not yet proven in any case", added Len-Wu, "it's not worth the risk. I suspect we're far too deep under water to be able to draw on the sun's energy."

"You don't know about the latest prototype I've developed."

"War is about to break out, Xian. This is not the time for prototypes."

"And when we're overrun with Potokans, what are you going to do?"

"Xian, Len-Wu, I've heard enough. I'll do what I can to convey your reservations, but I can't promise anything more."

Kuan could not believe that Tan's execution would be compounded by the extermination of the Potokans in the subterranean deck of *FSS Castle*. Not only was Tan innocent, but the Potokans he had seen could not be behind any plot to kill mauve elephants.

As soon as Chi-Ling had left with the Chief Engineer and Head of Security, Kuan turned back to the airflow system panel. With the help of Tan's surreptitiously obtained password he discovered that a secondary code was indeed logged for the erasure of the digital fingerprint of the one who tampered with the system at 00:46 that night. But when he sought to get a read-out of that secondary code to reveal who that was, the small screen simply said 'Deleted'. Of the identity of the true culprit, there was not a trace.

Chapter 9

<u>Betrayal</u>

Captain Ma, who appeared to have grown even greyer overnight, looked wearily around the courtroom. The gallery was packed with many members of *FSS Castle*'s Shiyanese crew, almost all in their cat form, large or small, except for Dr. Erica Lee and Xian. The doctor fidgeted with her stethoscope. Next to her, Len-Wu the lion ordered his guards to spread out. Xian the semi-morph stood by the main exit, using her long human fingers to pick out something that had got stuck between her leopard fangs. General Chi-Ling stationed himself near the front, chest out, legs apart, tiger head held high, his human physique stretching his army uniform.

The captain's eyes stopped at Kuan, crouching down by the black Chartreux cat, immersed in conversation. The boy kept nodding at Agent Tan who kept his eyes shut. He must be sharing his last words with his erstwhile charge. Ma waited for them to finish before he took his seat and called the court to order. He wasted no time in directing Kuan to the witness box. The trial must be swiftly wrapped up and all loose ends tied up for that exacting peacock, Governor Pui.

"Kuan, having reflected carefully, could you please tell us if you saw Agent Tan or not in the valley in Castle de Potoka on the night in question?"

"To answer your question, captain, I need to report a conversation I overheard last night when I went to pick up some equipment I had left in the engineering room. I was getting my things together when I heard voices. Couldn't really recognise them. I was worried that I might get into trouble, so I hid myself."

Len-Wu looked anxiously across to Chi-Ling at one end of the courtroom and Xian at the other. Xian scanned Len-Wu and Chi-Ling to see how they were reacting. The general subtly glanced back at the other two. Their visual crossfire was enough to intrigue Captain Ma, who decided to let Kuan go on.

"They were speaking about elephantium, which wasn't surprising since we were not far from the energy converter. And they said something about war with the Potokans. Then they seemed to have left, except after a short while, two of them came back."

Kuan paused as he had to rely not on any actual memory of events from that point, but on Tan's scripting. The optic intensity of the triangular exchange hit a new level, and he drew strength from it to continue.

"One of them said it was wrong to let Agent Tan take the blame. After all, they could open the panel and find out who was really responsible for the reprogramming at 00:46. The other one said the security code of that individual had been erased from the system. But the first one said to do that one would need a secondary code, which would be stored in a hidden drive, and it could still be accessed with the right password. And that password apparently was 'A4K8F9A1K'. The second one said in that case they must find out who it was."

The whole courtroom started to rumble. Kuan noticed Xian slip quietly out of the door at the back of the room. General Chi-Ling beckoned one of his lieutenants, a snow tiger bigger than the lion, to whisper an order to him. Len-Wu broke protocol by asking Captain Ma if proceedings should be halted as they were becoming highly irregular.

"Len-Wu, that's for me to decide. Do not interrupt the witness' testimony again. Go on, Kuan."

"One of them must have keyed in that password, and apparently got a read-out which one or the other of them noted down. Unfortunately, neither of them said aloud what the recorded secondary code was. But I assume they would want to pass that code to you, Captain Ma, so you could have solid evidence pointing to the killer."

Kuan's pulse was racing by now. The plan would only work if Tan's gambit on the 'Deleted' data were to pay off. Otherwise, he would have forfeited his chance to regain his freedom, and Tan would still be executed.

"Len-Wu, did you check the panel for this information on who tried to erase their digital fingerprint from the system?"

"No, Captain, I didn't have the password to interrogate the panel's restricted drive. As you didn't give me the password to do it, I assumed you must have done it yourself and found the secondary code to be Agent Tan's."

"Assumed? How can you make such an assumption? If there's someone else who should be the prime suspect in this case, I want him arrested."

"Captain Ma", General Chi-Ling cut in, "we may be talking about a *she*. I noticed Chief Engineer Xian sneaking out when the secondary code issue came up. I suggest we send out a combined team to hunt her down."

Chi-Ling's troops of tigers quickly huddled together, but Len-Wu's cheetahs stayed where they were, looking to the security chief for his instruction. Chi-Ling and Len-Wu glared at each other with tense anticipation.

"This is no time for hesitation." General Chi-Ling snarled.

Kuan could see that Len-Wu was reluctant to take any action. Did he think it outrageous to suspect a colleague he had come to know well over the years? Or was he troubled by the notion that she could turn out to be a traitor?

"Len-Wu, what are you waiting for? We must not let her get away." The tiger rallied for action.

"No one's getting away, General Chi-Ling," said Xian, bursting back into the courtroom. "I know who committed the murder. I've been down to the engineering room and entered the password Kuan recounted to us. It confirmed the use of a secondary code to erase the perpetrator's digital fingerprint."

"So whose secondary code was it?" demanded Captain Ma.

"It was marked 'Deleted'."

"The secondary code was also erased? Then this is a complete waste of time."

"Not just erased, but specifically marked 'Deleted'."

"Xian, is that supposed to mean something?"

"Yes, Captain, only senior commanding officers can use and remove secondary codes. But when they do, it is recorded as 'Deleted'. That is in the official protocol. I checked."

"It would appear that only one official on this submarine qualifies for that", Chi-Ling observed, "and that would be you, Captain Ma."

Ma was astounded.

"General Chi-Ling, are you suggesting I have something to do with the murder? That is preposterous."

"We must follow the evidence where it leads us. Len-Wu, discharge your duty and arrest the captain."

Sweeping his head between his captain and the general, the lion was now even more paralysed by indecision. As his guards looked intently at him for a sign of what they were to do, the Chartreux cat calmly offered his advice.

"Len-Wu, General Chi-Ling has given you an order, which he is entitled to give because as a general, he brings with him the authority to act as a senior commanding officer on any military base or naval vessel. He has shown remarkable consistency in trying to pin the murder on any remote suspect so long as it kept him out of the frame. He lied about what I said regarding Mauveans to concoct a false motive for me to commit a crime I had nothing to do with; with the flimsiest excuse, he tried to get Xian hunted down for the same crime; and then he turned on Captain Ma, who has shown nothing but deference and diligent care towards all the Mauvean guests on board his submarine all the time he's been at the helm. If anyone is the prime suspect in this case, wouldn't you say it has to be the general?"

With blazing fury, Captain Ma rose and ordered the general's arrest. Len-Wu's hesitation vanished, and his band of cheetahs surrounded the general. Chi-Ling's gentle demeanour rapidly gave way to a rage-filled eruption.

"Enough of this! You fools have no idea how you're putting Shiyan in grave danger. I've been advising the President that she must declare war on the Potokans, but she wanted more time to discuss options with the Council of Mauveans. She insisted that we must seek a consensus on how to move forward. But we can't afford to waste time when the Potokans are threatening our very existence right now. So I took an executive decision. Sacrifice a few to bring about a greater good for us all. The murder of Mauveans on board this submarine, which Potokan agents would have gladly carried out if given half a chance, leaves the

President no choice but to launch a war immediately. You are not going to stand in the way of that."

The general had confessed his crime. Kuan's faith in Agent Tan's stratagem appeared to have paid off. Chi-Ling would be arrested and Captain Ma would surely agree to return the boy to his home by the rocky beach. But perpetrators of the most vicious crimes were not known for their deference to the law, in Shiyan or any world.

Black and blood orange fur sprouted over his combat uniform as General Chi-Ling morphed into his full tiger form. It was the signal for his reinforcements to pour in from the back. The tigers attacked indiscriminately, their jaws crushing any creature that got in their way, their claws shredding all those now branded the enemy. Chi-Ling led with his ruthless example as he ripped the face off a mountain cat which just happened to be next to him. Howls and shrieks fused into a pandemonium of fear and rage.

Kuan, petrified by the sight of mass slaughter, remained standing in the witness box. He was not greatly assured by a lean cheetah sent over by Len-Wu to protect him. The clash between the tigers and the *Castle*'s crew continued unabated. He held his breath when Erica Lee was knocked sideway by one of the tigers. She fell like a red blur and transformed into the Abyssinian cat as she skipped away into a corner. As far as he could tell, she was unharmed. He wanted to run over to protect her but knew he would not make it through the gauntlet of claws and incisors.

Len-Wu found himself surrounded by three tigers drilled to slay without question. The lion could just about hold off two of them when the third one attempted to leap over his comrades to clamp his fangs on the back of Len-Wu's neck. But in mid-air he was knocked over by Xian who, having transformed completely into her leopard form, was more than a match for her adversary. She seized the tiger's skull and smashed it with a loud crunching sound against the floor. At the same time, Len-Wu had surged forward and pushed his two opponents up against a wall, his claws puncturing their lungs.

The tide was turning against the tigers. Kuan glanced ahead at Agent Tan whose eyes reflected back on him. The black cat seemed not to be bothered by the bloodshed choreographed with macabre precision all around him. He watched for any possible threat directed at the boy and was ready to strike in his defence any moment.

Captain Ma tried to shout over the mayhem, calling on Chi-Ling to surrender, but it only attracted the response of two jaw-gaping tigers descending onto him from right and left. Detecting the vulnerability of the captain, the Chartreux cat morphed into a gargantuan rhino and ploughed into the two assailants without mercy. Unfortunately, once Tan moved out of the way, it left a gap for Chi-Ling to hurtle through towards the witness box. His momentum toppled the sentry cheetah. The security guard tried to get back on his feet, but Chi-Ling had stabbed him in the throat with his incisors. Death was instant. Kuan wanted to run but he was backed into a corner. The general wrapped his paw around the boy's neck. He extended a solitary claw to point at Kuan's throbbing jugular vein.

"Stand down, everyone!" He roared.

Len-Wu growled and his trusted guards moved back. Captain Ma was standing up as boldly as he could though faintness was pulling him down. The rampaging rhino changed back into a very still cat. Groans of pain echoed amidst the carnage.

General Chi-Ling changed back into his semi-morphed form except for one part of his human body –

his right arm was still the limb of a tiger with blood-drenched claws. He was dictating the terms.

"This diversion has gone on long enough. I must leave your submarine and submit my personal report to the President. There will be no delay to our war on the Potokans. I will help her see through the irrelevant details and grasp the simple truth – Shiyan will never be weak again, because we have learnt not to hesitate in showing our strengths. None of us should ever forget the humiliations piled on our world when our timidity betrayed us. From now on, Shiyan must expect obedience and command respect, without exception."

Kuan glanced up at the tiger's face, consumed by delusional righteousness. Looking down at the fistful of claws clamped around his throat, he could see that any attempt to slip out of that grip would sever the arteries in his neck.

"Captain, if you want this boy to live, let me and my troops leave on our combat submersible. I'm in no mood for negotiation."

Captain Ma wanted to bargain for an alternative. Kuan turned his eyes to Agent Tan, who in total stillness was thinking frantically about what could be done.

"Captain, you know how easy it would be for me to cut his throat open. Don't make me do that."

The general tightened his grip around Kuan's neck. In a futile yet involuntary gesture, the boy raised his hand to hold back the blood that might any moment be gushing out of his severed throat.

If he had accepted the captain's original proposition, he would be on his way home. But at the expense of an innocent life? At least his action should mean that Tan would now be spared. Yet dead bodies were strewn across the courtroom, their spilled blood merely heralding the greater slaughter to come. Had he done the right thing? Was it going to make any real difference in the end? Such burden should not be put on the shoulders of a ten year old. It was the end for him in any case. Chi-Ling was dragging him towards the docking station to board his own underwater carrier.

Tan called out to Kuan.

"You were sent here for a reason. No one can harm you, Kuan, if you stay true to what you're meant to do. Embrace your mission."

Did Tan really say that? Or was it just Kuan's own fear-fuelled delirium? There was no mission. Just a hopeless predicament, seized by a bloodthirsty killer who would take you hostage and then dispose of your worthless body once he had made his escape.

Alongside the Chartreux came the red Abyssinian cat with her sad soulful green eyes. She must know that here was another one she had failed to save. Kuan wished she would morph back into her human form one more time before he was pulled away. She didn't.

The connection hatch was closed. Inside the small but technologically advanced combat submersible, General Chi-Ling stood his remaining troops to attention and ordered an immediate retreat. The army boat detached itself from *FSS Castle* and veered off on its own course. Kuan was thrown into a corner. He was a puny child, incapable of posing any physical threat, and it would be a demeaning waste of time to keep watch on him. Kuan could be freely torn apart once they were out of *FSS Castle*'s torpedo range and confident that Ma's crew could no longer track them.

The boy sat alone at the back of the submersible, arms locked around his knees. Rocking to and fro, he tried to imagine one or another of Chi-Ling's lieutenants revealing himself to be Tan or Len-Wu. In the past, he had heard tales of bravery in different forms, set in diverse traditions. But confronted by the face of deadly menace, of overwhelming destruction, all the courage from heaven would not tip the balance one iota. Was he supposed to laugh defiantly at the imminent arrival of his painful demise? All he was capable of grasping was the fear that had filled him to the brim.

An improbable voice called to Kuan. It was barely audible. Just above him was a reflector, a gadget for transmitting visual messages, but it was not in operation. Kuan crept up and just saw his own image, a boy with forlorn eyes beneath straggly black hair, and lips drawn down by dread and disappointment. A glimmer of light appeared at the bottom of the reflector. It was Amo. She had somehow survived the downpour and found her way back to the main part of *FSS Castle*, and not long after that she had located a standalone transporter all ready to launch. She knew immediately that it would be the perfect vehicle to get her and Kuan away.

While Amo was working out the internal circuits of the submersible's navigation unit, she heard the commotion and discovered Kuan had been forced on board. The challenge was to override the boat's mapping system which, to her surprise unlike the main submarine's, had few effective electronic safeguards. In the end it was not at all a difficult task to accomplish. As she had promised she would get Kuan home, she had memorised from *FSS Castle's* databank the coordinates of where the boy was first found. Next she activated the submersible's autopilot and fed it the necessary data. The effect was instantaneous. Cries of panic could be heard from the cockpit of the underwater vehicle as it defied all control and started to speed towards a destination unknown to all those on board, bar two.

Chapter 10

Vanished

The Charybdis Vortex was well known to Shiyan's military personnel as the most dangerous place in open waters where seafaring vehicles could be pulled into oblivion. Currents deep in the ocean swirled with such intensity that any passing object, large or small, would be sucked in closer and closer until irresistible pressure would crush it to smithereens.

It would explain why the otherwise fearless troops of General Chi-Ling were terrified as their combat submersible inexplicably headed towards the deadly vortex. None of the controls would respond to their commands. It was too late to abandon ship as any ejected life-pod or individuals would just as likely be caught by the Charybdis grip. The band of tigers, loyal soldiers of Chi-Ling, braced themselves for their imminent destruction.

The submersible, travelling at top speed, suddenly veered away of its own accord. It turned so sharply that they all tumbled over. At the back Kuan sat tightly in his corner uncertain as to what might happen next. Amo assured him in a whisper that all was going according to plan. Indeed with the chaos, the general had quite forgotten about his hostage. His crew desperately tried to rectify the malfunction, but to no avail. Hulking muscles and steely discipline were no help in surmounting technical problems with the navigational system.

The narrow escape from the vortex had brought the fretful tigers no relief, for their boat appeared to be rapidly moving into uncharted waters, and nothing they tried could divert it from its destination. They did not know that they were now fixed on a straight course, which was to lead them to a desolate shoreline.

Waves lapped against the rocky beach under a grey autumn sky. A few seagulls were gorging themselves on their earlier catch. Behind them the landscape of dark sand, fragmented rocks and slimy seaweeds rose to a small ridge. A platoon of tiny red crabs scampered sideways to scattered holes in the sand and with startling rapidity disappeared down them.

The sound from the sea shifted to a different pitch. The seagulls gave the murky ocean a nervous stare. All at once, outstretched pinions lifted the frightened birds away from their unfinished meals. Crashing out of the water, the submersible punched through the air and landed with a thunderous clang.

Panels cracked, cables exposed, sparks flew ominously. Amo told Kuan to hit the emergency hatch button, and as he was almost out of the opening, she punctured a hole in an oxygen pipe with a concentrated beam, igniting an explosive fire which, engulfing the back of the submersible, provided perfect cover for the boy to run away unseen.

General Chi-Ling might assume the boy had been killed in the explosion. Under the circumstances, he would probably be less concerned with a worthless hostage than with escaping from Captain Ma and the entire naval hierarchy for his treacherous deeds on board *FSS Castle*. He had not been alone in wanting the President to launch an all-out war against the Potokans. Others would rally to his support if he could stay a few steps ahead of those seeking to capture him. He ordered his troops to set up camp on the beach while he considered how the submersible's navigation unit could be repaired.

Kuan crouched behind a black rock that was shaped like a tombstone. It was a familiar spot to him on the beach. Father never seemed to suspect his son would be hiding there. Each time, the boy would eventually crawl out from behind the rock and make his way back to the house. Father had long given up the search and was back in his study typing. Hide without much seek appeared to be the norm.

In the distance he could see the tigers disembarking from the submersible in their semi-morphed form wearing their land combat uniform. The sight of the most indomitable predators striding upright was chillingly disconcerting.

Kuan stayed low below the rock. He dug his hands into the sand to feel the grains with his probing fingers. He really was back where months previously he had strolled before he was swept out to sea. Safety would not slip away from him again.

Both he and father must now hide, at least until Chi-Ling had eventually taken his troops back out into Shiyan's territorial waters. He cast his eyes up along the gently sloping beach. At the top was a ridge beyond which was home. They could all go into the reinforced basement. No one would find them there.

Amo assured him Chi-Ling's troops had moved to the other side of the beach. It was time he made a run for it. He had no trouble dashing up to the ridge where he took a sharp turn down a neglected path covered in weeds. Halfway down the path, he began to get out of breath. He bent down with his hands on knees, disgusted with his lack of fitness. Amo, manifesting herself briefly as a small flame, asked if his father's basement would definitely be strong enough to keep out the tigers should they choose to pursue them. All he could think of was father putting volumes of his precious paperwork into the basement, and that could only be because nothing could damage or break into that safe haven.

Kuan started to sprint again. It could not be too far now. His heart was racing with anticipation. Nearly slipping, he regained his balance to continue up a slight incline leading to what he expected to be the old clearing. In the middle of it was where he and his father had lived all these years, in that drab building which was no longer there. He stared at the vacant space.

The building father brought him to after they left China for reasons that had never been divulged. The building he grew up in, where he spent time with father talking about serious matters, which he would occasionally grasp. Where they had their simple meals, and he had his imaginary adventures. How could it not be there anymore? He rubbed his eyes with the base of his hands. Where the building once stood there were uneven patches of grass and more weeds spreading in vicious entanglement.

"Are you lost?" Amo asked with as little hint of alarm as she could keep to.

"This is my home. How could it have vanished?"

"Kuan, are you sure this is the right place? Could it be further along the beach?"

"This is where I live, where I've always lived. What's happened here? Where's father gone?"

He felt a cold spade thrust into his abdomen, and all that mattered to him was shoveled out. Everything had been taken away from him. No home, no father, there was no conceivable life left. He dropped to his knees.

"Didn't you say there was a basement here?" asked Amo.

Father could be hiding down there after the building itself had for whatever reason been removed completely. Kuan dared not allow himself any hope of finding father below the ground he was on, but he bent down to inspect it meticulously. He tried to relate his bearings to the memory of where the front door once stood. Entering through it he would walk down a short corridor where on the left would be a doorway to a staircase leading down to the basement. He crawled to roughly where that staircase might be and started pulling away the vegetation and rubbing away the sand. He scurried to and fro searching for any hinge, button, handle, anything which might open up to a concealed basement. But however much he tried there was nothing to indicate there was any passage to a sanctuary underneath.

Amo floated across the ground when something caught her attention. As she followed what she had noticed in a semi-circular arc, it brought her to where Kuan had just spotted an unusual mark in the ground. It was not an isolated mark, but stretched further ahead so that together with the curve Amo had detected it formed a complete circle. He stood in the middle and looked around at it, a dark charred circle in the ground, five metres in diameter.

"Could this be caused by you burning the ground when you moved around it?" Kuan asked as he stared incredulously at the shape.

"My fiery form generates no heat unless I will it. This was burnt into the ground with considerable energy, and it did not happen recently."

"Amo, what could this mean? Something came and just took everything away?"

"Your father might have been out when it occurred. When he saw this on his return he would probably have sought alternative shelter. Do you know where he might go to?"

Kuan persuaded himself that what she said made sense. The house was not important. He didn't like living there that much anyway. The priority was to find father. He summoned up a new determination to scan every square centimetre of the terrain for a sign of him. His eyes had never been so focused. In only a few minutes he spotted a piece of paper half buried in sand. He pulled it out but it was blank. Still it was definitely the paper father used for typing. It had the unique watermark of a picture of the sun. It was a symbol of persuasion, something to do with a fable father was fond of. He desperately sought a clue that might hint at where father might be. But an hour had passed, and despite the most intense scouring, with every rock turned over for inspection, every blade of grass interrogated, there was not the faintest trace of evidence pointing to any human life in the vicinity other than Kuan's.

Amo could sense the boy surrendering his last sliver of hope. That sapped her strength. It was painful for her to witness the boy descending into irretrievable anguish. Even with the late afternoon breeze cooling the indifferent air, Kuan sweated profusely as his vain search continued.

Seagulls flew inland with supper for their eager chicks. Some things were still as they ever were.

By the time the fading sun was close to the horizon, exhaustion had caught up with Kuan. What if something terrible had happened to father? Kuan had no one to turn to. Father was a loner, with no friends or relatives. Where could this orphan go?

"I've never understood why father brought us here instead of staying in China. All he ever wanted to do was write, and that's something he could do anywhere. Why come to this isolated corner of nowhere?"

"He must have had his reasons." She spoke in her young yet mature voice.

"Now he's not here anymore."

"Kuan, we can wait to see if he comes back."

117

"What if Chi-Ling and his tigers come looking for us?"

"Last time I checked they were camped on the far side of the beach. They must have assumed you were killed in that explosion."

Kuan drew the outline of a radiating sun in the sand.

"Amo, if I can't find father again, can I go with you to your world?"

"My world is not structured for physical life."

Kuan stared at the flame flickering before him.

"It's a considerable strain on me to maintain any form of presence in your world. I am not by my nature a corporeal entity. Where I'm from, we exist as thoughts, perceptions, emotions, and anyone with a physical form would not be able to join us."

"Can't I discard my physical form temporarily?"

"That would be too risky. And you cannot just cast your body aside because without it remaining in a healthy state, you would disintegrate too."

It would seem that he either did not understand or he preferred not to.

"Kuan, you must stay in your world, with your mind and body intact. As for my world, I have no idea at present how I could get back to it."

"But you will find a way though. I know you will."

He watched his companion gently burning next to him.

"Kuan, what did you father write about?"

How would he even begin to recount the contents of so many typescripts? Father always spoke to him as though it would all make perfect sense to him. If it did once, he was much less certain now.

"They're always about threats. Threats we cannot readily see but would destroy us if we didn't deal with them. It's all too easy to get used to them, accept them as a fact of life, not recognise them for what they are."

"What exactly are these threats?"

"I'm not sure."

A vague recollection told him he did grasp what they were at certain points in the past. But whatever intellectual prowess he was supposed to possess had slipped away from him again. Father would be so disappointed.

Amo's burning form contracted a little. She became still like a crystalline glow.

"Kuan, do you think those threats were connected with his disappearance?"

If only he could remember what they were exactly, he might be able to answer Amo's question, which could in turn help him piece together a plan to find father again. That was why father wanted so much for him to pay attention to what he was explaining to him, and yet inevitably he would allow his mind to drift away. There was no reason why he couldn't concentrate now and recover what he once knew.

They heard a noise.

It could be footsteps. Kuan was terrified that it could be the tigers but there was a chance it was father. He crept over to a nearby row of shrubs to peep through as best he could. Something went by quickly. Too fast to make out what it was. Amo retreated into complete invisibility.

In the direction of the noise Kuan strained his eyes for the slightest movement. If father was out there, he must call to him as he might not find the boy otherwise. But if it were Chi-Ling or one of his underlings, it would be fatal to draw attention to his whereabouts. He stayed silent. Another move, edging closer. Kuan saw a part of it fleetingly, a pinkish red colour with a black stripe. It couldn't be human. He scrambled his legs to run as they skidded under him. There it was. Pink, black, with a blue patch on its side, a large jay was after some hopping insect. He fell to the ground in relief.

Amo reignited, but cautiously minute.

"Kuan, is there somewhere away from here your father might have gone?"

"There is the nearby town but he's always reluctant to go there."

"But it would be worth checking?"

The boy was considering what he should do when an even louder noise approached. He could not see anything through the shrubs.

Standing up he called out, "Father?"

There was no response.

He called out for father again.

Something was approaching from over the ridge.

His eyes were stretched wide open at the emerging figures of semi-morphed tigers in camouflage combat uniform, a blur of tan, gray and green, walking erect in a tight formation flanking their leader, General Chi-Ling. They had spotted Kuan. Chi-Ling pointed to two of his troops and waved them forward. Fur poured over their uniform as they assumed their full tiger form and galloped ahead on all fours. Streaks of blood orange lined by the menacing black stripes, they closed in on the boy.

"Amo, leave me."

"I can help you." She said as she turned invisible.

"There's nothing you can do."

The two vanguards sped into the clearing. Their fierce amber eyes fixed on Kuan. Their fangs poised to strike. Noticing the boy was making no attempt to flee, they paused for the general to give the final order. Chi-

Ling had caught up with them, anger simmering on his merciless face.

"Who would have thought a puny human could cause so much trouble. But that's the point, isn't it? You're not capable of anything by yourself. Someone put you up to all those lies you made up on the witness stand. Some traitor used you to disrupt my plan. Who was it? That old fool, Ma? I doubt it could be Len-Wu. Those who acquire the lion form are rarely equipped with guile. It must be Agent Tan. It wouldn't surprise me if he turns out to be a Potokan spy after all."

The mere sight of the tigers' gruesome faces was enough to fill Kuan with trepidation. Since early infancy he had been afflicted with the recurring nightmare of being chased by big cat predators and torn to pieces by them.

One of the tigers inched forward and was suddenly met with a single burst of flame. Startled at first, he then broke out in laughter, as did the others in the platoon. These were not diminutive Potokans who could be easily frightened away. They were hardened soldiers, killer beasts.

Chi-Ling was not impressed.

"Neat little trick, Kuan. Learnt that at school?"

The boy could hear a tiny whisper from Amo apologising for her ineffectuality.

"It doesn't matter", the boy muttered seemingly to himself.

"So those are your last words?" rhetorically asked the general as he clenched his fist and raised it above his head. The two tigers in front lowered their heads and wound their muscles up for the execution order.

Kuan noticed something happening overhead.

The general was about to drop his arm when bright sparks danced in the dimming sky. Blades of electricity were sharpening each other in readiness to deliver a crushing blow. They clashed radiantly, drawing everyone's eyes upward. In an instant, a thunderous explosion flashed through the two tigers barely three metres away from Kuan. Dark smoke rose from the ground and slowly dissipated to reveal that the pair of soldiers had vanished. Around where they had been a moment ago was a charred circle, similar to the one Kuan had earlier discovered.

Nobody moved for fear of provoking another attack. But the general was emboldened by the ensuing stillness.

"It's just another trick", bellowed Chi-Ling.

The other tigers, staring at the sky with fearful suspicion, did not share this dismissive claim. They were all rooted to the spot, but Chi-Ling ordered another two to terminate Kuan. These two looked at each other and knew they could not defy their command. Side by side they cautiously advanced towards their human target.

Kuan glanced up at the sky not to call their bluff but because sparks were once again entwined in random flight. The two tiger soldiers hesitated but it was too late. A blinding flash blasted directly at where they stood and when the smoke cleared, they were no more.

The boy looked down on the latest charred circle with a sad calmness that Chi-Ling mistook as sadistic satisfaction, not for the first time projecting his own mindset onto others. Now convinced the boy possessed secret powers, he beckoned his troops to retreat back to the shore side of the ridge. Faster than when they were in pursuit of Kuan, they disappeared.

Kuan took in a deep breath.

"Amo, was that your doing?"

"No, we should move away from here as quickly as possible."

By the fading light Kuan backed out of the clearing and headed further inland, where he scuttled down a long stony path before he came off it towards a thicket of tall bushes. He pushed his way through into what had the appearance of a maze but which lacked any intentional design. For all he knew, every opening could lead to a dead-end or bring them back to where they were. But it might give them time to react should anyone approach them from the rocky beach.

Kuan sat down in the midst of the protective bushes. If Amo had not caused the lightning-like strike, and it could not be a contraption installed by father who knew nothing of gadgets or weapons, it must be a device connected with whoever was behind the threats father was warning everyone against. Did father fall victim to it himself? He could not have suspected that an attack would come out of nowhere in the sky. Did he suffer when the bright light exploded around him? Or did it happen too fast for any sensation to register?

"Kuan, there's no point speculating. We don't know what caused that phenomenon."

"What do we do then? It might have followed us."

"We need more information."

"What was odd, Amo, was that it struck the tigers, but not us. Twice that happened. And it was when the tigers were making a move to hurt us that it struck. What does that tell you?"

"That it responds to certain types of movement, or threatening behaviour?"

"No, it means it regards Chi-Ling and his troops as the main enemy."

Kuan was actually more fearful of the mysterious force than even the tigers.

"The evidence does not necessarily support that. It is possible that it is not directly hostile to us. But we cannot take any risk."

Amo was conflicted by her instinct to give objective assessment and the negative impact it could have on Kuan. The proliferation of possibilities, to varying degrees pointing to unpleasant chains of events, were visibly tormenting Kuan who was desperate for a way out of the situation. But Amo wanted Kuan to have hope. She needed him to have hope.

Chapter 11

<u>Inescapable</u>

The darkened night conceded a small corner for the pale moon to keep watch. Leaning against a thick hedge, Kuan took out of his pocket the emerald pebble Batya, the orangutan outsider, asked him to pass to his son if he should ever come across him. The silver lunar light gently polished its rich green surface. A gleaming token of an emotional bond split asunder by thoughtless cruelty. The celestial moon could lose and regain its fullness with effortless certainty, but terrestrial wounds ran deep, and some might never heal again.

Kuan put the pebble back in his pocket. He had no idea where father might be, or if indeed he was still alive. But he would go and look for him in the nearby town, which was about two hours' walk away. There was a chance, however slim, that he would find him there. It would not be too difficult to make his way there even after dark. He knew the area well. Although the security guards might not be willing to help him find father, they would want to take action against intruders from another world.

Others in the town might be more sympathetic in giving him a hand with tracking father down. But any news about shape-changing tigers being nearby might set off a panic and drive everyone in the town away. What other option had he got? He had to give it a try.

Amo convinced Kuan that she should remain behind to monitor the tigers and distract them if they were to come in their direction. She would prefer to go with the boy, not being confident that whoever was responsible for the charred circles would not strike at Kuan next time. Keeping Chi-Ling's troops at bay, however, was a task only she could perform under the circumstances. If Kuan could find his father or obtain assistance from the town, it might repel the renegade Shiyanese and give her more time to explore how she could return home herself.

Leaving the tall bushes, Kuan relied on dusty memories to guide him towards an uneven path. Rock fragments underfoot were painful to tread on with the flimsy shoes issued to him on the submarine. The path reunited him with a row of Chinese Chestnuts father planted. He remembered the time father played football with him. It was a rare occasion, with the tree trunks serving as goal posts.

The bookish man was not into sports but once in a while he would indulge the boy's passion for what was described - incomprehensibly to him - as the beautiful game. Repeatedly pushing back those gold-rimmed glasses which were slipping down his nose, he would stand between the selected trees and block the odd shot that came close to him. To celebrate the young shooter's record-shattering victory, they treated themselves to a feast of roasted chestnuts, so memorably sweet and meaty. Now the bare branches of the trees silhouetted against the dark sky like outstretched skeletal arms.

Fallen leaves and discarded seeds lined the ground, necessitating lightened steps to avoid making the crunching sound that had formerly been a delight. He looked back to check that he was not being followed.

A soft trickling confirmed he had reached the shallow stream, and he hopped across it. In front of him lay a dormant shape on the ground. He could just about make it out to be a pile of dead leaves. But so neatly gathered? Against his better judgement he took a few steps closer to see if it was no more than that. He kicked at the leaves. A handless arm fell out. He recoiled in horror.

The shriveled vegetation appeared to be covering a body. Only his shortness of breath jerked his lungs back into action. He could not allow himself to walk away without being sure. So he steadied himself and walked slowly towards the lifeless object which had dropped into his view. But that was not so much a limb as a thick branch stripped bare. As he leaned cautiously close to the 'arm', he realised how stupid he was to scare himself over a discarded tree branch. Just then his heart was pummeled with a furry form shooting out of the crumpled leaves at him. Flat on his back he fell, and the creature brushed against his leg before speeding away.

Kuan's eyes tracked the moving shadow. He did not want to deceive himself with any imagined horror. And in the distance, it paused. A huge brown rat, the size of an otter, was sniffing furiously as though it had lost its way. Its head twitched skyward to where luminous slits were cut in the blackness, sparks danced and dotted around above the entranced rodent. Then came the intense flash, the smoke, and it was gone. Under the glow of the moon, he observed the remains of a charred circle.

What choice had he but to turn back instantly? The invisible force was everywhere waiting to strike. He could easily have been the target. Suddenly he felt hidden eyes spying on him. There was no way through to the town. It might well have been devastated by the electrical strikes already. All he could think of was to turn back whence he came. He ran as fast as his tired legs could take him.

The stream slipped by underneath him, followed by a rapid procession of Chinese Chestnuts. Without even a glance back, he drove himself forward until the moonlit outlines of the maze-like bushes came into view. He squeezed his way past the outer shrubbery. He barely noticed the scratches inflicted by the prickly branches. Finally he came to a standstill. It was like a tap had been hammered into his wooden body and left open until every drop of energy within him had been drained. Thirst and trepidation fought for his attention. Fatigue robbed him of the ability to accede to either.

In every direction he was trapped. An inescapable net had been cast around him. He scanned his mind for recollections that might point to a way out. Could father have foreseen all this and made plans for it already? He must have known about the approaching danger. He would therefore have arranged somewhere safe to put himself where he would be invulnerable to attack. There would have to be a clue for his son to find him. If he thought hard enough, he could figure out how to be with father again. But what if Kuan didn't manage to find the clue in time? He would succumb to brutal annihilation.

A bright light erupted before him.

"Amo?"

The flame drew nearer.

"Kuan, why have you turned back?"

"The way to the town is blocked. The lightning struck a rat on the path I was going to take. There's no way through. Whatever it is, it's waiting for us."

"Then we must try a different approach."

Kuan wasn't listening.

"Amo, you believe my father is still hiding somewhere, don't you?"

"He could be."

"Do you think he knows I'm back? Because if he does, I should stay put in one place to make it easier for him to find me. Otherwise we could keep missing each other."

Kuan sat down on the ground. He did not want to run anymore. Father must come and fetch him.

"Kuan, it's too dangerous to stay here."

"It's no more dangerous than anywhere else. We go in any direction and we could be struck down."

"It comes down to a question of probability." She stated in her matter of fact way.

Kuan's fingers crawled through his tangled hair as he was overwhelmed with tiredness.

"What is probable? Father once told me that we could not possibly judge if it was more or less probable that we were at any given moment stuck in a dream. I may think I'm trapped in this nightmare, but actually I'm lying in my own bed, safe and sound. Any second now, father could walk in and switch the light on, and I would wake up."

"And I would cease to exist, if I were part of your dream."

"Not necessarily. Amo, you could be there in the real world after I've woken up from this false one."

His mind was racing desperately to pluck some kind of coherence out of the ether, anything to shield him from the predicament into which he had sunk.

"Kuan, believe me, you cannot dismiss this as a dream."

"I want to be with father again."

"And you will, if you take decisive action."

He eyes fixed on the flickering glow.

"Kuan, our one chance is to head back towards the sea."

"What?"

"When you were trying to get to the nearby town, I carried out a quick reconnaissance. Chi-Ling had pulled his troops back to the camp they set up on the far side of the rocky beach, a good distance from the submersible, which they appeared to have abandoned."

"Why would they do that?"

"They cannot override what I have done to their navigational system and assume, wrongly, that the ship is of no use to them. In case the submersible is detected and comes under attack, they want to be far enough away from it. But provided we can make it on board without being noticed by them, I can get the submersible to take us wherever we want."

"But where?"

"Isn't anywhere better than here?"

Kuan understood the point. But for ten years he had lived there. There was never any question that he would end up anywhere else, and his mind could not readily process the prospect of leaving it behind.

"What about father?"

"Let's find somewhere safe first. Then we can work out how to locate your father."

Unable to argue with Amo's logic, the boy followed her in moving over the ridge and stealthily descending to the near side of the moonlit shoreline. At the opposite end they could see the uniformed tigers encamped around a large fire. Kuan and Amo sneaked into the submersible. Like a lamp she shone on where he needed to go and what he should do with the myriad of switches. Once Kuan had done his part, Amo's flame reached into the electronic circuitry and the system was cleared for new coordinates to be input. By her calculation, the tide would be sufficiently high within the next two to three hours, by which time the submersible could be reversed out into sea again.

Kuan stood by one of the opened hatches and stared at the beach bathed in cold reflected light. All his memories were covered by the vast sheet of pebbles and sand. Moonlight glanced off tiny silicon fragments that resembled his life in their incapacity to hold on to any permanent form. Whatever constituted his past had crumbled away. This could be the last time he would ever see this place. How would he find father again? Ten-year old boys don't cry, he reminded himself.

"Enjoying the moonlight, are we?"

Kuan swung to face the unexpected voice from behind him. He could not open his mouth before his throat was clasped by one of Chi-Ling's soldiers. A semi-morphed snow tiger, vicious stripes stretched across his pure white face, roared out a spine-chilling signal. He dragged Kuan out of the boat like a rag doll.

"Lieutenant Sung, excellent work!"

General Chi congratulated the snow tiger.

"But don't snap this pathetic twig quite yet."

Kuan's legs were just about touching the ground.

"General, the submersible is operational again. You were right - he must have sabotaged it before."

"And having lured us here where some hidden ally of his could attack us, he was going to take our boat and leave us behind. But to think I wouldn't anticipate that obvious move."

The boy looked into the stark amber eyes of the general and knew then he would be tortured if he did not comply with his wishes. But what Chi-Ling wanted from him was suicidal.

"Take me to whoever's set up this ambush with you against us. Tell them they can surrender and hand me their lethal weapon, and I'll let you live."

The general glared at the top of the ridge.

"General, I have nothing to do with those attacks. If we don't get away, it'd kill us all."

"Kuan, the Potokans are behind this, aren't they?"

"I don't know who's behind it, but we'll all be killed if we stay here."

"Am I meant to be frightened by that threat?"

"It's the truth."

"You're a consummate liar, Kuan, that I know. Don't waste any more of my time. Tell them what I want or Sung here will give you a slow agonising death."

The tall and muscular lieutenant shook Kuan by the neck. The boy felt the breath of the snow tiger on his face. Fear drenched him. Amo, who had not been seen by either Sung or Chi-Ling, held back from doing anything lest the boy's neck got instantly snapped.

"General, they won't listen to me."

"We'll soon find out, won't we? You ask them to surrender, and we'll discover if they're as keen to protect you as I think they are."

"What if they're not? You saw what happened to your troops."

"You can't bluff your way out of this, Kuan. Persuade your collaborators to give themselves up and Sung will spare you."

Kuan feebly called into the darkness.

"Anybody there?"

Sung tightened his grip.

The general stared at the night sky.

"Kuan, don't try to send any coded message. If even a spark touches me, Lt. Sung will break your head off. Now tell your conniving partner to make himself visible and hand over the weapon to us at once."

"Please show yourself!" The boy pleaded in the hope that he would go unheard.

Silence.

"If you don't come out, I'll rip off the head of your little friend," Chi-Ling snarled.

The night breeze faded into stillness.

"You're trying my patience!"

A spark flew up and bounced off another. Bright lines scratched the night's colourless screen. Rapiers of light slashed ferociously above them. They looked up and a blinding flash engulfed them as the air around them imploded. Smoke filled their orifices while their very being seemed to have disintegrated. All sensations were wiped out.

Nothingness. An eerie tranquility shrouded Kuan's mind. The proverbial bright light lifting his eyelids, opening his vision to a world of smooth, unremitting white. He had been stunned. He pushed his back against a wall and unsteadily got to his feet. He was in a long, wide and windowless corridor. Above him, light panels covered the entire ceiling. There were sounds coming from further down.

Kuan noticed there was an empty compartment with nothing but a stainless steel operating table in the middle of it. Was it a hospital? Had he been rescued? He could not see Amo around him. There was a chance that the electrical force could not touch her amorphous form. As for the general and his sidekick, he wished they had perished.

He wandered on and came to another compartment. On the operating table he saw a blood-soaked creature with its internal organs spewed out of its body. It was a large brown rat.

Kuan stumbled back. He walked on, not wanting to even think about what he had just seen. But then the next compartment seized his attention. On this operating table lay a tiger held down by a host of mechanical arms extended from the walls. He was shaking his head and moving his mouth, but with a clamp around his throat, no sound was coming out.

The robotic tentacles performed with gruesome finesse the intricate tasks each had been assigned. In callous harmony they danced about slicing open his abdomen; injecting substance into one limb while extracting sample fluid from another; peeling off patches of fur and skin and drilling into his skull.

A camera eye swiveled around on a separate arm watching proceedings. Scattered below the operating table were the shambled remains of a second victim. Though the limbs and torso had been thoroughly mutilated, the severed head was unmistakably that of another tiger. In fact, these two were the first pair Chi-Ling had ordered to slay Kuan before they were blasted away by the mysterious light. The boy braced his nose for the most revolting stench, but there was no smell. None whatsoever.

The camera eye rotated towards the boy.

"*Kuan, our paths cross again.*"

The voice came from loudspeakers embedded along the walls. He did not recognise it.

"How do you know me?"

"*Have you forgotten me already?*"

"Who are you?"

"*Call me the Curator.*"

Chapter 12

<u>Reversal of Fortune</u>

Kuan was transfixed by the camera eye. Behind it, somewhere, was the Curator who consumed the lives of all those Potokans in the valley.

"*I think you owe me an apology.*"

"What have I done?"

"*You rejected my offer of a second chance. And you betrayed Max after all he had done for you.*"

"He should not have been giving out Blessing."

"*Without Blessing there would be no hope.*"

"What do you want from me?"

"*Your assistance with an on-going experiment. This is where I explore the transition from one doomed state of existence to another. Here I delve into the excruciating thread linking those of us condemned to an eternity of exile to the living world beyond.*"

"You're exiled from the living world?"

"*Exile. Death. Being here is to be deprived of an authentic existence. That applies to everyone without exception. The only difference is that with the help of what I learn in my purgoratory, I shall return to my former life. For those I capture, on the other hand, the journey is very much in the other direction.*"

"You killed all those Potokans for an experiment?"

"*The Potokans were given a second chance, to become part of the collection. You could have found out for yourself if you had not rejected the final blessing. But we all serve the greater cause in our different ways. Your destiny has brought you to my purgoratorial experiment.*"

"Have you captured my father too?"

"*Max told me about your father obsession.*"

"Is father here? Can I see him?"

"*I have no recollection of individual subjects. But if your father lived around the test site, then at some stage he would have been brought in for our experimentation.*"

Kuan looked to the mutilated carcass on the floor in the compartment and a nauseous sensation sank into his stomach. Father must have suffered a horrible fate.

The camera eye turned to Kuan's right and the voice issued a command.

"*Guards, escort Kuan to compartment 101.*"

Three white panthers, tongues ventilating, fangs gleaming, trotted in from the far end of the corridor. Against the white background they were almost invisible apart from their piercing red eyes, all converging on the boy's face. He took a few steps back and slowly started to run away from his pursuers.

The vicious guards accelerated their pace, with salivating jaws ready to strike. Kuan pushed his legs as hard as he could. The excruciating strain on his muscles told him there was no faster speed he could muster. But each step seemed to be dragged back by a thickness in the air. The guards were closing in on him.

Out of one of the compartments some distance ahead came two semi-morphed tigers. They recognised Kuan and immediately sprinted towards him. It was General Chi-Ling and Lieutenant Sung. Kuan's legs collapsed beneath him. He was certain he would be torn apart. An image of mangled bodily parts splattered across his mind. A hideous death would finally reunite father and son.

Sung's human body along with his uniform dissolved into a huge tiger frame, and he hurtled forward on all fours. Riding on the great roar that surged before him, the snow tiger leapt above Kuan and grabbed a white panther in each of its forelimbs.

The two guards sank their teeth into the tiger. Sung tried to shake them off but they clenched their jaws more tightly. The tiger snapped at the back of the neck of one of his adversaries and bit right through to his victim's windpipe. The other panther struggled to break free of the tiger's grip. It was no match for Sung's size or strength and for all the flesh wounds it inflicted on him, the tiger held it down and ripped open its throat.

At that moment the third white panther stole past Sung and headed straight at the immobilised boy. Kuan could see those seething red eyes bearing down on him. Instinctively he raised his arms up against the streak of pristine white hurtling towards him. A fist flew in front of him and hammered the panther's head to one side.

The dazed guard tried to retaliate against its assailant, but a booted foot crashed into its face. Two hands clamped down on the panther's muzzle and swung its head hard against the wall, painting a bloody red stroke against the pure white surface. It was Chi-Ling who had saved Kuan. The semi-morphed general picked him up in one arm and together with the snow tiger they ran towards the darkness at the other end of the corridor.

When they finally came to a stop, at the edge of a long stretch of unlit corridor, General Chi-Ling put Kuan down. Lt Sung prowled behind them to make sure they were not being followed.

"Kuan, we've seen what they do here. And they'll do it to you and me if we don't find a way out. So we must put aside our differences and work as a team."

The boy looked up at the general towering over him.

"You know your way around electronic controls, otherwise you could never have forced my submersible to change course like that. You must put those skills to unlocking whatever controls are in place to keep us here. Can you do that?"

He would not be able to tell one electronic circuit from another without Amo. But as he pondered what he could say to his unlikely rescuer, he felt a tingling on the back of his hand. Subtly glancing down, he noticed a tiny flicker. She had after all been transported too, and she was right next to him.

"It could take some time." Kuan spoke hesitantly.

If Chi-Ling did not think the boy would be of use to him, he would have killed him as swiftly as he did that white panther guard. Believing him to be key to their escape from the lair of the Curator, however, would mean that the general and his lieutenant would continue to give him protection.

"I don't think we're going to have much time."

"But General, suppose I can get us out of here, won't you be coming after me again?"

Sung turned around and narrowed his eyes at Kuan and Chi-Ling.

"Circumstances change, and priorities with them. Help us find a way out of here, and you can go free."

Kuan stared intently at the general's fierce yet indecipherable face.

"Kuan, you have my word." Chi-Ling was adamant.

The snow tiger lay down and licked the blood off its front paws, ignoring the cuts and gashes on his body.

The boy believed he would have the cooperation from the two tigers, at least until they broke free of their captivity.

"General, I'll get to work, if you and the lieutenant could keep a close watch."

Kuan walked away from them towards an alcove perpendicular to the back wall of a deserted compartment. Amo was directing him to a particular panel in the wall. She could sense the presence of accessible circuitry there. With his back to his military companions, the boy watched the minute flame float up to the panel. He had no idea what she was about to do.

Sung stared at the back of the boy quizzically.

"Lieutenant, what's on your mind?" asked Chi-Ling.

The snow tiger retreated further into the dimmer part of the corridor.

"General, what if the boy can't get us out of here? We don't even know where we are. You hear these stories about alien abduction, with unsuspecting victims being zapped away by spaceships hovering overhead. It's not an uncommon pattern, bright light transporting the captive away, and smoke gradually clearing with nothing left behind. What if we were on one of those spaceships? We break out and we could find ourselves dead within seconds without oxygen."

"Sung, don't be so gullible. There's no such thing as alien abduction. This place has to be something the Potokans have put together. They've been testing its capability in the human world, but their real objective is to launch an attack on Shiyan. We must take control of it somehow. It has immense potential for use in torturing information out of captives, not to mention eliminating opponents without even being seen. It's the most ingenious contraption I've ever come across. If we can get to the President and tell her about what we have found here, then despite our setback on *FSS Castle*, we could still persuade her to authorise a preemptive strike against all Potokan targets."

"But shouldn't we see if there are space suits and oxygen tanks around here we can use, just in case? I can check further down the unlit areas to see what I can find."

"We need to stick together."

"Perhaps the boy can help us. If he can get into the system here, he might be able to locate the equipment we need."

"Lieutenant, the boy has got enough to deal with as it is. Take it from me, we're not on a spaceship."

The snow tiger bowed his head and resumed his sentry duty.

Kuan overheard the conversation and asked Amo in a whisper who she thought might be right. Now in the form of sparkling electrical energy, she was interacting with the cables behind a wall panel. The boy moved his hands vaguely so that Chi-Ling would think he was effecting some changes.

"I don't know, Kuan. This is a very unusual system."

"We're not out in space somewhere?"

"Not so much space as cyberspace."

"We're in a computer?"

"It's some kind of reconstructed reality, but anchored to the shoreline area that was your home. In essence, the beach and its surroundings were turned into a potential portal into this virtual world where we're held."

"Amo, can you get us back onto the beach?"

"If I could reverse the polarity of the signals."

"Is that a 'yes'?"

"I cannot be sure."

"What do you mean when you called this a 'reconstructed reality'? The Curator claimed that this was away from the living world. Is this real or not?"

"Kuan, there are different levels of reality."

The boy was used to a simple reality – a basic life, regular routines, the certainty of home. He was not made for the fragmenting of reality leading to him being tangled up in a world dominated by shape-changing cats and then transported to some form of cyberspace laboratory run by a psychopath calling himself the Curator. Indeed the one pointing out the complexity of reality to him was a being of pure energy who did not know how she had ended up here herself.

"Amo, how likely is it that you can get us out of here?"

"I have not got sufficient information to calculate a meaningful probability. But it's definitely possible."

"Would you be able to find out if father was ever captured and brought here?"

"There is a databank of the experiments they have carried out. But don't you want me to concentrate on finding a way out of here rather than going through those data?"

"If father's here, we can't leave without him."

"How are you getting on?" asked Chi-Ling.

Kuan moved his hands purposefully.

"I need more time."

The general glanced into the totally darkened corridor ahead of them. At the very heart of it was a flash, barely perceptible at first, which began to grow larger. They were lights coming on, section by section, and they were closing in on the captives.

"Time may not be on our side." General Chi-Ling sardonically remarked as the entire corridor had been lit up.

At that moment steel partitions dropped from the ceiling to seal them off from either end, leaving them in a rectangular space covered by the clinical white panels.

Out of the wall came a dozen mechanical arms followed by a camera eye slowly swinging from side to side.

"I trust you've had a good rest. The experiment can now commence."

"What sick experiment have you got in mind? Injecting us with venom, electrocuting us, cutting us to pieces, or a deranged mix of the lot?" The general spoke defiantly with arms behind his back while the snow tiger stood guard beside him.

Kuan frantically hoped that Amo could work out a solution soon.

"Those were just minor tests, and it's regrettable that the survival rate is so low. But the main experiment is different. For this I need the three of you to work together. I'm giving you thirty minutes to agree which of you will come forward for vivisection, without anesthetics of course; another one will volunteer to be executed, swiftly and painlessly; and the remaining one will be safely returned to the surface world. If you cannot reach an agreement, then all of you will have to endure whatever painful operations I choose for you."

"So this is an underground facility." Chi-Ling said nonchalantly as he racked his brain to devise a response.

"Above, below, these are only metaphors for us. To live in Schloss 22 is to forego the dimensional formalities you would have taken for granted in your former life."

"Tell us more about Schloss 22. Does it encompass this entire complex and the device that transported us here?"

Amo was flitting like a miniature lightning storm around the panel in front of Kuan. They both knew Chi-Ling would not be able to deflect the Curator for long.

"When Schloss 1 was constructed, long before my time, it was just a portal to download and contain reconfigured entities. But since then, particularly under my stewardship, it has developed substantially, so much so that Schloss 22 is now the hub of something far beyond your comprehension. You should know the countdown has started, and you're only wasting precious time with your questions."

"On the contrary, having a better understanding of Schloss 22 is vital to working out a sensible strategy for deciding how we should act in your experiment."

"If you want to run down the clock with more of your ponderous queries, that is your call."

"Listen," the tiger's word sounded more like a command than a plea, "what if I tell you now how the three options you set out are to be divided between us."

The camera eye moved close to Chi-Ling's face.

"What have you in mind?"

"Suppose I kill these other two. Would I qualify as the only one left to be released then?"

Kuan assumed the general was trying to keep the camera eye distracted, but it was hard not to suspect treachery in him.

"Of course not. This experiment is all about how you reach agreement. If you kill the other two, you would just be condemning yourself to be the sole vivisection subject."

"That's fair enough. But what if I can get them to agree to a trial by combat?"

"If you kill them, then you would be the only one left to be the vivisection subject."

The mechanical arms extending out of the wall twitched ominously.

"I don't have to kill them. Say we agree that whoever can knock the others down, without killing them, is the winner who will get to be released by you.

And the other two can fight it out, if they agree, to determine who will get the torture and who will get a quick execution. Does that comply with your terms?"

The camera eye fixed on the tiger's deadpan face and pulled back with an impatient response.

"Yes, if you could get the others to agree."

"Who's to say you won't throw us all to your torture machine anyway. You could just be making us agonise over who would be willing to sacrifice himself, but never have the intention of releasing anyone."

"You don't have to trust me. Time will be up soon for you at this rate, and you will see if just one or all three of you will end up on the operating table. And tell Kuan to stop cowering in the corner and show some courage."

Kuan lowered his head and Amo halted her activities. Chi-Ling walked over to the boy and leaned over him with his arms pressed against the alcove, shielding him from the camera eye's sightline. The snow tiger joined them while glancing at the menacing tentacles protruding from the wall.

Whispers were exchanged, and discreetly Kuan moved his hand to the panel once more as Amo resumed her electrical exchanges. As far as Chi-Ling and Sung were concerned, the boy was projecting some form of energy into Schloss 22. Its impact, if it had any, appeared not to be detectable by the mastermind behind the sinister experiment.

Kuan was desperate to escape from this grim purgoratory, but he wanted to know if father was also trapped there. If so, he must ensure he was released too. The thought that father might have fallen victim already to the mechanical tentacles was firmly banished.

Kuan could not tell if Amo was drawing her energy from him. As her interactions with the panel intensified, he felt increasingly sapped.

Chi-Ling could see the colours draining out of the boy's face. He rested a hand on his back and whispered words of encouragement to him. Kuan could barely remain standing. The snow tiger let out a slight whimper. The white light had switched to red. Out of the wall, the camera eye turned to the captives.

"*Time's up. The moment of reckoning is upon us.*"

An operating table rose from the ground, with six of the mechanical arms hovering above it immediately. On either side of them, one arm held out a hypodermic syringe, while another one carried what appeared to be a torch.

"*Take your position. The operating table for the vivisection obviously. Over to your right for the quick death with an injection. And on the left is the teleportation projector to take the lucky one back to the world of the living. Any delay could prompt me to change my mind and give you all a torturous death.*"

The snow tiger leapt onto the operating table. Unflinching, he held his head high.

The general patted the boy on the back and walked over to the right where a mechanical arm raised the syringe up to his neck.

Kuan walked up to the teleportation projector.

"How do I know this will take me back?"

As he spoke, invisible electrical transference flowed between Amo and the projector. Command codes which had been cracked earlier were now being fed in.

"*Kuan, it's a shame you won't be staying any longer, but I stand by my terms. You can go. Bid farewell to your brave comrades. How noble of them to sacrifice themselves for you.*"

The mechanical arms above the operating table plunged towards Lt Sung; the hypodermic needle moved towards the general's neck; and the projector shot out a beam at Kuan, but the beam at that instant widened to cover Sung and Chi-Ling. A lightning flash swept them away even as the scream of "*What have you done!*" receded into a void.

They were back on the rocky beach. Darkness was held at bay by the gentle moonlight caressing the silent sand and stone fragments. The night breeze combed the shoreline retreating from the quietly rising tide.

Kuan was on his hands and knees. Exhaustion had hollowed him out. He asked Amo in a low voice if she managed to check the databank of experimental subjects in Schloss 22. She whispered to him that as far as she was able to scan the information, no human lifeform apart from Kuan was recorded as having been captured for experimenting on. The fraying thread of hope was still hanging there.

Chi-Ling walked over to Kuan and helped him to his feet.

"Good work, Kuan. You're sure you've jammed the device?" asked the general.

Having been assured by a tiny spark from Amo, the boy confidently nodded.

"Lt Sung, go and get the rest of my troops. We're moving out."

Before the lieutenant headed off to round up the other tigers still camped by the fire on the other side of the beach, he looked up at Kuan and bowed towards him. The snow tiger had doubted that he could pull it off. Messing up the navigation system of a standard army submersible was one thing, but to hack into that mysterious compound and take control of its teleportation was not something even the top military cyber operatives might manage. Besides, even if the boy had the ability to do all that, he could have just saved himself and left Sung along with the general to their death. But despite everything that had happened on *FSS Castle*, the young human kept his side of the bargain.

None of it would have been possible if not for the general of course. He knew what had to be done and brought everyone together under the most trying conditions. With a powerful bond of trust, they fought off an implacable enemy. Without his leadership, Sung noted, their comrades-in-arms had been stranded without a clue what to do. At least, now having learnt of the return of Sung and General Chi-Ling, they were ready to regroup.

The soldiers made the quick march across the beach and saluted the general before boarding the submersible.

Sung was surprised to find the boy still standing there.

"Waiting to wish us *bon voyage*, Kuan?"

Kuan did not reply. His angry stare was fixed on Chi-Ling.

"You gave me your word."

"Circumstances change."

"General, is there a problem?" asked Sung.

"Leave us, lieutenant, we're coming on board shortly."

The snow tiger, his black and white coat gleaming in the stark moonlight, strolled in front of the boy.

"He could have left us behind."

"Have you lost your mind? Are you getting sentimental about this human? We have a war to fight."

Reluctantly but with firmness, the lieutenant stood his ground.

"Sung, this boy knows the secret of one of the most powerful weapons we have ever come across. We need him at HQ to help us learn everything we possibly can about it. We must turn it to our advantage in our war against the Potokans."

Sung would not budge.

"Lieutenant, I'm giving you a direct order, take him to the submersible."

"General, we owe him our …"

Chi-Ling pulled out his pistol and shot the snow tiger between the eyes.

"Kuan, move it."

"I'm not going. I've had enough of this never-ending nightmare. Shoot me if you want."

General Chi-Ling was about to step over Sung's body to seize the boy when a shower of bullets fell before him. A squadron of attack helicopters had broken out of the night sky. One circled above the boy while the others rapidly descended. The general was warned to step away and surrender. There was a short exchange of fire between the helicopters' crew and Chi-Ling's soldiers. The general kept pointing his gun at Kuan until he managed to jump on board the submersible, which reversed at full throttle into the rising tide and disappeared into the sea.

Out of one of the landed helicopters came the black Chartreux cat familiar to Kuan. Agent Tan was flanked by Shiyan's special force operatives in human form, who spread out across the beach and it was not long before they were able to signal they had secured the area.

"Kuan, General Chi-Ling has been found guilty of committing a treasonable act in murdering the Mauveans on board *FSS Castle* and destabilising our naval defence. Vice-President Dao has sent his personal emissary, Governor Pui, to thank you for your part in exposing this crime against Shiyan, and in recognition of your bravery, to offer you an opportunity to serve as an apprentice with Dao himself."

Kuan did not know what to make of this information when he spotted the peacock, in his resplendent blue and green feathers, grandly emerging from a transport helicopter just landed. The cat discreetly checked that the governor was still some distance away before he whispered to the boy who had to bend down low to hear him.

"This is the turning point. The chance for you to fulfill your mission has been presented to you. You must take it."

"Agent Tan. I don't know where my father has gone. He's vanished."

The cat did not seem unduly concerned.

"It's down to you now."

"I need to find father."

"You must go with Governor Pui."

"I'm not going anywhere without father."

"Kuan, your father was the one who sent you to us. You must carry out the mission."

"What mission?"

"He said you've discussed it. You may not remember now, but it will come back to you."

"Where's father?"

"It's not safe for his whereabouts to be known."

"But you know where he is."

"You must focus on the mission."

"Please get a message to him for me."

The black cat quietly moved aside as Governor Pui approached.

"Young Kuan, I trust Agent Tan has explained. I am here on behalf of the vice-president to bring you to him as his new apprentice. I will explain everything during our journey to his mansion. But one thing above all you must remember, in his presence, you must always address him as Chairman Dao, or simply Chairman. It is one of the highest honours in Shiyan to be selected as the Chairman's apprentice, and it is unprecedented for an outsider to be chosen by him. Come along, we must not keep him waiting."

"What about General Chi-Ling?"

"He'll be hunted down." The peacock casually replied and wrapped his wing around Kuan to guide him towards his personal helicopter.

The boy cast his weary eyes across the rocky beach. It was not a safe place anymore for him to stay with the Curator lurking in the area. In any case, with father gone, there was nothing left to stay for. Becoming Dao's apprentice, he might be able to find a way to track down father, and he could discover new means to help Amo who had given so much of herself to save him. He climbed on board for takeoff.

Chapter 13

<u>Circles of Challenge</u>

A faint glow shimmered above the horizon, filling the sky with a golden orange canvas dotted with specks of attack helicopters. Amongst them sat Agent Tan, who was tasked with leading the hunt for General Chi-Ling. Paramount on the mind of the taciturn black cat though was what the boy would do from now on. So much depended on him remembering the mission he was meant to undertake. There were so many variables. But he must put his trust in the plan, even if plans rarely unfold as intended.

Flying away from the attack squadron in the opposite direction was *Governor One*, Pui's luxurious private helicopter. Tangerines, apples, pears were laid out on a table before its eponymous passenger and his guest. The peacock pecked at a cup of aromatic tea held out for him by a fidgety white cat on her hind legs. He raised his small but decorated head to gulp the fluids down. With a nod from him, the cat put the cup down and jumped off the seat to withdraw to the back of the cabin. He stretched and fluttered his iridescent feathers, a multitude of mascaraed eyes stared at Kuan.

"You're sure you won't have any more?"

The boy shook his head. That was enough water and fruit for him for now. His mind was preoccupied with the 'mission' Tan claimed he must fulfil. He could not fathom why father would send him to Shiyan. Unless there were dangers in their own world they must flee from. Perhaps he anticipated the coming of Schloss 22. That could have been one of the threats he was perennially warning others about. Now father was in hiding somewhere, his home lost.

"Kuan, I appreciate you must have had a dreadful time with that traitor Chi-Ling, and you're bound to be somewhat traumatised. After all, you're only human. But for your sake, you should pay close attention to what I'm about to tell you."

The boy glanced at the airborne squadron disappearing into the distance, separating him from the one individual who might have answers to the questions weighing him down. Had Tan known father all along? All that time on *FSS Castle* was he just testing him to see if he could hold his nerve? But what was he supposed to do now? And how could he find a way to be reunited with father again?

"Kuan, Chairman Dao is immensely generous in giving the deserving few a chance to succeed."

Governor Pui discerned his monologue was not receiving the consideration it was due. As he dramatically paused, his snake-like neck stretched across to the child sitting opposite him.

"But he does not tolerate failures. If you do well as his apprentice and impress him, there is no limit to how high you can rise. You could even become a Mauvean and do whatever you like."

As a mauve elephant, he could do whatever he liked, including presumably instructing others to help him find his father.

"Now I have your attention."

"Governor Pui, is it really true that even an outsider can become a Mauvean?"

"Anything is possible, my boy, that's the beauty of today's Shiyan. We have thrown the old ways into the pit of history. No more relying on others to come together, because we've learnt that might never happen. Count on no one but yourself. Let the drive within you overcome any obstacle that may come your way. That's what you've got to show Chairman Dao. Whatever the

Chairman requires of you, you must be determined to achieve it. Hold on to that thought."

The governor peered at Kuan with those rich indigo eyes.

"What exactly will be required?" asks Kuan.

"What is required is securing what matters to the Chairman. And three things matter to him. First, the wellbeing of our homeland, Shiyan. That's why he agreed to serve as vice-president even though he has so many commitments already. President Zhou is immensely lucky to have such an outstanding individual as her deputy. As I'm sure you will recall, I produced the report on the Potokan Question to advise the Chairman in his vice-presidential capacity on how to deal with our detested enemy. If you come up with a way to get rid of this poisonous thorn in our side, you will be well rewarded."

"Next comes his role as Chairman of the Council of Mauveans. Now you may not know this, but with a few exceptions like our gracious Chairman, Mauveans are a fractious bunch. They can already pretty much trample on, literally, whomever they want, but that's not enough. They squabble amongst themselves as to who possesses more of this, or who has the authority to acquire more of that. Only Chairman Dao has the standing to bring them all to order and make sure they work sensibly together."

"Above all else though, he has dedicated his life to his own organisation, Plutopia, on which the entire future of Shiyan depends. He will tell you about it when you meet him, and you must listen to every word carefully. Understand how to serve Plutopia and you'll understand how to be of service to Chairman Dao."

Kuan felt he should know more about this Chairman before he met him, but the peacock by then had other things on his mind. Pui called out to Wu-yin, the white cat, to bring him some scented sunflower seeds. It was time for a snack before his mid-morning nap. He woke up later to take an early lunch, followed by a quiet siesta. For the rest of the journey he spent his time listening to Wu-yin reading out the latest bulletins to him, meditating to a soundtrack of water dripping, and enjoying an extended session of afternoon tea and strawberries.

Dusk greeted the arrival of *Governor One* at Rook Mansion. The landing pad was by the grand ruby-encrusted front gate, which was powerfully illuminated from below, and majestically crowned by a towering platinum archway. Kuan and Wu-yin followed the peacock out of the helicopter, along a long thickly carpeted walkway, into a large square dimly lit with gaslights and lined by curiously empty terracotta pots. The boy half expected to see mauve elephants roaming everywhere. But there was not a single one in sight. Instead a dozen or so Shiyanese in the form of wolf dogs were patrolling the grounds. The familiarity of the governor's scent assured them it was a routine visit.

Pui paid no attention to them and strutted towards the middle of the square where there was a small circular platform just wide enough for him, his aide and the boy to step on. Activated by Pui's voice, the platform lifted from the ground and flew gently over a stretch of dense woodland. The crowded trees masked complex equipment littering the ground. Unseen creatures screeched out calls below the leafy canopy.

Beyond the woods, they passed over a giant maze. Its intricate design and mathematical beauty shone under floodlights stationed at every corner. It was hard to imagine how anyone could ever find a way out of this botanical labyrinth. If they did, they would be rewarded with the sight of an ornamental lake adorned by dolphins which at that moment were intrigued by the round shape floating through the air above them. Willows gently swayed on the bank. At its destination, the round platform descended before a three storey, forty bedroom house, built with the finest imperial green marble excavated from Bastille de Potoka.

A golden brown lynx, with long elfin ears and a white beard, ambled down the steps to receive the peacock.

"Governor Pui, welcome back."

"Thank you, Denji. Do you know if the Chairman has received a report about the incident yet?"

"Actually, he is at this moment speaking with …"

The peacock stopped Denji from saying any more by not so subtly pointing his beak at the boy next to him.

The lynx tuned politely to the young guest.

"This must be Master Kuan. The Chairman has been greatly looking forward to meeting you. Let me show you to your room."

Denji whispered a few words to Pui, who upon entering the mansion disappeared to his right down a marble corridor with his aide and their echoes. The lynx then led Kuan up a spiral staircase, wide enough for a pair of elephants to walk up side by side, and guided him along the silk soft carpet to where the boy would be staying.

Stepping through the dark walnut door, Kuan found himself in an expansive room where the four-poster bed alone was bigger than the mere cubicle in which he had slept all his life. Next to the bed was a round table with a lavish variety of sweets and nibbles that were provided for casual indulgence. To counter any excessive calorific intake there was a suite of games and exercise equipment designed to improve physical fitness and mental alertness.

At the far end was a sliding double door to an ensuite bath pool, constantly being refilled with water, the temperature of which could be adjusted by simple voice command. With his almost pathological aversion to taking a bath, Kuan swiftly turned away to consider the unusual outside wall behind him. As Denji explained in his soothing voice, it was made entirely of glass, sub-divided into thirty-six reflectors, which could deliver individual visual items separately or operate as one giant screen. When they were not in operation, one could look through them onto the lake of tranquility outside. It was reputed to be one of the most captivating views. But Kuan had more pressing matters to explore.

"Denji, can you get any information you want on these reflectors?"

"What kind of information, may I ask?"

"Information about how to find your way around Shiyan, or how to find someone who may have recently arrived here."

"I believe so, Master Kuan. You'll find all you need to know with the help of the console on the table. It can get you to the vast store of information covering everything there is to know in Shiyan."

"I can work this out by myself?"

"Do try it, sir, when you have a moment. It is surprisingly easy to use."

Kuan had never been addressed as 'sir' before. Inspecting his personal chamber, it was clear that however much he had detested Shiyan up to that point, he was prepared to give it an extensive re-evaluation. He was tired of constantly trying to escape. If Rook Mansion could offer him some respite, he would readily embrace it.

"If there is anything else you need, just speak into one of reflectors, and ask for 'Denji'. A change of clothes has been left on the bed for you. And you may find your new shoes more comfortable. Dinner will be served at eight. The Chairman will speak with you then."

"Thank you, Denji."

The respectful lynx lowered his head and padded out of the room. Kuan walked over to the glass wall and Amo, revealing herself, glided down to the small mahogany table next to the spherical console. The flame burnt brightly.

"Kuan, what do you think this Chairman Dao wants with you?"

"He's giving me a chance to work for him. I understand he's very powerful."

"Do you plan to stay here long?"

"It's not a bad place, is it?"

"Will this become your new home?"

"I'll stay until I can find father. Tell me what you think of this equipment Denji spoke about. It may help you find a way back to your nebula home too."

Amo said nothing as she hovered in front of the wall of glass. Kuan flipped back onto the luxuriant bed. It had been so long since he was able to rest comfortably.

He wondered what the Chairman might say to him. From what Governor Pui said, he was expecting to meet with someone extremely demanding. It could be an unpleasant encounter. His only interactions with mauve elephants up to that point had consisted of collecting their priceless excrement. Not one of them had ever spoken to him.

The gong was sounded. Kuan had dozed off. He quickly changed into the purple tunic and matching trousers that had been left on his bed, and slipped on his new socks and shoes. From his discarded jumpsuit, he retrieved the emerald pebble entrusted to him by the orangutan, Batya. There was little chance the memento would ever return to the son. But he would hold on to it for the time being.

Leaving Amo to ponder in silence the potential of the console in connecting her to a galactic network of electrical impulses and data, he stepped out of his bedroom and found Denji waiting to show him downstairs to the dinning room.

Dishes worthy of a banquet were laid out at either end of a long oak table. Kuan sat down at one end, captivated by the appetizing meal that had been served up. The crispy squid, steamed garoupa, classic three-mushroom flourish, garlic prawns, fried aubergines, bean curd pot, baked chestnuts with bamboo shoots, were arranged in a flawless gastronomic symphony. He could be in heaven or, it then struck him, this might be the prelude to an assessment centre. Was this another attempt to lull him into a false sense of security before subjecting him to more torturous interrogation?

Kuan jumped up when a human figure entered the dimly lit room.

"Sit down, Kuan, don't be alarmed."

It was a tall man in his fifties, dressed in a similar purple tunic to Kuan's. His black hair, distinguished with white streaks, framed his broad and deeply lined face. He had strong inquisitive eyes.

"I'm Dao."

The boy stared at the human form of the renowned Mauvean and sank back into his chair.

"Kuan, do start. I have ordered this especially for you."

He noticed that even chopsticks had been put out at his place. He picked them up but still hesitated.

Dao started eating, expertly with his chopsticks.

"Chairman Dao, I'm not going to be taken to an assessment centre after this, am I?"

"Is that what you're worried about? Of course not. The navy has to deal in its own way with outsiders who trespass into Shiyan's waters. But here, you're my guest. Nothing bad is going to happen to you, I assure you."

Kuan took a prawn, sampled a chestnut, and then a piece of mushroom. His chewing accelerated. Before long he was absorbed in his feast. Dao could see that the boy was at last at ease in his company.

"Kuan, I know of few Shiyanese, let alone an outsider, who have displayed such courage and composure as you did in exposing that traitor Chi-Ling. You have exceptional potential, and that cannot be allowed to go to waste. That is why I want to give you the opportunity to serve as my apprentice. Do you know what that would involve?"

The boy ploughed on with devouring the food as he shook his head.

"You have heard of the Circles of Challenge?"

He swallowed the chunk of garoupa in his mouth and put down his chopsticks.

"Is that where even an outsider can become a Mauvean?"

"That would be ambitious but not impossible. Why would you want to become a Mauvean?"

"I have known life as an outsider in Shiyan. I don't want to go back to that. I have seen what comes with being a mauve elephant. To have the Mauvean status would mean that I don't have to be at the mercy of others anymore. I can get the life I really want."

"And what kind of life might that be?" Dao asked patiently.

Moisture blurred Kuan's vision.

"To have a life worth living, I must find father again. He's disappeared and I have no idea where he is. When eventually I find him, I want to have a place that is safe for us to live together, in reasonable comfort. It won't have to be anything like your grand mansion. Just a nice, decent home of our own."

"Do you know how difficult it is to become a Mauvean? There are nine levels in Shiyan's Circles of Challenge. Only those who get to the very top Circle are granted the powers and privileges that come with the Mauvean status."

"So what would it take to reach the highest Circle?"

Dao slowly walked to the side of the room and opened a glass door onto the mosaic-floored courtyard. He spoke to one of the reflector panels in the glass. Denji's lynx face appeared instantly.

"Denji, could you have them sent up now?"

"Yes, Chairman Dao. Right away. Incidentally, the President has called twice to speak with you."

"She can wait a little longer."

He beckoned the boy to join him. Dao was admiring the full moon.

"I do believe it's the night of the Mid-Autumn Festival in your world."

"How do you know about our custom?" asked Kuan as he dabbed his eyes dry with a sleeve.

"Your world fascinates me, Kuan. For years I read and re-read *The Human Way*, one of the best Shiyanese books ever written, full of remarkable details and insights about Homo Sapiens. The human world put ours in the shade for nearly two centuries. It was a terrible time for Shiyanese. A humiliating time. But at long last we began to learn from the advantages other worlds had over us, especially your world with its incredible wealth and technology. We studied how you built up resources, and leveraged control over others. We started to change the way we do things in Shiyan. In time we have come to surpass you. Still, it's important to remember that we must continue to grow stronger if we are not to become weak ever again."

The inner circle of a solid round marble table in the courtyard sunk low only to resurface a moment later with a tray of moon cakes. The boy had seen pictures of this festive delicacy but never tasted them before. Dao cut a piece and passed it to him.

"You know the story of moon cakes?" He asked the boy.

"It was when the Mongolians were ruling over China, and they treated the people harshly. Anyone found talking about standing up to them would be taken away, never to be seen again. Everyone was scared. Then a few brave men and women decided to use the Mid-Autumn Festival to put secret messages in moon cakes to trigger an uprising, and since the Mongolian rulers didn't eat moon cakes, they had no idea what was going on and the people were able to rise up and overthrow them."

"That's a very instructive story."

"Father told it to me every Mid-Autumn."

"Was he afraid that China would be stifled by oppression again?"

"I think he was afraid not just for China, but that terrible forces might overrun everywhere. He was deeply worried about the threats he saw coming and he wanted to warn others about them."

"He has taken on a heavy responsibility."

"He's had to go into hiding. I have no idea where he is."

"I'm sure you will find your father again soon."

Kuan looked up at the nocturnal beacon in the sky.

"Did your father ever share with you the ancient poem by Su Shi about friends and relatives who were sadly separated? On Mid-Autumn night they could view the moon from wherever they were and feel their bonds uniting them. Your father could be looking at the moon right now just as you are, Kuan. In this moment, you are together."

Kuan's attention remained transfixed on the lunar image. Father's eyes would be cast upon the very same illumination.

Dao clasped his hands behind his back and took a step closer to the boy.

"Kuan, there is no reason why you can't reach the top of the Circles of Challenge and win yourself all the entitlements that go with the Mauvean status. You would find then that you could get pretty much whatever you want. But they are difficult challenges to meet. And you have to be smart and determined to get through them all."

"How many challenges will I have to face?"

"There are nine Circles, each entitling you to a higher form of being. Given your ability, I'm confident you can take the fast track route and leap through them by meeting three challenges. These will be set by me, with the approval of the Council of Mauveans of course. If you meet the first challenge, you will rise to Minos, the fifth Circle; the second will raise you further to Asterion, the seventh Circle; and the final challenge will elevate you to Antaeus, the ultimate ninth Circle. Each challenge you meet will bring with it the privilege and power to morph into the forms available on the corresponding Circle. If you succeed with all three challenges, you will attain the status of a Mauvean, and with the resources at your disposal, I have no doubt you will quickly find your father again. And the two of you will be able to live a very comfortable life together."

"When can I start on the first challenge, Chairman Dao?"

"Governor Pui will explain things to you in the morning. For now, let us enjoy the moon while we can."

The purple-clad Dao and Kuan stood side by side, sharing a moon cake, gazing at the distant orb saturated in silver.

Chapter 14

<u>Capital</u>

Crowded streets crisscrossed the hectic landscape. A sea of creatures periodically parted for a haughty mauve elephant to stroll through, while its own elephantium attendants swept up the precious waste it dumped behind. Once it had moved ahead, waves of bodies crashed together again. Countless Shiyanese in their diverse forms were on the move to reach their morning destination. There were cats in varying sizes, some morphed into wolf dogs or greyhounds; a few walked upright with human bodies, and nearly all convinced they were running late. Yet at every corner they were distracted by new offers to improve their lives. Along every street they were reminded of the pledges they had made to those who granted their wishes. This was Bastille, their capital city.

A brownish tabby cat rushed from the back of Wuchang Tearoom, morphing into a smartly attired and attentive waiter to stand by the lone table on the pavement.

"Governor Pui, is there anything else I can get you or your guest?"

Perched on a golden stand, the peacock shook his head dismissively, and the waiter backed away.

"Kuan, are you watching carefully? This is the world Chairman Dao wants you to help improve even further. Day in, day out, we remind them what they need from us, and they pledge to give their time to us in return."

Glass covered every shop front, every wall along the streets, each divided into reflector units constantly ready to beam out images of what could be missing in a Shiyanese's life. One moment a puma was staring at his

164

own reflection in one of the glass panels, then suddenly the panel came to life showing a golden medallion with the words 'Can't rise to a higher Circle? Can't assume a more desirable form? Get a Mauve Medallion instead. Wear it and be proud.' The puma thought about moving on but the image of the medallion kept flashing until he put a paw on the screen. The message came up: 'A Mauve Medallion will be delivered to you in three days. You have pledged 10 hours to Plutopia.'

On the next corner, a greyhound was entranced by a reflector filled with images of a haughty steed galloping at speed. Along came the words: 'Drink Velocity and you too can rise to the challenge and reach the next Circle. Don't just dream about it. Drink it. Velocity.' The greyhound touched the reflector and immediately received the confirmation: 'Velocity will be delivered to you in two days. You have pledged 40 hours to Plutopia.'

"What are they doing?" asked Kuan.

"They are pledging their time to get something they want. In doing so they are indebted to Plutopia. We can call in that debt whenever we want. Whatever we want to get done, we ask those who owe us time to do what we ask of them. So the more time is pledged to us, the greater our ability to get what we want, when we want."

"So you come to own their time? The more they pledge, the more they have to do your bidding."

"Exactly. It's far more efficient than using force to get work done, though of course that might be necessary on occasion. On the whole, Plutopia's way is best. Shiyanese who might not otherwise be motivated to labour hard day and night are reeled in by the multitude of things they can't resist."

"Does that mean that the more time you pledge away, the more you have to do what others who own your time ask you to do?"

"That's the idea for the masses. For high ranking Shiyanese like me, and of course the Mauveans, we have so much time pledged to us that we rarely have to expend any of our precious personal time unless we want to. We can always get others to do things for us."

"And this is how Plutopia works?"

"Everybody gets something out of it. We come up with the irresistible offers, we get an endless supply of pledges, and we grow and become even stronger. A sublimely virtuous circle. Everyone is driven to give more and more of their time to do what we deem necessary to make ours the most powerful world. The Chairman wants you to become a part of our success."

Kuan wondered how many hours he would have to pledge to get someone to find father for him.

"Governor Pui, what will be my first challenge?"

Pui's shiny indigo eyes blinked with dismay, though it was directed not at Kuan but at the character with whom the boy would have to deal with soon.

"In every vat of fragrant ointment there always lurks an irritating fly, and in ours we have Lord Ou-Yang. An old fashioned Shiyanese who bitterly rejects our new way of life, a proverbial thorn that, in my view, cries out to be removed. But Chairman Dao wants us to join forces with him. Your first challenge, and the Chairman has handed you a tough one, is to bring his pompous lordship to the fold. He has refused to talk to any of us so far. Impertinent fool. You have to convince him, charm him, whatever it takes, into consenting to work with us. Can you do that?"

"I will do my best."

He could see a slight grin in the corner of the peacock's beak.

"Everything's set then. Wu-yin, any news on the renegade?"

The white cat padded up to one of the glass panels on the sidewalk and put a paw to her ear. A thin yellowy cat appeared in the reflector with a short message. When he vanished from the screen, a dramatic sequence came on with a miserable looking white cat prowling aimlessly, until a mist descended on it, and black stripes appeared on the cat which now resembled a miniature snow tiger. The words 'You don't have to change your form to change your looks' flashed brightly, and Wu-yin put her paw on the reflector and it responded: 'Stripes Spray will be delivered to you in four days. You have pledged 15 hours to Plutopia.'

She walked back to the table.

"Governor Pui. The bad news is that General Chi-Ling is still at large. There's been no sighting of him. The good news is that I'm getting the snow tiger look. Apparently it's very popular with the young demographic, especially since Lieutenant Sung was murdered by the general."

Pui looked down on the white cat with no hope of finding any sign of intelligence.

"Wu-yin, just fetch our transporter. It's time I headed to the office."

She took a sideways glance at Kuan and wondered if, when one day she could morph into another form, it might be worth trying that of a human. After she departed with the governor, the boy was finishing off his noodles when the waiter discreetly asked him to follow him into the kitchen. He was wondering what it could be about when the black Chartreux cat emerged from the corner. His copper red eyes were glazed with fatigue.

"Agent Tan, what are you doing here? I thought you were hunting down Chi-Ling."

"We'll get Chi-Ling sooner or later. I wanted to talk to you about your mission."

Kuan looked back at the waiter who was now standing guard at the kitchen door.

"He's with us. Now tell me, have you figured out what your mission is? The fact that Dao has brought you to his home in the capital must mean you're getting near. The future of Shiyan depends on it."

"The Chairman has asked me to talk to Lord Ou-Yang about joining forces. I don't know why they think he would speak with me when he has refused to speak to Chairman Dao or the governor. "

"I can't see how that can be significant. Think Kuan, what else is being planned?"

The cat circled him impatiently.

"Could you stop that, you're making me dizzy."

"You've got to try harder. It's what your father wants, and he's counting on you."

His heart was lifted.

"You've heard from father? You've seen him? He's safe, is he?"

The boy crouched down close to Tan as the black cat curled his tail round himself to halt his own relentless pacing.

"I haven't seen him, but I'm sure he's still alive, otherwise he couldn't have sent me a message."

"What message? How do you know it was from him?"

"It's typed on paper with a picture of the sun as its watermark. That is the paper he uses, isn't it?"

Kuan affirmed with fervent nods.

"And the message simply said, 'Beware when the right way turns out to be the wrong way. Unmask the hidden. Resistance is life'."

Kuan could almost hear father's voice in his head saying those words, but what did they mean?

"Have you got the piece of paper with you?"

"No, I've destroyed it. It's dangerous to be found in possession of something like that."

"When did you get it? How was it delivered to you?"

"I found it when I returned to base late last night. I don't know how it was sent to me, but no one but your father could have written it. He's been planning this a long time."

"Planning what? He never told me about any such plan?"

"It's about the change that must be brought to Shiyan. He must have discussed it with you, perhaps not explicitly about Shiyan, but about the growing threats that must be stopped."

"He was always worried about something, but he never really explained what they were to me. Or maybe I didn't pay enough attention."

"You've got to think back to what he said to you and what he wanted you to do here."

"What could he want me to do in a world that has nothing to do with ours?"

"Maybe he foresaw Shiyan affecting your world, that what happens here would spread to your world unless something is done to stop it."

The waiter clicked his fingers twice.

"Kuan, think on your father's words. And be careful, you're being watched and followed wherever you go."

"Wait, could you ask him when I can see him?"

The black cat had swiftly disappeared.

Where could father be? How did he avoid being captured by the Curator? Did he know about Schloss 22 early enough to leave home? Why had he not got in touch directly with his son? If Kuan had the support he could command as a Mauvean in Shiyan, he would be able to arrange for protection for father so that he could come out of hiding. It would be far easier then to work together on this mission which he was supposed to accomplish.

Those questions and more were swirling around in Kuan's head when he was on his way to meet Lord Ou-Yang.

All along the route, signs would appear on successive glass panels to point him in the right direction. At one junction where he hesitated, the reflector on the corner kept flashing 'turn left'. He followed the instruction. As he turned, he caught a shadow behind him. He swung around and saw a heavyset cat morphing into a bulldog, examining its look in a reflector. Shaking its head in disappointment it reverted to its cat form and padded away.

Continuing his journey, Kuan walked into a deserted underpass. His footsteps echoed eerily around him. When his eyes had adjusted in the shade, it was too late to back away from the jawful of daggers displayed by an approaching predator. Somewhere in a crevice of his mind, he recalled father's observation that a prey could sometimes escape detection if it kept very still. But he was not talking about the preys of creatures with the killer instinct of tigers.

"General Chi-Ling regrets having to leave you behind."

Kuan's immobile legs disconnected themselves from his brain.

"But no one's going to save you this time. Come quietly with me."

"Where's the general?" asked Kuan.

"You'll find out soon enough."

The tiger's paw was reaching out to the boy. Kuan wished he hadn't left Amo behind at Rook Mansion. She would come up with a way out of this predicament. Without her, he had no choice but to be taken captive again.

Kuan could not outrun the tiger. His muscles were tightening in anticipation of being dragged away to some place where he would be tortured for information he could not yield. No one would find him. Just as hope was at the point of being extinguished, from behind him, a surge of grey swept past. Like a dark cloak flourished by a matador from the underworld, it flashed before the tiger's eyes before revealing its unforgiving intent.

It was a pack of wolf dogs. The underpass was flooded with their soul-splitting howls. The wolf dogs leapt forward and tore into their quarry. The tiger reacted fast and clamped its teeth on the head of one of his attackers. Its claws sliced open the chest of another. But they kept coming. The whirling mass of jaws snapped and gnawed at the big cat. It fought with blind fury. But its equally fearless foes surpassed it in numbers. Ultimately there was no contest. Like a wave of piranhas, they stripped it to the bone.

The eyes in the midst of blood-drenched faces fixed in unison on Kuan. Dread gushed down his windpipe. He held his breath.

"Master Kuan, you're safe now."

It was Denji, the golden brown lynx from Rook Mansion.

"Chairman Dao was concerned that Chi-Ling might still be after you, so I brought our own security guards with me to keep tabs on you. You look rather pale, sir."

He had finally come back up for air.

"Denji", he gasped, "you should have kept him alive. He knew where the general was hiding."

"No need to worry about that. There's no hiding from the Chairman. The traitor will be tracked down soon. Would you like to sit down for a rest?"

"I'm fine."

"In that case, you must keep your appointment with Lord Ou-Yang. It would not do for you to be late for his lordship, sir."

The lynx with his white beard bowed low. Kuan took it as wise counsel from someone who knew the ways of Shiyan. In haste, he continued his journey.

The House of Ou-Yang, one of the most venerable institutions in Shiyan, was based in a vast plain looking barn. From end to end, it would take Kuan an hour to walk through it. Workers, large and small, morphed or otherwise, packaged food to send to those who had pledged their time in return for a dependable meal. At one point it was reputed to be feeding half of Shiyan. And nearly every Shiyanese, and even a few Potokans, had at some point had a meal prepared for them by the House of Ou-Yang. It was not always the tastiest of food, but it helped to keep hunger at bay.

In a secluded corner of the barn stood the holographic image of a much enlarged and glistening snowflake. Kneeling underneath was a bowed figure deep in meditation. Kuan waited in silence. When Lord Ou-Yang finally rose to face him, he could see a lean human frame immaculately dressed in a grey suit and shirt, dark blue tie, and a long black leather coat. The head was of a leopard, imposing yet weary. Approaching the boy with the aid of his ash walking stick, he breathed in the odour of Rook Mansion with marked distaste.

"You must be Kuan. Denji told me you were coming."

"Lord Ou-Yang, thank you for agreeing to see me."

The aged semi-morph viewed him with sunken eyes that had seen too many sunsets.

"I see Dao's had you dressed up in his uniform already."

Kuan glanced down at his purple tunic.

"Are you religious, Kuan?"

"It depends." He automatically repeated father's usual response to that question when it was put to him in the past.

His lordship lifted his stick to point to the hologram.

"Do you believe in the Beginning?"

"I don't know what that means."

"Few do. The question is do you nonetheless believe."

"I can't say I do if I don't know what it means."

"In the Beginning, there was no heat, just absolute coldness. From the one and only Beginning, came heat and our existence."

"So what is the Beginning?"

"The Beginning was nothing, and because of it, there is now everything."

Kuan hoped he was not stuck with another preacher. At least there was no trace of clowning irreverence on the stern leopard face.

"Nothing and everything, what's left for anyone to disbelieve?" the boy asked.

Ou-Yang sat himself down in a steel frame chair, resting the stick's crooked handle on its back.

"You studied metaphysics?"

"Some physics."

"We all flow from our own beginning, an effect begotten by a cause. That defines our nature. And because of our common Beginning, we are ultimately one, and should support each other. But those who try to sever themselves from the Beginning want to break free from their bonds with others. They claim to have no Beginning, but to have made themselves."

"Can't see how anyone can make themselves out of nothing."

"It's heresy to suggest such a thing, but Shiyan has been cursed with two who dare to dismiss the Beginning. First there was Amadeus, the self-style prophet who proclaimed the dawn of a New Beginning, when only those who followed him without question would be saved."

He broke into a prolonged cough. Shaking his head with raw resentment.

"Saved from what?" asked Kuan.

"Saved from the suffering inflicted on anyone refusing to follow him."

"He's not still around, is he?"

A ray of satisfaction fell on Ou-Yang's leopard face.

"For the murders he instigated, especially against a number of Mauveans, he was duly punished and Shiyan is rid of him forever."

"But there's another like him?"

"The second heretic? That would be your master, Chairman Dao. He's much cleverer than Amadeus. Nothing overtly subversive, no blatant violence. But little by little he's been destroying the old spirit of Shiyan, and now he wants to finish off the few obstacles that are still in his way. He's out to take control of the House of Ou-Yang, and you're here to seek my consent, isn't that right?"

"Lord Ou-Yang, I think the Chairman would like to work together with you."

The leopard bawled out a hollow laugh.

"Nobody works *with* Dao, you only get to work *for* him."

He grabbed his walking stick and pushed himself up from the chair.

"My family has for generations provided food for the most modest of pledges to everyone who needed it, be they Shiyanese or Potokans. There's no need for any to go hungry when they could so easily be fed. But Dao thinks he can do better. He despises everything we do."

He stabbed his stick on the floor.

"There was a short time when his wife died that I thought I glimpsed another side to him. After he lost Nestra, Dao started to rethink his life, questioning his many all-conquering schemes for Shiyan. Progress was put on hold. Then as quickly as it came, the veil of conscience lifted, and he was once more his old self. And now he's making a move for what my family has built up."

Kuan could see the rage seething in his eyes.

"Believe me, you have better things to do with your life than wasting it on a foul creature like Dao. Do nothing he asks of you. Leave him before it's too late."

Lord Ou-Yang turned away, his coat billowing an unspoken farewell. There was nothing more the boy could do but retreat. He had failed his first challenge.

Chapter 15

__Transformation__

The room was engulfed in blinding yellow. Cold radiance flooded away every dark shade, leaving a spotless clarity. Then fireworks of geometric patterns exploded across the glowing space. The boy stood entranced in the middle of Amo's visual demonstration of her latest discovery. Gripped by its ineffable brilliance, and intrigued by its complex simplicity, he sat down on the floor as the flame retracted into a thumb-sized flicker.

Through the console in Kuan's room, Amo had been able to reach into Shiyan's computer system and review information she drew together from a vast array of sources. On this occasion Kuan fully grasped the findings she spectacularly conveyed to him. Amo's home nebula was not in fact situated many galaxies away. Instead the only viable hypothesis would place it somewhere in Shiyan. It had to exist at a quantum level, in some form of inner space, rather than beyond the Milky Way in outer space.

"Amo, that means you're much closer to your home world than you thought, and you should be able to return to it very soon."

The flame brightened momentarily in affirmation.

"The probability has definitely improved."

"Is there anything else that can help you with your search? I can ask Denji to see if he could get it."

"Kuan, it is best if you remain the only one who knows of my presence here."

"If that is what you prefer."

"You should be aware that I have repeatedly sought to locate your father as well."

"And what have you found?"

"So far, nothing. There is just no evidence that he is in Shiyan. He could be outstanding in erasing any traces he might have left no matter where he has been. Or he never came into this world from yours."

"How could he be passing messages to Agent Tan if he hasn't made his way into this world?"

"You should put that question to Agent Tan."

But since that surreptitious meeting in Wuchang Tearoom, there had been no further contact from Agent Tan. Could he be making up everything about father to trick him into revealing some secret he was guarding?

"Amo, could you see what information there is on the system about Agent Tan?"

She returned to the console to delve into Shiyan's store of electronic data.

Kuan wondered if the black Chartreux's obsession with this mission father supposedly wanted him to undertake was a genuine concern or a devious ruse for something he had not so far suspected.

A knock came on the door. It was Denji.

"Master Kuan, the Chairman would like to have a word with you."

Ever since returning crestfallen weeks ago from his meeting with Lord Ou-Yang, Kuan had been anxious about what little time he might have left before Chairman Dao kicked him out of Rook Mansion for failing to meet his first challenge. He would be stranded with nowhere to live in Shiyan, and could hardly expect to find his father. Would he be given at least a couple of days' notice before he was thrown out on the street? What excuse could he come up with to explain his failure? It was clear to him that Lord Ou-Yang despised Dao with such intensity that no one could ever persuade him to join forces with the Chairman.

The lynx led the boy to the library and left him to enter alone. Reclining in a wide, leather armchair, Dao pinched the top of his nose and closed the book on his lap. The daylight brought out his worn features more clearly. The narrowness of his eyes, beneath the wizened contours of a high forehead, was matched by those thin, dry lips. His broad face rested on an indomitable jaw line. He gestured to Kuan to sit down opposite him.

"I would have spoken with you sooner had the President not been demanding more and more of my time. The vice-president role was only meant to be an honorary one. But she's under a lot of pressure with the growing threat of a Potokan attack on Shiyan."

Kuan wanted to ask if the threat was not more of a Shiyanese attack on the Potokans, but he was dreading that the conversation would suddenly turn to his failed challenge.

"If I have to give more of my time to affairs of the state, I'll need someone to help keep an eye on Plutopia."

He wondered if that was a roundabout way to get to the Lord Ou-Yang challenge. Dao was staring at him now.

"Kuan, have you heard of Peter Lu?"

An unpleasant massacre of some kind sprang to his mind, but the boy just shook his head.

"He was my uncle. Both my parents died when I was three, and he brought me up, taught me everything about growing strong by encouraging others to pledge their strengths to you. I worked for my uncle for many years but he insisted I should set up my own organisation. I wasn't sure at first, but then I met Nestra Opia, a genius who had a bold vision for making Shiyan indomitable again. She chose the human form to morph into – a most perfect human form."

Dao stared into the distance. Kuan turned round and noticed that every reflector panel on the glass wall of the library was showing the recording of an attractive dark haired woman dancing, laughing, and waving at the camera.

"After we were married, Nestra suggested we use the support of my uncle and the substantial resources she inherited from her grandmother, Tess Opia, to set up our own organisation to make Shiyan a better place. In memory of 'P Lu' and 'T Opia', we launched our dream of Plutopia, to bring about the transformation this world so urgently needed."

The reflectors went blank. Kuan turned to face Dao again. By now he believed the Chairman had meandered so far away that if he kept quiet, the subject of the House of Ou-Yang might not come up at all.

"Most Mauveans looked down on Nestra because she never reached the highest Circle of Challenge. But I pitied them for not valuing what truly mattered. In time, they had to accept Plutopia was leading the way. I wish Nestra had lived long enough to see them queuing up to cast their vote for me to be the Chairman of their precious Council even though I too insisted on taking on a human form despite acquiring the Mauvean status. Plutopia is the future, Kuan, and you're going to be a big part of it. I want you to know that."

Perhaps the challenge did not really matter after all. It might not be necessary to become a mauve elephant if Dao would give him an important position in Plutopia. At that point the lynx entered the library to announce an expected interruption.

"Chairman Dao, the doctor is here."

Dao stood up. Kuan followed suit, wondering if some serious illness had inclined the Chairman to talk about the past and the future in that strange way that those with limited time left tended to slip into.

A woman in an elegant green dress came through the door. She swept her long red hair back as she strode towards Dao. In her wake, a tender fragrance flowed.

"Dr. Lee, I'm delighted to meet you."

He shook her hand firmly.

"Chairman Dao, it's an honour to meet you. I wanted so much to come and thank you for the generous donation you gave to our clinic."

"There's no need. A reflector message would have sufficed. But I appreciate you coming, because it means I can tell you in person how impressed I am with what you're trying to achieve."

She smiled nervously. Her eyes caught his.

"Kuan, is that you?"

"Erica!"

The boy dashed to give her a hug that doubled his heart rate. She ruffled his hair fondly.

"You know each other?" asked Dao benignly.

"Yes, we were both on board *FSS Castle*."

"Of course. Rather harsh on Captain Ma to put him on indefinite leave for the mess left by Chi-Ling. The navy always overreacts when Mauveans are involved."

"The sub needs to be refitted after the incident anyway. Hopefully, Captain Ma will be back on duty when the *Castle* is ready for sea again."

"But I hope you will stay on at the new clinic."

"I intend to. In fact, I was wondering, Chairman Dao, if you would be interested in paying us a visit sometime, take a look at what we're managing to do with your kind support?"

"I'd love to, but I really can't spare the time. I can send a deputy though, can't I? Kuan, why don't you go with Dr. Lee to have a look at her clinic and report back to me?"

Kuan couldn't think of anything better.

"I'll give Deputy Kuan a guided tour in that case, and answer all his questions."

With a gentle push of his head, Denji nudged open the door for Dr. Lee and Kuan to exit. But once Erica was out of earshot, Dao had a parting message for the boy.

"Kuan, you won't forget Lord Ou-Yang, will you? The deadline for your challenge is midnight tonight."

Kuan was initially perturbed by Dao's reminder, but Erica's drastic change of demeanour once they left the grounds of Rook Mansion grabbed his attention. As soon as they sat down in the doctor's hover transporter, she erupted in agitation, not with him (to his relief), but with the fact that she had to present a supplicant face to the likes of Dao. If only President Zhou had stuck to the idea she had mooted - that all those with over a million hours pledged to them should be made to share them out a little more. Instead the pledge hoarders – Erica's term for the Council of Mauveans – immediately signaled their grave disapproval and the President backed down.

So the same old ways prevailed. And when Erica decided to open a clinic for Potokans in Bastille, she had to manoeuvre her way to get support from the well-pledged Shiyanese to gather enough resources to make it viable. Why did she take on such a task?

It all started with *FSS Castle* having to be overhauled following the Chi-Ling incident, and all the Potokans were evicted from Castle de Potoka. Admiralty wanted all damages inspected and repaired, and instigated a micro-search for the explosive devices it suspected Chi-Ling's troops might have planted on the boat. The submarine would be out of commission for months. Shiyanese could take shore leave back home, but for the denizens of Castle de Potoka, the submarine's subterranean deck was the only home they ever had. No alternative, temporary or permanent, was offered.

The doctor refused to stand by, and organised an exodus of those willing to follow her to the nearest area they were allowed to relocate to - Bastille de Potoka, the mining region at the outskirt of the capital. Since many of them were suffering from poor health, she realised a clinic which provided pledge-free care was essential, but it meant she had to put on a fake smile in meeting and greeting her Mauvean benefactors, lavishing them with gratitude for their paltry donations.

The doctor's jade green eyes brimmed with resentment. It riled her that so many should suffer so much for the smug satisfaction of so few. She clasped her hands together to stop herself wringing the neck of an invisible enemy. Things must change, she declared to Kuan. They could not be allowed to continue as they were.

As the hover transporter glided into Bastille de Potoka, they were submerged by a wave of elephantium stench. To ease Kuan's retching, Erica gave him a small tablet, and casually took one herself. This was not about a few spadesful to be picked up here and there. Grime-laden, smog-filled Bastille de Potoka was where all the spare elephantium of the capital city was collected and buried deep underground so it could undergo a toxic decaying process. After ten years it would be sufficiently enriched to double its potency as a fuel, and it would be mined by Potokans who had pledged their lives to carry out this work for the Council of Mauveans.

The grey, scarred landscape rolled by in desolate silence. A few isolated trees in the distance held up their emaciated branches, bearing witness to the pervasive sense of undernourishment. The cloak of dusk was fast descending. Coming into view was the Oran Clinic, named after the district in which it was located. Oran was infamous as the place Shiyanese most feared of being stranded in after dark. It also had the dubious distinction of having a higher concentration of Blessed Potokans than anywhere else.

Kuan followed Erica through the swinging double door at the entrance of the clinic. Instantly voices from all sides called out for Dr. Lee to help them with a multitude of tasks. She quickly told the boy to feel free to look around before she set off to attend to the many pieces of broken lives scattered around her.

In the crowded waiting room, he recognised the drained look of many six-legged Potokans, disorientated by the Blessing they had received. A group of them were running around in a circle muttering that it was time they were Blessed again. One stared at his own gaunt image in one of the reflectors on the wall and turned his white eyes away in dismay momentarily before returning to his pointless self-loathing.

Then Kuan noticed a long queue of thirty or more Shiyanese in ordinary cat form lying lethargically on their side. They shared an eerie bewilderment in their eyes.

"Why are you here? I thought you weren't keen to be in this area. It's going to be dark soon."

Nearly all of them closed their eyes wearily and lowered their heads. But one, a short light blue cat with a very round face and tiny ears half-lifted its tail and looked up at the boy.

"This is the only place for us now."

"You've been Blessed?"

"That will come soon enough. No, our fate has been sealed."

"You're dying of some disease?"

"Worse. We've all failed at the first hurdle in the Circles of Challenge."

"Isn't the deadline at midnight tonight?" Kuan asked in panic.

"The end begins at midnight, but there's nothing we can do to alter the outcome."

The round-faced cat put its paw across its eyes and turned away.

How could failure in the Circles of Challenge be worse than dying? Instead of waiting to find out, he knew he must give his own challenge one last try. He ran over to one of the reflectors in the clinic's reception area.

"Operator here. What can I do for you?" A smiley cat appeared on the glass screen.

"Can you put me through to the House of Ou-Yang, please? I urgently need to speak with his lordship."

"Just a moment, caller, putting you through."

The cat faded away until its grin was replaced by a scowling leopard face.

"Kuan, has Dao asked you to give me a last minute reprieve? Or are you calling to gloat on his behalf?"

"I just need to let the Chairman know if you would work with him."

"Spare me the euphemism of partnership. He and his friends have effectively cut off my elephantium supply, asking for a pledge of 2 million hours for a week's delivery. Without fuel, we can't do anything, and that's what he's counting on. So you can tell him I will let him have the House of Ou-Yang. He can take it all!"

The semi-morphed leopard put his hand on the screen.

"You've got my confirmation, Kuan."

The boy almost beamed in relief but the more sensitive part of him pulled his face down.

"I will let the Chairman know. I'm sure together we will make sure the House of Ou-Yang continue to do its good work."

The leopard-human raised his stick at the screen, and Kuan instinctively recoiled.

"Are you that self-delusional? Wake up! See what's happening around you."

The screen went blank and Kuan's baffled visage was staring back out at him from the reflector. He felt he ought to be worried about why Lord Ou-Yang was so upset, but he was more concerned about letting Chairman Dao know in time that he had succeeded with his first challenge. So he called on the operator to put him through to Rook Mansion.

"Denji, could you give a message to Chairman Dao for me?"

The lynx bowed his head.

"Of course, Master Kuan."

"Please tell him that Lord Ou-Yang has agreed to work with him."

"That's very good, sir. The Chairman has been expecting this news. Although his lordship would not speak with anyone connected with Plutopia, Chairman Dao knew he would make an exception with you. He asked me to pass on his congratulations for reaching the Minos Circle. He will tell you more about your second challenge when he next sees you."

The first challenge did not seem that hard to meet in the end. Perhaps it was all about the timing.

"Master Kuan, are we expecting you for dinner?"

"Denji, I think I'll stay here at the clinic to help Dr. Lee. They're having a busy night."

The lynx nodded approvingly and disappeared.

Kuan was still staring at the glass panel when a pair of Potokans pushed into the reception area. One was holding with its front paws a placard with the word 'New' scrawled over it, while the other held up a sign saying 'Beginning'.

"Good Potokans, join us", urged one of them, "the New Beginning will wipe out all who are unworthy. Join us and you will be saved."

"Embrace the prophecy of Lord Amadeus", shouted the other in a loud voice Kuan didn't think they were capable of.

"Death awaits our enemies."

"We are love."

Dr. Lee, now wearing a white coat over her emerald dress, peered from around the corner.

"Will someone get these buffoons out of my clinic?"

The boy wanted to be the first to carry out the doctor's order.

"Excuse me, would you mind leaving?" requested Kuan, who felt he ought to be polite as he was much bigger than the squirrel-sized creatures.

"Who are you to tell us what ..."

"Wait, brother. Look closely."

The two proselytisers exchanged glances quickly.

"Are you saying I should be seeing what I think you're seeing?"

"It is he who has been sent to us."

"Sent to destroy the unforgiven."

"To remind us of the infinity of love."

"Can you just leave?" Kuan interrupted."You're disturbing our patients."

"You are the one."

"No, I'm certainly not."

"He denies it. That's the sign."

"There can be no doubt, brother, he is the one sent to us."

"Denial is the affirmation."

"We have the sign."

"In that case, I order you to get out of here at once." Kuan found an imperious tone.

The two turned to each other, and then back at the boy, to whom they bowed. And out of the clinic they ran, joy overflowing.

Impressed by Kuan's display of authority, Dr. Lee asked him to help ensure no new patient would be left unattended for more than an hour. As there were new arrivals every few minutes, it was no easy task. Kuan took to it with relish, and as the clinic's closing time approached at midnight, he was exhausted but feeling content that he had done something father would have been proud of.

"Good job, Kuan", remarked Erica as she pushed a trolley lined with rows of half-filled hypodermic syringes towards the queue of Shiyanese in their ordinary cat form lying in the corridor.

"Can I help?"

The boy asked though he had no wish to handle those needles.

"Do you know what these are for?"

Kuan shook his head as the dark sky outside switched to a shade of crimson. The glass windows lit by their red backdrop flashed up '20', '19', '18' …

"Erica, what's going on?"

A siren in the distance wailed like a wounded banshee.

'14', '13', '12' …

It was a haunted, pitiful, and relentlessly piercing sound.

"Kuan, get ready to pass them to me."

"What's happening? Tell me."

'8', '7', '6' …

"An outsider once described this as 'the reflected-sound-of-underground-spirits'."

'3', '2', '1', and the wailing stopped. Outside, the sky reverted to normal. Inside, the transformation had begun.

The cats that had been lying still all evening started to convulse. They began to shrink, with their fur of different colours all turning dull grey. Worm-like movement crept along their abdomens until the sides burst open and an extra pair of legs drooped out.

Kuan watched in astonishment as their eyes first turned a bloody red but within seconds all colour drained away leaving a cold whiteness across the socket. They screeched in pain through the excruciating metamorphosis. Dr. Lee worked as fast as she could to sedate them. She had to wait until then as the drug would only work with their newly acquired physiology.

Drowsiness overcame them. For now the physical agony subsided. But for the clutch of new Potokans that had just been brought into the world, the mental anguish would linger for years to come.

Chapter 16

<u>Towards Asterion</u>

Fingers hovering to strike … 'when the right way turns out', … the keys were hammering away, 'to be the wrong way'. Words orchestrated in rousing defiance … 'unmask the hidden'. A final flourish on the old typewriter: 'Resistance is life'.

Silence.

At the far end of a long room, he could see the typewriter left on a decrepit desk. Father was not to be found anywhere. Kuan tried to stand up but found himself tied to a chair. A row of bath taps lanced through the wall and started to gush out water. He pulled against the rope encircling him but the knots were determined to anchor him to his asphyxiation. The water level was rising. His trembling knees were soaked. He cried out for help, but no sound came out of his mouth. The taps were turning by themselves, letting in more water, more quickly. It was now splashing on his chin. Was that not the splashing sound he heard on the beach that night? The typewriter had drowned. Water overwhelmed his face.

It was no more than a jug of water thrown over him. There were no gushing taps. It was a passing hallucination.

He sat up on the floor and spat out the tasteless fluid in his mouth. It tasted disgusting.

"Kuan, your father needs to know. Are you ready?"

The rusty brown eyes of the Chartreux cat stared through the darkened surrounding into the inner sanctum of his mind.

"Am I ready for what?"

Behind Agent Tan stood the waiter he had met before, holding an empty jug.

"The mission, Kuan. The time has come for you to make the move."

"Father told you this?"

"Yes."

"But he didn't tell you exactly what it is?"

"No, only you're supposed to know that."

"Why won't father talk to me directly?"

"He can't."

The boy stood up and brushed the dirt off his purple tunic and trousers. He fixed his gaze on Tan. The black cat turned his head away with a deep frown. Resting on his hind legs, Tan tried to explain.

"Because it's too dangerous for him to get in touch with you at this point. It could destroy everything. I'm the only one he can safely contact without being tracked down by his enemy. What he must know, as do all of us, is that you are ready to make the move."

"I'll make the move. I won't fail him."

That appeared enough to reassure Tan even if the Chartreux's face remained an inscrutable mask. He apologised for having to tranquilise Kuan earlier so he could be smuggled into their secret meeting place. It was a long, thin room behind a metal door. A dim light hung from the ceiling. No one could spy on them there. And should Kuan's clandestine role be exposed, and he was pressed to disclose where he had met the agent, he genuinely would not know. Tan warned him not to try to make contact with him via any reflector since all signals and images sent or received on any glass surface in Shiyan were now being monitored. When the time came, he would get in touch with Kuan again. For now the boy must once again be deprived of his consciousness temporarily so he could be returned to Wuchang Tearoom, where he was earlier pondering what Shiyan might have in store for him after his long night at the Oran Clinic.

A pungent smell raised Kuan from his slumber.

"Would you like any more salt or pepper with that?"

"I'm fine." He asserted the opposite of how he felt about everything.

The waiter stepped back and morphed into his tabby cat form as he disappeared back into the kitchen.

Kuan surveyed the bustling streets of Bastille city centre. Two Potokans were shouting at passers-by that the New Beginning would soon be cleansing Shiyan of the filth it had been mired in. He couldn't tell if they were the same pair he saw the previous night. Before he could take a closer look, they were being chased away by patrolling cheetahs. Nobody else seemed to have taken much notice of the incident.

Busy Shiyanese were trying to keep up with the proliferation of messages on every glass surface around them. Obsessively they checked what news was being relayed, what offers were being made, and how their own reflections appeared at different angles.

Whatever forms they possessed at that moment though, their failings could lead to their transformation under a blood red sky into the very Potokans they feared and despised. But they seemed oblivious of that prospect as they carried on devoting the fleeting hours of their lives to the endless curiosities that might attract them to pledge more of their time away.

And what a curiosity it was to behold a white cat prancing proudly with the faintest black stripes along her short body. Wu-yin put her paw to her ear, muttered something, and a floating metallic globe descended from the sky to hover just in front of the tearoom.

"Kuan, get in."

The boy stepped into the globe as instructed. Its interior was small but luxuriously comfortable. It took off at high speed once Wu-yin had boarded too.

"Where are we going?"

"Governor Pui wants to see you. You're a Minos Circle Apprentice now. Lots of important tasks to carry out."

"How did you know where to find me?"

The white cat looked around but where glass might have been there were now thick steel plates encasing them. She fixed her eyes on the boy with a degree of seriousness she had rarely exhibited.

"Kuan, tell me honestly, and I don't want you to hide your true feelings, what do you think of my snow tiger look?"

He had learnt that while honesty was a virtue, sometimes one had to find the right word to bridge the gap between truth and courtesy.

"It's different."

"You really think that?"

"Yes, definitely different."

Wu-yin was delighted with that assessment.

"It's going to help me get to the third Circle. You've got to look the part if you want the part. That's what I've heard. I've been stuck as an aide for too long. Time to move onwards and upwards."

"So what would you become when you get to the third Circle?" asked Kuan.

"It won't be high enough to be a snow tiger, so maybe I'll take the cheetah form. I'd look good as a cheetah, and such acceleration. Or I could try becoming a wolf dog. You get a lot of respect when you roam around as a wolf dog. Not so much respect as fear, but fear is good. And there are a few security guard positions going at Rook Mansion. What about you, Kuan, you've got lots of choice on the fifth Circle, besides the human form, which you've got already? What about an alligator? Alligators can take possession of any swamps they find on the east side of Shiyan. Prime estate of the future, trust me, I know these things. Or how about becoming a rhinoceros? There are some special posts in the military for those who can attain the rhino form. You're not going to just stay as a human, are you?"

"Chairman Dao said there would be three challenges for me. For now, I think I'll prepare myself for the next two. They will no doubt be much more difficult than the first."

The white cat did not know if Kuan was admirably focused on his work or plain stupid in not thinking through his morphing options. But her attention span had reached its natural limit and she dozed off.

By the time the metallic globe had landed, Wu-yin was still deeply asleep. Kuan stepped outside the opened door. He had been brought to the woodland within the grounds of Rook Mansion, outside a camouflaged building which he would never have noticed had he not been standing right in front of it. An entrance revealed itself, and he walked towards it across the ground vegetation, still glistening with morning dew.

Inside, a long passageway led him to a dark narrow room where Governor Pui was standing behind a thick blue glass wall. Crouching by him was someone he knew from *FSS Castle*. It was Chief Engineer Xian, in her semi-morphed form of leopard head and human body. Instead of her blue naval overall, she was now wearing a snug purple one. She rose slowly and walked towards Kuan.

"When you were at the House of Ou-Yang, did my father look well to you?"

He was not aware of the two being related.

"I just remember him being angry."

"With me?"

"No, not at all."

The momentary relief in her red eyes was pushed aside by a deeper anxiety.

"Did he ask about me?"

He was reluctant to upset her but in truth he had to shake his head.

"So what was he angry about? Don't tell me. His blind hatred of the Chairman, compounded by my agreeing to help Plutopia."

She turned to walk away but glanced back at the boy.

"But he didn't look unwell to you."

"He seemed fine, on the day I met him. Is he not well?"

"How would I know?"

Xian disappeared off a side door which slid open and closed behind her.

The peacock twitched his head and beckoned Kuan to join him.

"Family, Kuan, nothing but trouble. I know your father's missing, and you feel terrible about it. But that's my point. I'm an orphan myself, raised by lower Circle foster parents who were utterly indifferent to me. Taught myself everything, and achieved everything myself. The last thing I want is to have my own family. What a weight that would be to put around one's fragile neck. Anyway, make sure you don't talk about his dreadful lordship when Xian's around. I don't want her distracted. She's working on a very important project for us."

He pecked a button on the floor. A shutter on the other side of the glass wall rolled up, and the distant sun could be seen in its full radiating magnificence. The reinforced glass served its purpose in sparing the watchers the instant loss of their sight. Pui pecked again. Now a round disc emerged from the ground beyond the glass wall. It was no bigger than half a metre in diameter, made of a matt black substance and positioned to block the sun completely from the observers' view behind the blue barrier. It started to shine like a star as it absorbed the energy from the sun. The demonstration came to an end when the outer shutter was brought down again, and a bolt of energy was released from the sizzling disc to vaporise a hefty chunk of metal nearby.

Fanning out his vivid feathers in excitement, the peacock strutted up to Kuan.

"That's the future of Plutopia, Kuan. You can tell generations to come you were there when the prototype was tested."

"What is it? Some kind of weapon?"

"I'll tell you more in due course. For now, the Chairman wants you to be ready for your second challenge. It's good you've reached the Minos Circle. But next up is your chance to take the fast track to Asterion, the seventh Circle. Not many are given an opportunity to try for the steep jump onto the Asterion Circle. The Chairman has great faith in you."

"Governor Pui, will I be turned into a Potokan if I fail?"

"Of course not. Where would you get such an absurd notion from? It's not that Wu-yin babbling her nonsense again, is it? If Denji hadn't pressed me to take on his cousin's only offspring, I would have got rid of her long ago. It's family again, you see. Even a wise head like Denji loses it when family intrudes."

"It's not Wu-yin, governor. I was at the Oran Clinic last night, and I saw what happened to those who failed their challenge."

"They must have been lowly Shiyansese trying to stay on the first Circle."

"It was their first challenge."

The peacock impatiently closed up his tail as though its grandeur must be shielded from the mention of such detestable creatures.

"Kuan, all Shiyanese are born into the first Circle, but they must pass their fist challenge to remain on it. You've got nothing to worry about, because you're high up now. All those on the superior Circles are safe. Except for the idiots who fail consccutivc challenges and drop right back down to the very bottom, but anyone so useless deserves to be Potokanised."

"Is it true that it's the work of underground spirits, with some strange power of their reflected sound?"

"What superstitious nonsense. There are no such things as underground spirits."

"What makes it happen then?"

"It's simple. Once a month, the President flicks a switch and all the successes and failures in the Circles of Challenge are ratified. Nobody knows how it works exactly. The powers to morph and acquire associated abilities were built into the ancient foundations of Shiyan. In olden times, the Circles were less firmly divided and Shiyanese could try out different forms. But the Council of Mauveans improved them so that only the very best could move up, while the weaklings would be turned into lesser beings called Potokans. Shiyan's revival as a great power is due in no small measure to this ingenuous development."

Governor Pui's explanation only left the boy more disturbed.

"What will happen to them after they have become Potokans? They were all going out of their minds and Dr. Lee had to tranquilise them."

"They've only got themselves to blame."

"But the clinic can't cope. Dr. Lee needs more help. Maybe Chairman Dao can increase his pledges."

The peacock flew up onto a table so he could be level with the boy when he gave him a scorching stare.

"It's not for you to think what the Chairman should do. You are to do what the Chairman thinks needs doing. Do you understand that?"

The boy nodded. If he should ever succeed in reaching the highest Circle, he would not have to put up with that arrogant tone ever again.

"It so happens that your next challenge concerns Dr. Lee. There is an important joint project the Chairman wants to pursue with her. Chairman Dao is very impressed with how you handled Ou-Yang, and he believes you can help with a difficult problem we'll need to solve together with the doctor."

"What kind of problem?"

"A very tricky one. You'll find out soon enough."

The peacock winked and bounced off the table most inelegantly. As he left the room, a separate door to a lift opened with Denji appearing on its reflector, inviting Kuan to go down and take the underground shuttle hovercraft back to the Mansion.

Kuan was still worrying that Erica Lee would react as angrily as Lord Ou-Yang to an offer of collaborative working from Chairman Dao when he reached his destination. The mission he had to carry out for father, whatever it was, would only be more likely to be accomplished if he could attain the powers that came with being an elite Shiyanese. It would enable him to bring father out of hiding and they would be able to execute the mission together.

Erica might not be happy with whatever suggestion he had to bring to her from the Chairman to begin with, but she would listen to him. Eventually an agreement would be reached and he would be another step nearer to the highest level in the Circles of Challenge.

The basement of Rook Mansion was basically one giant wine cellar. As he was about to climb up the stairs, he noticed Dao in the distance strolling with hands behind his back towards a wall with a single bottle hanging on it in a glass case. He touched a number of points on the glass and the wall opened wide enough for the Chairman to walk through. Kuan headed stealthily towards the gaping wall. There was a bright glow that had just come on, and he could hear Dao raising his voice. He tried to edge closer but the wall had returned to its original position. Was Dao berating someone? Or was he talking to himself?

Speculations concerning Dao's secretive behaviour had to be suspended when Kuan could not find Amo anywhere upon entering his own room upstairs. She had assured him she would not leave the room unless it was with him. He ran up to the ensuite bath pool and scanned for any unwelcome evidence. If she had fallen into the water, her invisible corpse would be in the bottom, adrift, beyond retrieval. He shuddered at the thought of being entombed in a watery grave.

Back into his room he turned. She could be just having a rest since she was prone to go very quiet from time to time. Falling on his hands and knees, the boy embarked on a finger-tip search across the velvety carpet. She had to be there somewhere.

Outside a streak of light flashed across the sky. Kuan's eyes gravitated towards the glass wall overlooking the lake Amo seemed fond of observing. Electrified lines slashed wildly. It reminded the boy of the frightening powers of Schloss 22. Could the Curator's monstrous complex be heading to Shiyan's capital? Burning branches etched across his vision. But they were not out there in the sky. They were in the glass itself. He picked up the console and keyed in the message: 'Amo, is that you in there?'

A flame flickered across the screen.

Then came these words: 'Kuan, I'm trapped.'

'What happened?'

'I was looking at some restricted data, and there was a lock-down.'

'I'll get you out.'

'Use the blue falcon programme.'

'I will.'

'My energy level is low.'

'It won't be long now, I promise.'

Kuan clicked on an avatar programme Amo had previously explained to him. The blue falcon avatar could be directed to any part of the computerised world and capture objects for its controller. They had both used it to navigate through obstacles in the system and locate data to be pulled out in a holographic form so it could be read or examined more easily. But retrieving a living being, albeit one of pure energy, was not something that had ever been tried.

The blue falcon had barely emerged on the screen when red blotches appeared in the eight surrounding panels and converged on the avatar. In the top left corner of the glass screen an ember glow held out against succumbing to the final darkness.

Kuan ordered the blue falcon to cut through the encirclement to reach Amo. The redness poured forward like rivers of ink seeking to blot out its presence. The blue falcon's wings cut a swath of passage through which it flew. The dispersed red forms drained away.

Ahead another trap sprang into existence. Four green lines appeared out of nowhere. In one synchronised move, they elongated themselves until they confined the blue falcon in an inescapable square. Lacking a third dimension, it could not fly over the tightening stranglehold. But if it waited for the square to close in on itself to a vanishing point, it would disappear with it.

Kuan rapidly pressed buttons on the console hoping to multiply the falcon's strength so it could break out of the square, but what it brought about was the multiplying of the avatar which split into four smaller versions of itself. The miniature falcons fanned out and crashed into the four corners. The green square faded into black nothingness.

For a drawn-out moment, the four fragmented copies of the blue falcon lost their bearing and were rooted to the spot. But slowly three of the replicas started to circle the fourth, and they collided and became one again. It tilted its flight to the top left where there was still a faint shimmering.

From the edge of the screen came a white barrier erecting itself in an arc to separate Amo from her would-be rescuer. As the falcon approached, arrows flew out from the barrier like water through a burst dam, cutting the defenceless avatar into scattered pieces.

Kuan stared at the screen. The severed wings, motionless head, discarded talons, lay where they had been flung by the offensive torrent. And where Amo was supposed to be, there was barely a dot of light left.

He tried everything he knew. He had no idea if anything he did led to what happened next, but the blue remains of the falcon started to shudder. Each part dimly aware of the need to be whole once more. They gravitated towards the head. The blue falcon recovered itself and at Kuan's command, it flew in a circle, gathered speed and blasted itself like a missile at the white barrier. Crashing through, it did not pause but swooped towards the dying light. Target secured for download.

The blue falcon was gone. There was no sign of Amo. The console in Kuan's hand became intensely hot. The boy wanted to let it go but the heat was bonding it to his palm. Searing pain tattooed itself along his arm, jabbing his shoulder and burning currents engulfed his brain. He could not shake the scorching console off. He crouched on the floor as electrical pulses sank deep into his skull. An impulse to defuse the agony by cracking open his head seized him. He swung the incandescent sphere towards his temple. It slipped out of his grip and landed by the bed. A cool breeze blew through his mind. He sat up, exchanging blank glances with his reflection in the glass wall.

[You brought me back.]

"Amo? Where are you?"

[I'm where you are.]

"What do you mean? I can't see you."

[You don't understand. I'm in the place you're occupying.]

Kuan stood up weakly, leaning on his bed. He took a step back as he looked about him.

"You're not here."

[I don't know what happened. But in breaking out of the electronic data system I must have crossed over to an organic data processor.]

"I can hear your voice in my head."

[I'm in your head. Embedded somewhere in your cerebral cortex.]

"You can't be. This isn't possible."

Kuan soon discovered that without even speaking, Amo would be aware of his thoughts and he could hear her response in his head. That drove him to distraction. He would go insane with that constant dialogue going on.

Amo assured him that she could suspend her thoughts so she would not interact with his mind incessantly. As proof she went into silent mode, but Kuan protested that it was the idea that she was inseparable from his consciousness that he could not accept. He could not live with two minds in his head. She must find a way to leave him.

But even as Amo tried to explain the difficulties without prolonging their interior exchange, Kuan recognised that it was going to be a long and arduous task to release his friend from her internment, let alone returning her to wherever she came from. For now she would have to be lodged inside him.

[I will investigate thoroughly how to deal with our predicament. But there was something I should tell you. Before I was caught by a lock-down in an unknown part of the data system, I went to the Admiralty network to see what I could find on Agent Tan.]

K: Any information on him meeting with father? Could you work out where father was?

Kuan now spoke to Amo in his mind without uttering a word orally.

[There was no information on Tan.]

K: You couldn't get past the Admiralty's security?

[I did. That was an easy enough task. But while there were extensive files on all their personnel – I could tell you when Captain Ma obtained his first pipe, or the challenge Len-Wu met to obtain the right to the lion form – there was absolutely nothing on Agent Tan. Either no information had ever been recorded of him, or he, with or without authorisation, was able to erase everything.]

K: So has he been lying to me about father?
[We can't tell.]

K: Why would he come up with a story about father looking to me to fulfil a mission if that's not true? How would he know about the watermark on father's papers?

[Misdirecting and spying are what he does.]

Kuan didn't know what to believe. The only person he would totally trust was father. There was no point in speculating what mission he was supposed to be on until he had located father and heard first hand from him. Two more challenges and he could command others across Shiyan to find father for him. He managed to achieve the first one even though Lord Ou-Yang seemed impossible to deal with. The second challenge would involve Dr. Erica Lee. He had no doubt she would want to help him in any way she could.

Chapter 17

<u>Salvation</u>

For the next fortnight Kuan was confined to Rook Mansion to undertake an intensive course under the direct supervision of Governor Pui. As the rising star of Plutopia he was expected to learn quickly to prepare for his next challenge. Pui adopted a peripatetic style to showcase his rhetorical genius. The idea was that Kuan would rapidly acquire the skills to talk anyone into following the path Chairman Dao had planned for them.

As the peacock flapped towards one side of the morning lounge, his beak would suddenly swing upward as he paused dramatically, for a long time. Later, swaying in the opposite direction his colourful coat would be majestically swept aloft when he spoke about the glory of Plutopia's achievements. Alas, his golden phrases came across to Kuan as little more than verbal elephantium. And as the feathered pendulum strutted back and forth, Kuan felt more and more sick.

With a little help from Amo's calming presence, Kuan just about made it through those compulsory sessions. When at long last he was allowed to take some time out, he made his way to Wuchang Tearoom. He took a couple of deliberate wrong turns in case he was being followed. There had been no communication from Agent Tan.

As soon as the waiter spotted the boy approaching, he morphed into his tabby form and ran into the kitchen. Kuan caught up with him just before he was able to jump over a wall into the back alleyway. But instead of getting an answer to his question about Agent Tan's location, he received a stern scolding. He could be putting Tan's life at risk, not to mention that of his own father. He had been told explicitly not to seek out the black cat but to wait to be contacted. It was a simple instruction that must not be ignored.

Kuan wanted to say that he needed to know more from Tan, but the tabby was in no mood to indulge him. With a growl of irritation he crawled through a hole and disappeared down the alleyway behind.

Kuan thought about giving chase but a riotous noise in the main street diverted his attention. It was a ramshackle parade of Potokans, chanting about the imminent commencement of the New Beginning. The small cat-like creatures marched forward on four legs while using their two front paws to ring bells or bang cymbals. Some of them huddled together to sing in cringing disharmony.

Shiyanese onlookers watched the clamorous spectacle with a mixture of amusement and dismay. What they did not notice was that high above them hairline fractures were cracking open in the atmosphere at lightning speed. The grey autumn sky was splintering into dazzling shards. A Potokan at the head of the parade shouted out "Now!" and fervent acolytes swarmed out to grab any passerby they could and pull them into a crowded circle. A celestial explosion showered intense light on the circle, leaving it empty and charred.

If Kuan had unnecessarily dreaded the coming of Schloss 22 before, there was no doubt that the deadly entity had arrived in Bastille, the heart of Shiyan. The psychopathic Curator who tortured captives with vivisections and sadistic mind games was after more victims.

[Kuan, you need to move.]

The boy did not know where to turn. All round him were screams of "the Potokans are killing everyone!"

Creatures were running in all directions. He was pushed in one way and then back again. He could hear Amo urging him to move but he had no idea where safety was supposed to lie. A patrol of cheetahs had finally arrived and without mercy they tore into the Potokans who were still around. Another blinding flash and more than half the patrol had vanished along with those they were attacking. Panic was endemic, except for two wolf dogs striding imperiously towards Kuan. They stood by the boy without uttering a word as a metallic sphere with the crest of Plutopia descended before him. He boarded his transport. He turned to thank his protectors, but they were gone. So he alone, and Amo of course, were airlifted back to the security of Rook Mansion.

[Ask the autopilot to drop us off at that building where you said Xian was working on the secret project.]

"Why?"

[My last search on the system indicated there might be equipment there I could use to track down Agent Tan and your father.]

"I'm not supposed to go there on my own. If Governor Pui finds me there, I don't know what punishment I would get."

[It might also help me find a way to leave your head.]

But sometimes risks had to be taken.

"Autopilot, could you drop us at the camouflaged building in the woodlands of Rook Mansion?"

"There is no such building", came the reply.

"I was taken to that building a couple of weeks ago for a meeting with Governor Pui. You can check."

"That is correct. That building does not exist."

"Then take me to that building which does not exist."

"You do not have clearance for entering the building."

"I won't be entering a building which doesn't exist."

"Why?"

"Because it doesn't exist."

"New coordinates programmed for the building that doesn't exist."

Kuan thought there was a certain resemblance between the autopilot and Wu-yin, the governor's white cat aide.

[Isn't that a cruel comparison?]

K: For the autopilot?

[No, for Wu-yin, she can't help being the way she is.]

K: Why are you listening to my thoughts?

[Your thoughts are all around me.]

K: You said you could shut them out unless I'm explicitly talking to you.

There was no reply.

The metallic globe flew away, leaving Kuan standing before the building which, according to official records of Rook Mansion, did not exist. The door was locked, but the boy already knew what to do. Placing his hand on the security keypad, minute electrical sparks darted around the circuitry below, and entrance swiftly followed.

Inside, down the long passageway, there was not a sound anywhere. He crept along as quietly as he could. Just around the corner was the thick blue glass wall, and he had to duck when a voice came out of the glass. It was Dao asking for an update. From another room the semi-morphed Xian ran up to the glass wall. She stood to attention, her leopard face resolutely focused on the Chairman's image.

"Chairman Dao, further tests have confirmed the capability of the prototype. We can proceed with the launch as planned."

"Xian, the launch must be brought forward. Events are moving too quickly."

"But we're already pressing ahead as fast as possible."

"It would have to be faster still."

"There'd be too many risks if we rush the launch."

"Not as many as sticking with the original schedule. Xian, it was your vision for Shiyan to make better use of the power of our sun, to rescue us from a ruinous dependence on elephantium."

The human-body leopard for possibly the first time in her life appeared subdued. Head lowered, she breathed heavily with eyes narrowed.

"Xian, trust me on the timing. The opportunity to save our world would be gone forever if we don't have the launch by the middle of next month at the latest."

She looked up, forcing herself to repress her inner uncertainties.

"Chairman Dao, I will need more support. But I can do it."

"Tell me what you need, and I will arrange for it to be pledged to you. You're doing a great service to Shiyan. I need to attend to something else now, we'll talk again tomorrow."

Dao disappeared from the glass wall. Xian paused for a moment with hands on hips. She detested hesitation. The plan must be revised. Preparations around the launch had to be drastically accelerated. With a brief shake of the head she left the building.

Amo directed Kuan into Xian's room where the control panel for all her work was situated. Attached to

the wall was the gleaming silver white iridium panel,
thinner than Kuan's finger, half a metre long in depth,
and wider than the boy's arms' span. Its smooth surface
was decorated with seemingly random sequences of
numbers. Kuan glided his hands across the panel,
sending and receiving electrical signals indecipherable
except to his inner resident.

[This is far more powerful than the system
accessible via the console in your room.]

K: Can you get it to separate us?

[I had not anticipated such search capability.]

K: Don't go wandering off to do something else,
Amo. You need to concentrate.

[I'm concentrating. I have almost come to
believe that it would be impossible to find.]

K: What are you looking for now? Have you
found father?

[No, Kuan. It's my home nebula, I've picked up
traces of it.]

She was heartened by his genuine delight upon
hearing that.

K: That is good to know. How exact can you be
in locating it?

[The signals are closing in.]

K: You'll soon be able to return to your home.

A hint of melancholic loneliness, of being left
behind, flitted by. He couldn't tell if was too fleeting to
be sensed by his companion.

[Something cannot be right. I must recalibrate
the search parameters.]

K: Amo, what is it?

Kuan was about to pull his hands away from the
control panel.

[Stop. I've checked it twice. The quantum level
nebula I'm from has been narrowed down to what's

relatively a very small area, no more than a square kilometre or two.]

K: And?

[It's basically here, on the estate of Rook Mansion.]

K: This is where you were from?

[This technology is more advanced than any I've encountered, and it's traced my home to here. The probability of it being wrong is virtually zero.]

K: Can you pinpoint it more?

[Kuan, we must leave at once. The security system has picked up someone entering the building.]

The boy immediately retreated from Xian's room. He vaguely remembered his way down to the tunnel for the underground shuttle hovercraft that would take them back to the Mansion. His legs barely moved despite the overwhelming sense of urgency. But he had found the lift. He pressed the button. Someone was on their trail. Should he make a dash for the outside door instead? No, the lift door was opening. Kuan ran in and counted on the automatic descent to kick in except the door would not now shut because its sensor had detected a presence at its threshold.

"Kuan, what are you doing here?"

The indigo eyes batted in surprise. It was the peacock, stretching his neck to examine the unexpected intruder.

"I came here to look for Xian."

"This is a top security facility. You can't just drop in for visits."

"I wanted to ask her if there's anything she might want me to pass on to her father. I'll be speaking with Lord Ou-Yang about the new arrangements with the Chairman."

"That's a good idea. Keeping Ou-Yang sweet for the time being, while the transitional details are being sorted. But don't talk to Xian about her father. She'd just get upset, and we need her to be very focused at the moment."

"I just thought that …"

"You leave the thinking to me. Now where did you say Xian was?"

"She must have gone out. I couldn't find her."

"Just as well. The last thing we need is her getting caught up in some silly emotional turmoil with her father."

He backed out of the lift but stopped short as he remembered something.

"Kuan, tell me the truth."

The boy swallowed discreetly.

"Have you been practising the rhetorical skills I taught you to convince others what you want them to believe?"

"Every possible opportunity, Governor Pui."

"Excellent. Keep it up. The Chairman has very high hopes for you."

The peacock withdrew back into the building, and Kuan was on his way back to the mansion via the shuttle transporter. Walking up the stairs, he was informed by the mild mannered lynx that the Chairman wished to speak with him. Denji led him to the morning lounge. He listened carefully with his elfin ears for the right moment to nudge the door open for Kuan to go in.

The boy stepped into a large oblong room. The low-lying sun threw a sheet of light through the bay window at the far end. The two opposite walls were covered by scrolls of paintings of mountains sagely pondering the vicissitudes of life behind a veil of mist, reminiscent of pictures he had seen in father's book on the history of Chinese art.

Surrounding the centre of the room were life-size statues carved out of jade, casting twisted shadows on the white marble floor. They were all of human figures. One was pushing a giant rock up a slope, another lay on the ground with broken wings tied to his arms, and the youngest looking of all held up a severed head with snakes for hair. Kuan timidly turned away from the sculpture.

Ahead of him seated at an oval crystal table, with a porcelain cup and still steaming pot of tea, was Chairman Dao. He was speaking into a reflector unit hanging from the ceiling.

A female voice was pressing him to double what he had pledged. It was Dr. Erica Lee. Deftly he parried with the impossibility of spreading his resources so thinly. In that case she would go to the President and ask her to promise Shiyan's backing. That would be futile, the Chairman explained with the adroitness of a Tai Chi master, as the President would ask the Council of Mauveans for advice and no doubt the Council would thunder its opposition. Instantly she declared the President could show her strength by rejecting the Council's advice.

Chairman Dao leaned back and sipped his tea. No President, he declared with the most serene assurance, would dare set the precedent of turning down the Council's advice. But such a move, she insisted, would signal the President's courage and independence of mind. There was growing resentment against the Mauveans, and the election was just a few months away.

"Resentment is never a good thing. Sadly in Shiyan it's rising above all against the Potokans, and you want the President to help them in an election year."

With that the Chairman appeared to conclude that the bout of declamatory fencing had been settled in his favour. He beckoned the boy to come forward.

"I have to go to a meeting with the President now. Kuan, you know Dr. Lee."

He smiled at the screen. Erica reciprocated warmly but she appeared to have given up disguising her true feelings about her benefactors.

"Chairman Dao, whatever you think about Potokans, it's wrong that they have to endure the wretched lives they have. More and more are cursed with Blessing, and too many are getting caught up with this deranged New Beginning nonsense. The Oran Clinic is the only place where they can get help, and we need more pledges if we are not to collapse."

"Dr. Lee, the New Beginning may be just what we all need, and the excesses of some followers should not mar the integrity of a sincere faith. As for the Potokans, I don't want to see them suffer any more than you do. But pledging more hours, by me or anyone else, will not solve the problem. Look what happened in the centre of Bastille just earlier today. That's what the President wants to speak to me about."

"Are you saying Potokans should be blamed for that?"

Kuan wanted to say that from what he saw it looked like the work of Schloss 22, except that he wasn't sure if anyone would believe him. He had begun to wonder himself what exactly happened when he and the others were trapped in that purgoratorial experiment between life and death.

"We don't know all the facts yet. But we will find out who's responsible and bring them to justice."

The boy decided it was best to leave it to the Chairman to deal with that problem.

"In the meantime, Potokan suffering escalates." The frustration deepened in the doctor's voice.

"Which is why we all need to think differently to come up with a real solution." Dao explained with quiet authority.

"And you have a suggestion?"

She spoke in a calm but firmly challenging tone.

"I will give it more thought. I can't keep the President waiting. Tell Kuan what the clinic needs and rest assured I'll come back to you."

Dao left the room, his strides echoing behind him. Kuan sat in the chair the Chairman had vacated. He could see Erica still quavering with restrained rage.

"How could you put up with him? Whatever his appearance, he's still a Mauvean. And all they do is look after themselves, without a thought for anyone else."

"He's not that bad, Erica. He said he would think about how to help the clinic, and he always keeps his word. If you let me know what you need for the clinic, I'll go through it with him."

"You really are becoming his trusted deputy. I hope he treats you well."

"He does. He's most kind to me."

"That's good. It does make sense, I suppose."

"What makes sense, Erica?"

"Dao choosing you. I can see why you would be the one he's been looking for."

Kuan's wide eyes sought an explanation of what she meant.

Erica shifted to one side as presumably someone had entered the room she was in to relay some information to her. She nodded appreciatively as inaudible words were spoken.

[You're thinking of her and your father together. Why?]

K: Amo, I told you to leave my thoughts alone.

[It's difficult when their presence is strong.]

K: They might be happy together, father would stay at home more, and life would be better from then on.

214

[The doctor is not really human, just a Shiyanese who can assume human form.]

K: Why should that matter?

[It may not matter at all. But you shouldn't idealise something which might be fraught with difficulties. They may not even be able to remain together in the same world.]

K: I want her to meet father.

[Just beware of unexpected complications.]

"Sorry about that, now where were we?" asked Erica.

Kuan slapped the side of his head as though that was the best way to silent his inner companion.

"You were saying that I could be the one Chairman Dao's been looking for, and you didn't mean just being his apprentice."

"Did you know that Dao lost his wife ten years ago? She died in childbirth."

"He still thinks about her a lot."

"He was devastated by her death, and they lost the baby too, his heir, who would be your age now if fate had not cut short its life."

"He's never mentioned that."

"Dao would be looking to the future now. He wants to bring up someone who will take over his Plutopia one day. And you would fit the bill. You must have been aware of his obsession with all things human."

"He does seem to know a lot about the human world. And he's always encouraging me to prepare myself for new challenges. But I don't know about being his heir. I'm not sure how long I'll stay here."

"But your own home is gone, and there's still no news on your father."

He numbly shook his head.

"Erica, why don't we go through what you need to save the clinic, so I can talk to the Chairman about it later?"

He needed the distraction, and under the pressing circumstances she was facing at the clinic, she was not altogether reluctant to oblige.

Chapter 18

<u>The Long March</u>

The half-face moon hung in quiet surveillance. Its searchlight passed through the glass wall shielding the boy's room and inspected its monochrome interiors. Kuan lay motionless in bed. He was petrified by a sense of impending doom. His hands held on to the top of his blanket like they were in a slippery grip of the cliff edge.

[Why are you tormenting yourself like this?]

K: I'm going to make the wrong move.

[Unless you tell Dao you're giving up on your second challenge, you have no choice but to go through with it.]

K: I thought father would want me to take on all these challenges, because if I succeed I can have the power as a Mauvean to help him come out of hiding, and we can be together again. But father might want me to have nothing to do with any of it. It's only Agent Tan who claims that I must carry out some mission for father. And now Tan has disappeared.

[Even if your father was not involved in any mission or these challenges Dao is setting you, becoming a Mauvean could still be an important step forward.]

K: Would it? When I look in the mirror these days, I'm not even sure if that's really me I see. What am I doing trying to be a mauve elephant? I'm a human being, I don't want to get mixed up with all this.

[But you can do so much more once you have attained Mauvean status.]

K: What would father want me to do? I should have a sense of that, shouldn't I? But I don't. What I find most frightening is that I can't picture father anymore. I can't call his face up in my mind? Am I beginning to lose my memory of him?

Amo said nothing.

K: Why are you thinking what you might do if I were dead?

[I was considering how we could separate ourselves.]

K: If I should die.

[Dead or alive, I need to work out a way to leave you.]

A V-shaped formation stealthily crossed the night sky. It was time migratory geese flocked south to escape the looming change of season. Kuan could hear a familiar voice explaining the differences between the major types of goose, but he could not visualise father's face. He had been gone so long. Wasn't he clinging on to the belief that he would find father again only because the alternative would sink him in despair? He took in gulps of air to make sure he was not suffocating.

The V shape took a sharp turn in mid air. They were not geese. He recognised them from a report on the reflector earlier on. Attack helicopters sent to join in the hunt for General Chi-Ling. Some Shiyanese were beginning to clamor for his reinstatement, for the simple reason that a general who would do anything to plot the wipeout of Potokans had got to be a good general. Was Agent Tan badly injured when he got too close to the treacherous Chi-Ling? If Tan should perish, would father try to contact his son directly? Would that put him in too much danger?

After a restless night Kuan thought a hearty breakfast might revive him only to discover his appetite had most uncharacteristically deserted him. Having been told by the Chairman over a week ago what offer of help was to be made to Erica, he was given a reminder that the deadline for his second challenge was the end of that day, by which time he must not only explain to the doctor what Dao proposed but secured her assent to it. Why would she accept it?

He dreaded that she would be angry, or worse, disappointed with him. He went into the library and slumped into the large reclining chair.

The reflectors automatically started to relay the news of the day, but he asked them to switch off as he did not want to hear any more about vicious Potokan attacks and retaliatory killings across Bastille. No one seemed to have the slightest inkling that the Curator had anything to do with the crisis. No one was even aware of his existence. Kuan should tell someone about it. But images of pain callously inflicted, amplified by piercing screams, made him stay silent. The horror had to remain within him alone. Through the blank glass wall, he stared vacantly at the rusty, crumpled carpet of desiccated leaves outside.

Denji padded softly into the library.

"Master Kuan, I have a message from Lord Ou-Yang for you."

"I suppose he's furious about some of the changes the Chairman is bringing in."

"I believe he wishes to speak with you while there is still time."

"There's still time for what?"

"His Lordship is seriously ill."

"He was fine when I last talked to him."

"I'm afraid he's actually been quite unwell for almost a year. The condition improves for short periods, but then he would deteriorate again. The latest prognosis is most distressing."

"How bad is he?"

The lynx, eyes cast down to the floor, spoke frankly.

"I'm sorry to say that the vigour has been so sapped from him that he is confined to rest. Without his daily injections, he will barely last another week. Even with them, he is unlikely to get through winter which is upon us."

"I should go and see him. But Denji, I have to go to Oran today."

"I understand, sir. I will arrange a visit for you to the House of Ou-Yang as soon as your business in Oran is satisfactorily concluded."

"Thank you. And Denji, is Xian aware of her father being so ill?"

"I do believe his lordship does not wish his daughter to know about his poor state of health."

"Shouldn't someone tell her?"

A bleeping sound trailed the appearance in the reflectors of Wu-yin, the white cat aide to Governor Pui, with a hint of black stripes along her. She said the transporter for Kuan and his security escorts were ready. The journey to Bastille de Potoka would be a dangerous one and the governor wanted to wish Kuan the very best. Needless to say, the peacock would not be joining them.

Wu-yin had only just vanished from the glass when Denji fetched a thick coat in his mouth for Kuan. He gently placed it by Kuan's feet.

"Let me know, sir, when you're ready to go."

The Oran Pavilion was an old structure left behind from the days when mauve elephants took more of an interest in the processing of elephantium in Bastille de Potoka. It was made entirely of glass with eight Doric style columns holding up a large dome. One or two representatives from the Council of Mauveans would lounge around in the middle of the pavilion and look up from time to time to make sure the Potokans on duty would either be interring fresh elephantium quickly enough into the ground or extracting from enriched old seams in sufficient quantity. They would become quite excitable when slackers were spotted as these would be ordered to be buried alive with the latest elephantium deposit being made. A glass wall would be raised between the columns to magnify the gruesome execution for the benefit of the myopic watchers. The practice was eventually stopped because of the unexpected emotional impact it had on the mauve elephants who took part. Repeated viewing left them bored.

Now it stood in languid isolation, surrounded by a stretch of dark barren land, encased in a rancid stench. When Kuan arrived late afternoon on his deadline day with his very own phalanx of wolf dog security guards, there was a mixed reception from the grey mass of Potokans who had gathered.

Six-legged cats jostled to catch a glimpse of the boy. A few lambasted him as the stooge of Dao. But an even more vocal minority hailed him as the one who was heralding the New Beginning, screaming that he would pave the way for all true followers to be saved. Others ignored him altogether and chanted "Dr. Lee for President", which was strictly illegal as only Mauveans could become President in the Federation of Shiyan.

The doctor met him in the centre of the pavilion. While he dreaded every detail he had to unfold before her, she listened without comment until at the end she quietly intimated it was time for the gathered Potokans to make up their own mind. He walked down a few steps and stood with the crowd.

A glass screen rose between two of the columns so that she could be seen and heard in an amplified way by those who had been waiting. To Kuan's surprise, Erica began by saying that she was grateful to him for bringing to them a decent proposal from Chairman Dao. She proceeded to list the reasons why some might consider the Oran Clinic in Bastille de Potoka a lost cause.

Like an unpleasant herbal broth coming to the boil, sour rumblings in the crowd bubbled up to the surface. But she continued. Potokans getting tangled up with the fanatics and acts of violence had provoked such intense anger that far from expecting any more pledges of support for the clinic, the whole of Bastille de Potoka might soon come under attack from marauding mobs of Shiyanese.

Amidst shouts of "they're always making threats against us", the doctor calmly but ominously pointed out that there were well-founded suspicions that the recently disgraced General Chi-Ling would soon be returning to rid the capital of what he called 'degenerates'. A dangerous minority in Shiyan had become obsessed with securing the reinstatement of the semi-morphed tiger to put an end to disorder. The infamy of Chi-Ling, who murdered mauve elephants to stir up war against Potokans, induced a fearful silence.

"So what is to be done?" asked Dr. Lee.

White eyes stared at each other in bewilderment.

"We can fight them to the death!" rallied one voice in the audience, but no one leapt to second that particular idea.

"We could do that," said the doctor, "and death would certainly take us all with him. Or we could find another home, bide our time, and regroup when we are strong enough to build a future of our choosing."

"What new home?" came a question from the back.

"Is there somewhere worse than here they forgot about?" came another.

"We've been offered a new lease of life at Chengbao Island."

The doctor's announcement stirred up murmurs rippling rapidly to the edge and bouncing back with moans about deportation and indefinite confinement.

"There is no question of deportation or confinement." She felt compelled to clarify immediately. "It is entirely up to us if we want to take up this offer. Chengbao Island has a mountain range dividing lush forests to the north and fertile plains to the south. It belongs to the Council of Mauveans but Chairman Dao has obtained their agreement to allow us to move there, on the grounds that it would ease tension in Bastille and avoid further bloodshed. The rich and diverse habitat of the island would mean that all Potokans would find their own space to thrive in."

"If it's so good, how come the mauve elephants have kept away from trampling all over it?"

"Fair question. A number of years ago it was established by Dao as a sanctuary for feathered Shiyanese as a gift to his wife, who had been concerned with the drastic decline of their population. Their numbers had dwindled as they had not adapted well to life in our elephantium-fuelled cities. From then on, in deference to the chairman's wife, only those who had permanently adopted the bird form were allowed on the island."

"So where are they now?" a young Potokan called out.

"Not long after Nestra Dao's death, they disappeared. Some say that her spirit has taken them with her to a higher plain of existence. Others claim they discovered in the sky a portal to another world and escaped through it."

"Shame they left Pui the peacock behind!" someone shouted at the back and uncorked a burst of nervous laughter.

"For all we know, they simply came upon another continent beyond Shiyan and settled there. The island has been left uninhabited since. And it is ours to move to if we so wish."

"How far is it from here?"

"And how are we going to get there?"

Erica pushed her hair back as she did her mental calculation.

"Chengbao Island is off the northeastern coast of Shiyan, my best estimate is that it's about 3000 kilometers from Bastille de Potoka. The move would have to be done on foot as there's no other means of transport, and with winter arriving, it would take us a month or two to get there."

She could see the prospect of a long march to this far off land was not being readily embraced.

"You should be aware that no Blessing was ever allowed on the island and the Council has confirmed that this position would be maintained. They have also agreed with the President that the Shiyanese navy would guarantee the safety of the island. Dao has pledged more than enough hours for us to build a new Oran Clinic there, and we can call on the help of a multitude of Shiyanese who owe time to Plutopua. Potokans everywhere will be free to join us if we decide to move our settlement to Chengbao. That decision rests with you."

A vacuum sucked out all capacity to deliberate. Potokans had been pushed along, left behind, but to be offered a choice was a disorientating experience. Their eyes roamed. Their mouths gaped. Their minds splintered. Then someone broke the silence.

"I want to know what the boy thinks."

The sentiment was contagious.

"The chosen one must speak to us!"

"He knows Dao better than any of us, let him tell us, can we trust the Chairman?"

"Tell us, what shall we do?"

The cacophonic wave pushed Kuan onto the steps of the pavilion. Even with his thick black coat, he felt a chill. Erica came from behind the glass screen and whispered to him that there was no need for him to say anything.

He stood on the highest step and surveyed the gathered Potokans. He could relate to their predicament. From his heart, he spoke.

"You are in danger. If you stay as you are, your life ends here. But if you leave, you may not have a better future, but at least you will have a chance for something more. Other than that, I've got nothing more to say. A choice has to be made."

Inertia should now give way to what must be done. The tide retreated, mulling over the ramifications of life and death, and with pent-up momentum it surged forward. Voices pouring on top of each other.

"Is that all you've got to say, you stupid boy!"

"Don't speak of him like that. He was sent here to save us."

"We must listen to him."

"You're all blind, he's just a courier boy, sent to trick us into a futile journey which would get rid of most, if not all, of us before we got to our fabled destination."

"We can't trust anyone."

The fractious crowd hollered towards the pavilion. The snarling wolf dog guards barricaded themselves in front of Kuan. Erica Lee wanted to get Kuan to move away but they were completely encircled by the angry and bewildered.

A jet of air gushed down like a waterfall from the darkening sky to flush out a clearing between Kuan and the advancing Potokans. A metallic globe half as big as the pavilion landed. Its array of weapons, swinging side to side in contemplation of locking on any unruly target, secured a fearful stillness. The door opened to reveal a solemn Dao. He also wore a black coat over his purple tunic. With poise that commanded total attention, he told them that Shiyan's security forces were battling to hold back a deranged mob heading towards Bastille de Potoka. They had been stirred up by the twisted idea of decapitating a hundred Potokans as a sacrifice to ensure safe passage for General Chi-Ling's return. Time was running out.

"Dr. Lee", he turned to Erica who anxiously approached him, "there's nothing more I can do. If you insist on staying, the carnage would be unspeakable."

She declared that unless anyone had a reasoned objection, they were to set their evacuation plan into motion. There was no protest, no argument. The long march to Chengbao Island had begun.

Dao slowly walked up to Kuan and sat down on the step beside him. His face was framed with stern authority, yet his eyes could not conceal the sorrow beneath.

"I've done badly, haven't I?"

The boy sat down too.

"No, you've done very well, Kuan. I knew you would. The doctor and I have found an agreed way forward. You have met your second challenge, and come midnight, you'll be on the Asterion Circle."

"But something's wrong, though?"

"Kuan, I've just received a report."

The boy's whole being begged to be told the truth and at the same time spared its revelation.

"You need to know."

"The report …"

"It's from the navy."

"Agent Tan, what's happened to him?"

"It's not about Tan. There's still no news about him."

"What's the report about?"

"It's your father."

"You've found him?"

He should have known no joy could come from Dao's grave expression.

"We've found him."

"Where is he? When can I see him?"

"Kuan, your father is dead."

The boy could not hear anything.

"Reports can be wrong. Often they're wrong."

"*FSS Knight* was called to the area on a false sighting of Chi-Ling near the rocky beach he was last seen holding you hostage."

"There you go, a wrong report."

"What they found was a body floating in the sea."

"Father's in hiding."

"It was your father's body."

"How could they know? Do they know what he looks like?"

"What they do know is that under standard scanning, he was identified as a close kin to the young human picked up by *FSS Castle* about six months ago. Kuan, unless your father had an identical twin you didn't know about, he's dead."

"I must see him. He's alive until my own eyes tell me he's not."

Dao paused but he could think of no other way to convey what he wanted the boy to accept.

"I'm truly sorry, but they have buried him. His face and much of his body had been eaten away. What was left had badly decomposed. He had been in the water for a few months."

"I have to see him."

Dao put his arm around the boy, who sat like a jade statue, all animation withered. The soul-shattering scream was only heard by the companion in his head. Amo barely survived the maelstrom. Kuan no longer cared about surviving.

Chapter 19

<u>New Beginning</u>

Out of the grey condensed sky, snowflakes fell. Like paratroopers dropped by mistake behind enemy lines, they drifted silently to the ground. Motionless they lay, waiting for an instruction that never came. More would arrive and the layer of pristine paralysis thickened. In Kuan's world, every snowflake was different. In Shiyan, they were all identical, each one possessing the same solitary beauty as the holographic image projected in the virtual altar inside the House of Ou-Yang.

Kuan asked Denji not to cancel the appointment that had been made for him to see Lord Ou-Yang. He wanted nothing to change on account of the news about his father. The Chairman had told him father's body had been found. He had explained why it had been identified beyond doubt and buried due to its decomposed state. But Kuan sought to convince himself that as he had not personally seen any evidence himself, he did not have to believe that father was gone. Amo was left in a perpetual spin by the contradictory thoughts in the boy's head. Yet for all the turmoil within his brain, a new icy calm glossed his exterior.

Lord Ou-Yang was lying in his semi-morphed form on a thin mattress laid on the floor. His eyes were fixed on the suspended snowflake. It had been there since his great-grandparents built the barn and set up the institution that kept so many Shiyanese fed and nourished.

The anchor of eternity underpinned his faith that all might turn out well despite the many signs to the contrary. The Beginning could not end for it was immutable, unlike frail mortals who weakened with age

229

and crumbled back to nothingness. The once striking gold and black leopard spots were fading on his face. A young visitor came into view. He raised his dried and bony hand to beckon Kuan towards him.

"Kuan, it's good of you to come. I'm sorry to hear about your father."

"Lord Ou-Yang, who can tell what has really happened? I think he's still out there, in some form. If he didn't laugh at the idea as blind superstition, I would say he could be on his way back to me as a butterfly. It's not possible that he can simply be taken away and will never be seen or heard from again. He has got to be somewhere even if it is beyond our reach right now, waiting to return to the world of the living. I can wait for him. There's no reason why I should ever stop waiting for him."

Lord Ou-Yang took hold of his hand. A gentle but skeletal grip.

Kuan noticed the fragility of the semi-morphed leopard in his deteriorating body.

"I'm sorry to see you unwell." Kuan said.

"My time has come. We have to accept these moments."

The boy nodded without conviction.

"Kuan, I asked to see you because I believe you are the one who can stop this madness consuming Shiyan."

"What madness?"

"Dao is the madness. For thousands of generations we Shiyanese gradually made our way from primitive savagery to a kinder, more thoughtful way of life. From the original Beginning, we were meant to strive to become better. The Circles of Challenge were stepping stones for everyone to improve themselves steadily. Whatever our outward appearances, each would rise higher and share in the glory of Shiyan. No one would be left behind, least of all discarded with contempt. But Dao and his fellow Mauveans have made a mockery of it. Turning the Circles into a circus. Everyone will soon be at their mercy, pledging away their lives, ending up as slaves."

To Kuan, Lord Ou-Yang's hatred of the Chairman and his own imminent demise could be driving him to see madness where there was none. Worse still, he was turning to someone who could hardly have any influence over what the Chairman did. Even if having risen to the seventh Asterion Circle he could now lay claim to more power over the affairs of Shiyan, what changes should he be pressing for?

"Lord Ou-Yang, I have no idea what Shiyan is supposed to be like. You and Chairman Dao have for years clashed over things I can't begin to understand."

"Just open your eyes, Kuan. Can't you see that up and down the streets of Bastille, there are more hungry mouths unfed, more begging faces along the sidewalk? Plutopia is tripling the pledges required for a basic meal. Many can't afford it. It's quite shameful this can happen. Shiyan is where we should help each other to the best of our ability so that none will ever sink without trace. Dao is destroying all that is decent in our world."

"What can I do?"

"Make him stop."

"How?"

"Just put your mind to what needs to be done. You're not Dao's lackey. I knew that as soon as I saw you when you first came here. You shall become his nemesis. Do what you're meant to do."

Kuan felt the burden of expectations Lord Ou-Yang's waning eyes placed upon him.

"And Kuan, ask Xian to stop doing whatever she's doing for Dao. Even if she cannot bring herself to come back to the family, she should not be helping Plutopia, no good would ever come of it."

It was time for his injection. The drug's potency was declining by the day. Lord Ou-Yang thanked Kuan again as he bade him a final farewell.

The boy was on his way out of the monumental barn when a familiar tailless cat padded past him in the opposite direction. He turned around as the small Manx cat transformed into a tall, pale-faced man with swept back silvery hair. Though he was wearing a dark blue suit instead of his usual naval uniform, Kuan recognised Captain Ma.

The captain was on his way to see Lord Ou-Yang, an old family friend. One way or another they were unlikely to meet again because Ma had been summoned by the Admiralty to one of those hearings where he would be told that either he had been cleared of any wrongdoing on *FSS Castle* and he must resume command immediately to deal with some dire problem at sea, or he had been found guilty of gross deficiency in failing to protect the lives of the Mauveans on board his submarine and was to be executed. Either way it was better than being banished indefinitely to an ignominious civilian life.

Ma gave what was meant to be a gentle slap on Kuan's back and praised him for his integrity and courage in exposing the scoundrel Chi-Ling. He hoped the boy wouldn't hold his attempt to pressurise him into giving false testimony against him.

Even as Kuan's head was shaking, the captain had moved on to another subject. He asked if Lord Ou-Yang had enquired about his daughter. Years ago when Xian stormed out of the family home over a quarrel the substance of which neither father nor daughter could subsequently recall, Captain Ma took her under his wing in the navy, and at the same time assured his old friend that she would be kept away from the influence of his antagonist, Dao. Things had not turned out quite as they should, for anyone. Ma seemed reluctant to move on to his rendezvous. But the moment of final parting was ultimately unavoidable. With a wry smile he congratulated Kuan for still having his life ahead of him.

Sensing Ma would be glad of any excuse for a further delay, the boy probed him for any information he might have on Agent Tan.

The captain said there had been no news about Tan on all the official channels, but that was typical of the secretive agent. Tan would suspect Chi-Ling of having sympathisers in the military who would betray his whereabouts to the renegade general if these were known. Instead he would just keep up his hunt in stealth until he was ready to strike the fatal blow. Tan could be so ruthlessly focused, and utterly relentless in pursuit of any goal he set himself. In the captain's own defence, it was partly why he was so easily deceived into thinking that Tan was the murderer of those Mauveans on board the *Castle*.

Ma pulled out his pipe and put it in his mouth without lighting it. He waited for Kuan to fire more questions at him. But with his mind already dwelling on what he might have to do next, the boy left. Ma chewed on his pipe wistfully, then he clicked his heals and walked on to see Lord Ou-Yang, reflecting that very soon, one or perhaps both of them would be dead.

Without asking him what it was about, Xian buzzed the door of the secret building open to let Kuan in. The semi-morphed leopard in her purple overall was pacing up and down along the thick blue glass wall. Images of circles rose and fell in quick succession in the glass. Xian thumped the wall and stormed back into her room. She could be heard yelling mercilessly at herself.

On her return, the circles shot up higher and almost matched each other on their respective trajectories. Hands on hip, she calculated the gap she would have to close in the next simulation.

"You can tell the Chairman we're on schedule with the launch date."

It was Kuan's turn to sense the turmoil in Amo's mind. She wanted so much to use the equipment there to pinpoint her home nebula. Having narrowed it down to the estate of Rook Mansion, it would be relatively simple to get its exact location. She might be just minutes away from returning to where she yearned to be. But she had to accept that Kuan needed to speak with Xian.

"Why are you still standing there? Go tell the Chairman everything's going according to plan with the launch."

Kuan's face epitomised puzzlement.

"Don't tell me, he wants me to explain it to you! He's setting it as your final challenge, so why doesn't he explain it to you? Don't answer that. He wants me to do it so we can start discussing how you can help with the launch. Frankly, I don't see what you can do to help. But if the Chairman wants me to run it through with you, then that's what I'll do."

"I take it you already know about the Sun Disc. Pui showed you the prototype the last time I saw you in here. With that disc we could harvest the energy of the sun for the whole of Shiyan and would not have to rely on elephantium anymore, which you of all creatures must appreciate, is a positive change. Now some Mauveans may not appreciate that, and I believe that's where the Chairman wants you to get them to go along with it. I don't see why that would be necessary though. Once the Sun Disc is ready, they'll have to learn to live with elephantium being nothing more than the disgusting waste product that it is. What are they going to do? Refuse to use solar energy? But the Chairman likes to get agreement in whatever he does. And for some reason he thinks you have this special skill in reaching out to others who would otherwise disagree with him. I don't know what you said to my father or Erica Lee to get them to go along with Chairman Dao, but I can't say I detect any unusual ability in you."

"Xian, it's actually your father I wanted to talk to you about. I've just been to see him."

The leopard's fiery eyes bored into Kuan.

"He would very much like you to stop helping Chairman Dao."

"I'm sure he would. Anything which is progress, any improvement on the way the House of Ou-Yang has been doing things for generations, it must therefore be something terrible to be stamped out. He has no idea how stifling he is. Even now he's trying to stop me doing something that could transform life across Shiyan for the better."

"He's just not sure if it would be better. I'm not saying he's right or wrong. But you should go and see him. He's not at all well. He may have ideas about what you could become, which you think are just wrong. He may see the world in ways you can't even grasp. But if you wait in the hope that things will work themselves out, you'll soon find him gone, and you'll never be able to see him again, to talk to him. You will wake up one day to find an important part of you forever missing."

Fury filled Xian and for one brief moment he thought she might morph into a full leopard form and tear into him. But the anger was directed at herself.

"Go to my control panel and call up the information on the Sun Disc project. You can tell the Chairman I've explained everything to you. He'll no doubt talk to you directly about what he wants you to do.

I've got to go. I need to check on the production arrangements."

Xian left.

Kuan moved into her room and walked up to the silver white iridium control panel. He let Amo guide his hands. Even as facts and figures relating to the Sun Disc Project flowed through his right hand into his brain, electrical signals danced between the panel and his left hand communicating to Amo the most crucial piece of knowledge she had ever sought. Kuan understood there was no need to ask Amo to translate abstract coordinates into terms he could comprehend because travelling back to the mansion on the shuttle transporter, he knew they were heading to the very location she had finally identified.

Disembarking into the basement, Kuan followed Amo's direction which pulled him past rows of solid oak wine racks until he came to a blank wall. Blank except for the glass case with a single bottle of wine suspended in it.

K: Your world is in that bottle of wine?

[That bottle is an emotion-scanner. My world is behind that wall.]

K: There's a vault behind here. I remember seeing Chairman Dao keying in a code and going into it. Are you sure your world is in that vault?

[Did you see what code he used?]

K: I was standing too far away to see. Can't you just hack into it?

Footsteps could be heard approaching. Firm bipedal strides. Kuan hid behind the nearest wine rack. Dao walked up to the glass case and touched different parts of it, which lit up briefly with the letter he chose.

K: 'NESTRA'. I should have guessed. It can't be a top security place if he uses such an obvious password.

[You don't understand, Kuan.]

The wall swung slowly outward and Dao disappeared into the vault. A blue glow appeared inside. Dao's voice was heard as the wall started to close behind him.

K: Who could he be talking to?

[Kuan, we must get in there.]

K: Do you think he knows about your world? And he's communicating with someone there?]

[I can't tell what he may or may not know about my home nebula.]

K: Maybe your world has always existed here, but then Dao discovered it and decided to build his family home on this site.

[Why would he do that? None of us has had any direct interaction with entities outside until I somehow found my way here.]

K: Amo, it doesn't matter. We've got the code. We'll wait for him to leave, and we can go in. Maybe someone in your world can help transfer you from my head back to your home.

[Kuan, 'Nestra' is not a simple code for Dao to use. The emotion scanner would check if the word keyed in matches the emotional state evoked in Dao by that word. I don't believe anyone other than Dao can have the same range of powerful feelings the name 'Nestra' conjures up in his mind. Even if I can get into the security system for the vault, I would not be able to replicate those emotional patterns unique to Dao.]

The boy searched for an alternative.

K: Why don't I ask Chairman Dao? We can just be open about it.

[No, you mustn't. We can't tell if it's a coincidence that he has a secret vault here, but whether he knows of the existence of my home nebula or not, I don't want him to find out that a former inhabitant of that nebula has come into this world. He might want to keep me here to study me, or experiment on me.]

K: He might also want to help you.

[I'm not willing to take that risk.]

Soft footsteps sounded in the distance.

"Master Kuan, are you down here?"

It was Denji. He had been notified of Kuan's return to the mansion on the underground transporter, but there was no sign of the young man though a guest had arrived to speak with him. The dutiful lynx assumed he was lost in the extensive wine cellar for the boy was notoriously bad at finding his way around.

He patiently searched down one passageway after another, and was mildly surprised when he saw Kuan walking towards him examining a dusty bottle of wine. The boy was apparently considering rearranging the cellar's treasures according to the colour of their labels. Denji calmly though resolutely urged him to return the bottle he was holding to its original place, before informing him that Dr. Erica Lee was waiting for him upstairs. All other thoughts moved aside in that instant and he ran towards the staircase.

Kuan found Erica standing in the grand lobby with its marble columns and gold framed mirrors. Her sinuous red hair draped over her black coat and dress. As soon as she saw him, she wrapped her arms around him in a long embrace. An enchanting aroma momentarily detached his memory from the gloom he had sunk into. She deeply shared the pain of his loss so that he would not have to bear it alone. Without her having to speak, he understood.

He put on the black coat Denji had left out for him, and followed the doctor out of the front door. They strolled through the snow towards the edge of the frozen lake. She held him close to her.

The vast majority of residents in Bastille de Potoka were already on the move, marching towards the north east coast of Shiyan where they would cross a bridge and settle on Chengbao Island.

Before Erica was to board her transporter to join them on the outskirt of Bastille, where she insisted she too would complete the rest of the journey on foot, there was a question she wanted to ask Kuan. Would he leave Rook Mansion and go with her? He held Erica's hand. It was smooth and cold. He would dearly love to join her. Nothing was more likely to salvage some semblance of happiness for him. But he could not leave just now.

He must stay to help Amo find her way home. His inner companion had risked her own life to help Kuan when she could have gone off by herself. He could hardly bring her with him to Chengbao Island when Amo had just confirmed that the nebula whence she came was located behind the wall leading to that vault beneath the mansion. Besides, she was growing increasingly weak as a result of the separation from her home world.

But as Amo insisted her existence must not be revealed to anyone, Kuan could not spell out why he could not depart with Erica Lee straightaway. The doctor was adamant that he owed her no explanation. She would go ahead and wait for him when he was ready.

The dread of imminent separation made him ask her for something that would be most difficult for her to agree to. Kuan entreated with her to stay a few more days with him at the mansion, or even just one day. A room could easily be prepared for her. They would then have more time to talk together, about what would be needed at the new Oran Clinic to look after the Potokans, and how Kuan could help when he was finally able to go to Chengbao Island to be with the doctor. In case the Potokans were worried about what had happened when she did not turn up when she was expected, he was sure Denji would not mind sending a message to them informing them when she would be joining them on their journey. She gently placed a finger to his lips. Words suspended. Of course she could not stay. He understood. He pushed back those red tresses the icy breeze had swept across her face, and tried to memorise those sadly smiling green eyes.

A tapping noise came from behind them. It sounded like a rapid knock on a thick door. They both turned towards the lake only to be greeted by complete silence. Then the tapping resumed, hesitantly at first, then ferociously. A pod of dolphins were tapping their nose against the underside of the ice.

"They can't breathe," said Erica, "they're trapped under the ice."

The boy picked up a rock, ran onto the ice and started to thump it against the frozen deathtrap.

"Kuan, that's dangerous."

The doctor's warning went unheeded. He would not let them suffocate. The tapping from below grew faster in desperation. Yet another swing brought the rock crashing down. Cracks splintered across the surface.

"Kuan, stay still."

Erica Lee carefully stepped onto the ice to pull the boy back. He could see their eyes staring up through the murky water. Nobody was going to die on his watch. And he smashed the rock once more onto the ice, landing a critical blow. The ice was broken. The dolphins surged upwards to gasp for air. Kuan fell back. He was on firm ground, but the ice beneath the doctor broke up and she dropped into the water. Kuan screamed for her, but she had been swept away.

Chapter 20

<u>In Memoriam</u>

The faint winter sun wearily drifted over the lake's frosted glass surface. Cold air encased the silent stillness. The lake of Rook Mansion was built to commemorate the death of Nestra Dao. Its tranquility was intended to symbolise the inner peace the Chairman rediscovered once he had overcome his loss. But all calmness was gone once another part of the boy's life was snatched from him.

Kuan screamed as he ran after the body floating away underneath. He could see Erica struggling, pushing, kicking against the frozen lid of her sarcophagus. Her efforts were having no impact. He threw off his coat. With both hands he grabbed the rock and thrust it down. A tiny dent was made. Her face turned to him, bubbles leaking out of her mouth. He smashed at it again. A few cracked lines. Erica tried to hold on to her position but the current was dragging her away. He stood up to follow her but his right leg plunged through the ice. His thigh was cut. The pain barely registered. With all his energy he pushed himself out of the hole.

Erica's black clothes were indistinguishable in the water, but he could see her red hair waving in slow resignation. He followed the trail, running as fast as his constricted lungs would allow. He had almost caught up, but unless she was halted at some point, he could not begin to try to get her out. She was still desperately thrashing against her confinement, but with diminished vigour. The water had almost overwhelmed her. Kuan wanted to rip the lake open so much his hands were violently shaking. Still, she was being carried away.

He saw a thick branch lying on the side. If he could pierce the ice with it, Erica might be able to grab hold of it long enough for him to crack open a sufficiently big hole to pull her out. The picture in his mind of the branch spearing through the frozen lake did not match the unyielding hardness of reality. The branch recoiled from the solid surface and the only marks made were those on his own hand.

For a moment he lost sight of her. He could not give up. There was a dash of redness dissolving into the side of the lake, coming to rest. He ran up to it only to realise that it was a sheltered spot under an overhanging willow, the ice was doubly thick there. He stamped and hurled a stone with a cutting edge, all to no avail. Down below was a motionless red form.

Kuan's sorrow mingled with rage. A searing pain erupted in his head and burnt along his arms to fill his hands with blistering intensity. He stabbed them into the ice. Steam burst forth like a volcano. A large opening had been melted out of the frozen lake. He reached down to pick up the red Abyssinian cat which had now floated to the surface. He laid her on the snow covered grass. Smoke was still rising from his bare hands.

K: Amo, that was you?

[I wanted to help you save her.]

K: It's too late.

[If only I could channel my energy like that sooner.]

K: There was nothing more you could do. Nothing I can do. That's just how it is.

[Kuan, I'm truly sorry.]

His nerves had been ground to powder. He must not feel any more pain. Anything of emotional value that he had ever held close within him had been wrenched out of him. He was done with the agony of losing those who mattered to him. It was time to shut himself down.

His eyes drifted out of focus. Blurriness masked the void before him. He did not want to recollect her tenderness. He did not want to miss her quiet affection. It was best to have no feelings at all.

Numbingly cold air swirled around him.

Water splashed on the boy's face.

The red cat was shaking herself dry. Kuan looked on in total disbelief as Erica Lee resumed her human form. She coughed up more water, wiped her mouth with the back of her hand and hugged him tightly.

"Erica, I thought you were…"

"Some of us could hold our breath for a surprisingly long time. But without you, I wouldn't have made it."

"You're alive?"

"Yes, I am."

"Tell me again."

"Kuan, I'm alive."

The boy's smile was entrenched in grief.

He walked the disheveled doctor back to the mansion, where a frantically concerned Denji immediately took charge. The doctor was shown into one of the guest bedrooms where, in her cat form, she rested by a warm fire.

Kuan had a soothing liquid sprayed onto the cut in his thigh before he changed into a fresh pair of matching purple tunic and trousers. He patted his pocket to make sure he had remembered to transfer the green pebble Batya left with him. Then he went to check on Erica. Through the open door down the corridor, he saw the flaming red Abyssinian arch her back and roll on her side. She had been waiting for the boy and having spotted him, she rose to her human height with one set of features seamlessly sliding over the other. She smoothed her coat and dress to see if they were sufficiently dry. She must be on her way as any further delay could end up holding back the Potokan exodus. She told Kuan she would be waiting for him on Chengbao Island. Then following a kiss on his forehead, she disappeared down the majestic staircase.

Another day went by. Kuan counted eight since she left. He had no idea of what life on Chengbao Island would be like, but in his mind living there with Erica Lee was all he could possibly want. Working with her at the Oran Clinic that night, notwithstanding the horror of watching those Shiyanese transformed into Potokans, gave him a sense of purpose and an intimation of belonging. What could be better than dedicating oneself to the building of the new clinic on the distant island, alongside Erica? But he must find a way to let Amo leave his head and return to her own world.

Unfortunately, not the slightest progress had been made on that front. Kuan was not aware that the more he felt that he was mired in futility, the more difficult it became for Amo to think clearly. It drained her of energy to explore new possibilities and work through them systematically. At times her mind was darting around as randomly as the boy's when his capacity to focus was once more suspended.

As the separation from her home world was sapping her life force in any event, she had offered to let go of her consciousness. Kuan would then for all practical purpose have no other presence in his mind, and would be free to leave for Chengbao Island. She insisted she would only be quickening what was inevitable.

He would not hear of it.

To distract himself, Kuan slumped into the reclining chair in the library for another dose of news on the reflectors. Bastille de Potoka was now clear of its former residents. A small minority did refuse to join the long march, but they were caught by a vicious Shiyanese mob and none was spared in the ensuing massacre. That had led to widespread anger against President Zhou, not for her failure to protect the vulnerable Potokans, but for not taking action to stop the other Potokans escaping from the capital.

One after another, Shiyanese in diverse forms stared into the camera demanding to see General Chi-Ling and his noble tiger warriors given a heroes' welcome back at Bastille. It was time to wipe out all Potokans.

The camera cut to a human-shaped figure walking down the grand steps of the Presidential Building. Dao, as Vice President, reluctantly agreed to explain the Government's position. He wearily looked into the intrusive lenses and pointed out that the peaceful departure of Potokans from Bastille had prevented needless deaths on all sides, but most importantly, the terrorising attacks of lightning explosions had completely ceased. Whether or not the Potokans had been behind those attacks, the Government's swift action had restored peace and order.

Kuan tried to think of a reason why the Curator would work with the Potokans in unleashing the Schloss 22 on Bastille. Now all of a sudden there were no more strikes leaving charred circles behind. Could the Curator be waiting for the Potokans to leave so that he could then swoop on those remaining in the capital to capture them for his ghastly experiments? Or was he just a deranged mind with no coherent plan?

The boy's speculation was interrupted by a solemn announcement on the reflectors. Reports were coming in that the venerated master of the House of Ou-Yang had died after a long illness. A picture of Lord

Ou-Yang, his leopard face in its prime, appeared. The camera cut to weeping Shiyanese, cats with paws over their eyes, and also semi-morphs with hands over their faces. Some reminisced between sobs the kindness his lordship had shown them. Others, never having met him, were nonetheless overwhelmed by the rising tide of grief. Phrases such as 'the passing of a legend', 'there shall not be another one like him', saturated the incoming bulletins.

Two days later, the memorial service was held in a snow-covered field beyond the great barn. Lord Ou-Yang's body was laid on a glinting metallic slab. In his eulogy, Dao spoke generously of his old adversary: his inspiring faith, his dedication to the wellbeing of others, and his indomitable spirit in making the House of Ou-Yang a byword for reliability.

He told those gathered how the two of them, since their youth, had contested at every point to make Shiyan a greater place. Lord Ou-Yang wanted everyone in need of a meal to be sure to get one, whatever form or status, Shiyanese or Potokan. Dao admired him but wished he did not leave it so late before he would let Plutopia work with him to get more done for less. But his great legacy would continue. Hunger would not only be banished, Dao declared, but life in every respect would be enhanced further in the years to come.

As Dao continued, Kuan glanced at the gathered mourners, standing side by side on the soft white plain contemplating the clutches of mortality. Xian wore her old naval overall underneath her long blue coat. She never did visit her father even after Kuan spoke with her. She held her leopard face high, full of pride in the achievements of her father, but also stirred by defiance against waves of regret. He could have done so much more, she was convinced, if he would only let Dao help him. The Chairman was a bold visionary. Though a Mauvean himself, he was prepared to tap into the energy of the sun to cut Shiyan's dependence on elephantium. That alone was sufficient to vindicate her decision to support Dao no matter what her father might think.

Governor Pui fidgeted beside Xian. He fanned his feathers to shake off the snow, and impatiently checked the length and angle of the shadows to ascertain if the Chairman was really speaking as long as he felt it to be. A few polite words would surely have sufficed. Lord Ou-Yang was a highly respected figure, but he never reached beyond the seventh Circle. As an eighth Circle Shiyanese with a governor rank, Pui sincerely hoped Chairman Dao would give him twice as long a funeral oration as he was giving to that half-leopard. Then again, he was certain that he would outlive Dao, who was far too obsessed with his work, with building his great Plutopia, and not paying enough attention to a more refined, balanced life. The peacock, by contrast, knew all about the art of enjoyment and relaxation. Why lift even an eyelid, he would muse to his aide, to do anything when you had thousands who had pledged countless hours between them to serve you.

To the other side of Pui was Denji. A mere sixth Circle lynx would not ordinarily be allowed to stand so close to the Governor at such an important event. But Denji, head bowed low, ears pricked up following every word uttered by the Chairman, was trusted by arguably the most powerful Shiyanese. Technically, President Zhou had more authority but even she had to pay special attention to any request from Dao. So it was an unspoken privilege to be lined up next to Denji. Pui would not expect to learn much from the quiet lynx, but it was good to be seen by his side. Denji did not mind for his part. His focus at that moment was to carry out the Chairman's next instruction meticulously. And as planned, Dao closed with the phrase, "In the end, there is no final passing, but only a return to our Beginning."

That was the cue for Denji to go forward and press the discreet lever at the base of the metallic slab. He retreated back into the line as a bubble of heat engulfed Lord Ou-Yang, transmuting the body first into a blinding red glow, and then exploding it in a burst of molecules, which within seconds reconfigured in the form of snowflakes gently scattered along the ground's pale white shroud.

The temperature dropped further and those who had come to pay their respect began to disperse. Kuan felt a tug on his trouser leg. It was Wu-yin asking him to follow her. The faint black stripes had disappeared, apparently they were not as permanent as they were made out to be. She led him to the secluded corner where the snowflake hologram was projected and asked him to wait there. The boy sat cross-legged on the floor. When Chairman Dao appeared he adopted a similar position next to him.

"Kuan, I'm going to miss Ou-Yang. His beliefs, his very existence, pushed me to come up with new ideas. His determination to look after everyone, even those who had no time left to pledge for anything, made me realise that it was down to me to point to a different path. There is a cost to everything in life, and the only way to meet that cost is if enough people pledge their time to cover it. The only reason why in the end the House of Ou-Yang was on the brink of collapse and Plutopia grows stronger by the day is because we have billions of hours pledged to us from residents all over Shiyan, while they could not call on enough support to keep them going. With so many Shiyanese owing us their time, we could get much more done without draining our own energy. But we mustn't rest on our laurels. We have to come up with more ways to get even more pledges in."

"But Lord Ou-Yang said many of those going hungry had already used up all the hours they had. How could they pledge any more?"

"They could borrow the spare hours we have. I'm not going to use all those hours pledged to me. So they could borrow ten hours from me to get what they need, and simply give me eleven hours back in work that Plutopia needs doing. It is good for everyone."

"Nobody would lose out?"

"Nobody willing to work hard can lose. You'll see, Kuan. I want you to start learning about how Plutopia works day to day. You've nearly completed all your challenges, so it's time you prepare for a permanent role as my deputy."

"I'm not old enough to do that."

"Age has nothing to do with it."

"What's going to be my final challenge? Xian said it was about getting all Mauveans to agree to the use of the Sun Disc instead of relying on elephantium."

"Governor Pui has already got that under control. He knows the Council members well, and he's assured me they will go along with what he puts forward to them. The challenge for you is much greater. I need you to send a message to all reflectors in Shiyan and convince everyone that the Sun Disc marks the New Beginning, and they should embrace it."

"In what way will the Sun Disc bring about this New Beginning? Has it got anything to do with what that prophet was saying before he was executed?"

"The delusional Amadeus? I wouldn't call him a prophet. He was little more than a mindless fanatic. But just because a truth is distorted by some, it doesn't mean we should not respect it all the same. The New Beginning is a sacred truth. Shiyan would degenerate into squalor and chaos without a purposeful renewal, without our effort to make it stronger."

"Why would anyone listen to me? They're more likely to pay attention to what you have to say."

"Kuan, you don't realise it, but you have this ability to reach the hearts and minds of others. You can make them believe. And I want you to help me convince them of the coming of the New Beginning. You do that, and you will reach the ninth and highest Antaeus Circle. You can then acquire the Mauvean status. Your father would have been so proud of you."

Would he? Didn't father say one should worry about those at the bottom and be wary about those at the top? Wasn't that the theme of what he tirelessly typed out in different versions of his work? What would father have made of the New Beginning?

"Kuan, you should think about how you would use the powers which had already been added to you for reaching the Minos and then the Asterion Circle. You can take on any of the forms on those Circles and exercise the capacities associated with them. You've earned them."

"If I change into a lion form, when I change back to human, can I become a doctor with my own stethoscope?"

"What a curious thought. No, our morphing doesn't create new things out of nothing. Whatever clothes or equipment you had on you in your human form before you change into a lion or any other form, that's what you will have on you when you resume your human form. If you want to be a doctor, you have to study to become one and pledge the necessary time to get the appropriate clothes and equipment."

"I think I'll just stay as I am."

Dao drew a deep sigh.

"That's what Nestra said after she reached the fifth Circle and took on her human form. She rose further up the Circles of Challenge after that, but nothing could tempt her to abandon her human form."

[Kuan, ask him something about Nestra.]

K: Why?

[I can sense his feelings about her. If I could transcribe it into electrical pulses, we might get past the emotional scanner into the vault.]

"How did you meet?"

The lined face raised a smile.

"It was here actually, in the House of Ou-Yang. We had both pledged some of our time to help with getting food out. It was a bad year for crops all over Shiyan. Nestra and I were the only ones in human form working here and we both felt so much more could be done if we could get more Shiyanese to pledge their time. We talked and talked."

"You've never had difficulty picturing her in your mind, have you?"

"No, she's as vivid to me as the day we first met all those years ago. I can hear her voice, her raucous laughter."

"Do you still hope to see her?"

"Like you still hope to see your father. In a way, yes, though I know she's gone. I often see her in my dreams."

"Doesn't it just hurt more when you wake up?"

"It is better to feel the pain than to lose the memory."

K: Amo, can I stop now?

[Yes, I have a pattern I can use.]

Dao was standing up and Kuan followed suit. The Chairman dusted himself off and walked pensively over to Xian who was waiting to speak with him. She pointed to the sky and waved her arm through an arc.

The launch of the Sun Disc was imminent. It would herald the New Beginning, and life would never be the same again.

Chapter 21

<u>The Launch</u>

A small white cat padded down a main road in Bastille, shaking her head, muttering to herself. It was mid morning. Wu-yin was not pleased about being sent out to fetch some exotic berries for Governor Pui when she had been looking forward to watching the launch with her family. It was the event everyone in Shiyan had been eagerly awaiting. President Zhou had declared the day a public holiday, which was a grand gesture, though in practice anyone who had pledged their time to carrying out their masters' orders was expected to continue with their work.

It was almost time. Along every street, reflectors in the form of windows, glass walls, or communication panels were all automatically polished with a film of warm air to clear them of any ice or snow. Inside every building, reflector units embedded in every glass surface, in mirrors, partitions, screens flashed out a countdown sequence to focus attention.

Wu-yin slowed to a complete halt. She licked the snow off her paw to quench her thirst. The peacock would have to wait. She was not going to miss what everyone else would be talking about for years to come.

The show had begun. A rocket was seen surging skyward. Stirring music propelled its single-minded trajectory, hundreds of drums beating to march the heart forward with intensifying anticipation.

The rocket had moved beyond the atmosphere. Its tail component fell away, its sides split open to reveal a white globe drifting purposefully into the distance. Sky blue had given way to the total blackness of space. The music eased to a series of electronic notes pulsating as the rotating globe hatched open to release a dark metallic disc, which floated freely into a masterfully orchestrated orbit.

An angelic chorus infused the words 'New Beginning' with transcendent beauty. The disc's momentum carried it towards the sun, until contesting gravitational forces fixed its position exactly as planned. The sun was now perpetually eclipsed. Morning light vanished everywhere on Shiyan.

Superimposed on the black nothingness was the image of a human child. He looked out with an intense gaze and spoke to every watching soul:

"In the beginning, the way was set for all things. But in time, age catches up with everyone. You know in your heart that death waits in stagnant water. To thrive we must renew our world."

No light or heat from the sun would now reach Shiyan except through the disc which gradually turned a dull shade of violet. It was designed to absorb solar energy and channel it back to a processing centre run by Plutopia.

"Our sky is now darkening, but today marks not an end, but a New Beginning, because from now on, all that is precious in our star has been harvested and will be served up for each and everyone of us. None will ever again be scorched by unwanted heat or blinded by excessive light."

The Sun Disc was in place. An expanded chorus now reprised 'New Beginning' with baritonic resonance. The destiny of Shiyan, of each individual who dwelt in it, had been reconfigured.

"Go to your nearest Plutopian distribution point and ask for an energy pendant and wear it round your neck at all times."

The boy held up a globular piece of mauve coloured silicon.

"All the light and heat you need will be sent to you directly, exactly as regulated by you. All the food you seek will be produced and prepared with the abundant energy we now have and made available for you at your convenience. With these matters taken care of for you, you will be able to do so much more to enrich your lives and make Shiyan greater than ever."

The image of the boy faded with the softening music, to be replaced by snapshots of content Shiyanese strolling through the snow with their pendants. A small brown cat was jumping about playfully while its pendant lit up the surrounding area. A semi-morphed lioness walked in her human body carrying a bag of food she had just collected, while a ray of heat from her pendant cleared a path out of the snow in front of her. Another shot revealed a group of mauve elephants gathering in a park with the combined heat and light from their pendants rendering it almost a summer's day. Then came the final message: "Don't forget your energy pendant, brought to you exclusively by Plutopia."

In the sky above, the last of the sun's energy silently dissipated. Darkness accompanied the descent of heavy snow. On top of the Plutopian distribution points on every street corner, searchlights beamed down to ensure Shiyan's residents could find their way to where the mauve pendants were. Cheetah security guards had been issued with theirs so they could keep order on the day the sun was shut out, permanently.

Kuan sat on the steps outside Rook Mansion, which bathed in its own Plutopian light. When everyone else was watching the launch of the Sun Disc on reflectors, he had been down in the basement attempting to break into the vault. His 'New Beginning' speech was recorded days ago and he had already seen how the launch would unfold in Xian's simulations.

255

Earlier on in the basement, he could not at first even reach the glass case covering the bottle containing the emotional scanner. Having found a crate to step on, he keyed in 'Nestra' and waited for Amo to project the thought patterns she discerned in Dao when he spoke about his dead wife. But they had no effect. Amo was desperate to try again. The proximity of her home was pulling her like an irresistible gravitational force. Within a few metres behind that wall was the route back to her home nebula. Ultimately, she could have no life outside of it. A second, a third, a fourth go was still proving futile.

Kuan could feel Amo shifting her emotional patterns to mimic Dao's psychological state. But while it made him seasick with the bobbing of feigned joy and sorrow she stirred up, the scanner was left unmoved. In the meantime, he could see from the glass case, which was of course also a reflector, the launch broadcast was coming to an end. He sensed her aching disappointment when he had no choice but to leave the wine cellar behind.

He was wondering if he could persuade the Chairman to let him into the vault without mentioning the existence of Amo, when the lynx came upon the steps he had sat down on. Denji looked upon him attentively.

"Master Kuan, is the temperature to your liking? I can arrange for it to be warmer. Indeed with the Sun Disc now in operation, we can have spring early if you prefer."

"Denji, this is just fine. I wouldn't want to lose the seasons. It gives me a sense of time."

"Very well, sir."

"But what about Erica? She and the Potokans travelling on feet to Chengbao Island, how are they going to cope with this extra cold weather?"

"You don't have to be concerned about that. I arranged for energy pendants to be sent to Dr. Lee and her companions. I am certain they would have reached them by now."

"Each one would get a pendant?"

"Yes, indeed. We had quite a few spares delivered too just in case."

"That's very kind of you, Denji."

"It was the Chairman. He insisted Dr. Lee and all those with her should have safe passage to the island."

K: Amo, do you see how caring the Chairman is? I won't mention you, but I'll ask him to let me into the vault and I'm sure he'll say 'yes'."

[You can't judge an individual by a few isolated actions.]

K: You still insist we should have nothing to do with Chairman Dao?

[I stand by what I have said. If it still proves impossible for me to get into that vault with you or separate myself from you so I can go into it alone – and we should not wait for more than two more days maximum – then you should go and join Dr. Lee. That's what you really want. You've completed your final challenge now, but I sense whether Dao deems you to have met it or not, you don't really care anymore. Being on Asterion, the seventh Circle, gives you quite enough privileges that you can use to help build the new Oran Clinic. You know that makes sense.]

K: You'd die if you couldn't get back to your home world. I won't let that happen. I'm not going anywhere until I've got you into that vault.

"Would there be anything else, Master Kuan?"

He had almost forgotten the lynx, quiet and patient, was still there at the bottom of the steps.

"Denji, there's just one thing. I should get my own pendant, shouldn't I? I'm not always going to be on the grounds of Rook Mansion."

"Very wise, sir. I will fetch one for you straightaway."

"Actually, I'd like to go into Bastille centre tomorrow to one of the main Plutopian distribution points to see for myself how it's done. It's one thing for me to tell the world, 'go and get your pendant', but I should know first hand what it's like."

"I understand. I'll arrange for the transporter to take you tomorrow."

The next day Kuan was transported into Bastille centre as planned. Even though he was taken almost to the door of the main Plutopian distribution building, the short walk from the transporter was still numbingly chilling. By contrast, an atmosphere of gentle warmth greeted those who entered. Provided they continued onto the distribution desk, all was well. But anyone loitering just to escape from the cold outside would be promptly seized by the scruff of their neck by a wolf dog guard and ejected from the building.

Kuan headed straight to one of the distribution desks where a very old lion had just asked for his pendant. Standing on the desk behind a glass screen was a small cat with a long black and white, badger-like face.

"Welcome to Plutopia. For your energy pendant, please put your paw on the screen and pledge a million hours."

Incredulity crumpled the lion's face.

"How many hours did you say?"

"That would be a million hours, sir. Please make the pledge."

Badger-face grinned unconvincingly.

"But I haven't got a million hours. I doubt if I have a thousand hours left altogether."

"Pendants for pledges. It's the Plutopian way, sir. We mustn't hold up others in the line."

The lion shook his ancient crown.

"How am I going to survive this cold, with the sun blocked out permanently?"

"Your pledge, please, on the screen."

"I fought for Shiyan in the first Simian War, you know."

It was a deep but faltering voice. And it made no difference to the black and white cat.

"That must have been hard. You take care of yourself now. Next!"

Two wolf dogs escorted the frail lion out of the building. The assistant on the desk turned to Kuan.

"Welcome to Plutopia. For your energy pendant, please put your ...", he looked down curiously at the boy's forelimb, "hand on the screen and pledge a million hours."

"I think there might be a mistake. It can't require a million hours to get an energy pendant."

"And you would know, would you?"

"Actually, I would."

"Pendants for pledges. If you won't pledge, sir, I suggest you leave."

"Listen..."

"You listen! There's no bargaining with Plutopia."

Another cat jumped onto the desk.

"What is going on? Oh, it's you."

It was Wu-yin and she instantly recognised Kuan. The white cat turned her much displeased face to her belligerent colleague.

"Are you out of your mind? This is Chairman Dao's apprentice. Will you give him a pendant!"

"But he doesn't want to pledge a million hours."

"*He* doesn't have to pledge anything. Besides, as an Asterion Circle member, he should get a free gift. Put a hundred hours in his account."

The badger-like cat leaned over the screen and gave Kuan his pendant, bowing low as he handed it over.

"Thanks for clearing things up, Wu-yin. What are you doing here anyway?"

"I was late getting Governor Pui's precious berries to him for his mid morning snack, so he transferred me here for my *development*. I'm responsible for coordinating the on-going transactional arrangements."

"She's an assistant", added the other cat.

"Senior Assistant." Wu-yin clarified.

"Wu-yin, are you really asking ordinary Shiyanese to pledge a million hours to get a pendant?"

"If you want my opinion, which nobody ever does, it's ridiculous. But the Governor sets the terms. I just coordinate."

Kuan thanked Wu-yin and left the Plutopian building. This was not how he thought the Sun Disc would work. Just before boarding the transporter, he saw the elderly lion stumbling along the frozen street. He walked over to him, took his own pendant off and put it round the big cat's neck. A bright warm glow radiated from the mauve silicon. It would protect the old soldier. But there were many others who could not secure an energy pendant, and soon they might all perish in the intensifying cold.

He asked to be taken straight to the secret building in the woods of Rook Mansion. This time neither he nor Amo had the patience to argue with the auto-pilot about whether he could be taken there without special authorisation. He placed his hand on the navigation panel and electrical sparks swiftly overrode existing command codes.

He was surprised to find the door open. Xian was scrutinising the blue glass wall. Amongst the different floating images, a line coming from a flashing circle was moving towards a square box but then changed direction and split into a dozen lines going into a rectangular area on the right. The semi-morph put her hands behind her leopard head in puzzlement.

"I'm expecting Pui. Is he on his way?"

"I don't know. I was hoping to find you or him here. Something's gone wrong with the Sun Disc project."

"That's an understatement."

"You know about the problem? Plutopia is asking for a pledge of a million hours for each pendant."

"That's just a crass miscalculation. Governor Pui insisted that setting it at this ludicrously high level would mean all but a few elite Shiyanese would have to pledge their entire lives to working for Plutopia. Basically, his choice is freeze to death or give yourself over to slavery. But many Shiyanese won't stand for it. The election is coming soon. President Zhou can either overrule this stupidity, or Shiyan will tear itself apart. I know which she would prefer. The real problem, Kuan, is far more serious."

Xian went into her own room to the side, and the boy eagerly followed. She stood over her silver white iridium control panel, punching in various keys.

"The Sun Disc is supposed to absorb the sun's energy on its way to our planet and direct it to a processing centre which then makes it available for a very small pledge to everyone in the precise form and quantity it is required. No one would then be dependent on elephantium anymore. But someone has tampered with the system. I couldn't believe it at first, but I have checked it over and over again, and my worst suspicions have been confirmed. The energy harvested from the sun is not being sent to the processing centre I set up, but diverted to a number of mobile stations which have in just the last few days moved into what used to be Bastille de Potoka, the mining region with all the surplus elephantium buried for enrichment. These stations are using the sun's energy to accelerate the enrichment process, so the interred elephantium becomes richer in energy potential much more quickly. And the pendants are drawing their energy from these stations as they make use of the super enriched elephantium."

"Is that connected with the Potokans being urged to move out of the area?"

"They had to be made to move. They would have got in the way of the whole clandestine operation. Radiating them along with the elephantium would not work."

"Because it would have caused a public outcry?"

"No. It would have given some fanatics an excuse to organise a day of celebration, and that would have drawn attention to what's really happening with the sun's energy."

"But if all the sun's energy is being diverted to the enrichment of elephantium…"

"We're going to end up, not becoming less dependent on elephantium, but desperately, totally dependent on it."

"Could Chairman Dao have planned this or was it all Governor Pui's doing?"

Xian looked up at a screen showing the room with the blue glass wall. The peacock had just strutted in. She flicked a switch on and they could hear him calling out for her.

"Kuan, you can listen for yourself. I want to know what exactly he's been up to. If I don't get a satisfactory explanation, then the whole Sun Disc project must be shut down. You see the key which has lit up in red. If I give you the signal …"

She gave him a thumbs down gesture.

"… you hit that key, the countdown for a shutdown will commence. By default, with ten seconds to go, it will ask for confirmation to complete the countdown, you'd have to key in the name of the Security Chief of *FSS Castle*. You do remember his name, don't you?"

Kuan nodded, and Xian went out to interrogate Pui.

The peacock was preening his feathers when Xian entered. He did not like being summoned to meet with a lowly semi-morphed leopard. But she was the lynchpin of the Sun Disc operation, so he gave her one of his best superficial smiles. Xian ranted about all the abnormalities she had detected. She wanted a complete explanation, including how much Dao knew about the changes which had been made.

Pui launched into a long speech about the infinite wisdom of Chairman Dao, the intricacies of making Shiyan stronger, and how energy was a weapon that had to be handled with the utmost secrecy. It was an unmistakable prelude to telling her absolutely nothing. He stretched his wings and tail before suggesting they go up to the mansion to meet with the Chairman. He bowed and let her walk in front of him. She was now facing the camera Kuan was looking into on screen. She paused to consider if she should give him the signal.

Massive talons burst through her chest. Blood gushed out of Xian's mouth, reddening her fangs. Her unbelieving eyes stared into the camera and she pointed her thumb to the ground. The talons retracted. She fell to the ground. A giant eagle with the back half of a lion stood with its claws dripping in torn flesh. The griffin leapt over the motionless body and slowly morphed back into the peacock. He left the building.

Kuan hit the red key and ran out to see what could be done for Xian.

"Xian, I'll get help."

"It's too late. Just complete the shutdown."

Kuan didn't know what to do but Amo was adamant he must do what Xian asked.

He ran back into the room to see the countdown suspended with ten seconds to go as Xian said it would, so he keyed in 'Len-Wu' but nothing happened. He did it again, and the countdown was cancelled altogether.

Back out to Xian, he asked what he should do next.

For the first time he saw her smile.

"Father, I'm sorry it's taken so long. I'm ready now."

"Xian, the confirmation code didn't work. The shutdown's been cancelled completely."

"Kuan, don't worry. I thought they might have got into my control panel. But I have a back-up. Find it and end this Sun Disc madness."

"Where's your back-up?"

Xian's eyes lit up at some image they had come upon, and then they froze.

The door flung open. Governor Pui had returned with a pack of wolf dog guards.

"Arrest the boy, he's committed murder."

The wolf dogs pinned Kuan down.

"No, he's the one who killed Xian. You can check on the reflector in the control room, it's recorded in there, what Governor Pui did."

Pui disappeared into the room and when he returned he merely said, "the only evidence in the control room is that the boy tried to sabotage the Sun Disc project. Take him to Chairman Dao."

Kuan should have known that his protest would make no difference. The wolf dogs dragged him into the shuttle transporter, and when they reached the mansion's basement, they pulled him along the ground to the secret vault. He tried to pull himself up but they were too strong for him. The wall of the vault had already been moved out of the way. Inside stood Dao with the most unforgiving expression on his face.

He was left at Dao's feet. The vault had nothing in it except a large reflector screen and two black doors to either side of it. Amo immediately sensed that the door on the left opened onto her world. A few steps by Kuan and she would be back home.

"Kuan, I never thought you were capable of murder."

"Chairman Dao, you must believe me. I have nothing to do with Xian's death. Her chest was ripped open by a griffin's claws. How could I have done anything like that?"

"He's on the Asterion Circle, he could easily have morphed into a griffin." Pui observed.

"I have no idea how to morph. It was Governor Pui who killed Xian, and he tampered with the Sun Disc project so Shiyan is now more dependent on elephantium than ever. Xian found out and that's why he killed her."

"Kuan, no more lies."

"Why would I even want to hurt Xian?"

"Governor Pui has always been loyal to me. He would not deceive me."

"He did it. I saw it with my own eyes. You must believe me."

"Kuan, I treated you like a son. I wanted you to be the one to inherit Plutopia. Yet you have disgraced me. Murder is a terrible crime, but to attempt to sabotage the Sun Disc is to threaten Shiyan itself, and that is a dreadful offence punishable by death in Hades."

The door on the right was pushed aside and Kuan was thrown into the room. He vaguely recalled the Hades punishment being described as a fate worse than actual death.

"Give me a chance to explain what happened."

Amo pushed with all the energy she could summon to reach over to the door on the other side of the vault. If she could bring Kuan with her through that other door, she would do so instantly. But she along with Kuan were confined to the narrow room with banks of electrodes protruding along its walls.

Dao stared at the boy from outside, volcanic rage wrapped tight beneath his skin.

"Why have you done this? You leave me no choice. By the power vested in me by the President of Shiyan, I, Aegisthus Dao, hereby sentence you, Kuan, to Hades for eternal damnation."

"Chairman Dao, please listen to me. It was the governor. It wasn't me!"

The door was slammed shut. All was dark. The incongruous sound of water dripping began to trickle down all around him. But there was no water, just sharp electrical charges bombarding him, causing his lungs to contract. Each breath was getting harder for him to complete. Blue light danced around him with malicious intent. Intense rays whipped his face and stabbed into his head. The more he gasped for air, the more pain splintered across his constricted chest. He grovelled on the cold hard floor. Intense currents now tore into his body, slicing and splicing him, until they severed from him his final hold on consciousness.

Chapter 22

<u>Hades</u>

Death in Hades was no ordinary death. Instead of a final and total cessation, one was suspended in an other-dimensional realm for all time with no hope of release. It was the most severe sentence to be handed down in Shiyan for heinously unpardonable crimes.

The electrical charges which had ripped Kuan apart now reassembled and deposited him in a silent space, domed by a blue shade of darkness. All around him a depressingly bland emptiness prevailed. Every part of him, even the clothes he had been wearing, had been left unchanged. But in the inner void of his mind there was no hint of his companion.

Amo's consciousness had been weakening for some time, and now there was no trace of it left. He called out to her but she did not reply. If he had made a run for that other room in the vault, he might have delivered Amo back to her own world in time to save her. But he failed.

He failed to save his friend, failed to bring Xian's killer to justice, failed to shut down the Sun Disc, and left countless to freeze to their death. Whatever mission he was meant to fulfil for father, he must have failed that too. There was probably enough self-recrimination to last an eternity.

He would have liked to find out what father did after he discovered his son was missing. Did he try to find him on his own but became lost at sea himself? Did he communicate with Agent Tan and suggest some task Kuan was to carry out while he went into hiding? What purpose would that have served?

More than anything else he wished they had been together again, however briefly, so that he could hear father's admonition to him. He had not listened carefully enough when he had the chance.

In an endless loop he scolded himself. The false hope of attaining the Mauvean status only led to more disappointment. Had he made the wrong decision at every turn? If Amo would never have survived anyway, perhaps he should have gone with Erica to Chengbao Island. With the sun permanently eclipsed, conditions would no doubt be harsh, but he and the doctor could have built a new home, safe from vicious, arbitrary interference which would in a flash leave one's life in ruin.

Now no matter how many years he could endure, there would be no prospect of being with her again. Hades was designed to erase hope. He pulled out the emerald pebble from his trouser pocket and smiled wryly at it. A token of remembrance serving only to affirm the pain of unbridgeable separation.

Kuan surveyed the clinically barren landscape. He had been cut away from everyone he had ever cared for. Sealed in unbearable isolation, he screamed for acknowledgement, but there was not even an echo in reply. He trudged along the black, glass-smooth surface of Hades. In every direction, the distant horizon led to a featureless backdrop.

He ached to hear another voice, to feel the touch of another being. His legs kept moving as though their blind determination would suffice in carrying him to somewhere less oppressive. But the intense nothingness followed him every step he took. There was no respite. He screamed louder still, again and again. His throat hurt. That was at least a sensation. They had not robbed him of his pain. He slapped himself hard in the face. A tingly, sweet sting. He went for the other cheek. It hurt deeply, reassuringly.

His legs finally gave in. He fell to his knees. Bored with slapping himself, he turned his attention to wiping non-existent dirt off the perfectly flat floor. How long had he been there? It might have been minutes, hours, or even days. It did not matter to him. He remembered stories about people in ancient times in China smashing their heads against the wall when there were no other viable instruments around to precipitate their demise. There was no wall in sight, but the black solidity beneath him felt hard enough. He leaned forward placing both hands on the floor. His muscles tightened. How much time would he need to summon enough force within him, by which he meant courage, to propel his own head into the ground?

But then the whole idea struck him as absurd. If he could find enough courage within him, and sufficient determination to unleash such formidable power, why direct it against himself? He should destroy Pui for framing him, Chairman Dao for not believing him, even the whole of Hades for imprisoning an innocent victim. He recoiled from his morbid infatuation and sat back in angry contemplation of the causes of his predicament. Rage, he discovered, was an antidote to the loss of sanity.

Time meaninglessly passed. He held on to his furious indictment of each manifestation of injustice he had suffered. He would not let it slip. Wrongs must be corrected.

A shadowy shape loomed in the distance. Kuan could make out a vaguely human form, the torso and arms definitely, but not the head. It could be a semi-morph. A fellow prisoner? A guard? It would in any case be another living being. It was not to be solitary confinement after all. He stood up slowly in anticipation. The figure trotted up to him. It was an unusual centaur, a gleaming white steed with taut muscular human torso and biceps, but the head of a white panther. His red eyes scanned the young human.

"Welcome, Kuan. Once again you've ended up in my domain."

He seemed to have heard that voice before.

"Don't be perplexed. You will fit right in."

That tone was lodged somewhere in his memory, if only he could retrieve it.

"Let me show you around."

The stranger turned sharply to his right where space opened up like a sliding door. He led the boy through a narrow transparent passageway into a long corridor with spotless white walls on one side and brightly lit compartments to the other. Kuan squinted at the light panels above him. He was sure he had been there before.

The centaurian panther called back to the boy.

"Each time you think you've got away from me, only to end up before me once again."

Kuan had never seen those piercing eyes, but the voice was unmistakable.

"You must remember what's behind these walls."

It was the voice behind the camera eye overseeing those gruesome acts in the so-called purgoratory. It was only because of Amo that he managed to escape with his life that day, along with the treacherous General Chi-Ling and the snow tiger, Sung.

"You're the Curator!"

"Yes, the Curator of Lost Souls, my followers here call me."

"You're the one in charge of Hades?"

"I've never liked that name. The President renamed it Hades because for some absurd reason she thought it would impress the voters more. For me, it'll always be Schloss – from Schloss 1, the primitive contraption that greeted me on my arrival, to the multi-functional Schloss 22 I've reconstructed with the most sophisticated programming. In theory, no one's in charge of Hades, it was meant to be a place of anarchic randomness, where the damned would drift through infinity with no purpose or meaning. But I have ideas of my own."

The Curator continued with the guided tour and paused when they came to a compartment where a Potokan was held down on a stainless steel table by mechanical arms extended from the wall. The six-legged cat creature turned his white eyes briefly on Kuan.

"Still torturing those who can't defend themselves."

"I wouldn't call the administration of low level pain torture."

"You're going to cut him up and kill him!"

"Cut him up, yes, but not to kill him. What you saw when you were last here were experiments that had served their purpose. This is something quite different. This is about giving him a second chance, something you rejected before without even knowing what was being offered."

The mechanical arms projected blue light beams that swept through the Potokan causing him to shake violently. The brightness intensified and the creature began to disintegrate, rapidly breaking up into clouds of molecules, which were contained by an invisible force field and moulded into a new shape filled with pristine whiteness. The shape gradually solidified into a larger, stronger being – a fearsome white panther. The reborn creature shook his head, leapt to the ground and galloped away. The same thing happened in the compartments ahead and at the end of the long corridor, they went out into an open arena where hundreds of white panthers had gathered.

The panther-headed centaur trotted up the steps onto a raised platform. At the sight of him, his votaries below prostrated themselves. Row after row of devotees devoid of any thought but what their leader commanded them to believe and do. He surveyed them with unbridled pride before leading Kuan down a spiral staircase in the centre of the platform. At the bottom they went through an underground tunnel to a small chamber. Blackened walls enclosed the space.

"Kuan, what kind of strange creature are you? Time and time again you have got in my way. My offer of Blessing to the lost and wretched had brought many into my domain over the years, but at one of our special Final Blessing ceremonies in Castle de Potoka, you disrupted proceedings and caused the portal to shut off permanently. You deprived many of a second chance to attain an infinitely better life."

"All you ever offered them was a second chance in death. They didn't have much of a life in Castle de Potoka, but it was better than this. What good can come from being stuck here, whether you are given the form of a white panther or not."

"You have no idea, Kuan. Potokans arriving here are not trapped in death. They get to be reborn as the purest Shiyanese, ready for a new life. But I forgive you because you knew not what you were doing. Besides, my purgoratory work opened up new channels for me to get hold of fresh intake."

"So you used the lightning device to transport more victims here to experiment on them."

"Actually the experimentation was concluded thanks to you. It was only ever conducted to explore how one could leave here. With the earlier models, the link was thoroughly locked in an incoming direction.

But as I came up with successive reconfigured designs, the possibility of a return to life was opened up. And when I experimented with you, it proved beyond doubt that one could leave here and get back to the world of the living."

"So you weren't at all sure when you offered to return me to the beach that day, that you could actually do it?"

"I was fairly confident. Previous experiments had led me to believe that the protagonist's state of mind was critical. The punishment of eternal damnation works by ripping hope out of your soul, forcing you to turn your back forever on the life you had. But if you believe enough that the life you had was not over, that determination could rejoin you to the world you've been cut adrift from. Observing what you did, I was able to complete the upgrading of Schloss 22 and now everything is set."

"All I have to do is to want to leave here and I'd be free?"

"Of course not. However resolute the will, it must be connected to the right command codes, and only I can access them."

Kuan did not bother to hide his disappointment. He wished Amo was still in his head and she would assure him that she could override the Curator's system to secure their escape. But she was gone.

"No need for despondence. Even though you rejected my offer of a second chance once, it is not in my nature to turn anyone away. Just let me know when you're ready."

"What sort of second chance is it to become a white panther? Help you control new prisoners you bring down through your lightning strikes? I knew it was your doing in Bastille when all those Shiyanese vanished in a blinding flash of light. They blamed the Potokans, but it was all your doing. Don't deny it."

"Why would I deny it? Who else could master such technology but I? With the old portal disabled, I needed other means of expanding my pool of potential followers. And when I obtained the coordinates for certain parts of Bastille I could target, I made use of them to track down more recruits."

"All your captives have willingly accepted your second chance?"

"A few declined, but many have joined me. It's entirely up to them. I always leave others the freedom to choose."

"But I'm to be locked up in here unless I agree to be reborn."

"Kuan, why do you insist on misunderstanding me?"

The Curator clicked his fingers and a bed made out of solid blue light appeared. Another click and an opening carved itself out of the wall.

"You can leave this chamber any time you wish. It's here for your comfort and privacy. I appreciate it's a lot to take in. Why don't you rest, go for a walk, whatever you like, and we'll talk more another time."

The centaur sauntered through the opening in the wall onto the vast plain of nothingness outside. He stretched his arms and let out a thunderous roar. It was to summon his assistant who from nowhere swung into view.

"Look to Kuan for me. I don't want him rushing into the wrong decision. But we must be ready soon to instigate our New Beginning."

The assistant bowed deeply. It was Max. The chimpanzee was still wearing his old red tuxedo, and his green frilly shirt with a large hole torn out when Agent Tan in his black rhino form rammed his horn into him.

"You're right about him, Max. There's something different about that boy. Keep a close eye on him."

"As you wish, Lord Amadeus."

The Curator, Lord Amadeus, galloped away into the dark blue background. The reverential seriousness on Max's face evaporated. He turned his head towards Kuan with a huge grin. What a tale he had to share with his old crew mate. After being gored by Agent Tan in the valley of Castle de Potoka, he was brought into Hades by the Curator, on whose behalf he had been dispensing Blessing to recruit followers for the much maligned prophet. As soon as he had passed through the light, his near fatal injury healed – physical mortality was apparently not permitted in the penitentiary of psychological death.

In recognition of his dedicated Blessing service, Lord Amadeus made him his assistant. It was the happiest day of Max's life. He was full of admiration for the flamboyant prophet who had long been a thorn in the side of the authority before his reckless incitement to kill anyone disagreeing with his religious views landed him with the first Hades sentence to be passed in the history of Shiyan. Up until then the Schloss, as it was originally known, was just used as a threat to deter anyone foolish enough to contemplate harming Mauveans. However, killing lesser Shiyanese, Max added as an aside, was often punishable with a fine of just a few pledged hours, while murdering outsiders was not a crime at all. The chimp indulged in his indignant digression for a while before turning back to his story.

Such prejudice would have no place under Lord Amadeus. There would be no division by Circles of Challenge, just a simple distinction between pure Shiyanese and the rest. And anyone could be transformed into a white panther so long as they accepted the prophet's words as sacred.

To work towards his vision, Amadeus quickly turned Hades into his own base of operation. The few criminals sent there subsequent to him were swiftly converted. Gifted in manipulating electronic data, he started to strengthen Schloss' capability, including sending messages to willing accomplices like Max who would dispense Blessing and draw creatures with little hope in life into the light. Once there they would be offered a second chance to rise again as pure vanguards of Shiyan under its New Beginning. Those taking it up would be reborn as white panthers, ready to accompany the great Curator on his triumphant return.

The only stumbling block for a long while was the seeming impossibility of transporting out of Hades back to the world of the living. So a few experiments, quite necessary ones Max insisted, were organised in the purgoratory to find a way to travel back to the other side. It was during one of those experiments, bravely conducted on himself, that Lord Amadeus had a number of the physical forms he could morph into – horse, human, panther – mangled up, leaving him as he was now. Not a subject to bring up in his presence, Max noted with a wink. Anyway, the important thing was that he was finally ready to lead his followers back to Shiyan.

Kuan stared at Max clapping his hands in fervent expectation.

"What about those who don't want to go with Amadeus?"

"They're going to be left here, to languish for eternity."

"You're going with him then."

"Of course, I'm his assistant, I'm going to be very important by the side of the prophet."

"You'll become one of those pure Shiyanese then?"

Max hesitated for a moment.

"It's part of the deal. Just before we leave, I'll put myself through the converter."

"Shiyan's not going to welcome Amadeus' return."

"He will be giving everyone a second chance to join him."

"But not everyone will accept his offer."

"Only fools will turn down a second chance. If they refuse, and it is their choice, they will be banished to Hades."

"Not much of a choice."

"That's why you should think about it carefully. Lord Amadeus likes your defiant spirit, and he'd be most disappointed if you weren't amongst his army of followers."

Max squeezed the boy's face with both hands. Kuan was expecting to be engulfed with the chimp's unpleasant sweaty odour, but he smelt nothing. There was no smell, fragrant or foul, in Hades.

Kuan withdrew into the chamber to lie on the bed of light. Max asked him if he would like some Blessing to help him clear his head. He declined and rolled on his side.

"Good idea, have a shut eye. When you want to talk some more, just call out 'Max', and I will hear you. The acoustics are quite unbelievable here."

Amadeus' assistant stepped out of the chamber and scampered away with a self-satisfied smirk. Not for the first time since he became acquainted with him, not hearing any more from Max made Kuan treasure an otherwise lonely moment.

What was he to do? Could he endure the relentless isolation that lay ahead should he refuse to go along with the mad prophet? He was at a crossroads again, and he must not allow himself to take yet another wrong turn. No good could possibly come from resigning himself to eternal confinement in this nowhere land. But to follow Amadeus would be to submit to whatever he deemed the truth. There would be no room to question, to diverge, to lead one's own life beyond the path imposed by the Curator. How could such mental servitude be outweighed by the slim probability of retaining some semblance of independent thought? The preacher would tether your brain to his leash, while the clown would dance with a shrug of the shoulders. That just took the boy back to the bleak cul-de-sac he was already in. Here he would be free. He could forever do as he pleased, interacting with nothing, changing nothing, remaining nothing.

   His mind drifted off in many directions until he was lost in a mist of stupour. Released once more from unforgiving consciousness. Unfastened from anger. Detached from solitude. He embraced his sleep.

   A distinctive strike broke the muteness in the air. It was followed by another. Someone was hitting the typewriter keys with impatient ferocity. Kuan jumped up from his light-constructed bed. Hovering in front of him was a holographic typewriter. With rapid precision the keys appeared to depress by themselves, and words appeared in mid air: 'Kuan, you must stop Amadeus.'
   "Amo, is that you?"
   Kuan called out. There was no reply. He stared at the glowing form of the old-fashioned typewriter, and typed out his question on it: 'who is this?'
   Words flashed up immediately in response.
   'It's Agent Tan.'
   The boy was sceptical. He typed another question: 'How do I know it's really you?'

A few seconds went by and an answer appeared.

'When I told you about the message I got from your father, we were at Wuchang Tearoom just after you met with Governor Pui.'

'You said it was sent to you on a particular type of paper.'

'One with the watermark of the sun.'

'What did the message say?'

'Beware when the right way turns out to be the wrong way. Unmask the hidden. Resistance is life'

Kuan was convinced. He typed out his plea for help.

'You must release me. I was framed by Governor Pui. He killed Xian.'

'I know, and I'll deal with Pui. But first you must prevent Amadeus from escaping from Hades.'

'How can I do that?'

'You have to find a way.'

'Even if I can stop him, how am I going to get out of here?'

'Trust yourself.'

Kuan was impressed by Tan's confidence but nonetheless felt that it was misplaced.

'Have you caught General Chi-Ling yet?'

'We should have him cornered soon.'

He paused before he tapped out his next question.

'Is father really dead?'

No response.

'Agent Tan, are you still there?'

'Kuan, I must go.'

The boy wanted to press him for an answer, but the typewriter dimmed and disappeared.

Minutes, hours, drifted by. Tan didn't confirm father's death. He could interpret that as suggesting that father might still be alive. Why couldn't father have an identical twin whose body was the one discovered in the sea? The improbable could nonetheless be possible. He was still wondering what Tan might really know about father, and how he was able to communicate with Kuan in Hades when he received a big slap on his back.

Max had come to take him to see Lord Amadeus. What was he to do if he had to give an answer then and there? He could pretend to go along with the centaurian panther and then wait for a chance to sabotage his plan.

Kuan was led into a cycloramic room where a screen spanned 360 degrees around the circular wall. They walked through the transparent wall to the centre where they were greeted by the Curator.

On the screen they could see snow-covered plains surrounding them. Under the cold dark sky, a few indistinct creatures in the distance with what looked like energy pendants round their necks were moving slowly. A bubble of warm light sheltered them from the inclement weather. It was a not uncommon scene from Shiyan in these eclipsed times.

"Kuan, I want to share this moment with you. Because of you I was able to work out how we could leave Schloss 22, and now I can show you where we'll be going to."

On screen, the ground shook and giant shoots pushed out of the snow to unfurl themselves skyward. At the top of each of these mechanical plants a large bulb sprouted forth. Like glass onions the size of a basketball the bulbous receptors rotated on their stems until they all focused on a common point in the black atmosphere above. At that moment, streaks of energy rained down and the receptors lit up with a blinding glow. Day had displaced night. Spring was melting away the snow.

"Is this happening across Shiyan? Has the Sun Disc been shut down?" asked Kuan.

"Why would the Sun Disc be shut down? No, darkness still generally prevails. What you see is a gift to me, by one of my secret followers out there, an isolated piece of land which had been guaranteed its own provision of light and warmth, ready for my arrival. Everywhere else you would have to pledge your life to that damned Plutopia to get by, but on Amadeus' territories, you will have all you need."

On screen, all around could be seen the unsuspecting dwellers of that land emerging from their hiding places to rejoice in the remarkable change to their circumstance. Grey, six-legged, cat-like creatures sniff the air and dance around with celebratory excitement.

"Why have you sent them up when they're still in their Potokan form? I thought only those who convert into white panther followers of yours could return to the world of the living."

"These are not my followers, not yet. But they will soon discover their good fortune in being at the right place at the right time. Having been forced to leave Bastille, that corrupt heart of Shiyan, they have at this auspicious moment arrived at where my prophecy is about to be fulfilled."

In the midst of the Potokans, a human figure emerged, brushing the snow off her black coat, a pendant still faintly glowing around her neck. She pushed her red hair behind her ears and surveyed the sky with unbelieving joy.

"I will show myself to them and offer each a second chance to join me and become a pure Shiyanese. Those who're so unwise as to turn it down will fill the space we leave behind in Schloss 22. An eternity is probably just about long enough for them to reflect on their folly."

The boy stared at the screen. How could he save her?

"Kuan, Max, it is time to get ready for our ascent to Chengbao Island."

Chapter 23

<u>Time to Choose</u>

The Curator had divided up his flock of lost souls. In the arena stood those who would follow him wherever he led and had accordingly undergone the process of conversion into the pure white panther form. Beneath the arena was an underground dungeon holding those who turned down Amadeus' offer of a second chance. They were far fewer in numbers, but they would yield neither to temptation nor threat. All the promise of glory and dominion left them unmoved. Pain, solitude, deprivations failed to dent their tranquility. They had thought deeply about the prophet's vision of a New Beginning, and they resolved never to succumb to it.

They were the dungeonites, the twice-damned, the ones Amadeus wanted to make an example of to the rest of the world. Once he had led his devoted ones to Chengbao Island, Schloss 22 would countdown to a state called 'death-plus-one'. It was a state of being devised by the unstable genius, consisting of the mind being suspended one moment before its final demise. Instead of granting an infinity to think, it would accelerate the termination of any sentient being within the Schloss to that point just before the mortal precipice. It would be like being trapped forever in that moment when an innocent prisoner felt the barrel of the gun pressed against the back of his head. Amadeus knew that Hades had in fact afforded him the luxury of plotting his escape and revenge. Such a luxury must be denied to those in Shiyan he was to banish for rejecting him as their prophet. For them one and only one recurring thought would be allowed – *I'm about to die*.

When Kuan still expressed reservation about going along to one of the compartments to convert into a pure Shiyanese, Amadeus led him to the gate of the dungeon. After warning him not to make the mistake again of turning down a second chance, he trotted away and left the boy there to decide if he truly wanted to share the fate of the twice-damned.

Through the blue transparent yet impenetrable bars, the boy could see the stoic faces of around twenty Potokans, three or four Shiyanese in their small cat form, and another half dozen in their cheetah form captured when Schloss 22 attacked Bastille city centre. One of them in particular looked familiar. It was the Potokan who saved his life when he fell into the quicksand in what was known as 'the valley' in Castle de Potoka, and in return he tried to prevent her from entering into the light on the night of the Final Blessing.

"Kuan, I'm sorry to see you here. You've been presented with your choice?"

"Not much to choose between, is there? But why are you a dungeonite? I thought you wanted a second chance."

"I've had a long time to think about it. And when you're trapped in death with no distraction, some things do become clearer."

"But Amadeus's going to remove all scope for thoughts, anyone left here would be stuck in the single moment before death. You won't be able to think anymore."

"That doesn't change anything. Amadeus' path is unacceptable. He's obsessed with its rightness, but we must beware when the right way turns out to be the wrong way."

Kuan asked her to repeat the last sentence, and it was exactly the same as father's message. He demanded to know where she might have heard it from, but her reply was even more startling.

"It's an old Potokan saying. And 'when evil disguises itself, unmask the hidden; when evil threatens death, resistance is life'."

"My father wrote that."

"Perhaps he was learned in Potokan culture."

"That's not possible. You must have got those words from him somehow."

"It doesn't matter where those words came from, Kuan. Think what they mean and act by them."

He was in Hades, and here the doubt over father's death surfaced. There was something he must uncover. Something had been hidden from him. He must think, while there was still time. Agent Tan asking him to stop Amadeus, the danger to Erica Lee and the Potokans on Chengbao Island, the mission he was to fulfil for father, they were all connected. If he concentrated hard enough, he could work it out.

A strong arm pulled Kuan away from the dungeon and led him back to the corridor of the purgoratory. Max's chimp face was filled with inner conflict. The Curator had announced it was time for them to depart. There could be no further delay to his formal conversion.

The chimp ran his thick hairy fingers down his red tuxedo, displaying a strange attachment to his tatty garment. He screwed up his lips as he knew there was no choice about the matter. Patting the stainless steel table with his big hands, Max sighed deeply. The centaurian panther galloped by to see what was still holding things up.

The chimp hopped onto the table and lay down. Mechanical arms surged out of the wall. They shot out blue light beams that plunged into the latest convert. He screamed and convulsed. The disintegration of what he was had commenced. His face was contorted into a cloud of dark molecules along with the rest of his body.

An elongated shape flashed white and blue. The chimpanzee momentarily reappeared, gripped with intense fear. And it was back to the amorphous shape. A mouth was formed in the middle, screaming "Lord Amadeus, save me!" It sank back into a blob of light. White turned to black. The cloud burst into oblivion.

Mild puzzlement coloured the Curator's white panther face.

"So it doesn't work on outsiders. Works fine on Potokans and Shiyanese, yet not on outsiders."

"How could this happen? No one can physically die in Hades." Kuan queried what he had apparently witnessed.

"That's what we thought. The Schloss is full of surprises. Maybe he's not exactly dead, just dead-plus-one. No time to find out now."

"You killed him."

"It was his choice. What about you? Are you coming?"

"Absolutely not."

"Are you afraid the same might happen to you? You can't be sure. It might work for you. It's not an exact science."

"I've made my choice. I'm not going with you. Why don't you stay too and we can talk about making Schloss 22 even better?"

"With Max gone, I could do with an assistant like you. It's your choice. But if you decline, I'll have to find another. Stay if that's what you truly want, staring hopelessly into the abyss forever. It must be quite an exquisite experience. All that time I'll be leading the world forward on the crest of its New Beginning."

Amadeus' hooves clopped restlessly as he indulged in a reverie of the glorious future he was about to unleash.

"Suppose you have eventually turned everyone into a pure Shiyanese in white panther form, while all those refusing to side with you are banished here. What difference would that make?"

"The purity of our Beginning would have been renewed. All blemishes would be erased. What more can anyone want in life?"

The Curator looked incredulously at Kuan's stoney expression.

"I guess it's something about outsiders. You're not meant to be part of our world. Max was loyal to the end. Come and bid us farewell."

The centaurian panther pushed the back of the boy's head so that he walked along with him to the edge of the arena. Amadeus leapt over the barrier and stood at the head of his army of followers, hundreds of white panthers, some high on spiritual delirium, some eager to stamp out the impure, and not a few thinking it was better to go along with the mad prophet than to be his victim. Each was carrying a pack on the back containing the conversion equipment.

"Kuan, for the final time, our ways part. The moment we leave, the countdown to death-plus-one begins. You will have a day, long enough to relive the many regrets you have over your short life. Expect a few more to join you before your mind goes blank. Sadly there will be a foolish few on Chengbao Island who will refuse my offer of a second chance. I trust you won't mind explaining to them what they can expect once the countdown is completed."

Amadeus raised his arms and clapped his hands together. Ribbons of electricity floated above the arena. They intertwined with one another and shone more intensely as they began to cut through the air. The centaurian panther roared out in anticipation. Blades of light clashed and in one giant flash the prophet and his band of pure Shiyanese were gone.

A charred circle marked the empty arena. A day was all he had left. He sat on the steps pondering his limited future. A wisp of a call floated by him.

"Kuan, help me."

It was faint. Max had not died? In Hades, he could not die. Remnants of him were still around.

"Kuan."

Perhaps he could help restore Max. He followed the faded echo of a voice until he found himself back in the cycloramic room. He walked through the wall but the screen around it was blank. The chimpanzee might even know how to stop the countdown to death-plus-one. He listened intently. It seemed to have stopped. Perhaps Max could not hold his fragmenting existence together anymore. Languidly he moved to the centre of the room.

"Look down."

He obeyed the whisper. With a squint he could make out the tiniest flicker on a blue dot on the ground. On one knee, he cupped his hands around the minute flame and raised it to his eye level.

"Kuan."

It was a young girls' voice.

"Amo, is that you?"

"Sit with me for awhile."

The boy, eyes closed, sat cross-legged, his hands resting one on top of the other on his lap. A glimpse of hope had appeared, and slowly it spread across him. It did not have to end like that. His belief radiated towards his open palm. The flame intensified. It grew taller. He understood that it was his choice to make – never to surrender to despair. Resistance united them. Amo's fire soared brightly.

The virtual deportation of Kuan from the world of the living had blown Amo out of his head. It shot her towards the empty margins of Hades. At first she was relieved to find herself freed of the boy's mind, but very soon she realised it was his mental energy which had sustained her despite the prolonged exile from her home nebula. Desperately weakened she just managed to make her way to where she thought Kuan might be found. Fortunately the mere sight of her gave the boy such a lift that hope replenished them both.

Amo moved towards the blue dot in the middle of the cycloramic room. She sensed that underneath that point was the nerve centre of Schloss 22. She had been there before, when she got trapped during her exploration of Shiyan's data system via the electronic console in Kuan's room at Rook Mansion. Not realising she had stumbled into an isolated network that pulled her into Schloss 22, she became entangled in that system. It triggered a lock-down which held her captive until she managed to tell Kuan to send the blue falcon avatar to rescue her. The process freed her from Schloss 22, but resulted in her becoming stuck inside the boy's head, until now.

She believed she could work out how Schloss 22 functioned, if she had enough time. If she could stop the countdown to death-plus-one, she could turn her attention to getting them and the dungeonites released back to the world of the living. She had escaped twice from this facility. She should be able to do so again, and with that thought she disappeared below the surface.

Kuan stared anxiously as the flame vanished into the ground. Intentionally or otherwise she must have flicked some switches because the screen was lit up with images of Chengbao Island. He could see that the artificial dispensers of light and heat Amadeus had arranged to be placed on the island were accelerating the arrival of spring. Signs of renewed vegetation spread across the ground. A pair of white panthers marched Erica Lee, in a plain grey dress under her white doctor's coat, up a steep path until she was standing before the Curator, arms folded in front of him.

"Have you reached a decision, Dr. Lee?"

"We need more time."

"That's not an answer. I could just sever your jugular and be done with you, but I'm magnanimous and I want to give you all a chance to choose."

"This is not something any of us can decide lightly. You're asking us to give up being what we are."

The centaur lifted himself up high on his hind horse legs, while his front legs nearly kicked into Erica Lee's face. She took a couple of steps back but continued to glare unflinchingly at him.

"I'm giving you a chance to be a pure Shiyanese, to be a part of our great future, and you dare to treat it with such contempt!"

"I don't know who you are, or what you are …"

Kuan could see that Erica's reference to Amadeus' unusual form pumped anger into his blood red eyes.

"… but this island has been guaranteed to us as a sanctuary for Potokans, and we will build our new clinic here. Why don't you take your circus elsewhere and leave us alone, otherwise you'd have to answer to Chairman Dao."

"Dao, that fool, he's your protector? He spouts words of New Beginning, but he knows nothing of spirituality or purity. He's just a crass materialist. How he can protect you when he can't even get his own house in order?"

It was a shock for Kuan and the doctor to come across someone so dismissive of Dao whom few would dare defy.

"Do you know who offered me this island? Dao's trusted adviser, Governor Pui, right under the nose of your hoodwinked chairman. Pui respects my prophecy and he's been helping me ever since I was banished. He gave me the coordinates in Bastille to strike and secure more potential recruits, and he planned for me to take over Chengbao Island as the base to build my following. All he wanted in return was to be allowed, in a world of pure Shiyanese, to retain his peacock form. I can grant him that, for now."

"When Dao finds out, the navy will be here in no time. Your little army can hardly fight off gunboats and submarines."

"The navy is going to be kept busy with a few problems of their own. You need to accept a simple fact: you're at my mercy."

Amadeus stopped and leaned down towards Dr. Lee's face. He drew a deep breath and straightened his back again.

"Such fragrant vitality. How I've missed this world. And how it has missed me. This is your final ultimatum: by midnight tonight, stand with me and my followers on the narrow beach on the north side of this island, undertake your conversion to pure Shiyanese and you will be saved. Anyone standing elsewhere on the island will be banished to Schloss 22, better known to you as Hades. Don't waste time plotting an escape. You cannot reach the bridge to get off the island without coming through the north beach. Your pendants have been disabled so anyone trying to swim for it will freeze to death. If you want salvation, join me before the midnight hour is struck."

The Curator galloped away with a wave of white panthers in tow. The doctor stood motionless, overcome by the burden of having to relay the news to those who thought they had at long last found a home of their own.

They would seek her advice, but what could she say to them?

"Amo, we must help her."

His friend was too preoccupied with defusing the countdown to respond to him.

Kuan was working out a plan of his own. Amo would stop the countdown, giving them time to find a way to escape from Hades. They would go to Chairman Dao and tell him everything about the treacherous peacock who had been secretly plotting against him. With Amadeus turning everyone else into one of his submissive white panthers, there would be no mauve elephants left in the future, and Pui would have in his possession the only limited, but greatly enriched, stock of elephantium on which the whole of Shiyan would be dependent. In time he might even have the centaurian panther under his control. Only Dao could stop him before it was too late.

"Amo, how much longer before you can stop the countdown?"

Her voice came from below.

"Kuan, it's unlikely I can stop it. Amadeus did not build in a cut-out mechanism. The process cannot be reversed or slowed."

"There must be a way. He wouldn't put in place something like this. Imagine he starts the countdown and then finds for whatever reason he's stuck here himself. He must have thought about that and prepared a code or switch to stop it continuing."

"That is probably what a rational being would do. But how rational would you say the Curator is?"

" What else can we do? Can we destroy Schloss 22 so we're not frozen forever in that horrible moment just before death?"

"This construction is virtually indestructible."

"There has to be an alternative."

Amo did not respond.

Dr. Lee's despondent face gazed out of the screen. She pulled her red hair tightly back before releasing it with a disbelieving shake of the head. Hands in her pocket, she started to walk ahead, muttering to herself all the while. Kuan followed her around the cycloramic room.

"Erica" he gently called to her, but of course she could not hear him.

She paused and crouched down as half a dozen Potokans scurried up to her. Attempting her utmost not to reveal her distress, she explained to them what the strange centaur who had appeared from nowhere demanded of them. She asked them to gather everyone together for they needed to agree what they were to do before midnight.

Above Kuan, a pair of sparks clashed and shards of light splintered off. He looked up as bright lines scratched through the air around him.

"Amo, what's going on?"

A ray of solid light rose from the blue dot on the ground, with the living flame on top of it.

"Kuan, Amadeus did build in a supplementary mechanism for the countdown. If it detected any attempt to interfere with the countdown it would accelerate it. That's what has just happened."

"Accelerate?"

"We have about six hours left, taking us to just after midnight on Chengbao Island."

So if Erica Lee decided to reject the prophet and was sent to Hades, she and Kuan would barely have time with each other before their minds were sealed forever in solitary anticipation of imminent death.

Chapter 24

<u>Resurrection</u>

Bars of blue light knitted together like a bird's nest holding in its bosom the lost souls who, for their very different reasons in ending up in Hades, were now united in the dungeon for their final hours. The Potokans had initially been seduced by the Final Blessing and thought the Curator would give them a genuine second chance to make something decent of their lives. Unlike most of the other Potokans brought down to the Schloss, they balked at the offer to gain the supposedly superior form of a white panther in return for total submissiveness to every word and whim of Lord Amadeus. Their white eyes revealed their determination to retain their last strand of dignity.

By contrast, the quartet of ordinary Shiyanese in the dungeon were strolling around Bastille city centre when they were snatched by fanatical followers of the prophet and transported into Schloss 22. Many of the other abductees leapt at the chance of becoming white panthers since they were unlikely ever to move beyond level 2 or 3 in the Circles of Challenge. But these four detested the arrogance in assuming they would be grateful for the bulky panther form when they possessed such petite and delicate cat frames. By their aesthetic code, they turned their small but determined faces away from Amadeus.

The remaining cheetahs were on security duty in Bastille and got trapped in the course of trying to protect vulnerable Shiyanese. A few cheetahs, tempted by the new strength they would acquire, agreed to join the prophet, but these stood by their oath to serve Shiyan.

To this motley group of condemned prisoners, Kuan came to tell them the bad news. Countdown had been accelerated to complete in a few short hours. From then on, their minds would forever replay the single moment of impending nothingness. None of them, however, showed any emotion. He was surprised by their indifference. Again it was left to the Potokan who knew Kuan to explain to him.

"In our minds, we have long been dead. Trapped without any hope of release. In some ways, losing the last vestige of thought might even be an improvement on the present condition."

"Is there anything I can get you?" said the boy who was in no position to grant any last wish.

"No. The time has finally come."

He looked through the bars at the Potokan who had lay down on her side. She seemed genuinely free of angst.

"You're sure there's no way out of here that Amadeus might have mentioned or hinted at?"

"There is the ultimate reprieve."

Kuan excitedly darted forward and grabbed the bars which burnt his hands. He shook them furiously as though that would get rid of the searing pain. She sprang up to check on him, though staying well clear of the light barrier.

"Kuan, you're hurt."

Her kind voice was filled with soothing concern. He sheathed his hands under his arms.

"I'm fine. What's the 'ultimate reprieve'?"

"According to Amadeus, even the dungeonites could be pardoned. He has left just enough energy in the dungeon to transport us to his new base on Chengbao Island, so long as we agree to convert to pure Shiyanese. There are enough converters in here for us to become white panthers. And the moment the sensors pick up the emergence of such beings in here, we would be instantly released."

"So you submit to the conversion, even at this late stage, and you would be sent back to the world of the living?"

"But once we submit to it, we surrender ourselves to the commands of the prophet."

"You might be able to reject him *after* your conversion. That could be possible?"

"Would you give up your soul to the devil on the off chance you could sneak it back?"

"Not if you put it like that."

"Similarly there will be no ultimate reprieve. We are resolute about that, all of us."

Kuan could sense they would not change their mind.

"Why might the right way turn out to be the wrong way?"

"It's not always easy to see through the masks of those who seek to trick others into accepting their ploy. They tell you to go down one path, the right path, which actually leads to your undoing."

"Who began that saying? You're sure it has nothing to do with my father?"

"It's been around a long time. It's part of a bigger book. The original was long lost, but its ideas continued to be passed on."

"My father must have something to do with that book."

"Your father was a Potokan?"

Kuan was beginning to wonder about father's identity. Was he really human? He appeared to have sent secret messages to Agent Tan, and he might be responsible for Potokan sayings passed down many generations. His death was reported to him by no less a figure than Chairman Dao, but he was relying on a message from a submarine crew. They could be wrong. They could have lied.

"Could Potokans have human form?" asked Kuan.

"We acquire our form either through the transformation given to Shiyanese who fail to remain on the first Circle of Challenge, or from being born of those who have been thus transformed. As Potokans we could not change into any other form, certainly not human."

Kuan wanted to ask her more about the book when he saw a flicker in the corner of his eye. Amo needed him to assist her with some esoteric inspection she was carrying out. She gave him various instructions which he managed to carry out without comprehending what he was doing. He crawled around the arena, checked the wall panels in the purgoratory compartments, felt for secret switches along a series of dark passageways, before returning to the cycloramic room to report to Amo that he had found absolutely nothing. Was she just trying to distract him as the last few meaningful hours crumbled away?

"Kuan, you are sure?"

"I found absolutely none of the things you asked me to look for. I've double-checked."

"Then we have a chance."

"How can we have a chance when I've found nothing?"

"It means Amadeus is so confident that everything will go according to his plan that he made no contingency arrangement for any form of reversal. If we use what he has put in place to our ends, he cannot stop us."

"Amo, you have to explain to me what you have in mind."

She did not bother because Dr. Lee and the Potokans on Chengbao Island had appeared on screen as they prepared to tell the centaurian panther their decision. Kuan's eyes were fixed on Erica, standing under the dimmed glow of one of the heat-giving contraptions.

"We have discussed your offer carefully. A small number amongst us want to join you, but the rest of us can see no alternative but to stay true to ourselves and decline."

"Then you fools are going straight to eternal damnation."

As some of the Potokans scurried over to the Curator's side to be converted into faithful white panthers, the doctor drew a deep breath before responding. Calm courage filled her crystalline green eyes.

"Lord Amadeus, why don't we divide this island? You and your followers take the north side, and we'll confine ourselves to developing the new Oran Clinic in the south. You can show us how successful your way of life is, and if we fail to make much of ours, we suffer the consequences. There is no need to send us to Hades."

"Bargaining is the first sign of denial. Doctor Lee, you need to see that the very notion of comparing the New Beginning with anything else is flawed. My prophecy is incomparable because only my way is the right way, the true way. And it is part of that prophecy that all who reject me shall be banished to eternal damnation. The prophecy has to be fulfilled. But you can change your fate simply by joining me."

"Or you can change your prophecy? After all, everything depends on your decisions. Say that anyone not following you shall have to learn the consequences by themselves, and it will be so."

"And you will learn the consequences of your blind defiance, locked in your own head, staring over the precipice of death, forever. There is no way out of what I have proclaimed. The midnight hour is drawing near.

We will retire to the beach on the north side. Join us before it is too late for you. No one can escape the Schloss unless I will it."

Amadeus trotted away. A few of the newly converted glanced back at their former Potokan comrades as though they pitied them for not making the right choice. Soon they had all departed, leaving Erica Lee and the trembling cat creatures behind. They were struck by the gleaming white panther form that the converts had acquired, how it contrasted with their misshapen six-legged appearance. They braced themselves for the dreaded fate of Hades. The doctor stood amongst them, resigned to her inability to save those left in her charge yet again.

Kuan's moistened eyes could not look away. He could feel himself standing under an intensifying shower, each droplet wearing him further down. It was turning into heavy rain. He and father were returning from the town after another seemingly futile visit. No one wanted to be seen with them for long. Perhaps the boy was the problem, the adults kept staring at him suspiciously. Father could not deposit him anywhere safely though. The preacher was off sick, and the church door was locked. No sanctuary today. The clown and the rest of the circus were touring elsewhere. So he followed father everywhere until, disappointment etched on his face, the tired writer said it was time to head home.

They were not that far from the Chinese Chestnut trees when heavenly hoses unleashed a downpour so vicious that the ground which had been baked to a crisp dryness in the preceding weeks turned muddy almost instantaneously. Father opened his briefcase to check if his typescript was getting wet and water smudged the title page. They carried on trudging forward. He could not understand why father kept looking back nervously. The drumming of the rain would have drowned out any footsteps.

Father crouched down by the boy, holding his briefcase tightly to his chest. He said he wanted to protect him, but he had other responsibilities he could not neglect. He wished he could explain more but time was not on their side.

Wearing only his soaked through orange T-shirt and shorts, the sudden drop in temperature left the boy shaking uncontrollably.

Father passed the briefcase to his son, who was to take it home, put it in the study and then shut the door. He must not look inside the briefcase. It was for his own good that he knew nothing about what had been written. Father took off his gold-rimmed glasses and pointlessly wiped them in his shirt as the rain kept up its bombardment. He patted his son's arms to reassure him that everything would be alright.

The bespectacled man stood up and scanned furtively around. While he checked something out by himself, the boy must run ahead home and lock all the doors. No time for questions. He must just go and promise he would not look back. In obeying his father, did he desert him? The rain nearly washed all his energy away but he made it home. He slipped the briefcase into father's study and shut the door.

After drying himself he stared at the study's door debating with himself if he should have a peep at what father had typed up. Pros and cons battled valiantly. His mind liked the thought of a confrontation, but it was to be one between the Monkey King and the evil demons. Into his imaginary war the young hero vanished. By the time victory was beyond dispute, he was so tired he climbed onto his top bunk bed and stared at the comforting blankness of his ceiling. The rain had stopped, and soon it was like an oven in that little room of his. Night had fallen but it was too hot to sleep. Was father home already? He could not recall hearing him come in. Father would not forget the test he had planned for the boy the next day. Then there was that peculiar splash.

"Kuan, I need you to listen now."

Kuan turned to face Amo whose flame was shooting electrical sparks down to the column of blue light she was floating on.

"The transportation programme for exit and entry is extremely complex and would take months to override. But the designation for exit or entry is relatively simple."

The boy intensified his concentration, or so he thought, but was none the wiser.

"If I can switch the markers for what's to come and what's to go, I can get you out of here."

"Get me out of here? What about you?"

"Someone has to remain here to coordinate the switching."

"Then you'd be trapped here."

"Kuan, it's better than all of us being trapped. I want you to go and join the dugeonites now. If my plan works, all of you would be removed from here at midnight back to the world of the living."

"I'm not leaving without you."

"You go ahead first. I could find another way to join you later."

"No, Amo, we go together or not at all."

"Kuan, you know it is easier for me to deal with a world like this than you. I have escaped from the Schloss before. If you go, I can concentrate ..."

"You're right."

"I am?"

"Yes, in this world, there are all kinds of barrier I cannot cross. I've just remembered, the dungeon is protected by the light energy. I can't get past it, but you can easily slip through the gaps between the bars."

"But…"

She was reluctant to concede the point.

"Amo, you tell me what I have to do, then you go off to join the dungeonites. There's no need for both of us to stay."

"In that case, I should stay here too." Amo said.

"No, when you thought I could escape with the others, you insisted I should go with them. But now as I couldn't, you must accept that you should go with them. There's no point wasting your life as well as mine."

"It's different. If I agree to go, then you have no chance of getting out of here. Your brain can't work things out the way I can. That's a fact."

"Amo, be honest with me. You can talk me through how to coordinate the controls. You know I can do it and that would guarantee your escape. And once you're out of here, you will have all the time to work out how to rescue me. But if you stay, your mind would no longer function and that would be the end for both of us."

Amo could think of no counter-argument. She explained to Kuan what he must do which was in fact quite simple. He just had to press certain points on the ray of blue light rising from the centre of the cycloramic room in a specific sequence, and the switching Amo had planned would unfold. The boy demonstrated to her twice that he knew exactly what he had to do and urged her to join the dungeonites. She was about to say something but then quietly moved out of sight.

Kuan was all alone again. The departure of Amo left a void in him. He had no doubt she should leave when she had the chance, but it was like casting away a precious part of himself. Her mere presence had made him believe that he could put his life back together.

The final seconds were ticking away and he could see on the cycloramic screen blades of light slicing through the night sky above Chengbao Island. The Schloss was primed to strike. Kuan knelt down beside the thin column of blue light at the centre of the room. As if playing the clarinet at high speed, he ran his fingers up and down the solid ray of light pressing at the exact points he had learnt from his departed friend. Invisible signals fanned out from the electronic nerve centre. Imperceptibly, sets of codes were being switched.

He could see Amadeus on the north side of the island raising his euphoric panther head to the heavens. The prophet was poised to unleash the first of many lessons for unrepentant souls. To defy him was to succumb to eternal suffering. Everyone in Shiyan was about to learn that.

On the other side of the 360 degrees screen, Erica Lee and the Potokans at the opposite end of the island stared at the approaching lightning storm. Fear saturated their being, making their courage all the greater.

One of the elderly Potokans started reciting lines to those gathered: "Beware when the right way turns out to be the wrong way. When evil disguises itself, unmask the hidden. When evil threatens death, resistance is life. We will stand together. And oppression shall be overturned."

The chilling slashes of pure light intensified. Now the doctor and the rest of the Potokans joined in repeating those lines. Every phrase imbued Kuan with a warming sensation under his skin. Father's words. He knew them all along even if for some time he had forgotten them.

Spears of lightning cascaded from on high. Kuan watched Erica's eyes gently closing. A blinding flash. The entire screen was blanked out. Amo had warned that the countdown to death-plus-one would reach its end not long after the transportation programme was completed. He must not hesitate. The next set of points must be pressed in rapid succession.

The blinding light faded. Erica Lee's unbelieving eyes blinked, soon to be accompanied by a nervous smile. She and the Potokans had remained where they were on the island. The lightning had landed, not on them, but the north side of Chengbao. Where the Curator and his pure followers had stood, nothing but a charred circle was left. In that instant, the white panther creatures were torn into billions of particles, beamed through an other-dimensional portal and in micro-seconds reassembled inside Schloss 22.

Amadeus never suspected that the target areas would be switched. Worse still, as he and his acolytes were being reconfigured in the dungeon, the emergence of their 'pure' form caused the 'ultimate reprieve' sensors to register, as Amo thought they would, that the existing occupants of the dungeon had undergone a last minute conversion into white panthers. Automatically that triggered the release of the Potokan and Shiyanese prisoners to Chengbao Island just as Amadeus promised. By the time the astounded prophet and his followers were fully rematerialised in the dungeon, the former captives were gone, and no further exit was authorised.

The Curator needed time to reprogramme Schloss 22 to open up another escape route, but time was precisely what he did not have. In making the countdown to death-plus-one irreversible, he had sealed his own fate.

Kuan could see the plan had worked because the freed captives were seen on screen arriving out of nowhere next to Erica Lee and the joyfully relieved Potokans. In fact, joy and relief were filling the hearts of everyone on Chengbao Island, except for Dr. Lee, crouching down to listen to one of the released Potokans telling her about the young human who was their saviour. Proud emotions stirred in her only to be extinguished by the realisation that he was lost forever. A cold potion coursed through her veins.

For the boy, it was almost over. It could only be a matter of seconds. He heard a commotion nearing. Amadeus had broken out of the dungeon.

"Kuan, I should have known you would sabotage my plan. My kindness was once again my undoing. I should have strangled you before I left."

"You must stop the countdown to death-plus-one before it's too late for all of us."

"You fool, it's irreversible. What I put in place, no one can alter."

"Think, there has to be a way."

"The only thing left to do is to end your worthless life."

Kuan stepped backwards but there was no escape. Two white panthers leapt up and pinned him to the ground. Amadeus bent down to clutch his small neck. All he wanted to do was to crush that windpipe. But he and the two panthers were blasted back by a raging flame.

Kuan sat up and there was Amo aglow on his knee. Why didn't she go with the dungeonites when she had the chance? Why did she come back for him? The countdown was approaching its end point. The centaurian panther fell to his horse's knees, his union with the moment of death began to dawn on him. The face on every one of his followers was filling up with similar horror.

Kuan could hear his own thoughts slurring. But as his vision blurred, a transparent blue object flew into view. It was a falcon, an avatar, like the one he sent to rescue Amo all those months ago when she was held by a lockdown in what turned out to be Schloss 22. The blue falcon shot into Kuan, and a burst of energy radiated outward, tearing him apart. Was that the moment of final disintegration he was destined to focus on for the rest of eternity? His consciousness was gone.

Chapter 25

<u>Know Thyself</u>

From particles to particles. From nothingness to self. Elements of what he once was gravitated with accelerating momentum towards a single point. They collided, and out of the impact his form emerged. His purple tunic was torn and singed. Smoke drifted up to him. He could smell it. Never had burnt odour meant more to him. It was pungently real. He must have returned to the world of the living. But where exactly?

Somewhere on Chengbao Island perhaps? He must find Erica and tell her that he managed to escape after all. They could settle on the island together and build the new Oran Clinic with the surviving Potokans and the released Shiyanese. Tranquility at last beckoned. Then it occurred to him that Governor Pui might come after them once he discovered his plan with Amadeus had been thwarted. But without the Curator and Schloss 22, he would not be able to stand up to Chairman Dao. Once the Chairman discovered that the treacherous peacock had been lying and plotting against him, he would deal with him and no doubt clear Kuan of the murder he did not commit.

"Amo, where are you?"

It was dark and he could do with the brightness of his friend.

"Amo?"

She was close to him when the blue falcon struck him. She must have been transported back too. The force might have thrown her some distance away from him.

He cautiously crawled along what felt like a damp stoney floor. Pitch-blackness surrounded him.

"Amo! Tell me you're alright!"

His call echoed back but no reply.

What if she had been left behind? He berated himself for selfishly thinking about making a home on Chengbao Island when Amo was still unable to return to her home. She was certain that the room to the left in the vault down in the cellar of Rook Mansion would lead her back to where she belonged. It must be Kuan's duty to help her get there above all else. And if she had been left in Hades, he would have to find a way to go back for her. But who else apart from Amo knew how to escape from there? Agent Tan did manage to get messages to and from Hades, so he might help him figure out what he should do.

The more he tried to explore the possibilities, the more an invisible band seemed to tighten around his head. Too many thoughts to deal with.

"Amo, please show yourself!"

Loud echoes swept back at him, with a cold silence trailing. Fear of losing her began to creep up on him. He scanned the darkness, desperate now for a glimpse of the tiniest flame.

And a flicker appeared. It materialised in mid air and slowly descended before Kuan. It was not a flame, but a minute glass creature, with a glowing bulb of a head, and twitching fiberglass legs and wings. Like electric sparks, rapidly more popped into sight, until a large cluster of them lit up the semi-circular stone platform he was prostrate on. They were the fireflies of Castle de Potoka, and he was in the valley where he once disrupted the Final Blessing ceremony. The disruption broke down the light portal the Curator had used to lure Blessed Potokans into Schloss 22. Did Amo find a way to reactivate it so they could be transported back?

The radiant cloud of fireflies moved forward but then stopped to wait for Kuan to follow. He stood up in the middle of the platform and surveyed the deserted oasis. Ever since *FSS Castle* was taken into dry dock for inspection and repairs, all the Potokans had been evicted, most of them ending up on Chengbao Island with Dr. Lee. He realised there would not be a reunion for him with Erica any time soon, but the dock was on the edge of Bastille, and it would not be too difficult for him to take Amo to Rook Mansion – once he had found her.

If he followed the fireflies he might come across Amo or at least make his way out of the submarine to get help with a proper search for his friend. If he stayed, he would be stuck in the unremitting darkness he could still recall from the time he lived down in the subterranean deck.

The fireflies took off again and Kuan chased after them, calling out for Amo all the while. He refused to believe that she could have perished. Hades had taught him never to give up. Of course father had always tried to impress that on him.

For a long time father insisted that with effort he would discover a deep well of potential within him, to be drawn on in grasping and solving the many problems he would face in life. Yet for reasons unknown he could only rise ever so fleetingly above the fog, before sinking back into incomprehension.

As an alternative to facing up to his recurrent failings, he found diversion through games and imaginary battles. Most of the time he succeeded in losing himself completely. Every now and then, though, he felt that another part of him might surface to take charge. He would like to think that deep down he possessed intelligence beyond his age. If he applied himself, he might yet discover that his was more than the mind of an ordinary boy. He would work out a way to find Amo and safely return her to her home.

The fireflies bobbed rhythmically in their shimmering formation and led Kuan up the sloping path into a familiar tunnel. It was here he once bore witness to the Potokan who hammered his front paws into the wall, to prevent himself from succumbing to the draw of the Blessing. At least the Curator had now been locked away in the eternal suffering he had contrived for others. But Governor Pui was still at large. He must be exposed for his crimes.

Out of the tunnel he arrived at the small cavern where he and Amo first encountered the Potokans. What exactly was their connection with father? The writings he guarded so carefully were common knowledge amongst them. The words he determinedly typed out had been stamped into their consciousness, giving them strength in their moment of need to stand firm.

He thought he saw a movement ahead of him. He darted forward to feel for any sign of life on the ground. It was only a flickering shadow cast against inorganic rocks and crevices. The bramble of hope was as ever cutting to embrace.

Crestfallen, he followed the cloud of light into the narrow opening through which he walked out onto the vast cave that had been home to generations of downtrodden white-eyed, six-legged cats. The whole place had been stripped bare.

Fuelled by groundless suspicion of Potokan involvement in the murder of the mauve elephants on board *FSS Castle* – which was actually perpetrated by the Potokan-hating General Chi-Ling – the inspection process must have destroyed and removed what little vegetation there was in Castle de Potoka. It would never be habitable again. But why should anyone be forced to live at the bottom of a submarine their entire life?

At least the Potokans now had a chance to start a new life on Chengbao Island. Who could have foreseen that when Chairman Dao secured the agreement of the Council of Mauveans to give the island over to the

Potokans, the deceitful peacock was preparing for it to be turned into a base for the Curator to wage his deranged campaign against Shiyan. But how was Kuan to persuade the Chairman to see through Pui when Dao had previously trusted the governor's words over the boy's regarding the murder of Xian?

Persist and find a way. That was what father would say. Acquiescence in evil must not be tolerated. He could picture him slamming his papers down once when he railed against some news he had picked up. The face was still a blur, just those gold rimmed glasses were in focus. He thundered against the wrongs that were being done to the nameless victims. Kuan knew he must follow father's path. The threats could not be allowed to hide behind their masks any longer. They had to be exposed and the just cause pursued.

He had reached the steep slope leading up to the large crimson stone. He glanced back at the dark expanse behind him and resolved to return to look for Amo once he had reported Pui's treachery to the Chairman.

Wearily he completed the final part of his journey and climbed onto the crimson stone. He remembered where the concealed metal pad was to its side, but a code was needed. He keyed in various sets of digits. None of them worked. The light brigade overhead waited impatiently as their charge was running low.

There was the code he memorised for the trial: 'A4K8F9A1K'. There must be a reason why that had stayed in his head. He tapped it in and jumped down from the stone expecting it to move aside. Nothing. One of the fireflies swooped down to the metal pad and its fibreglass limbs pressed out the necessary code and Kuan could at last step inside onto the circular disc. It steadily rose upward until it reached the subterranean portal, through which he walked out to deck 4 of *FSS Castle*, where the black Chartreux cat was waiting for him.

"Agent Tan, I thought you were out hunting down General Chi-Ling."

"We're closing in on our prey as we speak."

"We're not in dock?"

"I located Chi-Ling's hiding place two weeks ago, and *FSS Castle* has been recommissioned to ensure we have enough fire power for the final assault."

Tan led the boy into a small room.

"Kuan, you've kept Amadeus in Hades?"

"He'll never be able to escape again."

He wanted to say that the credit should go to Amo but remembered she always wanted to keep her existence a secret from everyone else.

"I'm glad you found a way out yourself. I knew you would."

"Agent Tan, you must have helped with opening up some escape route?"

"What do you mean?"

"Since you could get in touch with me in Hades, I thought you were able to tamper with its system."

"Kuan, if I had the means of getting in and out of that place, I would have got rid of Amadeus long ago. Sending and receiving messages is one thing, but other than the self-proclaimed prophet, you're the only one who's ever been able to defy Hades."

The boy sat down on the bottom of two bunk beds and rubbed his eyes.

"Agent Tan, will you tell me now, is father still alive?"

"Who told you he was dead?"

"Chairman Dao."

"And did he see your father dead?"

"No, he got the information from one of your submarines."

"*FSS Knight*?"

"How do you know?"

"We're rendezvousing with *FSS Knight* soon. I can arrange for you to meet the crew and see who has evidence to back the claim that your father's dead."

"So you don't think father's dead?"

"He's alive as far as I'm concerned, unless there's clear evidence to say otherwise."

"When was the last time you heard from him?"

"A month or two ago? He was in hiding, and I've been off tracking down Chi-Ling, it's not conducive to communications. But your father is a very resourceful person. I see him in you."

High praise indeed for a boy whose abiding regret was being nothing more than a pale reflection of his father.

The Chartreux looked up at the timer on the wall.

"Kuan, you should get some rest. There are naval overalls and boots in the locker you can change into later. We've still got a lot to do, but your mission can soon be fulfilled."

Tan left. The boy was too tired to confess that he still did not know what his mission was. He climbed on to the top bunk and fell deeply asleep. In his dream he kept hearing Amo calling out to him. The flickering of her flame slowed to utter stillness and there she was alongside Amadeus and his flock of white panthers, forever locked in the split-second before death. He vaguely heard the door to his room slide open and then close. He told himself to believe that when he opened his eyes, he would see the small fire burning brightly. Slowly, he lifted his eyelids, fearful that reality and dreams would not mix together to produce the desired effect.

But his friend remained decidedly absent. The only thing to have entered the room was a tray of food. A bowl of soup noodles, assorted dishes of dumplings, and plenty of sweet buns for dessert. Melancholy was no cure for hunger. He jumped off the bunk bed and dived in with his chopsticks. It had been a long while since he had a proper meal. On a full stomach his rational prowess could reach astounding levels. Maybe he could surprise himself one more time and work out what he should be doing next.

Fed and changed into his naval outfit, Kuan left his room to look for Agent Tan. He was pondering which corridor he should take when he heard his name called out. It was Captain Ma, once more in his resplendent uniform, who clasped him on both arms.

"Good to see you, Kuan. Tan told me about your latest exploit. You're quite the escapologist."

"Captain Ma, the Admiralty has put you in charge again?"

"They were getting very nervous about Chi-Ling remaining at large. President Zhou herself said there must be no more delay in bringing the renegade in. So the old *Castle* is back in action again. Dr. Lee put me in quite a quandary when she sent us a distress call about Amadeus landing on Chengbao Island. Should we go to her or stay on course and deal with Chi-Ling first? But then we got another message to say that you had saved the day. Dr. Lee was devastated when she thought you had sacrificed yourself in the process."

"Can you tell her I got out of Hades after all? There's no need for her to be upset."

"I've sent a message to her reflector already, and she was overjoyed to hear the news."

To think that he was happily in Erica's thoughts gave Kuan a sense of warm contentment.

Ma fumbled in his pockets. He pulled out his pipe with one hand and retrieved a gleaming rectangular object with the other. He handed the latter to Kuan. It was the size of a playing card with the thickness of about half a deck, light and encased in iridium.

"Xian asked me to give this to you."

"When did you see her? You know it was Governor Pui who killed her?"

"Agent Tan told me. Don't ask how he knows. Poor Xian, her father asked me to look out for her. You remember Lord Ou-Yang, a great Shiyanese. Once I found out the Admiralty wasn't going to court-martial me after all, but was giving me back the command of *FSS Castle*, I went to see her. I told her my chief engineer was needed again, but she was determined to finish the project she was working on for Chairman Dao. You can't talk to her if she's got her mind set on something. She wouldn't listen to me either about visiting her father. Not that he would have wanted that. They were both awfully stubborn. But as I was leaving, she gave me this and made me promise I'd get it to you if anything should happen to her. I asked her if she suspected she was in some kind of danger, but she just said it was essential to have a back-up plan. Do you know what it's all about?"

Kuan held up the silver card and ran his fingers across its plain surface. A back-up plan? Minute sparks weaved between fingertips and the iridium. Electrical pulse surged up his arm to splinter across the back of his head.

"I think this has something to do with the Sun Disc."

"Are you sure? Can you use it to get more power into our engine core? Ever since the Sun Disc was launched, our entire fleet has been converted to this enriched elephantium. On the plus side, we don't need mauve elephants as 'special' guests to accompany every voyage we take anymore. Each consignment of enriched elephantium's supposed to last the entire mission – and the Admiralty has to pledge millions of hours more to Plutopia – but it's not as enriched as it's made out to be. I thought the Sun Disc was supposed to channel energy to us directly, not making us depend even more on elephantium."

"That was Governor Pui's doing. Xian found out and he killed her."

"Kuan, once we've captured Chi-Ling, we'll deal with Pui."

The boy looked at the pristine corridors.

"So you've dispensed with using outsiders for collecting elephantium?"

"On our subs, yes, but with the Potokans gone, outsiders are sent to work on extracting and transporting enriched elephantium."

"Will I be sent there too?"

"Of course not, look at you, you're one of us now."

The Chartreux cat appeared without a sound from behind them. He spoke gravely.

"Captain Ma, we've reached the rendezvous point. The Captain of *FSS Knight* wants to speak with you."

Ma put his pipe in his mouth for a couple of seconds and removed it again. He pressed a button on the wall and it lit up in red.

"*FSS Knight*, this is Captain Ma of the *Castle*. Have you located Chi-Ling?"

A deep female voice replied through the loudspeaker.

"This is Captain Fei, *FSS Knight*. We've done better than locating the traitor. We've captured him. Our order is to place him in your custody so you can proceed with interrogation on your way back to Bastille."

Ma's face lit up with delight. He had fought enough sea battles in his long naval career. He was content to take responsibility for an important but relatively simple delivery job. Agent Tan's copper brown eyes tensed with vicious intent. He would be in charge of the interrogation. The semi-morphed tiger general had tried to frame him for the capital offence of murdering Mauveans.

"Captain Fei, that's excellent news. You must tell me how you caught the general when I come over with a team to collect the prisoner."

"Another time, Captain. I've already dispatched a submersible to bring Chi-Ling to you. In return can you have ready for us the prisoner we've been assigned to take into custody?"

"What prisoner are you talking about?"

"Captain Ma, we've been informed that you have the fugitive Kuan on board. Admiralty has instructed us to take him to Vice-President Dao."

"I have received no such instruction."

"You can check with Admiralty yourself, if you wish. Having just narrowly escaped one court-marshal, it's not advisable to disobey a direct order."

"Captain Fei, your concern is appreciated. I *will* confirm with Admiralty their instruction."

"Thank you, Captain Ma. Once Chi-Ling has been handed to you, please be sure Kuan is handed to us."

Ma pressed the button again and its red light went out. He wiped his forehead with the back of his hand.

"Tan, what should we do? We can't hand Kuan over to them. He would just be locked up somewhere else without trial. Who would have leaked his whereabouts to Fei?"

"The moment he came through the subterranean portal it would have registered with Admiralty central. But no one would look at such information on the vast database unless someone was tasked specifically with tracking Kuan."

"I'll get on to Admiralty to clear this up."

"All communications with headquarters are being jammed. You should refuse to let the *Knight*'s submersible dock."

"Captain Ma," interjected Kuan, "let them take me to Chairman Dao. I'll tell him what Amadeus said about Governor Pui's plot. This time I'm not the only witness."

Ma would not hear of it. He did not share the boy's faith in the Chairman's judgement.

An onboard siren sounded. The submersible was approaching the docking station off deck 1 of *FSS Castle*. The three made their way to the upper deck, still arguing what they should do about the request to hand Kuan over.

The docking station was no more than a narrow passage leading from the outer hatch. Two cheetahs from the security team were there to seize Chi-Ling upon his delivery into Captain Ma's custody. Ma put his pipe away, brushed his silver mane back, and stepped over the threshold into the tight docking space. He told Tan he could not turn the submersible away and jeopardise the priority mission of holding Chi-Ling pending trial. But he agreed Captain Fei's team would have to return to *FSS Knight* without Kuan. If Admiralty had really issued an order for Kuan's capture, he would deal with the matter himself.

Kuan was told to stay clear of the docking station in case Captain Fei's team was tempted to snatch him. He looked on from a distance at Captain Ma, arms behind his back, rocking on the heel of his feet, waiting for the submersible to dock.

The boy whispered to Agent Tan about the opportunity it would give him to question the crew of *FSS Knight* about his father if he were taken into their custody. The cat wearily closed his eyes and assured Kuan that if he were taken into custody on board the *Knight*, he would be the only one questioned. With a shudder he remembered what happened when he was first dragged on board *FSS Castle*.

The light in the docking station turned green. The submersible was locked onto the outer hatch. Captain Ma nodded to the cheetah guards by his side and stepped up to open the hatch. Kuan stared from outside awaiting the sight of the general whose ruthless duplicity knew no bounds, going so far as killing his own lieutenant when the snow tiger Sung had the temerity to suggest that Chi-Ling should fulfill his promise of letting the boy go after Kuan had saved their lives.

The outer hatch swung back. Ma waited. The cheetah guards growled uneasily. No one emerged from the submersible. The captain cautiously took a look inside. He leapt back and shouted "get out!"

The submersible exploded. The blast rocked the whole of *FSS Castle*. It devastated the docking station. Water flooded in. The cheetahs were killed instantly. Captain Ma, barely alive, was trapped under a pile of debris. The gushing fluid jerked him to consciousness only for him to experience the ebbing away of what little life there was left in him. He was choking on the water he was confusingly gulping in.

"Close the hatch, Kuan!"

He was so transfixed he didn't seem to hear the Chartreux shouting at him. There it was, the image of Captain Ma, submerged in water, lungs leaching out air bubbles, eyes blanked out excruciatingly by suffocation. Kuan couldn't look away, let alone move.

The water was lapping across the threshold of the docking station. A dark shape dashed past the boy. The hatch door was slammed shut, the wheel rapidly turned to lock it tight. Agent Tan had morphed into human form wearing a black and green camouflage uniform, with a balaclava revealing only his eyes. But Kuan knew those eyes.

Chapter 26

<u>Battle Station</u>

"Attention! This is Agent Tan. We're under attack from *FSS Knight*. Captain Ma is dead. Fire on the enemy sub. When they take evasive action, pull us away with all the engine power we've got. I'm on my way to the control room."

Kuan, in a daze, followed Tan. The shock of witnessing Ma's death was compounded by Tan's transformation into a figure with familiar eyes he was more accustomed to seeing behind smudged lenses. It could be no more than a case of similarity.

Presumably the Shiyanese could morph their features any way they liked so long as they were associated with a form they were entitled to, having reached the necessary level in the Circles of Challenge. If Tan had been in contact with a certain man, he might subconsciously adopt some of his features when he took on the human form. Were there other explanations for that? He would have to ask Tan.

Agent Tan had more pressing matters to deal with. The explosion in the docking station had damaged *FSS Castle*, though not as badly as it could have been. *FSS Knight* had opened its torpedo tubes with the apparent intention of finishing off the *Castle* when it had been destablised. But it did not count on the instant counter-offensive Tan launched, and it had to turn away rapidly to avoid being blown apart. That gave the *Castle* just enough time to accelerate in the opposite direction.

In the control room, Len-Wu, the former security chief who had been promoted to second in command for this mission informed Tan of the loss of life they had suffered besides Ma and the two guards. Water had flooded the section underneath the docking station and claimed another thirteen victims before the area was sealed off. Len-Wu shook his lion head. He had switched into a semi-morphed form with his human body bulging under a blue naval tunic. Although with Ma's death, he was now formally in charge of the *Castle*, the agent was the leader of the taskforce to capture Chi-Ling, and he must follow Tan's orders.

"Agent Tan, are you sure the explosion was instigated by *FSS Knight*? They have moved steadily away from us."

"Len-Wu, they sent the bomb to us on their submersible. They wanted to eliminate us before they turn their attention to something else. How quickly can we turn back and catch up with them?"

"At current speed, twenty minutes at least. But once they have detected us, they are capable of accelerating to go twice as fast, and we would never catch them. Or worse, they could turn round and come after us. I don't think we can outrun them a second time."

Len-Wu stared at the monitors tracking *FSS Knight*'s movement.

Tan paced up and down. Determination raged in his eyes.

"Len-Wu, this is Chi-Ling's doing. *FSS Knight* didn't capture him, he captured them."

"That's not possible. How could he and his bedraggled platoon outgun one of our Class A submarines?"

"He didn't capture them in a fight. He turned them with some treacherous promise no doubt. A chance for greater naval glory, or rapid promotion in the military hierarchy."

"But he's not in a position to promise any such things." The semi-morphed lion observed.

"Depends what he's been promising. My sources tell me that at least half a dozen generals could throw in their lot with Chi-Ling should he return to Bastille and call for a change of government. He has fewer supporters in the navy but it would appear that Captain Fei has turned out to be one of them."

Kuan stood to one side observing Tan in his human form. He was still shaking from the explosion he had just witnessed. He could do nothing about the drowning of Captain Ma. Then came that moment when Tan stared at him through the narrow slot of his balaclava. The height, the physique, they were just improbably similar. That would explain so much, how he knew the watermark of the sun, what had been written in secret. But other questions came to mind. He just needed a couple of seconds to ask him directly.

Len-Wu pulled Tan over to the monitors.

"They're heading for the surface."

"Len-Wu, turn us around. We must stop them. Send them a warning message."

"They're not responding. We can't be sure they were responsible for the explosion. Someone could have planted a bomb on the submersible without their knowledge."

"If they were not behind it, why have they gone into radio silence?"

Len-Wu ordered the crew to do as Agent Tan instructed. *FSS Knight* continued to ignore all communications sent from the *Castle*. It increased its speed which meant that the damaged submarine had no chance of catching up with it.

"Agent Tan, it's leveling off beneath the surface. They're holding the depth which would keep them safe from any aerial fire. Are they expecting an attack from the air force?"

"They're holding that depth because that would be close enough to the surface to launch their long range missiles."

"Who could they be attacking?"

"Len-Wu, who does General Chi-Ling hate above all?"

"Potokans."

"And are they not all conveniently gathered now on Chengbao Island? A perfect target."

"We can never get to them in time."

"Is communication with Admiralty still jammed?"

"We're on our own."

"We must surface ourselves."

"That would make us vulnerable to their torpedo attack."

"Len-Wu, have our anti-missile rockets ready. As soon as their missiles surface, I want them shot down."

"Agent Tan, you know that at best we have a 20% chance of destroying their missiles once they have been launched."

"We'll destroy their missiles, and we'll destroy them too unless they surrender."

Kuan wished there was something he could do. The idea that Erica Lee and the Potokans were at last safe from the mad prophet, Amadeus, had been the one consoling thought for him. Now he had to helplessly witness their extermination. Agent Tan in his bellicose human form might be incapable of contemplating failure, but even the boy could see that there was no way *FSS Knight* could be prevented from annihilating life on Chengbao Island.

Tan caught Kuan's eyes. He understood his anxious concern for the doctor, but he knew there was more on his mind. The monitors were bleeping furiously with incoming signals. The agent bent down and whispered to him.

"Kuan, we're almost there. Let's deal with Chi-Ling first. We can then make sure your mission is completed."

The boy stared into those dark unfathomable pupils.

"Agent Tan, are you my father?"

"There's something you need to understand, Kuan."

Len-Wu called for Tan. *FSS Castle* had surfaced just in time as missiles from the enemy sub burst out from the ocean's face and soared skyward. Tan authorised the full deployment of their anti-missile arsenal. The four rogue missiles were already surging away imperiously. A battalion of *Castle*'s rockets closely harangued them. Kuan could not bear to watch the monitors, but he heard Len-Wu confirming that one of the missiles had been downed. There was faint hope they could stop any of the remaining three. But the anti-missile rockets did not give up on the chase. Against the odds, one of those rockets clipped the tail of its prey, causing it to veer from its course, and even more fortuitously crashed into a second missile. The resultant explosion left just one of the *Knight*'s missiles still in flight.

"Len-Wu, why have we stopped firing?"

"It's out of our range. There's nothing more we can do."

"How long before it lands on Chengbao Island?"

As the lone surviving missile reached the pinnacle of its trajectory across the blackened sky, the denizens on Chengbao far below were still celebrating their escape from the gruesome fate the psychopathic Curator had planned for them. They would have been added to his eternal collection of living corpses if not for the bravery of the boy who, according to an earlier communiqué from Captain Ma, managed to break out of Hades too just in time.

Erica Lee glanced up at the sunless firmament, contemplating a happy reunion with Kuan in the not too distant future. Together they would not only set up and run the new Oran Clinic, but would help the Potokans build their own home on the island. The sea breeze brushed her long red hair back and gently caressed her face of hope and contentment.

The missile had commenced its final journey.

Kuan clutched his own hands tightly, flesh squeezed without mercy. He had to be prepared for the pain.

"Len-Wu, haven't you got a readout for the time to impact?"

The semi-morph's lion face contorted in disbelief.

"Agent Tan, it's not heading towards Chengbao Island."

"Are you sure?"

Kuan opened his eyes, but the signals on the monitors meant nothing to him.

"Len-Wu, if Chengbao's not the target, where's it going?"

"Tan, it's heading for northern Bastille, the Presidential Building."

President Zhou and Vice President Dao were meeting there to announce their intention to run for a second term.

Tan slammed on the button for the communicator.

"Captain Fei, this is Agent Tan of *FSS Castle*. Whatever Chi-Ling has said to you, you must self-destruct the missile now. I can guarantee you a full pardon. Otherwise there's no way back from high treason."

Momentary silence was broken by a response from *FSS Knight*. But it was not the voice of Captain Fei.

"Tan, this is General Chi-Ling. I would like to inform you that Captain, and soon-to-be Admiral, Fei, is busy preparing her next mission. Nothing can save President Zhou or Chairman Dao now. They were given a chance to reinstate me, but instead they persisted with coming after me, when everything I've done is for the good of Shiyan. They have only got themselves to blame. But you, Agent Tan, have one more chance to save yourself and your crew. Hand Kuan over to me, and I'll let the rest of you go free."

The agent stepped back impassively. Len-Wu shook his head as his muscular frame was deflated. The flashing dot denoting the Presidential Building had vanished from the screen.

"Tan, in case you missed it, there's just been a change of government. If you don't want to be tried for treason, send the human boy to me at once."

"General Chi-Ling, I'll send him over in a submersible. Would you like to gather at your docking station and wait for him?"

"Humour in the face of adversity. I could use someone like you on my staff. Put Kuan on a life raft, and move out of our mutual firing range. Once it's clear that neither of us can cause any damage to the other, I'll have the boy picked up. Do this right, Tan, there might even be a promotion in it for you."

Kuan walked up to Agent Tan, who pulled the boy close to him.

"Captain Len-Wu, *FSS Knight* has locked its torpedoes on us, hasn't it?"

"Tan, if we didn't comply with Chi-Ling's demand, we would be fired on."

"In that case, we have no choice."

"What about negotiating with Chi-Ling? Offer me as a hostage instead."

"Len-Wu, they don't want the boy as a hostage. They want to kill him."

"There must be another way."

"You can't negotiate with a treacherous murderer like Chi-Ling. Unless he gets what he wants, he won't have any compunction about killing all of us."

The masked agent held Kuan tightly.

"Len-Wu, get a life raft ready."

With all natural light blocked by the Sun Disc, the sea was frozen over except for the vicinity where the two submarines had manoeuvred in close proximity to each other. In that clearing was left a rubber life raft and its well wrapped occupant. *FSS Castle* closed its hatch and dived below. Once it reached the requisite safety distance, *FSS Knight* surfaced. Its guns emerged at its side, turned towards the life raft, and delivered a barrage of fire until shreds of rubber and body parts were left floating on the dark water.

Before the *Castle* left the raft behind, Agent Tan said these words to Kuan:

"Sacrifices have to be made when there is no alternative. When there is no other means of stopping the strong destroying the weak, preventing the ruthless from crushing the defenceless, it is then up to us to step in and resist to the end. Someone very close to me once risked his life in order to help others fight against an enemy so evil that they did not only hurt him physically, they destroyed his mind. I promised him the fight would continue, wherever it took me. And no matter how long it takes, I'm going to make him whole again. I know you understand what it is to sacrifice yourself when the cause is just. You were prepared to do it in Hades, and you would not hesitate to do it again. That means you are ready."

Kuan watched the life raft lowered into the water. Tan wrapped a thick blanket around the shivering boy.

"Agent Tan, I've been wanting to tell you. I have no idea what my mission is. You kept saying father wanted me to carry out a mission. But I don't know what it is."

"You knew once."

"When?"

"You'll remember again."

"Father told me, did he? And he's still alive?"

Tan straightened his balaclava so he could stare clearly into Kuan's eyes.

"We have to believe he's still alive. We can't give up now."

"When can I see my father's face again?"

"It won't be long now."

"Agent Tan, you're not my father, are you?"

"Kuan, have you ever wondered who really is your father?"

"Who are you then?"

"You should ask yourself the same question."

The *Knight* loomed over the flotsam swaying on the sea's chilled surface. The scent of dismembered flesh and blood spread through the gentle waves alerting fish of all sizes of a ready meal. General Chi-Ling stepped out onto the bridge and inspected through a pair of binoculars his latest accomplishment.

A hand, a leg, and the torso with the head still attached. The head of Captain Ma.

"Fei!" the tiger general roared, "find *FSS Castle* and destroy it!"

As *FSS Knight* was preparing to dive, its antagonist had been moving away at speed. If the *Castle* could get to the central naval defence zone off the Bastille coast, other submarines would come to its rescue, assuming they had not all defected to Chi-Ling's side.

Tan handed Captain Ma's pipe to Kuan, who placed it in the empty torpedo tube. Len-Wu fired it into the solemnity of a sepulchral ocean. They bowed their heads. Whether Ma's crew would survive him for long now depended on if there was enough fuel left to help them outrun their pursuer.

Having followed Tan back to the control room, Kuan quietly reflected on the agent's words. Who was father? Who was his son? Incoherent thoughts were cutting through his brain. Blistering sensations were erupting. Phantom of a life adrift like a thousand jigsaw pieces. Glimpses of a lamented past, echoes of a familiar voice, hints of repressed memories, swirled around too quickly. He sat down in a corner, with hands to his head.

Tan, arms folded, scrutinised the three dimensional map projected in front of him. Shiyan's Navy built artificial caves near the ocean floor for their submarines to hide in special circumstances. Each sub would have its own designated hideouts which would be unknown to others in the fleet. Could the *Castle* reach one of its assigned caves before *FSS Knight* had caught up with them?

Len-Wu insisted they had no choice but to try. The enemy boat was gaining on them, and their own fuel was running low. The agent accepted his proposal to steer their submarine into the first hideout they could access.

FSS Castle came to a complete rest in a vast underwater cavern, invisible to any surveillance from above. Its perfect tranquility contrasted with the turmoil bubbling up in Kuan's head.

Tan and Len-Wu stood immobilised, awaiting fate's decision. *FSS Knight* approached. It sailed over the cavern. No one was noticing the agony on the boy's face. What he would give to crawl under a rock and be left alone. Father was all he had. The one person he could leave everything to so that he would not have to worry about a thing. He could be the young boy, playing his games, battling in his imaginary adventures. But without the father he was always counting on, he would have to face up to it all on his own. It was too much to ask of him.

The enemy sub was circling and coming back. Its torpedo tubes were opened. Chi-Ling knew exactly where they were hiding.

Tan put his hand on Len-Wu's mountainous back.

"It's time, old friend."

The semi-morphed lion understood. The two subs were locked in a showdown. Torpedoes on both sides were ready to be fired. *FSS Castle* surged forward. The *Knight* accelerated. They unleashed their destructive power on each other. Two deadly archers racing towards one another, shooting and dodging arrows with fatal intent. The *Knight* weaved through the assault it faced and came through unscathed. Its prey took one explosive puncture in its side. By the time the damaged sections were sealed off, nineteen more of *FSS Castle*'s crew were dead.

The *Knight* had managed to turn round and resume firing. A series of near-hits forced the *Castle* to swerve onto an unacceptable course.

"Len-Wu, it's a trap."

"I know, Tan, but if we deviate even by a single degree either way, we would be hit."

"But this course is taking us to the Charybdis Vortex. The *Castle* will be torn apart."

"We haven't got enough power to outrun them."

"There must be something we can do." Tan enquired in desperation.

"If Xian were still with us, maybe. But our only chance now is to run through the vortex and hope for the best."

Len-Wu knew there was no hope except for a swift death. *FSS Castle* was heading towards certain doom. The vortex might just offer a quicker exit than drowning in a slowly sinking sub. Kuan dropped to the floor and pulled out the iridium card Xian had asked Captain Ma to pass to him. His fingers danced involuntarily over the gleaming face while dots of light flashed in sequence. He could visualise lines connecting the Sun Disc to the hunted submarine.

[That would bring the sun's energy down to us.]

It was that serious young girl's voice, inside his head.

K: Amo, is that you?

[I thought the transportation out of the Schloss might fuse me into your brain again. I didn't anticipate that it would almost obliterate me completely.]

K: Is it really you? How do I know I'm not just talking to myself?

[Kuan, the blue falcon you saw, that was the same avatar you used to rescue me when I was trapped in the Schloss. The entire sequence was in the system's memory. I managed to get it to replay the programme to get us released.]

He did not bother with pressing Amo to explain how that was supposed to have worked. He was just ecstatic to find her alive.

K: But you're stuck in my head again?

[We know that's not necessarily permanent. For now, we've got to save *FSS Castle*.]

K: We can't get away from Chi-Ling. We haven't got enough fuel.

[The Sun Disc has absorbed all we need.]

K: You think the Sun Disc can be made to send some of the sun's power directly into our energy converter?

[By my calculation that is perfectly feasible.]

Sparks flew from Kuan's hand before he pressed down decisively on the iridium card. Out of the shrouded atmosphere far above them, a beam of concentrated energy shot down from the Sun Disc, burning a tube of steam through the sea, missing the port side of *FSS Castle* by just a few metres. It blasted a crater in the seabed and the repercussion violently rocked the submarine.

Len-Wu and Tan were thrown onto the ground where they instinctively morphed into their respective lion and Chartreux forms. The lion rose, recovering his semi-morphed shape, and rallied the crew to stabilise the boat. The black cat tumbled towards the boy and in the blink of an eye resumed his camouflaged human appearance.

"Kuan, what are you doing on Xian's back-up control card?"

"Am … I am trying to direct the Sun Disc to send solar power into our energy converter."

"That would melt us down!"

[He's right. This submarine is not robust enough to withstand a direct injection of power of that magnitude. And we haven't got time to rebuild the engine to receive an external solar boost.]

"What else can I do?"

Tan thought and then his eyes lit up.

"Melt *them* down. Target *FSS Knight*."

The agent then turned to Captain Len-Wu.

"How much longer before we breach the safety limit for the vortex?"

"Seven minutes."

"Tell Chi-Ling to back off within two minutes, and steer us away in three."

"What if they don't back off?"

Tan crouched down to Kuan.

"We can't let them destroy us. It's up to you now."

Len-Wu shouted out across to them.

"Chi-Ling is not responding! All their torpedoes are locked on us."

The boy knew what he must do.

Kuan walked up to the monitor showing the position of *FSS Knight*. Complex calculations flashed through his mind. Electrical impulses flowed between him and the iridium card. There was no response from Chi-Ling. Kuan pressed down and executed the command.

The orbiting Sun Disc took aim and hurled its radiant spear through the air, drilling into the sea, piercing the armour of its unbelieving prey. Searing heat cut deep into the *Knight*, severing its bow along with its weapons. Fatally wounded, it drifted too close to the clutches of the Charybdis Vortex. Its propellers screamed in vain.

General Chi-Ling delivered a defiant speech for posterity. Outraged that he could go down in history as a traitor, the semi-morphed tiger roared out that the truth must not be concealed. He had done nothing but obey orders. His final moments were duly recorded and transmitted to his would-be vindicator. Proclaiming that he was from first to last an honourable soldier, he saluted his troops, and they followed him to an ignominious death.

Chapter 27

In the Name of the Sun

Sheets of ice were unceremoniously cast aside. Like a blue whale having at last outpaced its predator, *FSS Castle* wearily rose to the surface. Winter should have given way to spring by now if the Plutopian Sun Disc had not blocked off all sunlight and diverted solar energy into the enrichment of elephantium. The new climate had certainly enriched the mauve elephants, getting a thousand times the pledges for the same old bowel movement.

For those who could afford to keep an energy pendant, life was just about tolerable, though only the most well-pledged could expect to get hold of enough warmth and light to ever experience again a gentle, sunny day. For the rest, existence was cold, dark and short.

The open deck of the *Castle* was lit up by rows of light along each side. An unforgiving coldness filled the air. Len-Wu, now donning the captain's jacket, stood in front of his assembled crew – in their diverse Shiyanese forms. They were gathered to pay their last respect to those who had fallen in the battle with *FSS Knight*. One by one, the encased heroes were claimed by the deferential waves carrying them to their final resting place fathoms below.

Kuan stayed at the back with Agent Tan, who was barely visible in his black and green camouflage uniform. Now the task of dealing with General Chi-Ling had been irrevocably concluded, command of *FSS Castle* lay fully with Len-Wu. The agent's most important undertaking, however, was yet to be fulfilled. He had taken the boy so far. He must ensure Kuan has the opportunity to work the rest out for himself. Success or failure hung on the capacity of his mind to grasp the truth which would be unspeakably painful for him.

Stoic and dignified, the lion face of Len-Wu bowed low in silence until the last of the burials at sea had finished. He slowly raised his head.

"Today we have bidden farewell to comrades-in-arms who gave their lives to defeat a traitor against Shiyan. It is fitting that we should also remember a former member of *FSS Castle* who also lost her life because she stood up against another who betrayed the trust Shiyan placed in him. Chief Engineer Xian was known to all of us as a dedicated and outstanding naval officer. She discovered that the Sun Disc she helped to develop for Plutopia to bring energy to all Shiyanese was subverted to gratify the greed of a few, and in trying to rectify it she was brutally killed by someone I will bring to justice. Before she died, she entrusted the task of shutting down the Sun Disc to Kuan. But he was falsely accused of her murder and sentenced to Hades. Thankfully he has returned to us."

Len-Wu beckoned Kuan to join him. The boy walked up to the captain, and took out Xian's back-up iridium control card. His hand followed Amo's invisible guidance. Bright charges erupted from the glistening metal, launching signals which flew through the stratosphere to burrow into the central processing unit of the Sun Disc. The order to shut down was issued.

The Disc glowed a deep red as countdown commenced. The entire crew stared skyward. Winter's reign had long exceeded its mandate. A final confirmation had to be given with ten seconds left. Kuan glanced up at the captain, who nodded to him, and he keyed in Len-Wu's name. The process was complete.

The usurper in the heavens began to fade and drift out of its orbit. The long eclipsed star stretched out its rays. Shafts of glorious light sliced through frozen blackness. Ubiquitous ice began to sweat profusely and loosen its grip on vulnerable life. Warmth was racing across space to grace the world once more with its desperately missed presence. Echoes of joy could be heard across Shiyan, from *FSS Castle* off the west coast to Chengbao Island in the east. There was rejoicing everywhere, except in the Council of Mauveans. The sun's exile was over.

Kuan moved to the edge of the open deck and sat down. The biting wind was mellowing into a gentle breeze. It was time to sort out his priorities.

K: Amo, let's work out how we'll get you home.

[What about your mission?]

K: That can wait. I must get you home first.

[You have to complete your mission if you and your father are ever to be reunited.]

K: Why do you say that?

[Wasn't Agent Tan trying to tell you that your father's in trouble, and he needs your help.]

K: I don't know what he was trying to tell me. Why did he ask me to think about who father was?

[And who you are.]

K: I know who I am. And father is a writer, always typing away, day and night. We used to live a very simple life together. Then we were split apart. What else is there to know about us?

[It may come to you eventually. What is not obvious at first can suddenly become unmistakably clear. You just have to keep looking.]

The sun continued to ascend towards its midday apotheosis while majestically proclaiming its restoration. Warm air groomed gleaming white clouds passing over their reflections on the mirror afloat the ocean surface.

K: What is it I'm supposed to see? I'm who I am, though I'm told I could be much more. It's like staring at clouds. You can see whatever you want to see.

[The clouds in my world are not visible, but they can cause a lot of interference. Sometimes we have to wait patiently for them to pass over.]

K: I can try to be patient, but only father can clear all this up. Until then I must help you get home.

[How are we going to get to Rook Mansion?]

K: I'm sure we can find something suitable from the selection of transporters on board this submarine.

[I couldn't find a way round the emotion-scanner last time to open the vault.]

K: Chairman Dao's gone now. We'll have more time to find another way into the vault if necessary.

[If ultimately we cannot get into the vault, you will agree not to pursue it anymore?]

K: If we cannot find a way into the vault between us, I will ask Agent Tan to help me blow it open. Amo, you're going home. The nebula you're from is definitely behind that door on the left in there?

[Of that I'm certain.]

He casually moved his fingers over the iridium card.

[Stop. Xian has hidden something here.]

K: What is it?

[Encryption codes to protect what she didn't want erased, and codes she had stealthily copied to unravel secrets of a suspected enemy.]

K: What secrets have you found?

A few long seconds passed and her voice returned.

[You must talk to Agent Tan about this.]

The boy looked up to find the agent deep in conversation with Len-Wu. They had their backs to him. Tan tried to calm the much agitated captain. Len-Wu growled angrily but eventually he departed. The agent pulled off his balaclava. He rummaged through his own short black hair, stretched his arms and back, before carefully putting the mask back on. He turned away from the shimmering horizon and walked over to Kuan.

"Kuan, Pui is on his way here."

"You can have him arrested for Xian's murder. He mustn't be allowed to get away with it again."

"It's not that simple."

"He can't be a match for you and the entire crew of *FSS Castle*."

"We won't be able to get near him if we don't come up with a plan quickly."

"If he's coming onto the submarine, just get a few guards ready to throw him into a cell."

"Kuan, he's now the President."

The brightening sky painted a pale blue backdrop for the V-shaped formation approaching from over the horizon. The attack helicopters were flanking the airborne carrier known simply as *President One*. Shielding their eyes from the sun, those on the open deck started to move back to clear a space for the imminent landing.

Tan exchanged further words with the boy, who nodded hesitantly before climbing back down into the sub. Kuan wished he had gone to Rook Mansion for the sake of his inner companion, but Amo insisted on dealing with Pui first. The perfidious peacock must be brought to justice.

Its rotating blades came to a gradual stop. The grand helicopter's deep mauve door slid open. A dozen Shiyanese soldiers in human form disembarked tightly gripping their automatic weapons. The lurid colours of the flamboyant peacock followed behind them. One of the soldiers knelt down and rigged up a microphone with military precision. He switched it on and with due gravity announced:

"Attention, *FSS Castle*, the President of Shiyan will now address you."

The soldier stepped away and held out a camera to record proceedings.

Pui pecked at the microphone to test that it was working. He fanned out his luminous feathers, and they gleamed magnificently as he fluttered his dainty crown.

Len-Wu was standing barely a metre away from Pui. Ever since he learnt the truth about Xian's death from Kuan, he had wanted to track down her killer. Now all he had to do was to dart forward and wring that sinuous neck, but Tan warned him not to openly defy the chain of command. Pui was thus able to pour out his oleaginous words.

"I want to thank you, Agent Tan, and Captain Len-Wu and your crew, for your brave endeavour in defeating the disgraced General Chi-Ling and his attempted coup d'état. Unfortunately, both President Zhou and Vice-President Dao were amongst the victims when the Presidential Building was destroyed by one of *FSS Knight*'s missiles. In accordance with the protocol they put in place, I have been promoted to the Antaeus Circle, granted Mauvean status, and duly installed as acting President until the election which, under the state of emergency I have declared, will be postponed to a future date."

"More than anything else, we must restore law and order. And we can only do that with the dedication of fearless officers such as Agent Tan and Captain Len-Wu. It is therefore my privilege to award the Medal of Valour to our two heroes."

Len-Wu's fingernails morphed into enormous claws, but Tan subtly restrained him. Grudgingly they both walked forward and one of the po-faced soldiers pinned a medal on each of them. They exchanged bows with the President and were about to step back into line when Pui whispered to them.

"We must speak about the fugitive you're harbouring."

As President Pui strolled off to wave his wings at crew members of *FSS Castle* who would also have wanted to strangle him had their captain not kept the identity of Xian's killer to himself, Len-Wu and Tan threw their medals into the sea.

Increasingly filled with rage, the semi-morphed lion was prepared to give up his life if he could be certain of crushing the peacock. But Tan reminded him that any sign of harm to the commander-in-chief would immediately lead to the attack helicopters hovering above them battering the *Castle* with heavy fire, even to the point of scuttling the submarine. They must accede to Pui until there was a viable alternative.

Assured that enough footage had been captured for a later broadcast across Shiyan's reflectors showing the new President paying tribute to the crew of *FSS Castle* who destroyed the renegade Chi-Ling, Pui summoned Agent Tan to assist him in the delicate matter of securing the cooperation of young Kuan in solving a top secret problem. Tan explained that the boy was already being held. He took Pui down to deck 4, along a narrow corridor, followed by two of the President's armed guards, leading them into a padded cell with a single stainless steel chair.

Kuan was standing anxiously in the opposite corner.

Pui, resisting the urge to give his immaculate feathers another quick inspection, signalled with a tilt of his head, and one of the soldiers dragged and pushed Kuan into the chair where metallic bands instantly clasped around his waist and wrists. The detainee was not unfamiliar with the set-up – give a satisfactory response or sample the smell of one's own burning flesh. He pulled on the wristbands but he realised nothing would loosen their grip.

[Can we really trust Tan?]

K: It's a bit late to have doubts, Amo.

[I can still locate the ammunition on this submarine and set them off to create a diversion. I'm reasonably familiar with the circuitry on this boat, and there are enough connections passing below this chair for me to trigger an explosion. It might take some time, but I can do it.]

K: You mustn't. The *Castle* has taken too many hits already. We'd all sink and die.

[Let me know when you want me to do something.]

K: You've uploaded to the submarine's system what you found?

[But that can't protect you if Pui presses the electrocution button.]

K: If I die, would you die with me? Or would it release you from my body?

[You're not going to die. I won't allow it.]

The peacock strutted up to Kuan. Without looking back he told Tan and the two soldiers to leave, and the agent was escorted out. The door was shut.

"Kuan, time as you know is a most precious commodity. I have lots of it because others have to keep pledging their time to me, and I rarely give mine away to anyone. So I'm not going to make an exception with you. There is something you are going to do for me. Convince me you can get it done quickly, I will let you live out the rest of your life scrubbing the decks on this submarine, or whatever outsiders are meant to do here these days. Needless to say, if your response disappoints me, you would have to endure a great deal of pain before you die from your burns. I seem to remember you like the odour of fried cuisine."

[Ignore him, Kuan. How long can you hold your breath?]

K: Not very long at all. Why?

[I've just found I could shut off the oxygen supply to this cell. So long as Pui passes out first…]

K: No, Amo, I'm not good at holding my breath.

Pui narrowed his malevolent eyes.

"Return the Sun Disc to its intended orbit and get it back online. I take it you can do it as quickly as you shut it down?"

"Why do you assume I had anything to do with it being shut down?"

"I know Xian got you involved with her plan to sabotage the Sun Disc. Besides, you were hardly discreet when you did it openly on the open deck here. Did you think one of our satellites wouldn't pick you out immediately?"

"Shutting it down was easy, but getting it back would be extremely difficult."

"Just tell me how quickly you can rectify your act of sabotage."

"It was you who sabotaged the Sun Disc. The energy harvested should be for everyone to use, not diverted to enrich elephantium, which only benefits you and your friends."

"What's good for us is good for Shiyan."

"You're as mad as Amadeus. No wonder he was pleased to have you working for him."

"*He* was working *for me*."

"That's not what he said."

"What else did he say about me?"

"Not much. You weren't that important to him."

"He could never have escaped from Hades without me. I knew he would be ungrateful."

"So I did you a favour then putting him back?"

Pui paused and grinned with self-satisfying menace.

"I taught you well, Kuan. Diversionary rhetoric well deployed. It probably was no bad thing you got rid of that psychopath before he got out of control, as it doesn't look like I need his assistance after all. But your time is running out. So this is your last chance: how long before the Sun Disc is reactivated?"

"That won't be possible."

Pui was aghast with the boy's response and stared theatrically at the electrocution button on the floor.

But after all that he had been through, Kuan found that he was actually not afraid to die anymore. Even the severe pain that could soon be inflicted on him roused little fear in him.

"The shutdown cannot be reversed. It's what Xian wanted, and the whole of Shiyan should thank her."

"If you don't bring it back, Shiyanese would only end up suffering more."

"How? Unless you've already dreamt up something even worse than leaving everyone in freezing darkness until they drop dead."

"All they have to do is to make the necessary pledges to Plutopia. We don't live in a something for nothing never land."

"I was tricked into helping you with launching the Sun Disc once, but it won't happen again."

"You leave me no choice, Kuan."

[Say something to deflect him.]

"As the President of Shiyan …"

[All the circuits in this cell have been re-routed. I can't reach the ammunition section.]

345

K: Amo, I hope this will release you from my body.

"... I hereby sentence you to death."

Pui furiously pecked at the eletrocution button in front of him.

Teeth gritted, fists clenched, Kuan closed his eyes.

Nothing happened, except the metallic bands were released, and a screen emerged from the ground.

Kuan jumped out of the chair, but blocking his way was no longer a peacock. Pui had morphed into his gruesome griffin form, and his massive eagle talons reached for the boy's heart.

The screen started to play a message from Captain Len-Wu:

"All crew members and comrades from the President's guards, it has come to my attention a fugitive from justice is on board the *FSS Castle*. See for yourself, and help me apprehend him."

The screen cut to an excerpt of what Amo found on Xian's back-up iridium card, and which Kuan had earlier arranged to upload onto the submarine's system. It showed Xian, the former chief engineer in her semi-morphed leopard form walking ahead of Pui. The peacock could be seen morphing into his griffin form and ripping out Xian's chest with his talons. It was what took place in the secret research building on the estate of Rook Mansion after Xian confronted the governor. They were images Pui thought he had permanently erased, not aware that the incriminating security footage was automatically backed up remotely.

Acting President Pui shrunk back to his peacock form. There was more on show. Another recording quickly followed. It was a transmission sent from *FSS Knight* just before it was pulled into the Charybdis Vortex. It was encrypted for Pui's eyes only, but since the peacock used his encryption codes on Xian's control panel when he tampered with the distribution of energy from the Sun Disc, once they were uploaded to the *Castle*'s system, they could be accessed in decoding the scrambled transmission which had earlier been picked up. It was revealed to be what General Chi-Ling, his tiger face filled with righteous fury, bellowed at Pui just before his demise:

"Governor Pui, or are you President already, you owe me and all those who have unwaveringly followed me, the recognition we deserve. We will not be branded traitors. Everything I have done, the murder of the Mauveans on *FSS Castle*, attacking my fellow military officers, launching the missiles against the President's Building, it was all to make Shiyan great again, and executed exactly as your ordered. Honour us as heroes once your Presidency is established. I expect nothing less."

When that faded out, the recording looped back to the message from Captain Len-Wu about seizing the fugitive on board – a murderer, an assassin, the treacherous instigator of a coup d'état.

Pui flopped onto the floor.

The door opened and Agent Tan slipped in without a sound. He locked the door tightly behind him.

"You've seen what's being shown to everyone on the boat."

"It's all fabricated."

"The Admiralty's experts have authenticated everything."

"These are all lies, I'm telling you."

"There are also rumours circulating that you helped Amadeus escape from Hades."

"I can explain everything."

"You're welcome to go out and give a different story, if you think anyone will believe you. The *Castle*'s crew want to avenge Xian's death, and the President's guards now believe you ordered her assassination."

The quivering peacock blinked his pathetic indigo eyes.

"Agent Tan, help me escape and I'll lead you to the one who's really behind all this, the one I take my orders from."

"So it's someone else's doing? You're just a lackey carrying out instructions."

"You don't understand, Tan. I'm willing to risk my life and take you to the one who's been plotting to take over not just our world but the boy's world too. Who do you think has been holding Kuan's father?"

The bolt struck the boy.

"What has father got to do with this?"

The peacock explained in the most earnest tone he could muster.

"Your father sometime ago began to suspect that someone from Shiyan was planning to secure domination over your world. And he tried to enlist help in our world to stop it. But he was not careful enough and got captured by a foe far more formidable than he could imagine. He has been languishing in a cell ever since. I can help you get him back, but only if Agent Tan agrees to let me go afterwards."

"Why should we believe you, Pui?" asked Tan with a glacial stare.

"I'll take you to where Kuan's father is held. There is minimum security because no one's supposed to know where it is. You can get him out and take with you all the evidence you need to charge the real mastermind behind all the things I had to organise. When you need my testimony, I'll send it to you via a reflector."

"And the identity of this mastermind? The one to be blamed for everything, leaving you free to start a new life?"

"We only communicate via coded messages, so I can't tell you who he, or she for that matter, is. But I'll help you set a trap for the megalomaniac. Once I'm safely away, and you've got the boy's father back, you can bring your own taskforce to seize his captor."

"I don't detect much loyalty there, Pui. Are you not flipping rather easily?"

"Agent Tan, you know very well that with those recordings being shown, I'd be instantly killed if I'm seen by any member of this submarine's crew. I have no choice. But you've got to smuggle me out of here, or else there won't be much of me left to help you with anything."

Kuan grabbed the agent's arm.

"Tan, we must go and rescue father."

"Pui, you fail to get the boy's father back alive and well, you don't lead us to the real culprit you claim to exist, you try to trick us in any way, …"

"I'm well aware what would happen to me."

Tan released a secret door and morphed temporarily back to his black Chartreux cat form as he led them along a hidden passage to where they undocked from *FSS Castle* in an underwater speedboat. Only about an hour ago, Amo thought she would be making her way to the vault underneath Rook Mansion where the door to her home world was. Now she was once again diverted elsewhere. But she understood. How could Kuan not pursue this chance of reuniting with his father. Besides, the exertion in directing the Sun Disc to strike at *FSS Knight* and then shutting it down completely had taken its toil. There was not much time left for her. She resolved to do all she could to help her host. At least one of them should attain the reunion they had desperately sought.

Chapter 28

<u>The Art of Dissemblance</u>

The unrelenting rain poured down on Kuan. He was holding the briefcase. Father had asked him to take it home. So he took it home. Placed it in the study and shut the door just as he was instructed to. Father would return after he had checked whatever was so urgent he must attend to in the middle of a monsoon attack. Except he didn't return. Not that day, nor the next. Weeks of unexplained absence were truncated in the boy's mind into one and the same day. Father was just delayed a little. He would not forget the test he had set his son the next day. Tin after tin of canned food was consumed. There was no one he could contact.

Left in isolation, he turned to companions he could conjure up in his juvenile mind. The comic book stories of the Monkey King and other heroes opened a gateway to endless imaginary battles until he was too tired to stay awake any further. Then one night he was caught in the twilight of dream and consciousness. The sweltering heat was real enough, but the voice was ethereal. It told him to listen out for the splash. Not an ordinary splash. He would notice it when he heard it. Be prepared and go to it. Forget these words that had drifted through in a trance. He was not to remember why he wandered into the territorial waters of Shiyan, but at the critical point he must recall the life he must save. It would all depend on him.

Water scattered in all directions off the elegant surface of the naval speedboat emerging out of a dimly lit pool. The cockpit cover slid open. Pui flapped his decorative wings clumsily to reach the pier. Kuan, with a helping arm from Agent Tan, jumped across too. Tan, in his crumpled black and green camouflage uniform, straightened his balaclava.

The peacock pecked at a switch and a dull light seeped across a narrow underground archway which stretched into the dark distance. Steel girders stretched haphazardly to a high rocky ceiling. Weaving through them a path led to a giant hourglass, the bottom half was oddly empty. Tan and Kuan were behind Pui when he stopped in front of the contraption. An opening in the glass appeared.

The peacock raised his wings to signify that no one should step forward. The opening was closed, and at once sand from the top chamber poured down at great speed. When the bottom half was full, the entire hourglass sunk halfway into the ground, leaving the now empty top chamber directly in front of them. An opening appeared. This time Pui stepped into it. Kuan rushed in impatiently, but Tan, crouching down to get in, was more cautious. The opening they had stepped through closed abruptly. In front of them a circular shutter peeled back to reveal a long tunnel. The chamber in which they stood detached itself from the buried half of the hourglass and sped down the tunnel.

As shapeless patterns flew past, Kuan was torn by his guarded hope of soon seeing father again and the need to tend to Amo's deteriorating condition. It was the closest he had come to being reunited with father so he must take a chance, even with the devious peacock. Agent Tan would not allow him to trick them in any way.

By that ineffable sensation of a gentle warmth fading in his head, he knew Amo was weakening to the point of no return. It was not merely solitude that came with being exiled from her world, but extinction. It was too late to change course. Nonetheless he resolved then and there that he would insist on Agent Tan getting them to Rook Mansion once father was safely with him. Even if Amo could not find a way into that vault, he was sure Tan could get them in. That resolution would go ahead, he firmly told himself, even if it turned out Pui was not leading them to father. If that were the case, however, what would he and Tan be letting themselves in for?

At the end of the tunnel the glass transporter slowly halted and they stepped out into a dusty square hall, lit by quavering candles lined up along opposite walls. Stone columns in each corner held up Atlas-like a gargantuan boulder protruding through the ceiling. At the far end was an inert reflector standing two by two metres.

Kuan scanned for signs of his father.

"Where is he?"

Pui said nothing but glanced towards the reflector.

"Answer him." Tan commanded.

The peacock twisted his neck as if it pained him to speak.

"Please, you must trust me. I'm taking a huge risk bringing you here to set the boy's father free."

"You said security here is minimal. Why should you be worried?"

"I'm just being cautious. You can never be too cautious."

"Take us to Kuan's father." Tan's stern stare pressed for a response.

"I have to check the time-lock first."

The peacock pecked at various points on the bottom of the screen, and the reflected images of the three surreptitious visitors were replaced by a white on black message: 'time-locked cell next accessible for inspection in 47 minutes.'

"He's in a time-locked cell below us. We have to wait 47 minutes before I can open it."

[Beneath us is just water, I can sense it.]

K: Are you sure? What about father? Any sign of him?

[I can't tell you that. But I can sense the water.]

"Is father still alive? Or have you drowned him?" Kuan asked with intense alarm.

"Drowned him? Why would I do that?"

"What have you done with him?" Tan moved menacingly closer to Pui. The acting President might be tempted to morph into his deadlier form, but even for a griffin the charge of a rhinoceros could be lethal.

"Agent Tan, there's no need for all this suspicion. The watertight cell is submerged in water for extra security, to stop the prisoner escaping. But it's easy when it's unlocked to get him out."

Kuan searched for a grain of sincerity in the peacock's blinking eyes.

"Override the time-lock. I want to get father out now."

"You don't understand, Kuan. The time-lock can only be overridden by the one who brought your father here."

"You're lying", the boy fired back.

"Pui, I'm beginning to wonder if there is anyone besides you who plotted the assassination of President Zhou and Vice-President Dao, or ordered you to commit all those crimes you perpetrated. I should take you back to *FSS Castle* and hand you over to Len-Wu."

"Wait, you must wait. It's not that long now. Very soon you can both see for yourselves. If it turns out I've been lying to you, you can put me on trial, execute me, as you like. But if we leave now and what I've been saying is the truth, you'll be leaving the boy's father to rot in his miserable cell. To show my good faith, I'll start pulling together some of the evidence that will help you arrest and convict the real mastermind behind all the atrocious deeds. You will see that I'm but a minor instrument at someone else's beck and call."

The peacock's beak rapidly tapped out instructions which led to a long series of symbols and numbers appearing on the reflector.

"What you are seeing is a selection of the more substantial pledges I received for carrying out the instructions sent to me."

"This is just gibberish, Pui."

"They are in a coded form, Agent Tan. Pass them onto whoever has been cracking my encryption codes for you, it'll all become clear. Let me pick out a few examples which may be of particular interest to you: a million hours for arranging for Chi-Ling to kill the Mauveans on *FSS Castle*; two million hours for reaching various agreements with Amadeus; another million to make sure Chi-Ling gets the necessary information to evade capture by you; three million hours for secretly altering the Sun Disc's energy distribution; a million hours for getting Chengbao Island ready for Amadeus; six million hours for silencing Xian after she threatened to shut down the Sun Disc; and fifty million hours for the missile attack on the Presidential Building."

"This is supposed to impress me of your innocence?"

"Greed is my sin, and I have to account for it to my maker. But what these data will do for you is to identify the account holder who has been pledging all those hours to me, and connecting the pledges to specific instructions I have meticulously recorded. With this evidence, conviction is virtually guaranteed."

As Tan scrutinised what was before him, Kuan quietly walked up to the reflector. He touched the screen. He sensed pain, but not his own.

K: Amo, what's wrong?
[I'm fine.]

He could hear repressed agony in her voice.

K: You're not. I should have tried to get you back to your home world first.

[You must stay here for your father.]

K: But there's probably no cell in the water underneath us.

[Wait another 42 minutes and you'll know for sure.]

K: You're not going to last that long, are you?

[I can be unpredictably resilient.]

K: Why don't I ask Tan to hold Pui here and we'll go to Rook Mansion. It doesn't matter if you can't leave my head. I'll go with you into your world. We can worry about what to do next later, but we must get you back first.

[Kuan, I appreciate what you're trying to do. But you must make sure your father is safe. That's all that matters now.]

K: You're flinching from your pain. I can feel it, Amo.

[It was just the shock from these data Pui has put up on the reflector. They are genuine records, and the pledges do come from a single source. But that cannot be true.]

K: Who's sent these pledges to Pui?

[Someone from Rook Mansion.]

Kuan could not process Amo's revelation to him. How could Chairman Dao be behind it all? He was killed. Who else could direct communications from Rook Mansion? At that moment the symbols and numbers disappeared from the reflector to be replaced by the image of a lone figure walking up close to the camera.

It was Denji, the lynx who had been in the service of Dao for almost ten years. He and the peacock bowed to each other. Denji spoke first.

"Tan and Kuan were not followed. They have made no attempt to communicate with anyone back on *FSS Castle*, and the scanner confirms there is no tracking or recording device on them."

"So once again we have outwitted our enemy," declared Pui waving his wings and tail with a self-satisfied flourish.

Kuan stepped back to be close to Agent Tan who put his arm around the boy's shoulder.

"All that remains is for the wolf dogs to be released to enjoy their meal", said the grinning peacock.

Like a fleeting shadow, Tan had crept up on Pui before he even noticed the agent had moved. His hand closed tightly round his adversary's slender neck.

"I can snap your neck before you can morph one feather. So don't try anything."

Denji immediately intervened.

"Agent Tan, if you don't release President Pui this instant, not only you, but the boy also will be fed to the wolf dogs. They have completely surrounded you."

Tan swept his eyes across the interiors of the candle-lit hall. He detected nothing.

"If I see one wolf dog, I'm breaking Pui's neck. Now give us the boy's father and let us leave."

The unperturbed lynx narrowed his eyes but gave no response.

Pui tried to speak without success.

Kuan felt indifferent about being put to death. Father had probably been killed soon after they last spoke to each other in that downpour. He must have known he was in imminent danger, as he would never otherwise give his briefcase to the boy. But if it was too late for him and father, Amo deserved a chance to return to her home. Was there any point in appealing to Denji?

"Denji, if my father is still alive, please release him to me."

Denji chose to stay silent.

"Do what the boy asks", Tan pleaded, "and you can keep me to bargain with the authority."

With grave reluctance, Denji spoke.

"Agent Tan, we are the authority. You're the lone agent who has a personal grudge against President Pui and fabricated evidence against him."

"The evidence we have will stand up to examination."

"Not if the President embargoes their use."

"Denji, I don't for one moment believe you're behind all this. It's all Pui's doing. He's just using you. Testify against him."

"For the last time, let the President go."

"If you want him to live, you have to listen to me."

The lynx gave Tan an enigmatic stare, and neither of them was going to give ground to each other.

Kuan asked Amo what he should do but there was no response from her. He could barely register her faint presence.

Pui made a muffled sound about dying. It was duly ignored by the agent.

From the other side of the hall a deep voice took charge of the stalemate.

"Denji, you can leave it to me now."

It was the voice of Chairman Dao who emerged from the dark in his customary purple tunic and trousers, hands clasped behind his back.

"Pui, you've done well to avoid being taken into custody and instead lure them into helping you escape back here. You see why we always need a contingency plan."

The peacock's throat was too constricted to reply but he nodded.

There was not the slightest sign of any injury on Dao.

"But you were killed in the Presidential Building." A startled Kuan remarked.

"Death, life, as one who's been in Hades you should know, it can all be very misleading. I just had Denji confirm one of the mutilated bodies in the rubble was mine and the gullible media took care of the rest."

"You weren't even in the Presidential Building, were you?" Tan observed.

"I went there earlier to make sure President Zhou was going to be in her office. Then I left in good time to go to a secret bunker of mine."

"Dao, how do you expect to get away with all this?"

"In a week or two, Denji would announce that detailed tests have revealed that there had been a mistaken identification, and I was actually buried in another part of the ground. Fortunately, the doctors performed a miracle and I would make a full recovery. Acting President Pui would step down and as the surviving Vice-President I would succeed Zhou as President. Plutopia would at last have complete control over Shiyan."

"But you've always been content with your honorary role of Vice-President. Why suddenly go to such length to remove the President?"

"I'll tell you, Agent Tan, because it's important you understand. Shiyan is at a crossroads. Fools like Lord Ou-Yang wanted us to stick to the old ways, sharing out responsibilities, pooling resources, everyone working together for some so-called common good. And there are the blind idealists like Kuan's friend, Dr. Lee, calling for Shiyan to look after Potokans, those deformed failures who are of no value except as a reminder to the rest why they must work harder every day. But President Zhou started to listen to them. She wanted more help for Potokans. She was forgetting that she was a Mauvean herself. She even suggested that the Circles of Challenge should be reformed. And when she found out that the Sun Disc was channeling energy not to everyone but just to the enrichment of elephantium, she had the temerity to ask me to rethink what I was doing. When I refused, she said she would not have me as her running mate in the coming election. I threatened to stand against her, but she claimed the lower order Shiyanese were gravitating towards her and she was confident of getting a winning majority. So I had to take action to remove her. Besides, my ambition goes beyond Shiyan. Once I've got this world firmly under my control, I want to see Plutopia expand into other worlds, such as Kuan's. I find human culture most congenial."

"But someone found out about your plans and tried to stop you. So you had him locked up."

"You're talking about Kuan's father?" asked Dao.

"You know who I'm talking about." Tan rejoined.

"He'll never be released."

"Dao, if you don't release him at once and let us go, I'll kill your underling."

"Go ahead, Tan, if you want, but I wouldn't advise it. In any case, I have a more important proposition for you. You've seen the resources I'm prepared to pledge to those who serve me loyally. You could become as well-pledged as most Mauveans if you work for me. For Plutopia to control Shiyan and other worlds, I need the best lieutenants. Of late I've lost both Chi-Ling and Amadeus, though the prophet could be somewhat unstable, so I need to recruit new blood. And you're top of the list."

"I'm flattered."

"Why don't you let Pui go? I can so easily have the boy torn apart. Even you can't stop thirty wolf dogs at once."

Tan tightened his grip around the peacock's neck. Pui gasped.

"Denji, at my signal." The Chairman intoned.

On screen, the impassive lynx lowered his head in acknowledgement.

Kuan looked over to Tan who forcefully threw Pui aside. The peacock crawled off to choke as dramatically as he could.

"Wise choice, Agent Tan. It shows that we can work together. I've read your naval records: tenacity, outstanding mental agility and ferocious combat skills. You will be an asset for Plutopia."

"You've achieved all you wanted. You've used Amadeus to strike fear into Shiyan, causing panic about a dreaded Potokan conspiracy; had Xian murdered by Pui for trying to reverse what you did with the Sun Disc; and even initiated a coup d'état by ordering General Chi-Ling to kill President Zhou. What else is there left to do?"

"There is plenty more to do to secure complete domination here and in the human world. There're too many twisted minds set on opposing Plutopia. By whatever means necessary, they must be silenced."

"Have you got anyone in mind?"

"The trouble-makers in Shiyan have been largely taken care of. It is the enemies I'm going to encounter in Kuan's world that concern me. Unless they are stopped, they would stir up animosity and slow Plutopia's progress."

"You want them all killed?"

"Killing is a crude last resort. Some will undoubtedly merit it. But for the majority, being intimidated or discredited would suffice. As an experienced agent, I'm sure you are well versed in the most effective techniques to use."

Tan glanced at Kuan by his side. The boy looked back at those eyes peering out of the agent's concealed face.

"If I agree to work for you, you'll let Kuan go?"

"No, if you agree to work for me, your first task would be to kill him to convince me you are truly committed."

"You want me to kill an innocent boy?"

"Innocent?" Dao retorted, "I gave him a home, helped him rise up through the Circles of Challenge, and would have passed Plutopia on to him one day. But what did he do? He might have unwittingly helped me with acquiring the House of Ou-Yang or evicting the Potokans to Chengbao Island when we needed access to the buried elephantium in old Bastille de Potoka, but he was always going out of his way to help the Potokans. He scuppered my plan to bring Amadeus out of Hades with his army of 'pure' Shiyanese so that as President I could later crush them. Worst of all, he robbed us of the Sun Disc. He's not innocent, and he will not be spared."

Kuan walked up to Dao.

"What have you done with father?"

"Your father? You really don't know who your father is, do you? I tried to help you, Kuan, to start a new life. But you couldn't let go of your past. Now you have nothing."

"He's still alive?"

"In a manner of speaking, yes."

"Can I see him just one last time?"

"I do pity you, Kuan."

"Let us have just a few minutes together."

Dao turned away from the boy.

"Agent Tan, if you want to take my offer, then it's time to carry out your first assignment. Unless you want to die along with Kuan."

Kuan told Tan to do as Dao asked and save himself. There was no point both of them dying.

"Kuan, neither of us has to die."

The agent turned to Dao and the peacock, who had just about recovered his supercilious deportment.

"Chairman Dao and Governor Pui, you are both under arrest for conspiracy to murder, terrorism and treason. All the evidence we have previously gathered on Governor Pui and the evidence you, Chairman Dao, have just provided in front of the reflector will be used to indict you."

"Agent Tan, an impressive bluff, but I don't see how this is going to get you anywhere. You think I'm going to believe you can use one of my own private reflectors to record what has just transpired in here? None of them could be used against the parameters I have set, and any transgression will be immediately notified to me."

"That's why we've never used any of them until now. We have one shot and we want to get it right, and your confession was perfect. It's been recorded and transmitted to all concerned. And my back-up should be here any minute now."

"Denji, I'm tired of this, send in the wolf-dogs."

The lynx, charged with unusual animation, stared ominously out of the screen.

"Chairman Dao, I've had all the wolf dogs tranquilised. Agent Tan, your back-up team is entering the hall as arranged."

"Thank you, Agent Denji."

Chapter 29

<u>Recovery</u>

Out of the hollow boulder looming large over the darkened hall, holes were drilled and through them cats leapt balletically to the ground below, where instantaneously they morphed into heavily armed soldiers in human form. They clutched their weapons with tense precision, aim focused on the powerful figure of Chairman Dao.

One nod from Agent Tan they would shoot the supreme chief of Plutopia into tiny fragments. Dao stood firm and still, his face stoked by the erupting anger beneath. Denji, in whom he had placed complete trust in the running of Rook Mansion over the last ten years, turned out to be a government agent under deep cover to expose his subversive activities against Shiyan. He could not abide by such flagrant betrayal.

Sheltering behind the Chairman, the peacock transformed himself into a small turquoise cat and slipped away while all the attention was on Dao. He had almost reached the transporter in the shape of the top half of a giant hourglass. At his approach, an opening appeared. But as he was in midair jumping towards it, he was seized by the scruff of his neck.

Len-Wu in his full lion form had caught Pui. A split second hesitation held him back from crushing his quarry. The ball of turquoise exploded into a griffin matching Len-Wu in size and ferocity. The eagle talons cut into the lion's back. Len-Wu stabbed his fangs into the griffin's side. They grappled with each other, spiralling in a helix of blood. The talons flew down on a brave but defenceless chest. A jet of red spewed calligraphically across the dusty floor. One of the antagonists was gaining the advantage. Len-Wu received another cut to his face.

A soldier took aim at Pui, but Tan signalled to him to wait. Len-Wu craved to avenge Xian's death. The fight must conclude with a fatal end. Beyond the dichotomy of vengeance and death, Len-Wu wanted nothing else.

The griffin pushed the lion onto his back, fastening dripping claws onto the neck. With a thunderous roar, the lion rose to clamp his jaws around Pui's eagle head.

In such contests, with strengths evenly matched, it would always come down to instincts in the end. Would the approach of death bring on fear or fury? Pui was filled with dread as the lion's mouth closed in and he slackened his grip on Len-Wu's throat. But the touch of the sharp cold claws around his windpipe drove the lion on with redoubled determination to kill. In that crucial moment, Pui the murderer, more than metaphorically, lost his head.

Kuan did not want to rejoice in a loss of life, but another of Dao's hydra-like fiends had been severed. Perhaps the evil of Plutopia could now be extinguished.

"Cunning was his forte. Never good at a real fight though." Dao noted dryly.

"What about you, Dao? Are you any good at combat yourself? You've got no lieutenant left to do your dirty work for you now."

"Constitutionally, Agent Tan, you have just allowed your friend to carry out a most propitious act. In ending the life of acting President Pui, the position is automatically conferred on the next-in-line to the office, and that as you know is either the President-elect, which we haven't got as we have not had the election yet, or the Vice-President, which of course is me. Since I have not been put on trial, let alone convicted of any crime, I can legitimately take on the Presidency. Indeed by the oath I have taken, I am obliged to exercise the power of that office with immediate effect. So I suggest you all point your weapons away from me, and by my executive order take Agent Tan and the boy Kuan out and shoot them for insurgency."

For a moment, the puzzled troops looked at each other and at Tan.

Kuan could not believe that by some technicality Dao could turn the table on Agent Tan and seize control of Shiyan after all. Just as he thought the battle against Plutopia had been won and he could ask Tan to rush him to the vault where Amo might be revived, Dao might triumph.

"Would it help", Dao added, "if I declare anyone refusing to comply with my order as an accomplice of the insurgents, to be executed along them?"

The soldiers sought desperate guidance from Tan, who just calmly turned to the reflector.

"Agent Denji, could you relay to us the news reports we might have missed while we've been down here?"

"Agent Tan, I'm putting them through now. These are being shown on all external reflectors across Shiyan."

The screen switched from the image of the lynx to a succession of reports with the backdrop of a hospital heavily guarded by cheetahs and soldiers in human form. It had been officially confirmed that President Zhou survived the missile attack. Having suspected a plot by her embittered Vice-President, she had prepared an escape route to her own underground bunker. Though she sustained injuries, these were not serious and she had been recovering well. Most importantly, she had been able to respond decisively to the attempted coup by formally stripping Dao of his Vice-President position, and ordering his arrest for treason. A new Vice-President had been appointed to lead a reform programme to reintegrate Potokans, restructure the Sun Disc technology, and put an end to the excesses of Plutopia.

Blistering venom coursed through the veins of the disgraced Chairman. His life ambition was to build up Plutopia to be so powerful that Shiyan itself would become but one of its compliant subsidiaries. He wanted to demonstrate that ultimately none would dare challenge his vision for the world, and all would depend on his mercy for even the most basic provision of food, light, and warmth. Now he had been routed. The serene appearance held up in the past by hegemonic confidence was crumbling away.

"Have you seen enough, Dao?" asked Tan.

"I don't know how you turned him, but tell Denji, I don't forget those who betray me."

"Agent Denji was always one of us. We sent him to gather evidence from the inside on how you operated. So he's familiar with how you deal with your enemies. Indeed he's compiled a comprehensive list of those you call on to deal out your retribution, and of course they're all being rounded up as we speak."

"You, most of all, Agent Tan, will come upon your reckoning soon." Dao spoke in a low voice with hateful menace.

Tan waved his arm and Dao was taken away.

Kuan asked Tan to help him get to Rook Mansion.

"But you're here already. This whole area is just below the Mansion's cellar."

"You knew this was Rook Mansion, and it was Dao behind it all along?"

"We've suspected Dao for a long time of all kinds of wrongdoing, but it wasn't easy to get enough evidence to bring him and Plutopia down."

"The mission was to bring Plutopia down. Father wanted Plutopia exposed and stopped."

Tan's eyes affirmed his realisation.

Kuan wanted to tell Amo but there was a sad emptiness in his mind.

"Kuan, which part of Rook Mansion do you want to get to?"

The boy hoped in vain for a flicker of his inner companion. He would still take her back to her world, but he sensed it was too late for anything except a memorial service, whatever form that might take in the nebula that was her home.

From the reflector, Agent Denji sought their attention.

"Agent Tan and Master Kuan, the Vice-President would like to have a word with you."

They turned to the screen and were greeted with the ebullient visage of Vice-President Erica Lee. Kuan's felt a surge of melancholic joy.

"The President asked me to pass on her thanks to you both. Without your courage Shiyan would have fallen to Dao."

"Thank you and congratulations, Dr. Lee", said Tan, "the President has made a bold and wise choice."

"It was a complete surprise to me. One moment we had just escaped from being sent to Hades, and the next a helicopter arrived to take me to see the President."

"You have your security guards with you?" asked the agent.

"I can't go anywhere without them. I don't know if I can ever get used to this."

"They must know where you are at all times. Dao has so many insidious contacts, he can still be a threat to you and the President."

"Do you ever stop worrying, Agent Tan? Take your team out for a long celebration after what you've achieved."

"In time perhaps. There is still much to be done."

Tan paused to glance at the boy whose gaze was fixed on Erica Lee.

"I'll let you speak with Kuan."

The agent walked away towards Len-Wu who, remaining in his lion form, stared pensively at the corpse of the decapitated griffin, while mourning another.

Kuan looked up at Erica's beaming face on the reflector as she gently pulled her long red hair behind her ear. If only he could just walk through the glass to be with her. But he needed to be elsewhere.

"Without you, all the Potokans on Chengbao Island and I would have ended up in Hades. We'll never forget what you did for us. You must come and see us when we lay the foundation for the new Oran Clinic."

"Erica, are you still going to be working with them on Chengbao? You're the Vice-President now."

"I accepted President Zhou's offer because she wanted me to bring in reforms which will really help the Potokans. Not just building clinics and better living accommodation for them, but changing the system so Potokans could morph back into their previous forms if they wished, and no Shiyanese will ever again be forced to become something that everyone else recoils from. The Circles of Challenge will be completely transformed. All Shiyanese will be permitted to morph into any form provided they have cultivated the relevant aptitude for it. So long as they can improve their lives or those of others through the forms they adopt, they can freely do so, but there will be no special privileges attached to any of them, mauve elephant or otherwise. Those who have learnt to generate high energy fuel by altering their physical constitution will be welcome to share their resources with others on fair terms. But we are planning to adapt the Sun Disc technology to give every Shiyanese a Sun Cloak so that in addition to the natural light and warmth from the sun, extra brightness and energy can be readily conserved for later use for free."

Echoes of ideas rebounded in Kuan's mind. Thoughts typed out long ago came flooding back to him.

"What about the terrible treatment of outsiders? The use of Blessing in deceiving the downcast with false hope? Or the demand for extortionate pledges? You're not going to allow them to go on?"

"We will stop these not just with new laws, but with better enforcement to protect the vulnerable. We will particularly control the way some Shiyanese have virtually enslaved others by getting them to pledge away all they had."

"Plutopia cannot be permitted to continue."

"And it won't be. Its power will be broken up for a start. Those who actually do the work in the different constituent parts of Plutopia will be able to take control of their part and run it on their own. So those who make and distribute food in the House of Ou-Yang, for example, will take charge of it independently. Anything that Plutopia has done up to now which could be used to hold others to ransom, such as heat, light, water and life-saving medicine, will be overseen by the government from now on. We have to explore how best to do that, but we won't repeat the mistake of letting a few megalomaniacs dictate terms to the rest of us."

"Then there's hope."

"Only if we win the next election. The Council of Mauveans has always gone along with Dao under sufferance, because however rude he was to them at times, he would always make them better off. But they loathe President Zhou, especially since she has come out insisting that Mauveans and other Shiyanese are all equal. We suspect the Council will put up their own candidates to run for President and Vice-President. If they win, none of our reforms will see the light of day, and Plutopia will be on the ascendancy again."

"Do you think you and President Zhou will win?"

"It's difficult to tell. It's one thing to explain to a small group what needs to be done, but where millions are concerned, they can easily be distracted and manipulated by others. The Council of Mauveans will use everything at their disposal to make Shiyanese fear and hate what we put forward."

Kuan sighed deeply and then spoke as much to himself as to Erica Lee.

"But you mustn't give up. You have to keep making your case as best you can."

There was a subtle change to his demeanour which intrigued her.

"Kuan, why don't you join me later on today? We should talk more."

"I would really like that, but I need to take someone back to a special place. It's something I have to do."

She felt it was not opportune to press him to explain.

"Some other time perhaps?"

Kuan nodded but he knew he would never see Erica again. He tried his best to imprint her face, the flowing red tresses, those captivating green eyes into his memory.

"Goodbye, Kuan."

Her image faded. An irretrievable loss passed through him like a ghost.

He was still staring at the blank screen reflecting back a curious image he seemed not to recognise, when Agent Tan offered to take him to whichever part of Rook Mansion he wanted to get to.

The secret vault of Chairman Dao was not at all far away. Up a spiral passageway, then twenty minutes' walk at most along tunnel 13 and they would be there. Kuan did not say why he wanted to go there. Tan did not ask.

The agent picked up one of the burning candles off the side of the hall and a narrow entrance opened to a spiral passageway. Unlike the dusty floor outside, the black marble wall and steps were immaculately clean. Reverberating footsteps accentuated the silence of their gradual ascent.

Occasionally a solitary picture would be found hanging on the wall. The agent paid no attention to them but Kuan observed the subject of each one as he came upon it. A magnificent waterfall with a butterfly darting between the fluid curtains. A flower battered by incessant rain. A snowball melting away on top of a piece of paper, smudging its words. And finally by the door to tunnel 13, a tranquil river flowing by with a lamb lying serenely at the bottom.

Tan slid the door to one side, and flicked a switch to bring the lights on. Ahead of them was a large tunnel seamlessly covered by dark wood panels. He blew the candle out, put it down on its side, and adjusted his balaclava.

"You know what happened to him, don't you?" asked Kuan.

"Yes."

Tan continued to stride forward with the boy in tow.

"Why didn't you tell me?"

"The realisation has to come from you." Tan explained.

"Dao and Plutopia have been defeated now."

"For now, in this world. But the bigger battle is still to come."

"In my world?"

"Yes, and that's why you must go back and stop Plutopia corrupting your world as it almost succeeded in this."

"Words. Pages of typed up words. That's all I've got."

"Those words helped the Potokans."

"Erica helped the Potokans."

"Words have their part to play. When all hope appears lost, you need words to rekindle the spirit of resistance. Dr. Lee couldn't have done it all by herself."

"Why can't I see her again?"

"Don't torture yourself. You must accept some things can't be changed. Devote the time you have left to fighting for what can be changed."

"I miss her."

"I know."

They continued to walk down the wood paneled tunnel. Muffled noises seemed to rumble in the distance. Tan hit a button on his uniform to ask for a report and was assured all areas remained secure. He signaled Kuan to stop, but neither of them could hear anything unusual. Ambulation resumed, albeit with more caution.

"That was my own voice, wasn't it, telling me to leave that night? I knew he had gone, and it would have been too much for me to stay where I was."

"You couldn't have coped otherwise." Tan confirmed.

"You knew what my mission was then?"

"I wasn't certain. I didn't even know how much you would recover from your past. If it had all gone, you might have got stuck in this world."

"It's started to come back to me now, more and more quickly. I can feel it. Is it a good thing though?"

"It's the truth."

Kuan did not know how much of the truth he could take. The infantile psyche had to be peeled away, and the ugliness of what had been hidden would be inescapably with him once more. It had been a bewildering sojourn from home. He was on the verge of losing sight of what really mattered. He was about to surrender. But he realised he could not turn away from the struggle.

"There's nothing to be afraid of. You've come through the worst." The agent wanted to be assuring.

"Can I face what I ran away from?"

"You're more resilient than you think."

"Will you be here if I need to escape again?"

Tan squinted to check that it was the correct exit which had just come into view.

"Will *FSS Castle* come and snatch me from the water again?"

"Kuan, you won't need me anymore. Your time here is done."

"I can go to him now?"

"You feel you're ready?"

"Almost. There's just one other thing I need to do. Then I want to be with him again. It's been too long."

"I've made the necessary arrangements."

"So where is he being held?"

A loud bleep coming from Tan's uniform interrupted them. He hit the button again but this time all he heard back were indistinct noises. He told Kuan to stay close to him but they must move forward quickly to get out of the tunnel.

They ran towards the exit of the tunnel. The agent glanced back to check if they were being followed. In that split second one of the wooden panels ahead of them erupted into splinters. A dark mammoth object charged in and swung its python-like trunk viciously across the face of Agent Tan, knocking him back as though a shotgun had discharged a round into him. The agent pushed himself off the floor, but the trunk came flying through the air and smashed into the back of his head, catapulting him face-down into the ground.

The assailant shifted into his human form. Dao tore into the stricken Tan with his malevolent stare.

"Wishing you had accepted my offer now?"

Tan slowly stood up. He lifted the bottom of his mask to spit blood out.

"Fugitive Dao, I should have taken you in myself."

"Because you are a match for me?"

"More than."

But before Tan morphed a single molecule of his body into his rhino form, the mauve elephant in front of him had already unleashed its trunk like a whip and thrashed him hard in the face again. The agent fell to his knees. Kuan ran in front of him.

"Leave him alone. Surrender yourself. There's nowhere for you to run to."

The human-shaped Dao bent forward and spoke softly.

"That's where you're wrong, Kuan. I'm going into your world, where Plutopia will expand and reign unchallenged."

Dao grabbed the boy by his naval overall and threw him to one side. He stepped up to Tan.

"Tan, I want you to regret everything you've done."

"My life is too fulfilled to have regrets. Best of all has been your defeat."

"Defeat? I have a whole new world to exploit."

"You can't win, Dao. You'll be exposed wherever you go, whatever disguise you adopt."

"Words. Mere words."

Tan attempted to rise and morph, but Dao was too fast for him. The mauve elephant lashed another blow across Tan's battered head. The agent fell on his back, powerless to stop the elephant foot stamping down on his chest. A splash of red gushed out of his mouth. Kuan screamed in horror. The purple killer turned towards him.

"I will turn the weaklings in your world into pathetic Potokans. Everyone will be fearful of my power, and no one can rein me back as I will possess more resources than the rest combined."

"There is no place for you in my world or anywhere else."

The boy hesitantly stepped back away from Dao.

"Have you forgotten Plutopia is already in your world?"

"Then it will be brought down there as it has been here."

"For all that you've been through, Kuan, you still haven't learnt anything, have you? Opposing me only brings pain. I am strong, and because of that I get even stronger. And to challenge me is unforgivable."

Dao in his menacing elephant form took another step forward.

"It's you who should seek forgiveness."

"I gave you a chance to be something more. I helped you reach the Antaeus Circle, the Mauvean rank was yours if you hadn't decided to sabotage the Sun Disc. In time, I'll have another Sun Disc built, but once you've lost my trust, that can never be rebuilt."

"Agent Tan is badly hurt. Let me help him."

"He's as good as dead, and you deserve to be too."

"Have you no sense of remorse?"

"To think I seriously considered you becoming my successor one day."

"I can help you, if you're willing to change."

"I should have known the old man's influence could never be removed from you."

"Tell me where he is."

"I've had enough of you, Kuan."

The murderous elephant tensed his muscles and charged mercilessly at Kuan. The boy fell and a massive foot was poised to crush his head. Dao took aim as an intense brightness radiated out of his intended victim. Then a fireball exploded, propelling him against the wall of the tunnel and at the same time engulfing him in scorching heat. He was wrapped tightly in the raging fire. In vain he tried to break free as every muscle in him was being melted away. The flame carved its way into the exposed skin and consumed the living tissues with gluttonous combustion.

Shifting in agony between his human and elephant form, Dao rolled along the ground. The fire burnt relentlessly until his spine-chilling yell trailed off and it was finally over. Ashes floated above the residual smoke.

[You are not to be harmed.]

K: Amo, you're still there? You saved me.

[Go to Agent Tan. He needs you.]

Kuan ran up to Tan. Blood was streaming down the uncovered lower part of his face. The boy tried to push a button on the dying agent's uniform, but there were just interference sounds.

"How do you get this to work?"

"Kuan, he must have jammed the communications in here. No one can help me now anyway."

"You're coming with me."

Tan could see one of the wooden panels had caught fire.

"Kuan, head for the exit, and you'll be in the secret vault. When the reflector comes on, say you've got Agent Tan's delivery, and you'll be taken through a simple procedure which will show you how to get back to him."

"Do I need a code?"

"You already know it."

Tan reached into his pocket and took out a small object.

"I've been meaning to give this back to you. You must have dropped it when you changed into your naval overall."

He pressed it into the boy's hand. It was the green pebble Kuan was supposed to be holding in trust for Batya the outsider, to return to his son.

"Kuan, recover yourself, find him, and be together again."

The blaze began to spread voraciously along the wood paneled tunnel.

Tan's hand slipped out of the boy's. Those eyes which had reminded him so much of another's were now forever closed.

Kuan held the pebble tightly and ran away from the pitiless inferno.

Chapter 30

<u>Beneath a Burning Sky</u>

Kuan pushed his way through the exit barrier and the thick metal door clunked shut behind him. No light, no sound. He stretched his arms out to feel his way around.

K: Amo, do you know where we are?

[We're close. But I can't help with the lack of visibility. I can't summon up any more energy.]

K: You rest. I'll get you home.

[I'm sorry about Agent Tan.]

K: I owe him, and you, my life.

Returning Amo to her home was his last task before making his own way back. She had been his companion from the beginning. Without her he would never have made it this far. Yet while their thoughts might mingle each time she found herself in his mind, he still had little understanding of this nebula world she hailed from. She had said that Kuan could not be in it, but somehow she had survived in Shiyan. Why the asymmetry?

As the memory of what happened after he ran home with the briefcase gradually flowed back into him, he began to catch glimpses of a nebula form in which consciousness could be discerned.

His concentration wandered in the dark and he did not expect there to be steps going down. One foot plunged into emptiness. It was only his reflex shooting an arm out to grab a railing that saved him from a sharp fall. Slowly he made his way to the bottom. He followed the contour of a stony wall, leading him through a semi-circular turn towards a door which slid open quietly as soon as he touched it. He entered.

The door slid closed and a bright light came on. It was the secret vault in the basement of Rook Mansion. In the centre was the large reflector screen. The room to the right was where Kuan was thrown into when Dao sentenced him to Hades. To the left behind the black door was where Amo said her home world was to be found. Kuan pulled on the handle.

[We're almost there.]

But the door wouldn't budge. He tried turning it in different directions. He pushed hard against the door. Not the slightest impact.

[Touch the reflector.]

Kuan placed his palm on the glass screen. The reflector lit up with the image of a half-asleep Wu-yin, the white cat who was once the aide to Governor Pui.

"Wu-yin, what are you doing there?"

She dragged her paw across her face a couple of times before answering.

"Denji asked me to keep an eye on the vault in case he needs to be alerted to anything. My mother is his cousin on his father's side, you know. Or is it my father on his mother's side? Once the Sun Disc was shut down, and I was out of a job giving out energy pendants to the few who could afford the pledges, I asked him to help me find something else to do. So he put me in charge of the reflector in Dao's old vault. With Dao gone, nothing much is going to happen really."

"But Dao escaped."

"What? I must sound the alert!"

"No need, Wu-yin, Dao's dead."

"Dao's dead?"

"So is Agent Tan."

"I must report it to Denji. I'll need to look in the procedural manual to see how I'm supposed to do that."

Kuan found himself reflecting on those last moments with Agent Tan, but Amo reminded him of the problem with the door.

"Wu-yin, I need your help."

"That's what I'm here for."

"There are two rooms in this vault. You can't see them from where you are. One is to the right of the reflector as I look at it, and one is to the left of it. I need you to open the door to the left. Can you do that?"

"I'm sure I can. Just bear with me."

The white cat's face was overwhelmed with concentration.

K: Amo, are you making any headway with the door? We can't rely on Wu-yin.

[It's more complicated than anything else I've come across.]

K: You can find a way, can't you?

[I can't be certain. It is in essence a gateway between two worlds. That could be why it would be particularly difficult to unlock.]

Wu-yin suddenly glanced at Kuan with a most animated look.

"Kuan, you must see this."

Nothing happened to the door, but on screen, the white cat morphed into a human child, a girl with long blonde hair, wearing a blue dress with a white pinafore on top. Yet her head was disproportionately large and her feet decidedly too small.

"What do you think? You're on all the news, and the human child look is so in. And now we can change our appearance if we have practised enough to do it. Impressive, wouldn't you say?"

"Very impressive, and keep practising."

Wu-yin's girlish face grinned broadly.

"Wu-yin, how's the door going?"

"Almost there. Press this one here, followed by that one. There you go."

The door on the right sprang open. Sparks shot across the empty room. Kuan held his breath. Into that very room he was bundled by Dao's wolf dogs before he was dispatched to Hades. Trepidation slashed across his chest. Electricity cracked the air. He ran up and slammed the door shut.

"Wu-yin, please leave all the controls as they are."

[Kuan, I can't do it without help.]

K: Amo, is there anything you haven't tried?

"Kuan," called out Wu-yin reverting to her white cat form, "we've got a problem."

The boy tried not to lose his calm.

"What is it?"

"Tunnel 13 is on fire."

"I know. I was there."

"But do you know the vault you're in is right underneath tunnel 13, and it's burning through?"

Kuan looked up and noticed smoke seeping through the ceiling of the vault.

"The vault must be evacuated. The message is flashing up on my monitor. I must ask you to leave immediately."

[Kuan, you must leave. You are not to risk your life.]

K: Keep trying. I have something else I must find out while I'm in here.

"Kuan, the fire will bear down on you in under five minutes."

"Wu-yin, I've got Agent Tan's delivery."

"Agent Tan's delivery? Yes, of course, I must take you through security."

"What security?"

"Unmask the hidden."

"Resistance is life." Kuan replied.

"Correct. Now I just need to input the required details. Who's making the request for this delivery?"

"Me."

"And your name is?"

"Kuan."

After all he had been through, he thought how absurd it would be to perish in a fire because he was held up by Wu-yin's inane questions.

"And the delivery is on behalf of?"

"Tan."

"Just one more question, Kuan."

"I thought you said the fire will be getting through any minute now."

"Is there any other passenger travelling with you on this delivery?"

Amo, thought Kuan, would not want to her existence to be known.

"It's just me."

"That's all been confirmed with the system. You're set to go."

The fire was gnawing through parts of the ceiling. Sizzling heat was creeping down on him.

"Wu-yin, you haven't shown me where to go. I was supposed to be told how to get to the place Agent Tan located for me."

[Kuan, I think she has.]

K: What do you mean, Amo?

[The door's been unlocked.]

Kuan tried the door to the room on the left and was able to open it.

"Wu-yin, are all the directions I need in that room? Is there anything else you should tell me?"

"I've processed your request exactly as instructed. To escape the fire, you must leave the vault now."

Above him fiery cracks appeared, raining down a mist of glowing dust and smoldering embers.

[Kuan, we must leave the vault. While going through this door could take me home, you would be trapped by the inferno.]

Without hesitation Kuan charged into the room and shut the black door behind him. A comprehensive darkness confronted him. He stretched his arms forward but could feel nothing. He was apprehensive of falling down unseen steps again.

K: Amo, whereabouts is your world? You have to direct me to it.

[It's straight ahead, Kuan.]

He slid one foot slowly forward, and then repeated the move with the other foot.

[Can you smell that?]

K: Smoke?

[It's coming through the door. You won't be able to go back out.]

K: Agent Tan must have left in here the directions I need. Once I've got them, I can go with you to your world until we work out a way for me to bypass this room to get to where I have to go.

The smoke was thickening.

[What if Wu-yin made a mistake? And the directions Agent Tan left you are not in this room.]

Kuan coughed drily.

K: Knowing Agent Tan, the information would be in some electronic form. Can you sense anything which might contain the data I'm looking for?

[There's no electronic pulse of any form in this room.]

K: Was that a wince? You're in pain.

[I have been trying to conserve what life force I have left, but the burst against Dao took out more than I thought.]

Kuan shuffled his feet more quickly. He must get Amo back to her world where they would know how to revive her. The smoke crawled subtly like a boa constrictor around the boy's feet, then twirling ever higher towards his torso until it was ready to squeeze the life out of him. His lungs spluttered.

[Kuan, I'm sorry to have led you to this.]

His hands were halted by a cold barrier. It was a wall of ice. He desperately checked the surface for a handle, an opening, anything to escape from where he was. But its chilled smoothness was devoid of any feature.

Baked air was filling up the room. Repeatedly he choked, his watery eyes staring at pitch-black nothingness. He thumped against the frozen barricade before him. His fists sank into a slushy dent. It must be melting. Ferociously he struck against it. He took a few steps back and charged shoulder first into it. Was Amo's world hidden in deep freeze? What lay behind the wall? A captive in suspended animation? Was that where he was being kept?

One more charge. Kuan crashed through the glacial rampart and fell headlong into a deep pool of water. He was sucked under. The sensation of water swallowing him up saturated him with fear and disgust. Must hold his breath. He was tumbling further and further down. His mind flashed back to Erica trapped under the ice in the lake, bubbles leaking from her frozen lips; and to Captain Ma gazing with resignation as the hatch was locked and rising water flushed the last vestige of life out of him.

He could not take it anymore and at that moment he was spat out of the sea onto a rocky beach. He retched on all fours for minutes. Slowly clearing his head, he pulled out from his pocket the green pebble

Agent Tan found and returned to him. A token of hope, memento of death.

A couple of hundred metres away was a drab one storey building, all painted in grey.

[Kuan, you've brought me home.]

K: This is your home?

[It's right ahead of us, in that building.]

K: Will they be expecting you?

[We'll soon be together again.]

Kuan pushed himself up and walked with weary limbs towards the building. It was sweltering under the midday sun. His feet crunched across the rock and sand. There was no one else in sight, except for a few seagulls gliding by seeking shelter from the burning sky.

He stepped through the front door.

[Over there, in that tiny room.]

A daunting familiarity descended on him. Entering the windowless room, he saw the back of a man handcuffed to a chair. He was clothed in an orange coloured overall. An intensely bright light was targeted at his face. In front of him was a table with sheets of paper scattered haphazardly. Resting on top of them were a pair of gold-rimmed glasses.

K: This is your home?

[His nebulous mind is my home. I remember now I was sent to find you, to bring you back safely. In the end, we helped each other return home.]

K: You're part of his mind?

[He couldn't hold it together, and we split into fragments. But we'll be whole again, because you're back.]

K: How can I help him?

[You've helped him defeat Plutopia in the other world. Now you've come back. You must stay. The fight must go on here.]

K: What am I supposed to do?

She was gone. Reabsorbed into a cerebral nebula which had threatened to self-destruct with a super-nova. But the galactic storm of a troubled mind was passing. Order was being restored.

Voices were heard. There were at least two other men in the room. Kuan could not see them. But he could hear a loud slap, and the captive's face was flung to one side.

"Should you be doing that?" asked one of the voices.

"Sir, we were told to use whatever means necessary to get him to talk."

"Let me talk to him."

"Yes, sir."

"Listen, I can make sure there's no more beating. Just answer our questions. These papers you had with you when you were captured. They would suggest you were inciting dangerous activities against the government and important institutions the government must protect. 'Plutopia' is obviously a code word for your target. The Potokans, I assume, refer to terrorist cells primed to attack us. And the phrase, 'Unmask the hidden, resistance is life', must be the trigger command to order some covert operation. Tell me all you know about them, and you'll have a much easier life."

Not a word came from the man in the chair.

"Is he always like this?"

"Yes, sir. He's been totally uncooperative since he was captured and brought here."

"And how long ago was that?"

"He's been here ten years, sir."

"Ten years? And he just sits there."

"A few years ago a doctor examined him and alleged that he was suffering from some form of catatonic breakdown."

"What happened then?"

"The doctor was discharged for making an unfounded diagnosis."

"And the questioning continued?"

"Yes, sir. It had to. He was flagged as a major terrorist suspect."

"On what basis? Has he actually been charged with anything?"

"No, sir. He has refused to provide us with any evidence to charge him with conspiracy against this unspecified target of 'Plutopia'."

"What does the warden say about all this?"

"He said we must follow protocol and apply all authorised interrogation procedures."

"You do what you have to do. I'm going to grab a coffee. Give me a shout if he's ready to talk."

"Yes, sir."

The senior officer left the room, leaving the other to push the chair along with the prisoner onto the floor. Kuan involuntarily fell on his back too. He braced himself for what would come next.

A towel was soaked in a bucket of water and thrown over the captive's face. Kuan instantly felt the stifling wetness as well. But there was nothing he could do. A tap was being squeakily switched on. The water gushed through a hosepipe and splashed onto the ground. A peculiar splash. Meticulously the stream of running water was directed onto the towel. He held his breath for as long as he could, but eventually he had to take a gulp of air even though he knew it would not be air but water that flowed remorselessly into his lungs. He choked. He retched. And the water kept coming. He was almost passing out when the chair was at last pushed back up and the drenched towel fell off his face. Kuan looked down on himself, handcuffed to the chair.

Water dripped out of his nostrils and his eyes. He knew where he was. The voice of the senior officer was back.

"Did he say anything?"

"No, sir."

"That's not the first time he's had the procedure administered to him?"

"I've lost count, sir, but it definitely wasn't the first time."

Kuan glanced down at the papers spread across the table in front of him. They were all somewhat blurred. He heard someone pull up a chair behind the bright light.

"Kuan, let me help you. We don't have to keep doing this. I can call all of this off. I've been authorised to suspend all special interrogation procedures, so long as you cooperate with us. I've been through your papers, and you're clearly orchestrating some movement against this 'Plutopia' enemy. What I want specifically from you is the real identity of a number of people whose names, or codenames, appear frequently in your notes."

Kuan peered at the dazzling lamp bombarding him. He could not make out who was asking the questions. But it did not really matter.

"So tell me, who are Winston, K, Rieux, and Alice? What is their role, and where can we find them? I know you have close connections to all of them."

He wondered what his interrogator knew about literature.

"You're not helping yourself, Kuan. But I'm a patient man. I'm going to show you some photographs. I want you to tell me what you know about them, especially in relation to your plot against Plutopia."

A picture was placed in front of Kuan. He screwed his eyes up.

"Put his glasses on for him."

"Yes, sir."

Clarity at last. It was a picture of someone he had never seen before. He shook his head. The response gave the questioner tremendous encouragement. Another picture. Nothing. Another picture. A shake of the head. Then came the picture of a red-haired woman, with the most enchanting green eyes staring out at Kuan.

"You know this woman, don't you? Who can forget a face like that. Kuan, who is she? Is she Alice?"

The fissure in his heart was threatening to open again. Kuan was determined to hold himself together.

"Kuan, tell me about this woman."

He sat rigidly still.

"I can tell you're familiar with her."

He must learn to face reality.

The questioner lost his patience and slammed the table.

"Don't play games with me, Kuan! Who is this woman and where can we find her?"

"Sir, that's his wife."

"Where is she now?"

"She was with him when he was captured. She was shot."

"Killed?"

"Yes, sir. She wasn't a suspect herself. Just collateral damage."

After a long pause, the interrogator spoke in a vacant tone.

"That will be all for today. We'll resume tomorrow. Take him back to his cell."

Kuan was uncuffed from the chair. He silently bade farewell to her smiling image on the table.

Someone seized his arm and escorted him back to his cell.

He stood alone by the tiny window listening to the waves. Looking up, he could see the moon was almost full again. His palm slowly opened to reveal that the green pebble had gone.

The fight could be resumed.

He was home.

****

Far away, beneath a burning sky
Onward and inward dreamily
Restrained by a lie –

All the characters nestle near,
Listening with a willing ear,
Learning to weave a tale to hear –

Incarcerated under that burning sky:
Memories fade and echoes die:
Pain has long ago slain 'I'.

Remember the foolish and the wise,
Imagine smiles instead of cries,
Seen never by waking eyes.

One or two or three to hear,
Never without a willing ear,
Everyone shall nestle near.

Down in Wonderland they lie,
Morphing as the days go by,
Igniting as oppressors die.

No more drifting down the stream –
Doubt not the golden gleam –
Survive beyond the dream.

****

5702138R00232

Printed in Great Britain
by Amazon.co.uk, Ltd.,
Marston Gate.